NERVE
&
SMOKESCREEN

Dick Francis has written forty-one international best-sellers and is widely acclaimed as one of the world's finest thriller writers. His awards include the Crime Writers' Association's Cartier Diamond Dagger for his outstanding contribution to the crime genre, and an honorary Doctorate of Humane Letters from Tufts University of Boston. In 1996 Dick Francis was made a Mystery Writers of America Grand Master for a lifetime's achievement and in 2000 he received a CBE in the Queen's Birthday Honours list.

Dick Francis

NERVE
&
SMOKESCREEN

PAN BOOKS

Nerve first published 1964 by Michael Joseph Ltd.
First published by Pan Books 1976
Smokescreen first published 1972 by Michael Joseph Ltd.
First published by Pan Books 1974

This omnibus edition published 2004 by Pan Books
an imprint of Pan Macmillan Ltd
Pan Macmillan, 20 New Wharf Road, London N1 9RR
Basingstoke and Oxford
Associated companies throughout the world
www.panmacmillan.com

ISBN 0 330 43916 2

1 3 5 7 9 8 6 4 2

A CIP catalogue record for this book is available from
the British Library.

Phototypeset by Intype, London Limited
Printed and bound in Great Britain by
Mackays of Chatham plc, Chatham Kent

NERVE

CHAPTER ONE

Art Mathews shot himself, loudly and messily, in the centre of the parade ring at Dunstable races.

I was standing only six feet away from him, but he did it so quickly that had it been only six inches I would not have had time to stop him.

He had walked out of the changing-room ahead of me, his narrow shoulders hunched inside the khaki jerkin he had put on over his racing colours, and his head down on his chest as if he were deep in thought. I noticed him stumble slightly down the two steps from the weighing-room to the path; and when someone spoke to him on the short walk to the parade ring, he gave absolutely no sign of having heard. But it was just another walk from the weighing-room to the parade ring, just another race like a hundred others. There was nothing to suggest that when he had stood talking for two or three minutes with the owner and trainer of the horse he was due to ride, he would take off his jerkin, produce from under it as he dropped it to the ground a large automatic pistol, place the barrel against his temple and squeeze the trigger.

Unhesitating. No pause for a final weighing-up. No goodbyes. The casualness of his movement was as shocking as its effect.

He hadn't even shut his eyes, and they were still open as he fell forwards to the ground, his face hitting the grass with an audible thud and his helmet rolling off. The bullet had passed straight through his skull, and the exit wound lay open to the sky, a tangled, bloody mess of skin and hair and brain, with splinters of bone sticking out.

The crack of the gunshot echoed round the paddock, amplified by the high back wall of the stands. Heads turned searchingly and the busy buzz and hum of conversation from the three-deep railside racegoers grew hushed and finally silent as they took in the appalling, unbelievable, indisputable fact that what remained of Art Mathews lay face downwards on the bright green turf.

Mr John Brewar, the owner of Art's prospective mount, stood with his middle-aged mouth stretched open in a soundless oval, his eyes glazed with surprise. His plump, well-preserved wife toppled to the ground in the graceless sprawl of a genuine faint, and Corin Kellar, the trainer for whom both Art and I had been about to ride, went down on one knee and shook Art by the shoulder, as if he could still awaken one whose head was half blown away.

The sun shone brightly. The blue and orange silk on Art's back gleamed: his white breeches were spotless, and his racing boots had been polished into a clean, soft shine. I thought inconsequentially that he would have been glad that – from the neck down at least – he looked as immaculate as ever.

The two stewards hurried over and stood stock-still, staring at Art's head. Horror dragged down their jaws and narrowed their eyes. It was part of their responsibility at a meeting to stand in the parade ring while the horses were led round before each race, so that they should be both witnesses and adjudicators if anything irregular should occur. Nothing as irregular as a public suicide of a top-notch steeplechase jockey had ever, I imagined, required their attention before.

The elder of them, Lord Tirrold, a tall, thin man with an executive mind, bent over Art for a closer inspection. I saw the muscles bunch along his jaw, and he looked up at me across Art's body and said quietly, 'Finn . . . fetch a rug.'

I walked twenty steps down the parade ring to where one of the horses due to run in the race stood in a little group with his owner, trainer and jockey. Without a word the trainer took the rug off the horse and held it out to me.

'Mathews?' he said incredulously.

I nodded unhappily and thanked him for the rug, and went back with it.

The other steward, a sour-tempered hulk named

3

Ballerton, was, I was meanly pleased to see, losing his cherished dignity by vomiting up his lunch.

Mr Brewar pulled down his unconscious wife's rucked-up skirt and began anxiously to feel her pulse. Corin Kellar kept passing his hand over his face from forehead to chin, still down on one knee beside his jockey. His face was colourless, his hand shaking. He was taking it badly.

I handed one end of the rug to Lord Tirrold and we opened it out and spread it gently over the dead man. Lord Tirrold stood for a moment looking down at the motionless brown shape, then glanced round at the little silent groups of the people who had runners in the race. He went over and spoke to one or two, and presently the stable lads led all the horses out from the parade ring and back to the saddling boxes.

I stood looking down at Corin Kellar and his distress, which I thought he thoroughly deserved. I wondered how it felt to know one had driven a man to kill himself.

There was a click, and a voice announced over the loud-speaker system that owing to a serious accident in the parade ring the last two races would be abandoned. Tomorrow's meeting would be held as planned, it said, and would everyone please go home. As far as the growing crowd of racegoers round the ring were concerned, this might never have been said, for they remained glued to the rails with all eyes on the concealing rug. Nothing rivets human attention as hungrily as a bloody disaster, I thought tolerantly, picking up Art's helmet and whip from the grass.

Poor Art. Poor badgered, beleaguered Art, rubbing out his misery with a scrap of lead.

I turned away from his body and walked thoughtfully back to the weighing-room.

While we changed back from riding kit into our normal clothes the atmosphere down our end of the changing-room was one of irreverence covering shock. Art, occupying by general consent the position of elder statesman among jockeys, though he was not actually at thirty-five by any means the eldest, had been much deferred to and respected. Distant in manner sometimes, withdrawn even, but an honest man and a good jockey. His one noticeable weakness, at which we usually smiled indulgently, was his conviction that a lost race was always due to some deficiency in his horse or its training, and never to a mistake on his own part. We all knew perfectly well that Art was no exception to the rule that every jockey misjudges things once in a while, but he would never admit a fault, and could put up a persuasive defence every time if called to account.

'Thank the Lord,' said Tick-Tock Ingersoll, stripping off his blue and black checked jersey, 'that Art was considerate enough to let us all weigh out for the race before bumping himself off.' Tick-Tock's face emerged from the woolly folds with a wide grin which faded comically when no one laughed.

'Well,' he said, dropping his jersey absentmindedly in a heap on the floor. 'If he'd done it an hour ago we'd all have been ten quid out of pocket.'

He was right. Our fees for each race were technically earned once we had sat on the scales and been checked out as carrying the correct weight, and they would be automatically paid whether we ran the race or not.

'In that case,' said Peter Cloony, 'we should put half of it into a fund for his widow.' He was a small, quiet young man prone to over-emotional, quickly roused and quickly spent bouts of pity both for others and for himself.

'Not ruddy likely,' said Tick-Tock, who disliked him openly. 'Ten quid's ten quid to me, and Mrs Art's rolling in it. And snooty with it. Catch me giving her the time of day, you'll be lucky.'

'It's a mark of respect,' said Peter obstinately, looking round at us with rather damp large eyes and carefully refraining from returning young Tick-Tock's belligerent glare.

I sympathized with Tick-Tock. I needed the money, too. Besides, Mrs Art had treated me, along with all the other rank-and-file jockeys, with her own particularly arctic brand of coolness. Giving her a fiver in Art's memory wouldn't thaw her. Pale, straw-haired, light-eyed, she was the original ice maiden, I thought.

'Mrs Art doesn't need our money,' I said. 'Remember how she bought herself a mink coat last

6

winter and used it as a hedge against all of us who didn't measure up to her standards? She hardly knows two of us by name. Let's just buy Art a wreath, and perhaps a useful memorial, something he would have appreciated, like some hot showers in the washroom here.'

Tick-Tock's angular young face registered delight. Peter Cloony bent on me a look of sorrowful reproof. But from the others came nods of agreement.

Grant Oldfield said violently, 'He probably shot himself because that whey-faced bitch short-changed him in bed.'

There was a curious little silence. A year ago, I reflected, a year ago we might have laughed. But a year ago Grant Oldfield would have said the same thing amusingly and perhaps vulgarly, but not with this ugly unsmiling venom.

I was aware, we all were, that he didn't know or care a jot about the private practices of Art's marriage; but in the past months Grant had seemed more and more to be consumed by some inner rage, and lately he could scarcely make the most commonplace remark without in some way giving vent to it. It was caused, we thought, by the fact that he was going down the ladder again without ever having got to the top. He had always been ambitious and ruthless in character, and had developed a riding style to match. But at the vital point when he had attracted public attention with a string of successes and had begun to ride regularly for James Axminster, one of the very top trainers, something had happened to spoil it. He had lost the Axminster job, and other trainers booked him less and less. The race we had not run was his only engagement that day.

Grant was a dark, hairy, thick-set man of thirty, with high cheek-bones and a wide-nostrilled nose bent permanently out of shape. I endured a great deal more of his company than I would have liked because my peg in the changing-room at nearly all racecourses was next to his, since both our kit was looked after by the same racecourse valet. He borrowed my things freely without asking first or thanking afterwards, and if he had broken something, denied he had used it. When I first met him I had been amused by his pawky humour, but two years later, by the day Art died, I was heartily sick of his thunderous moods, his roughness and his vile temper.

Once or twice in the six weeks since the new season had begun I had found him standing with his head thrust forward looking round him in bewilderment, like a bull played out by a matador. A bull exhausted by fighting a piece of cloth, a bull baffled and broken, all his magnificent strength wasted on something he could not pin down with his horns. At such times I could pity Grant all right, but at all others I kept out of his way as much as I could.

Peter Cloony, paying him no attention as usual, indicated the peg on which Art's everyday clothes hung, and said, 'What do you think we had better do with these?'

We all looked at them, the well-cut tweed suit neatly arranged on a hanger, with the small grip which contained his folded shirt and underclothes standing on the bench beneath. His almost obsessive tidiness was so familiar to us that it aroused no comment, but now that he was dead I was struck afresh by it. Everyone else hung up their jackets by the loop at the back of the neck, hooked their braces on to the pegs, and piled their other clothes into the tops of their trousers. Only Art had insisted on a hanger, and had provided his valet with one to bring for him.

Before we had got any further than an obscene suggestion from Grant, a racecourse official threaded his way down the changing-room, spotted me, and shouted, 'Finn, the stewards want you.'

'Now?' I said, standing in shirt and underpants.

'At once.' He grinned.

'All right.' I finished dressing quickly, brushed my hair, walked through the weighing-room, and knocked on the stewards' door. They said to come in, and in I went.

All three stewards were there, also the clerk of the course, and Corin Kellar. They were sitting in uncomfortable-looking, straight-backed chairs around a large, oblong table.

Lord Tirrold said, 'Come along in and close the door.'

9

I did as he said.

He went on, 'I know you were near Mathews when he ... er ... shot himself. Did you actually see him do it? I mean, did you see him take the pistol out and aim it, or did you look at him when you heard the shot?'

'I saw him take out the pistol and aim it, sir,' I said.

'Very well. In that case the police may wish to take a statement from you; please do not leave the weighing-room building until they have seen you. We are waiting now for the inspector to come back from the first-aid room.'

He nodded to dismiss me, but when I had my hand on the door-knob he said, 'Finn ... do you know of any reason why Mathews should have wished to end his life?'

I hesitated a fraction too long before I turned round, so that a plain 'No' would have been unconvincing. I looked at Corin Kellar, who was busy studying his fingernails.

'Mr Kellar might know,' I said, non-committally.

The stewards exchanged glances. Mr Ballerton, still pallid from his bout of sickness by Art's body, made a pushing away gesture with his hand, and said, 'You're not asking us to believe that Mathews killed himself merely because Kellar was dissatisfied with his riding?' He turned to the other stewards. 'Really,' he added forcefully, 'if these jockeys get so big for their boots that they can't take a little well-earned criticism, it is time they looked about for other employment. But to suggest that Mathews killed himself because of a few hard words is irresponsible mischief.'

At that point I remembered that Ballerton himself owned a horse which Corin Kellar trained. 'Dissatisfied with his riding,' the colourless phrase he had used to describe the recent series of acrimonious post-race arguments between Art and the trainer suddenly seemed to me a deliberate attempt at oiling troubled waters. You know why Art killed himself, I thought; you helped to cause it, and you won't admit it.

I shifted my gaze back to Lord Tirrold and found him regarding me with speculation.

'That will be all, Finn,' he said.

'Yes, sir,' I said.

I went out and this time they did not call me back, but before I had crossed the weighing-room the door opened again and shut and I heard Corin's voice behind me.

'Rob.'

I turned round and waited for him.

'Thanks very much,' he said sarcastically, 'for tossing that little bomb into my lap.'

'You had told them already,' I said.

'Yes, and just as well.'

He still looked shocked, his thin face deeply lined with worry. He was an exceptionally clever trainer but a nervous, undependable man who offered you life-

11

long friendship one day and cut you dead the next. Just then, it appeared, he needed reassurance.

He said, 'Surely you and the other jockeys don't believe Art killed himself because ... er ... I had decided to employ him less? He must have had another reason.'

'Today was supposed to be his last as your jockey in any case, wasn't it?' I said.

He hesitated and then nodded, surprised at my knowing what had not been published. I didn't tell him that I had bumped into Art in the car park the evening before, and that Art, bitterly despairing and smarting from a corroding sense of injustice, had lowered the customary guard on his tongue enough to tell me that his job with Kellar was finished.

I said only, 'He killed himself because you gave him the sack, and he did it in front of you to cause you the maximum amount of remorse. And that, if you want my opinion, is that.'

'But people don't kill themselves because they've lost their jobs,' he said, with a tinge of exasperation.

'Not if they're normal, no,' I agreed.

'Every jockey knows he'll have to retire some time. And Art was getting too old ... he must have been mad.'

'Yes, I suppose so,' I said.

I left him standing there, trying to convince himself that he was in no way responsible for Art's death.

Back in the changing-room the discussion on what

to do with Art's clothes had been ended by his valet
taking charge of them, and Grant Oldfield, I was glad
to find, had finished dressing and gone home. Most of
the other jockeys had gone also, and the valets were
busy tidying up the chaos they had left behind, sorting
dirty white breeches into kit bags, and piling helmets,
boots, whips and other gear into large wicker hampers.
It had been a dry sunny day, and for once there was
no mud to wash off.

I reflected as I watched the quick, neat way they
flipped the things into the baskets, ready to take the
dirty ones home, clean them and return them
laundered and polished on the following day, that
possibly they did deserve the very large fees we had
to pay them for the service. I knew I would loathe,
after a day of travelling and of dressing jockeys, to
have to face those hampers and bags when I reached
home; take out the grubby piles and set to work. Ugh.

I had often seen Art paying his valet, counting
through a wad of notes. At the height of the season it
always amounted to over twenty pounds each week.
My own valet, Young Mike (in his middle forties),
twitched my helmet up from the bench and smiled at
me as he went by. He earned more than most of the
dozen or so jockeys he regularly looked after, and
decidedly more than I did. But all the same ... ugh!

Tick-Tock, whistling the latest hit tune between his
teeth, sat on the bench and pulled on a pair of very
fancy yellow socks. On top of those went smooth, slim-

13

toed shoes reaching up to the ankle bone. He shook down the slender legs of his dark tweed trousers (no turn-ups), and feeling my gaze upon him looked up and grinned at me across the room.

He said, 'Look your fill on the "Tailor and Cutter's" dream boy.'

'My father in his time,' I said blandly, 'was a Twelve Best Dressed man.'

'My grandfather had vicuna linings in his raincoats.'

'My mother,' I said, dredging for it, 'has a Pucci shirt.'

'Mine,' he said carefully, 'cooks in hers.'

At this infantile exchange we regarded each other with high good humour. Five minutes of Tick-Tock's company were as cheering as rum punch in a snowstorm, and some of his happy-go-lucky enjoyment of living always rubbed off on to the next man. Let Art die of shame, let the murk spread in Grant Oldfield's soul; surely nothing could be really wrong in the racing world, I thought, while young Ingersoll ticked so gaily.

He waved his hand at me, adjusted his Tyrolean trilby, said 'See you tomorrow,' and was gone.

But all the same there *was* something wrong in the racing world. Very wrong. I didn't know what; I could see only the symptoms, and see them all the more clearly perhaps, since I had been only two years in the game. Between trainers and jockeys there seemed to be an all-round edginess, sudden outbursts of rancour,

14

and an ebbing and flowing undercurrent of resentment and distrust. There was more to it, I thought, than the usual jungle beneath the surface of any fiercely competitive business, more to it than the equivalent of grey-flannel-suit manoeuvring in the world of jodhpurs and hacking jackets; but Tick-Tock, to whom alone I had in any way suggested my misgivings, had brushed the whole thing aside.

'You must be on the wrong wavelength, pal,' he said. 'Look around you. Those are smiles you can see, boy. Smiles. It's an O.K. life by me.'

The last few pieces of kit were disappearing into the hampers and some of the lids were already down. I drank a second cup of sugarless tea, lukewarm, and eyed the moist looking pieces of fruit cake. As usual it took a good deal of resolution not to eat one. Being constantly hungry was the one thing I did not enjoy about race riding, and September was always a bad time of the year, with the remains of the summer's fat still having to be starved off. I sighed, averted my eyes from the cake, and tried to console myself that in another month my appetite would have shrunk back to its winter level.

Young Mike shouted down the room from the doorway through which he had been staggering with a hamper, 'Rob, there's a copper here to see you.'

I put down the cup and went out into the weighing-room. A middle-aged, undistinguished-looking policeman in a peaked cap was waiting for me with a notebook in his hand.

'Robert Finn?' he asked.

'Yes,' I said.

'I understand from Lord Tirrold that you saw Arthur Mathews put the pistol against his temple and pull the trigger?'

'Yes,' I agreed.

He made a note: then he said, 'It's a very straightforward case of suicide. There won't be any need for more than one witness at the inquest, apart from the doctor, and that will probably be Mr Kellar. I don't think we will need to trouble you any further.' He smiled briefly, shut the notebook and put it in his pocket.

'That's all?' I asked rather blankly.

'Yes, that's all. When a man kills himself as publicly as this there's no question of accident or homicide. The only thing for the coroner to decide is the wording of his verdict.'

'Unsound mind and so on?' I said.

'Yes,' he said. 'Thank you for waiting, though it was your stewards' idea, not mine. Good afternoon, then.' He nodded at me, turned, and walked across towards the stewards' room.

I collected my hat and binoculars and walked down to the racecourse station. The train was already waiting and full, and the only seat I could find was in a compartment packed with bookmakers' clerks playing

16

cards on a suitcase balanced across their knees. They invited me to join them, and between Luton and St Pancras I fear I repaid their kindness by winning from them the cost of the journey.

CHAPTER TWO

The flat in Kensington was empty. There were a few letters from the day's second post in the wire basket on the inner side of the door, and I fished them out and walked through into the sitting-room, sorting out the two which were addressed to me.

As usual, the place looked as if it had lately received the attentions of a minor tornado. My mother's grand piano lay inches deep in piano scores, several of which had cascaded to the floor. Two music-stands leant at a drunken angle against the wall with a violin bow hooked on to one of them. The violin itself was propped up in an armchair, with its case open on the floor beside it. A 'cello and another music-stand rested side by side like lovers along the length of the sofa. An oboe and two clarinets lay on a table beside another untidy pile of music, and round the room and on all the bedroom chairs which filled most of the floor space lay a profusion of white silk handkerchiefs, rosin, coffee cups and batons.

Running a practised eye over the chaos I diagnosed

18

the recent presence of my parents, two uncles and a cousin. As they never travelled far without their instruments, it was safe to predict that the whole circus was within walking distance and would return in a very short while. I had, I was thankful to realize, struck the interval.

I threaded a path to the window and looked out. No sign of returning Finns. The flat was at the top of a house two or three streets back from Hyde Park, and across the rooftops I could see the evening sunlight striking on the green dome of the Albert Hall. The Royal Institute of Music, where one of my uncles taught, rose in a solid dark mass beside it. The large airy apartment which was the headquarters of the Finn family was held by my father to be an economy, as it was within walking distance of where so many of them from time to time worked.

I was the odd one out. The talents with which both my parents' families had been lavishly endowed had not descended to me. This had become painfully clear to them when at the age of four I had failed to distinguish between the notes of an oboe and a *cor anglais*. To the uninitiated there may not seem to be much difference between them, but my father happened to be an oboist of international reputation, against whom other oboists were measured. Also, high musical talent, if it exists, is apparent in a child from an extremely early age, earlier than any other form of inborn ability, and at three years (when Mozart began composing), concertos and symphonies made less impression on me than the noise of the men emptying the dustbins.

By the time I was five my shattered parents had reluctantly faced the fact that the child they had bred by mistake (I had caused an important American tour to be cancelled) was unmusical. Unmusical, that is, in their pure sense. I was not tone deaf and soaring flights of melody had drawn from me childish tears, but I never had, and still have not, their complete understanding, intellectual, emotional, technical and spiritual, of the effect of putting certain sounds in certain orders.

My mother never being one to do things by halves, I had henceforth been shuffled off from London between school terms to a succession of long holidays on farms, ostensibly for my health, but in reality, I knew later, to free my parents for the complicated and lengthy concert tours in which they were engaged. I grew up into a sort of truce with them, in which it was tacitly agreed that as they had not intended to have a child in the first place, and as he had proved to be less than a (musical) credit to them in the second, the less we saw of each other the better.

They disapproved of my venture into jockeyship for no other reason than that racing had nothing to do with music. It was no use my pointing out that the one thing I had learned on the various holiday farms was how to ride (for I was enough my father's son for farming itself to bore me stiff), and that my present occupation was directly due to their actions in the past. To what they did not want to hear my acute-eared parents were sublimely deaf.

There was still no sign of them down in the street, nor of the uncle who lived with us who played the 'cello, nor the visiting uncle and cousin, violin and clarinet.

I opened my two letters. The first informed me that my income tax returns were overdue. I slit the second envelope with a smiling and complacent anticipation of enjoyment, which just shows how often life can get up and slap you when you least expect it. In a familiar childish hand the letter said:

Dearest Rob,
I am afraid this may come as a surprise to you, but I am getting married. He is Sir Morton Henge, who you may have heard of, and he is very sweet and kind and no cracks from you about him being old enough to be my father etc. I don't think I had better ask you to the reception, do you? Morton doesn't know about you and you will be a great dear not to let on to anybody about us, if you don't mind. I shall never forget you, dearest Rob, and all the sweet times we had together. Thank you for everything, and goodbye.
Your loving Paulina.

Sir Morton Henge, middle-aged widower and canning tycoon. Well, well. I wondered sardonically how his serious-minded son, whom I knew slightly, would enjoy the prospect of a cuddly twenty-year-old model for a stepmother. But being in a lopsided way able to laugh at Paulina's catch made it no less of a blow.

In the eighteen months since I had first met her she had progressed from mousy-haired obscurity to blonde blossoming on the cover of at least one glossy magazine a week. In the last month her radiant eyes had smiled at me (and eight million other men) from a cigarette advertisement in every underground station in London. I had known that it was inevitable that one day she would forsake me if she struck gold in her profession, and our whole relationship had from the start been based on that assumption; but a future without her happy inanity and her generous love-making seemed all of a sudden more bleak than I had expected.

I went through to my bedroom and putting down Paulina's letter on the chest of drawers, caught sight of myself in the oval mirror on the wall above it. That is the face, I thought, that she has been pleased to see beside her on her pillow, but which was no match for a title and a canning fortune. Looking objectively at my reflection I noted the black hair, black eyebrows and lashes, brown eyes ... not a distinguished face, nor handsome; too thin perhaps. Not bad, not good. Just a face.

I turned away and looked around the little sloping-ceilinged room which had been converted for me from a lumber room when I came home from my travels. There was very little in it; a bed, the chest of drawers, an armchair and a bedside table with a lamp on it. One picture, an impressionistic sketch of racing horses, hung on the wall facing my bed. There were no other ornaments, few books, no clutter. In six years of wandering round the world I had become so used to living with a minimum of possessions that although I had now occupied this little room on and off for two years, I had amassed nothing to put in it.

A clothes cupboard had been built for me across one end of the room. I opened the door and tried to look at its contents as Paulina must have looked, the twice she had been there. One good dark grey suit, one evening jacket with black trousers, one hacking jacket, two pairs of grey slacks, and a pair of jodhpurs. I took off the suit I was wearing and hung it at the end of the meagre row, a tweed mixture of browns. They were enough for me, those clothes. They covered every situation. Sir Morton Henge probably counted his suits in dozens and had a manservant to look after them. I shrugged my shoulders. There was no profit in this melancholy stocktaking. Paulina was gone, and that was that.

Picking up a pair of black sneakers, I shut the

cupboard door and changed into jeans and an old checked shirt. That done, I contemplated the desert of time between then and the next day's racing. The trouble with me was that steeplechasing had got into my blood like a drug addiction, so that all the normal pleasures of life, and even Paulina herself, had become merely ways of passing as quickly as possible the hours away from it.

My stomach gave an extra twist, which I would like to have believed was due to romantic desolation at my blasted love life, but which I knew very well was only the effect of not having eaten for twenty-three hours. Admitting wryly that being jettisoned had not spoiled my appetite, I made for the kitchen. Before I reached it, however, the front door of the flat banged open and in trooped my parents, uncles and cousin.

'Hello, darling,' said my mother, presenting a smooth sweet-smelling cheek for a kiss. It was her usual greeting to everyone from impresarios to back row chorus singers, and when applied to me still utterly lacked any maternal quality. She was not a motherly person in any way. Tall, slender and immensely chic in a style that looked casual but was the result of much thought and expenditure, she was becoming more and more a 'presence' as she approached fifty. As a woman I knew her to be passionate and temperamental; as an artist to be a first-class interpretative vehicle for the genius of Haydn, whose piano concertos she poured out with magical, meticulous, ecstatic precision. I had seen hardened music critics leave her performances with tears in their eyes. So I had never expected a broad motherly bosom to comfort my childish woes, nor a sock-darning, cake-making mum to come home to.

My father, who treated me always with polite friendliness, said as a form of greeting, 'Did you have a good day?' He always asked. I usually answered briefly yes or no, knowing that he was not really interested.

I said, 'I saw a man kill himself. No, it wasn't a good day.'

Five heads swivelled towards me.

My mother said, 'Darling, what do you mean?'

'A jockey shot himself at the races. He was only six feet away from me. It was a mess.' All five of them stood there looking at me with their mouths open. I wished I hadn't told them, for it seemed even more horrible in memory than it had done at the time.

But they were unaffected. The 'cello uncle shut his mouth with a snap, shrugged, and went on into the sitting-room, saying over his shoulder, 'Well, if you will go in for these peculiar pursuits...'

My mother followed him with her eyes. There was a bass twang as he picked up his instrument from the sofa, and as if drawn by an irresistible magnet the others drifted after him. Only my cousin stayed long enough to spare Art a thought, then he too went back to his clarinet.

I listened to them re-tuning and setting up the music stands. They began to play a jigging piece for strings and woodwind that I particularly disliked. The flat was suddenly intolerable. I went out and down into the street and began to walk.

There was only one place to go if I wanted a certain kind of peace, and I didn't care to go there too often for fear of wearing out my welcome. But it was a full month since I had seen my cousin Joanna, and I needed some more of her company. Need. That was the only word for it.

She opened the door with her usual air of good humoured invitation.

'Well, hello,' she said, smiling. I followed her into the big converted mews garage which served her as sitting-room, bedroom and rehearsal room all in one. Half of the roof was a sloping skylight, through which the remains of the evening sun still shone. The size and comparative bareness of the room gave it unusual acoustic qualities; if one spoke ordinarily it was like any other room; if one sang, as Joanna did, there was a satisfying illusion of distance and some good amplification from concrete walls.

Joanna's voice was deep and clear and resonant. When she liked, in singing dramatic passages, she could colour it with the suggestion of graininess, a very effective hint of a crack in the bell. She could have made a fortune as a blues singer; but having been born a true classical Finn, so commercial a use of her talent was out of the question. Instead she preferred songs which were to me unmelodic and unrewarding, though she seemed to be amassing a fair-sized reputation with them among people who enjoyed that sort of thing.

She had greeted me in a pair of jeans as old as my own and a black sweater streaked here and there with paint. On an easel stood a half-finished portrait of a man, with some brushes and paints on a table beside it.

'I'm trying my hand at oils,' she said, picking up a brush and making a tentative dab at the picture, 'but it's not going very well, damn it.'

'Stick to charcoal, then,' I said. She had drawn with flowing lines the racing horses which hung in my bedroom, short on anatomy, but full of life and movement.

'I'll finish this, at least,' she said.

I stood and watched her. She squeezed out some carmine.

Without looking at me she said, 'What's the matter?'

I didn't answer. She paused with her brushes in the air and turned and regarded me calmly for some seconds.

'There's some steak in the kitchen,' she said.

A mind reader, my cousin Joanna. I grinned at her and went out into the long narrow lean-to where she both took her bath and did her cooking. It was rump steak, thick and dark. I grilled it with a couple of tomatoes and made some french dressing for a lettuce

27

I found already prepared in a wooden bowl. When the steak was done I divided it on to two plates and took the whole lot back to Joanna. It smelt wonderful.

She put down her brush and came to eat, wiping her hands on the seat of her pants.

'I'll say one thing for you, Rob. You cook a mean steak,' she said, after her first mouthful.

'Thanks for nothing,' I said, with my mouth full.

We ate every scrap. I finished first, and sat back and watched her. She had a fascinating face, full of strength and character, with straight dark eyebrows and, that night, no lipstick. She had tucked her short wavy hair in a no-nonsense style behind her ears, but on top it still curled forward on to her forehead in an untidy fringe.

My cousin Joanna was the reason I was still a bachelor, if one can be said to need a reason at twenty-six years of age. She was three months older than I, which had given her an advantage over me all our lives, and this was a pity, since I had been in love with her from the cradle. I had several times asked her to marry me, but she always said no. First cousins, she explained firmly, were too closely related. Besides which, she added, I didn't stir her blood.

Two other men, however, had done that for her. Both were musicians. And each of them in their turn in a most friendly way had told me how greatly having Joanna for a lover had deepened their appreciation of living, given new impetus to their musical inspiration, opened new vistas, and so on and so on. They were both rather intense brooding men with undeniably handsome faces, and I didn't like hearing what they had to say. On the first occasion, when I was eighteen, I departed in speed and grief to foreign lands, and somehow had not returned for six years. On the second occasion I went straight to a wild party, got thoroughly drunk for the first and only time in my life, and woke up in Paulina's bed. Both adventures had turned out to be satisfying and educational. But they had not cured me of Joanna.

She pushed away her empty plate and said, 'Now, what's the matter?'

I told her about Art. She listened seriously and when I had finished she said, 'The poor man. And his poor wife . . . Why did he do it, do you know?'

'I think it was because he lost his job,' I said. 'Art was such a perfectionist in everything. He was too proud . . . He would never admit he had done anything wrong in a race . . . And I think he simply couldn't face everyone knowing he'd been given the sack. But the odd thing is, Joanna, that he looked as good as ever to me. I know he was thirty-five, but that's not really old for a jockey, and although it was obvious that he and Corin Kellar, the trainer who retained him, were always having rows when their horses didn't win, he hadn't lost any of his style. Someone else would have employed him, even if not one of the top stables like Corin's.'

29

'And there you have it, I should think,' she said. 'Death was preferable to decline.'

'Yes, it looks like it.'

'I hope that when your time comes to retire you will do it less drastically,' she said. I smiled, and she added, 'And just what will you do when you retire?'

'Retire? I have only just started,' I said.

'And in fourteen years' time you'll be a second-rate, battered, bitter forty, too old to make anything of your life and with nothing to live on but horsy memories that no one wants to listen to.' She sounded quite annoyed at the prospect.

'You, on the other hand,' I said, 'will be a fat, middle-aged, contralto's understudy, scared stiff of losing your looks and aware that those precious vocal cords are growing less flexible every year.'

She laughed. 'How gloomy. But I see your point. From now on I'll try not to disapprove of your job because it lacks a future.'

'But you'll go on disapproving for other reasons?'

'Certainly. It's basically frivolous, unproductive, escapist, and it encourages people to waste time and money on inessentials.'

'Like music,' I said.

She glared at me. 'For that you shall do the washing up,' she said, getting to her feet and putting the plates together.

While I did my penance for the worst heresy possibly in the Finn family she went back to her portrait, but it was nearly dusk, and when I brought in a peace offering of some freshly-made coffee she gave it up for the day.

'Is your television set working?' I asked, handing her a cup.

'Yes, I think so.'

'Do you mind if we have it on for a quarter of an hour?'

'Who's playing?' she asked automatically.

I sighed. 'No one. It's a racing programme.'

'Oh, very well. If you must.' But she smiled.

I switched on, and we saw the end of the variety show. I enjoyed the songs of the last performer, a vivacious blonde, but Joanna, technique-minded, said her breath control creaked. A batch of advertisements followed, and then the fluttering urgent opening bars of 'The Galloping Major', accompanied by speeded-up superimposed views of horses racing, announced the weekly fifteen minutes of *Turf Talk*.

The well-known good-looking face of Maurice Kemp-Lore came on the screen, smiling and casual. He began in his easy charming way to introduce his guest of the evening, a prominent bookmaker, and his topic of the evening, the mathematics involved in making a book.

'But first,' he said, 'I would like to pay a tribute to the steeplechase jockey, Art Mathews, who died today by his own hand at Dunstable races. Many of you have watched him ride . . . I expect nearly all of you have

seen televised races in which he has appeared ... and
you will feel with me a great sense of shock that such
a long and successful career should end in a tragedy
of this sort. Although never actually champion jockey,
Art was acknowledged to be one of the six best
steeplechase riders in the country, and his upright
incorruptible character has been a splendid example
to young jockeys just starting in the game ...'

Joanna lifted an eyebrow at me, and Maurice Kemp-
Lore, neatly finishing off Art's glowing obituary,
reintroduced the bookmaker, who gave a clear and
fascinating demonstration of how to come out on the
winning side. His talk, illustrated with films and
animated charts, described the minute by minute
decisions made daily in a big London starting price
office, and was well up to the high standard of all the
Kemp-Lore programmes.

Kemp-Lore thanked him and rounded off the
quarter of an hour with a review of the following
week's racing, not tipping particular animals to win
but giving snippets of information about people and
horses on the basis that there would be more interest
in the outcome of a race if the public already knew
something of the background of the contestants. His
anecdotes were always interesting or amusing, and I
had heard him called the despair of racing journalists
since he so often beat them to a good story.

He said finally, 'See you all next week at the same
time,' and 'The Galloping Major' faded him out.

I switched off the set. Joanna said, 'Do you watch that every week?'

'Yes, if I can,' I said. 'It's a racing must. It's so full of things one ought not to miss, and quite often his guest is someone I've met.'

'Mr Kemp-Lore knows his onions, then?' she said.

'He does indeed. He was brought up to it. His father rode a Grand National winner back in the thirties and is now a big noise on the National Hunt Committee; which,' I went on, seeing her blank look, 'is the ruling body of steeplechasing.'

'Oh. And has Mr Kemp-Lore ridden any Grand National winners himself?' she asked.

'No,' I said. 'I don't think he rides much at all. Horses give him asthma, or something like that. I'm not sure . . . I only know him by sight. He is often at the races but I have never spoken to him.'

Joanna's interest in racing, never very strong, subsided entirely at this point, and for an hour or so we gossiped amicably and aimlessly about how the world wagged.

The door bell rang. She went to answer it and came back followed by the man whose portrait she was attempting, the second of her two blood stirrers, still stirring away. He put his arm possessively round her waist and kissed her. He nodded to me.

'How did the concert go?' she asked. He played a first violin in the London Symphony Orchestra.

'So so,' he said; 'the Mozart B flat went all right

33

except that some fool in the audience started clapping after the slow movement and ruined the transition to the allegro.'

My cousin made sympathetic noises. I stood up. I did not enjoy seeing them so cosily together.

'Going?' asked Joanna, detaching herself.

'Yes.'

'Good night, Rob,' he said, yawning. He took off his black tie and loosened the neck of his shirt.

I said politely, 'Good night, Brian.' And may you rot, I thought.

Joanna came with me to the door and opened it, and I stepped out into the dark cobbled mews and turned to say good-bye. She was silhouetted against the warm light in the studio room where Brian, I could see, was sitting down and taking off his shoes.

I said flatly, 'Thank you for the steak . . . and the television.'

'Come again,' she said.

'Yes. Well, good night.'

'Good night,' she said, and then in an afterthought added, 'How is Paulina?'

'She is going to marry,' I said, 'Sir Morton Henge.'

I am not sure what I expected in the way of sympathy, but I should have known. Joanna laughed.

CHAPTER THREE

Two weeks after Art died I stayed a night in Peter Cloony's house.

It was the first Cheltenham meeting of the season, and having no car I went down as usual on the race train, carrying some overnight things in a small suitcase. I had been engaged for two races at the meeting, one on each day, and intended to find a back street pub whose charges would make the smallest possible dent in my pocket. But Peter, seeing the case, asked me if I were fixed up for the night, and offered me a bed. It was kind of him, for we were not particularly close friends, and I thanked him and accepted.

From my point of view it was an unexciting day. My one ride, a novice hurdler revoltingly called Neddikins, had no chance of winning. His past form was a sorry record of falls and unfinished races. Tailed-off and pulled-up figured largely. I wondered why on earth the owner bothered with the wretched animal, but at the same time rehearsed in advance some

35

complimentary things to say about it. I had long ago discovered that owners hated to be told their horses were useless and often would not employ again a jockey who spoke too much unpalatable truth. It was wiser not to answer the typical question, 'What do you think we should do with beautiful Neddikins next?' with an unequivocal 'Shoot it.'

By working hard from start to finish I managed to wake Neddikins up slightly, so that although we finished plainly last, we were not exactly tailed off. A triumph, I considered it, to have got round at all, and to my surprise this was also the opinion of his trainer, who clapped me on the shoulder and offered me another novice hurdler on the following day.

Neddikins was the first horse I rode for James Axminster, and I knew I had been asked because he had not wanted to risk injury to his usual jockey. A good many of that sort of ride came my way, but I was glad to have them. I reckoned if I could gain enough experience on bad horses when nothing much was expected of me, it would stand me in good stead if ever I found myself on better ones.

At the end of the afternoon I joined Peter and we drove off in his sedate family saloon. He lived in a small village, scarcely more than a hamlet, in a hollow in the Cotswold Hills about twenty miles from Cheltenham. We turned off the main road into a narrow secondary road bordered on each side by thick hedges. It seemed to stretch interminably across bare farm land, but eventually, turning a corner, it came to the edge of the plateau and one could see a whole village spread out in the small valley below.

Peter pointed. 'That bungalow down there is where I live. The one with the white windows.'

I followed his finger. I had time to see a neatly-fenced little garden round a new-looking house before a curve in the road hid it from view. We slid down the hill, rounded several blind corners with a good deal of necessary horn blowing, and at the beginning of the village curled into an even smaller lane and drew up outside Peter's house. It was modern, brick-built, and freshly attractive, with neatly-edged flower beds and shaven squares of lawn.

Peter's wife opened the white front door and came down the path to meet us. She was, I saw, very soon to have a child. She herself looked hardly old enough to have left school. She spoke shyly.

'Do come in,' she said, shaking my hand. 'Peter telephoned to say you were coming, and everything is ready.'

I followed her into the bungalow. It was extremely neat and clean and smelled of furniture polish. All the floors were covered with mottled soft blue linoleum with a few terra-cotta rugs scattered about. Peter's wife, she told me during the evening, had made the rugs herself.

In the sitting-room there was only a sofa, a television set, and a dining-table with four chairs. The bareness of the room was to some extent disguised by one wall being almost completely covered in photographs. They had been framed by Peter himself and were edged in passe-partout in several different bright colours, so that the effect was gay and cheerful. Peter showed them to me while his wife cooked the dinner.

They were clearly devoted to each other. It showed in every glance, every word, every touch. They seemed very well matched; good natured, quickly moved to sympathy, sensitive, and with not a vestige of a sense of humour between them.

'How long have you two been married?' I asked, biting into a wedge of cheese.

Peter said, 'Nine months,' and his wife blushed beguilingly.

We cleared away the dishes and washed them, and spent the evening watching television and talking about racing. When we went to bed they apologized for the state of my bedroom.

'We haven't furnished it properly yet,' said Peter's wife, looking at me with anxious eyes.

'I'll be very comfortable indeed,' I said. 'You are so kind to have had me at all.' She smiled happily.

The bedroom contained a bed and a chair only. There was the blue linoleum on the floor, with a terra-cotta rug. A small mirror on the wall, some thin rust-coloured curtains at the window, and a hook and two hangers on the back of the door to serve as a wardrobe. I slept well.

In the morning, after breakfast, Peter did a lot of household jobs while his wife showed me round the small garden. She seemed to know every flower and growing vegetable individually. The plants were cherished as thoroughly as the house.

'Peter does most of my housework just now,' she said, looking fondly back to the house. 'The baby is due in six days. He says I mustn't strain myself.'

'He is a most considerate husband,' I said.

'The best in the world,' she said fervently.

It was because Peter insisted at the last minute on driving down to the village shop to fetch a loaf of bread to save his wife the walk that we started out for Cheltenham later than we had intended.

We wound up the twisty hill too fast for prudence, but nothing luckily was on its way down. At least, it seemed to be lucky until we had streaked across the farm land and were slowing down to approach the turn into the main road. That was when we first saw the tank carrier. It was slewed across the road diagonally, completely blocking the way.

Peter's urgent tooting on the horn produced one soldier, who ambled over to the car and spoke soothingly.

'I'm very sorry, sir, but we were looking for the road to Timberley.'

'You turned too soon. It's the next road on the right,' said Peter impatiently.

'Yes, I know,' said the soldier. 'We realized we had turned too soon, and my mate tried to back out again, but he made a right mess of it, and we've hit the hedge on the other side. As a matter of fact,' he said casually, 'we're ruddy well stuck. My mate's just hitched a lorry to go and ring up our H.Q. about it.'

We both got out of the car to have a look, but it was true. The great unwieldy articulated tank carrier was solidly jammed across the mouth of the narrow lane, and the driver had gone.

Pale and grim, Peter climbed back into his seat with me beside him. He had to reverse for a quarter of a mile before we came to a gateway he could turn the car in: then we backtracked down the long bend-ridden hill, raced through the village and out on to the road on the far side. It led south, away from Cheltenham, and we had to make a long detour to get back to the right direction. Altogether the tank carrier put at least twelve miles on to our journey.

Several times Peter said, 'I'll be late,' in a despairing tone of voice. He was, I knew, due to ride in the first race, and the trainer for whom he rode liked him to report to him in the weighing-room an hour earlier. Trainers had to state the name of the jockey who would be riding their horse at least three-quarters of an hour before the event: if they took a chance and declared a jockey who had not arrived and then he did not arrive at all, however good the reason, the trainer was in trouble with the stewards. Peter rode for a man who never took this risk. If his jockey was not there an hour before the race, he found a substitute; and since Peter was his jockey, the rule was a good one, because he was by nature a last-minute rusher who left no time margin for things to go wrong.

We reached the racecourse just forty-three minutes before the first race. Peter sprinted from the car park, but he had some way to go and we both knew that he wouldn't do it. As I followed him more slowly and walked across the big expanse of tarmac towards the weighing-room I heard the click of the loud speakers being turned on, and the announcer began to recite the runners and riders of the first race. P. Cloony was not among them.

I found him in the changing-room, sitting on the bench with his head in his hands.

'He didn't wait,' he said miserably. 'He didn't wait. I knew he wouldn't. I knew it. He's put Ingersoll up instead.'

I looked across the room to where Tick-Tock was pulling his boots up over his nylon stockings. He already wore the scarlet jersey which should have been Peter's. He caught my eye and grimaced and shook his head in sympathy: but it was not his fault he had been given the ride, and he had no need to be too apologetic.

The worst of it was that Tick-Tock won. I was

standing beside Peter on the jockeys' stand when the scarlet colours skated by the winning post, and he made a choking sound as if he were about to burst into tears. He managed not to, but there was a certain dampness about his eyes and his face had changed to a bloodless, greyish white.

'Never mind,' I said awkwardly, embarrassed for him. 'It's not the end of the world.'

It had been unfortunate that we had arrived so late, but the trainer he rode for was a reasonable man, if impatient, and there was no question of his not engaging him in future. Peter did in fact ride for him again that same afternoon, but the horse ran less well than was expected, and pulled up lame. My last glimpse of him showed a face still dragged down in lines of disappointment and he was boring everyone in the weighing-room by harping on the tank carrier over and over again.

For myself, things went slightly better. The novice chaser fell at the water jump, but went down slowly and I suffered nothing but grass stains on my breeches.

The young hurdler I was to ride for James Axminster in the last race on the card had as vile a reputation as his stablemate the previous day and I had made completing the race my sole target. But for some reason the wayward animal and I got on very well together from the start, and to my surprise, an emotion shared by every single person present, we came over the last hurdle in second place and passed the leading horse on the uphill stretch to the winning post. The odds-on favourite finished fourth. It was my second win of the season, and my first ever at Cheltenham: and it was greeted with dead silence.

I found myself trying to explain it away to James Axminster in the winner's unsaddling enclosure.

'I'm very sorry, sir,' I said. 'I couldn't help it.'

I knew he hadn't had a penny on it, and the owner had not even bothered to come to see the horse run.

He looked at me broodingly without answering, and I thought that there was one trainer who would not employ me again in a hurry. Sometimes it is as bad to win unexpectedly as to lose on a certainty.

I unbuckled the girths, pulled the saddle off over my arm and stood waiting for the storm to break.

'Well, go along and weigh in,' he said abruptly. 'And when you're dressed I want to talk to you.'

When I came out of the changing-room he was standing just inside the weighing-room door talking to Lord Tirrold, whose horse he trained. They stopped talking and turned towards me as I went over to them, but I could not see their expressions clearly as they had their backs to the light.

James Axminster said, 'What stable do you ride for most?'

I said, 'I ride mainly for farmers who train their own horses. I haven't a steady job with a public trainer, but I have ridden for several when they have asked me. Mr Kellar has put me up a few times.' And that,

I thought a little wryly, is the true picture of the smallness of the impression I had made in the racing world.

'I have heard one or two trainers say,' said Lord Tirrold, speaking directly to Axminster, 'that for their really bad horses they can always get Finn.'

Axminster grinned back at him. 'Just what I did today, and look at the result! How am I going to convince the owner it was as much a surprise to me as it will be to him when he hears about it? I've told him often that the horse is pretty useless.' He turned to me. 'You have made me look a proper fool, you know.'

'I'm sorry, sir,' I said again: and I meant it.

'Don't look so glum about it. I'll give you another chance; several in fact. There's a slow old plug you can ride for me on Saturday, if you're not booked already for that race, and two or three others next week. After that . . . we'll see.'

'Thank you,' I said dazedly. 'Thank you very much.' It was as if he had thrust a gold brick into my hands when I had expected a scorpion: if I acquitted myself at all well on his horses he might use me regularly as a second-string jockey. That would be, for me, a giant step up.

He smiled a warm, almost mischievous smile which crinkled the skin round his eyes and said, 'Geranium in the handicap chase at Hereford on Saturday, then. Are you free?'

'Yes,' I said.

'And you can do the weight? Ten stone?'

'Yes,' I said. I'd need to lose another three pounds in the two days, but starvation had never seemed so attractive.

'Very well. I'll see you there.'

'Yes, sir,' I said.

He and Lord Tirrold turned away and went out of the weighing-room together, and I heard them laugh. I watched them go, the thin angular Lord Tirrold and the even taller trainer, a pair who had between them won almost every important event in the National Hunt calendar.

James Axminster was a big man in every sense. Six foot four and solidly bulky, he moved and spoke and made decisions with easy assurance. He had a big face with a prominent nose and a square-looking heavy lower jaw. When he smiled his lower teeth showed in front of the upper ones, and they were good strong teeth, evenly set and unusually white.

His stable was one of the six largest in the country: his jockey, Pip Pankhurst, had been champion for the past two seasons; and his horses, about sixty of them, included some of the best alive. To have been offered a toe-hold in this set-up was almost as frightening as it was miraculous. If I messed up this chance, I thought, I might as well follow Art into oblivion.

I spent most of the next day running round Hyde Park in three sweaters and a wind-cheater and resisting the temptation to drink pints of water to replace what

I had sweated off. Some of the other jockeys used dehydrating pills to rid their bodies of fluid (which weighs more than fat and is easier to shift) but I had found, the only time I took some, that they left me feeling almost too weak to ride.

At about six o'clock I boiled three eggs and ate them without salt or bread, and then removed myself hurriedly, for my mother was entertaining some friends to dinner, and the girl who came to cook for us on these occasions was beginning to fill the kitchen with demoralizing savoury smells. I decided to go to the pictures to take my mind off my stomach; but it wasn't a great success as I chose the film somewhat carelessly, and found myself watching three men staggering on their parched way through a blazing desert sharing their rations into ever dwindling morsels.

After that I went to the Turkish baths in Jermyn Street and spent the whole night there, sweating gently all evening and again when I woke in the morning. Then I went back to the flat and ate three more boiled eggs, which I no longer cared for very much, and at last made my way to Hereford.

The needle quivered when I sat on the scales with the lightest possible saddle and thin boots. It swung up over the ten stone mark and pendulumed down and finally settled a hair's breadth on the right side.

'Ten stone,' said the clerk of the scales in a surprised voice. 'What have you been doing? Sandpapering it off?'

'More or less,' I grinned.

In the parade ring James Axminster looked at the number boards where the weights the horses carried were recorded, if they differed from those printed in the race cards. He turned back to me.

'No overweight?' he asked.

'No, sir,' I said matter-of-factly, as if it were the easiest thing in the world.

'Hm.' He beckoned the lad who was leading round the slow old plug I was to ride and said, 'You'll have to kick this old mare along a bit. She's lazy. A good jumper, but that's about all.'

I was used to kicking lazy horses. I kicked, and the mare jumped: and we finished third.

'Hm,' said Axminster again as I unbuckled the girths. I took my saddle and weighed in – half a pound lighter – and changed into the colours of the other horse I had been engaged to ride that afternoon, and when I walked out into the weighing-room, Axminster was waiting for me. He had a paper in his hand. He gave it to me without a word.

It was a list of five horses running in various races during the following week. Against each horse's name he had put the weight it had to carry and the race it was to run in. I read through them.

'Well?' he said. 'Can you ride them?'

'I can ride four of them,' I said. 'But I'm already booked for that novice chase on Wednesday.'

'Is it important? Can you get off?' he asked.

I would dearly have liked to say yes. The paper I held was an invitation to my personal paradise, and there was always the chance that if I refused one of his mounts, the man who got it might corner all the future ones.

'I . . . no,' I said, 'I ought not to. It's for the farmer who gave me my first few rides . . .'

Axminster smiled faintly, the lower teeth showing in front. 'Very well. Ride the other four.'

I said, 'Thank you, sir. I'd be glad to.' He turned away, and I folded up the precious list and put it in my pocket.

My other ride later that afternoon was for Corin Kellar. Since Art's death he had employed several different jockeys and moaned to them about the inconvenience of not having a first-class man always on call. As it was his treatment of Art which had driven a first-class man to leave him in the most drastic possible way, Tick-Tock and I considered him a case for psychiatry; but both of us were glad enough to ride his horses, and Tick-Tock had ridden more of them than anyone else.

'If Corin asks you,' I said as we collected our saddles and helmets ready to weigh out for the race, 'will you accept Art's job?'

'If he asks me, yes,' said Tick-Tock. 'He won't harass *me* into the hereafter.' He looked up slantwise from under his rakishly tilted eyebrows, the thin-lipped, wide mouth stretched in a carefree grin. A vivid,

48

almost aggressive sanity moulded the angular planes of his face, and for a moment he seemed to me more than ever to have been born too soon. He was what I pictured twenty-first century man should be – intensely alive, curiously innocent, with no taint of apathy or anger or greed. He made me feel old. He was nineteen.

We went out together to the parade ring.

'Paste on a toothy leer,' he said. 'The eye of the world has swivelled our way.'

I glanced up. From its draughty platform a television camera swung its square snout towards us as it followed the progress of a grey horse round the ring. It tracked briefly over us and moved on.

'I'd forgotten we were on the air,' I said indifferently.

'Oh, yes,' said Tick-Tock, 'and the great man himself is here somewhere too, the one and only M. Kemp-Lore, no less. Puff pastry, that man is.'

'How do you mean?' I asked.

'A quick riser. And full of hot air. But rich, man, and tasty. A good crisp flavour, nice and crunchy.'

I laughed. We joined Corin and he began to give us both our instructions for the race. Tick-Tock's mount was a good one, but I was as usual riding a horse of whom little was expected, and quite rightly, as it turned out. We trailed in a long way behind, and I saw from the numbers going up in the frame that Corin's other horse had won.

Corin and Tick-Tock and the horse's owner were

conducting a mutual admiration session in the winner's
enclosure when I walked back to the weighing-room
with my saddle, but Corin caught me by the arm as I
went past and asked me to come straight out again,
when I had dumped my saddle and helmet, to tell him
how the horse had run.

When I rejoined him he was talking to a man who
had his back towards me. I hovered, not wanting to
interrupt, but Corin saw me and beckoned, and I
walked across to them. The man turned round. He
was in his early thirties, I judged. Of average height
and slim build, with good features and light hair. It
never ceases to be disconcerting, meeting for the first
time in the flesh a man whose face is as familiar to
you as a brother's. It was Maurice Kemp-Lore.

Television is unflattering to everybody. It fattens the
body and flattens the personality, so that to sparkle
from the small screen an entertainer must be positively
incandescent in real life, and Kemp-Lore was no
exception. The charm which came over gradually in
his programme was instantly compelling when one met
him. Intensely blue eyes looked at me from a firm,
sun-tanned face; his hand-shake was quick and strong,
his smile, infectious and warm, indicated his delight in
meeting me. But it was a professional delight, and
even as I responded to him I recognized that the effect
he had on me was calculated. His stock in trade. All
good interviewers know how to give people confidence
so that they expand and flower, and Kemp-Lore was

a master of his art. Dull men had shone as wits in his programme, taciturn men chattered, bigoted men thought again.

'I see you were last in the race,' he said. 'Bad luck.'

'Bad horse,' said Corin, put into smiling good humour by his presence.

'I've been wanting for some time to do a programme on – if you'll forgive me – an unsuccessful jockey.' His smile took the sting out of his words. 'Or at least, a jockey who is not yet successful. Perhaps that would be a fairer way of putting it?' His blue eyes twinkled. 'Would you consider coming on my programme and telling viewers what sort of life you lead? I have in mind your financial position, your reliance on chance rides, insecurity ... that sort of thing. Just to give the public the reverse side of the coin. They know all about big retainers and fat presents and jockeys who win important races. I want to show them how a jockey who seldom wins even unimportant races manages to live. A jockey on the fringe.' He smiled his warm smile. 'Will you do it?'

'Yes,' I said, 'certainly. But I'm not really typical. I ...'

He interrupted me. 'Don't tell me anything now,' he said, 'I know enough about your career to find you suitable for what I have in mind, but I always prefer not to know the answers to my specific questions until we are actually on the air. It makes the whole thing more spontaneous. I have found that if I rehearse with my subject what we are going to say the programme comes over stiffly and unconvincingly. Instead, I will send you a list of the sort of questions I will be asking, and you can think out your replies. 'O.K.?'

'Yes,' I said. 'All right.'

'Good. Next Friday then. The programme goes out at nine o'clock. Get to the studios by seven-thirty, will you? That gives time for seeing to lighting, make-up, and so on, and perhaps for a drink beforehand. Here is a card which will tell you how to get there.' He produced a card which had 'Universal Telecast' printed in large capitals on one side and a simplified map of Willesden on the other.

'Oh, and by the way, there will be a fee, of course, and your expenses.' He smiled sympathetically, letting me know that he knew that that was good news.

'Thank you,' I smiled back. 'I'll be there.'

He spoke a word to Corin and strolled away. I turned to Corin and caught on his face as he watched the retreating figure of Kemp-Lore, the same expression that I saw so often on hangers-on round my parents. The smug, fawning smirk which meant 'I am on speaking terms with a famous person, clever me.' It would have been more impressive, I thought, if like most other trainers he had taken knowing the illustrious Kemp-Lore entirely for granted.

'I know Maurice quite well,' said Corin aloud, in a self-satisfied voice. 'He asked my advice about whether you'd be any good as his – er – unsuccessful jockey, and I told him to go ahead.'

'Thanks,' I said, as he waited for it.

'Yes, a grand fellow, Maurice. Good family, you know. His father won the National – an amateur of course – and his sister is the best lady point-to-point rider there has been for years. Poor old Maurice, though, he hardly rises at all. Doesn't even hunt. Horses give him the most ghastly asthma, you know. He's very cut-up about it. Still, he'd never have taken to broadcasting if he'd been able to race, so perhaps it's all for the best.'

'I dare say,' I said. I was still in lightweight silk colours and breeches and the afternoon was growing cool. I dragged the conversation back to the horse I had just come last on, got the post-mortem over, and eventually went back to the weighing-room to change.

The jockeys had already gone out for the last race, but several others were standing about in various stages of undress, gossiping and putting on their street clothes. As I went down the room I saw Grant Oldfield standing by my peg, holding a paper in his hand, and I was annoyed to find, drawing nearer, that it was the list of horses James Axminster had given me. Grant had been going through my pockets.

My protest was never uttered. Without a word, without any warning, Grant swung his fist and punched me heavily in the nose.

CHAPTER FOUR

The amount of blood which resulted would have done credit to a clinic full of donors. It splashed in a scarlet stain down the front of my pale green silk shirt and made big uneven blotches on the white breeches. There were large spots of it on the bench and on the floor and it was all over my hands where I had tried to wipe it out of my mouth.

'For God's sake, lay him down on his back,' said one of the valets, hurrying over. His advice was almost unnecessary, since I was already lying down, mostly on the floor but half propped up by the leg of the bench. It was where that one blow, catching me off balance, had felled me.

Grant stood at my feet, looking down as if surprised to have caused so much mess. I could have laughed if I had not been so busy swallowing what seemed like cupfuls of my own blood.

Young Mike thrust a saddle under my shoulders and pushed my head backwards over it. A second later he was piling a cold, wet towel across the bridge of my nose; and gradually the breath-clogging bleeding lessened and stopped.

'You'd better stay there for a bit,' said Mike. 'I'll go and get one of the first-aid men to see to you.'

'Don't bother,' I said. 'Please don't bother, it's all right now.'

He came back irresolutely from the door and stood by my head. He looked upside down to me, as my eyes were level with his ankles.

'What the hell did you do that for?' he said to Grant.

I wanted to hear his answer too, but Grant did not reply. He scowled down at me, then turned on his heel and pushed his way out of the changing-room against the incoming tide of the jockeys returning from the last race. The list of Axminster horses fluttered to the floor in his wake. Mike picked it up and put it into my outstretched hand.

Tick-Tock dumped his saddle on the bench, tipped back his helmet, and put his hands on his hips.

'What have we here? A blood bath?' he said.

'Nose bleed,' I said.

'You don't say.'

The others began crowding round and I decided I'd been lying down long enough. I lifted the towel off my face and stood up gingerly. All was well. The fountains had dried up.

'Grant socked him one,' said one of the jockeys who had been there all the time.

'Why?'

'Ask me another,' I said. 'Or ask Grant.'

'You ought to report it to the stewards.'

'It's not worth it,' I said.

I cleaned myself up and changed, and walked down to the station with Tick-Tock.

'You must know why he hit you,' he said. 'Or was it merely target practice?'

I handed him Axminster's list. He read it and gave it back.

'Yes, I see. Hatred, envy and jealousy. You're stepping into the shoes he couldn't fill himself. He had his chance there, and he muffed it.'

'What happened?' I asked. 'Why did Axminster drop him?'

'I don't honestly know,' Tick-Tock said, 'you'd better ask Grant and find out what mistakes not to make.' He grinned. 'Your nose looks like a vulgar seaside postcard.'

'It's good enough for the goggle box,' I said. I told him about Maurice Kemp-Lore's invitation.

'My dear sir,' he said, sweeping off his Tyrolean hat, and making me a mocking bow. 'I am impressed.'

'You're a fool,' I said, grinning.

'Thank God.'

We went our ways, Tick-Tock to his digs in Berkshire and I to Kensington. The flat was empty, the usual state of affairs on Saturday evenings, a busy night for concerts. I took half the ice cubes from the refrigerator, wrapped them in a plastic bag and a tea towel and lay down on the bed with the ice bag balanced on my forehead. My nose felt like a jelly. Grant's fist had had the power of severe mental disturbance behind it.

I shut my eyes and thought about them, Grant and Art; two disintegrated people. One had been driven to violence against himself, and the other had turned violent against the world. Poor things, I thought rather too complacently, they were not stable enough to deal with whatever had undermined them: and I remembered that easy pity, later on.

On the following Wednesday Peter Cloony came to the races bubbling over with happiness. The baby was a boy, his wife was fine, everything was rosy. He slapped us all on the back and told us we didn't know what we were missing. The horse he rode that afternoon started favourite and ran badly, but it didn't damp his spirits.

The next day he was due to ride in the first race, and he was late. We knew before he arrived that he had missed his chance, because five minutes before the deadline for declaring jockeys his trainer had sent an official into the changing-room to find out if he was there, and he wasn't.

I was standing outside the weighing-room when Peter finally came, forty minutes before the first race.

He was running over the grass, anxiety clear on his face even from a distance. His trainer detached himself from the group of people had he been talking to and intercepted him. Fragments of angry remarks floated across to me.

'Is this your idea of an hour before the first? ... I've had to get another jockey ... very stupid of you ... second time in a week ... irresponsible ... not the way to go on if you want to keep your job with me ...' He stalked away.

Peter brushed past me, white, trembling and looking sick, and when I went back into the changing-room a short time later he was sitting on a bench with his head in his hands.

'What happened this time?' I asked. 'Is your wife all right? And the baby?' I thought he must have been so busy attending to them that he had forgotten to watch the clock.

'They're fine,' he said miserably. 'My mother-in-law is staying with us to look after them. I wasn't late setting out ... only five minutes or so ... but ...' he stood up and gazed at me with his large, moist-looking eyes, '... you'll never believe it but there was something else stuck across the lane, and I had to go miles round again, even further than last time ...' His voice trailed off as I looked at him in disbelief.

'Not another tank carrier?' I asked incredulously.

'No, a car. An old car, one of those heavy old Jaguars. It had its nose in the hedge and one front wheel in the ditch, and it was jammed tight, right across the lane.'

'You couldn't have helped its driver push it straight again?' I asked.

'There wasn't any driver. No one at all. And the car doors were locked, and the hand-brake was full on, and he'd left the thing in gear. The stinking bastard.' Peter seldom used such strong language. 'Another man had driven up the hill behind me and we both tried to shift the Jag, but it was absolutely hopeless. We had to reverse again for miles, and he had to go first, and he wouldn't hurry a yard ... he had a new car and he was afraid of scratching it.'

'It's very bad luck,' I said inadequately.

'Bad luck!' he repeated explosively, apparently near to tears. 'It's more than bad luck it's – it's awful. I can't afford ... I need the money ...' He stopped talking and swallowed several times, and sniffed, 'We've got a mortgage to pay off,' he said, 'and I didn't know babies could cost so much. And my wife had to stop working, which we hadn't reckoned on ... we didn't mean to have a baby so soon.'

I remembered vividly the new little bungalow with its cheap, blue linoleum, its home-made terra-cotta rugs, it bare, bare furnishings. And he had a car to run and now a child to keep. I saw that the loss of a ten guinea riding fee was a calamity.

He had not been booked for any other ride that afternoon, and he spent the whole day mooching about the weighing-room so as to be under the eye of any trainers looking hurriedly for a jockey. He wore a desperate, hunted look all the time, and I knew that that alone would have discouraged me, had I been a trainer. He left, unemployed and disconsolate, just before the fifth race, having done himself no good at all in the eyes of every trainer at the meeting.

I watched him trailing off to the car park as I walked down from the weighing-room to the parade ring for my own one-and-only ride of the day, and I felt a surge of irritation against him. Why couldn't he pretend a little, make light of his misfortune, shrug it off? And why above all didn't he leave himself a margin for error on his journeys, when unprompt arrivals cost him so much? A punctured tyre, a windscreen shattered by a flying stone, anything might make him late. It didn't have to be as unforeseeable as a tank carrier or a locked Jaguar wedged immovably across his path. And what a dismal coincidence, I reflected, that it should have happened twice in a week.

James Axminster smiled his disconcerting, heavy-jawed smile in the parade ring and introduced me to the owner of the horse I was to ride. He shook hands and we made the usual desultory pre-race conversation. The middle-aged handicap hurdler plodding sleepily round the ring was the third Axminster horse I had ridden during the week, and I had already grown to appreciate the sleekness and slickness of his organization. His horses were well schooled and beautifully turned out, and there was nothing makeshift or second-best in any of his equipment. Success and prosperity spoke from every brightly initialled horse rug, every top quality bridle, every brush, bandage and bucket that came to the meetings.

In the two earlier races that week I had been riding the stable's second string while Pip Pankhurst took his usual place on the better horses. Thursday's handicap hurdle, however, was all my own because Pip could not do the weight.

'Anything under ten stone six, and it's yours,' he told me, cheerfully, when he found I was riding some of his stable's horses. 'Anything under ten six is hardly worth riding, anyway.' ·

By eating and drinking very little I had managed to keep my riding weight down to ten stone for a whole week. This meant a body weight of nine stone eight, which was a strain at my height, but with Pip in that ungrudging frame of mind it was well worth it.

James Axminster said, 'At the fourth hurdle, you want to be somewhere in the middle. About three from home, providing they're not too strung out, you want to lie about fourth. He takes some time to get into top gear, so start him moving going into the second last. Keep him going, try to come up to the leader at the last and see how much you can gain in the air there. This horse is a great jumper, but has no finishing speed. Very one-paced. See what you can do, anyway.'

He had not given me such detailed instructions before, and it was the first time he had mentioned anything about what to do at the last obstacle. I felt a deep quiver of excitement in my stomach. At last I was about to ride a horse whose trainer would not be thoroughly surprised if he won.

I followed my instructions to the letter, and coming into the last hurdle level with two other horses I kicked my old mount with all the determination I could muster. He responded with a zipping leap which sped him clean past the other horses in mid-air and landed us a good two lengths clear of them. I heard the clatter of the hurdles as the others rapped them, and basely hoped they had made stumbling, time-wasting landings. It was true that the old hurdler could not quicken. I got him balanced and ran him straight to the winning post, using my whip hardly at all and concentrating mainly on sitting still and not disturbing him. He held on gamely, and still had half a length in hand when we passed the post. It was a gorgeous moment.

'Well done,' said Axminster matter-of-factly. Winners were nothing out of the ordinary to him. I unbuckled the girths and slid the saddle off over my arm, and patted the hurdler's sweating neck.

The owner was delighted. 'Well done, well done,' he said to the horse, Axminster and me indiscriminately. 'I never thought he'd pull it off, James, even though I took your advice and backed him.'

I looked quickly at Axminster. His piercingly blue eyes regarded me quizzically.

'Do you want the job?' he asked. 'Second to Pip, regular?'

I nodded and dragged in a deep breath, and said, 'Yes.' It sounded like a croak.

The hurdler's owner laughed. 'It's Finn's lucky week. John Ballerton tells me Maurice is interviewing him on his television programme tomorrow evening.'

'Really?' Axminster said. 'I'll try and watch it.'

I went to weigh in and change, and when I came out Axminster gave me another list of horses, four of them, which he wanted me to ride the following week.

'From now on,' he said, 'I don't want you to accept any rides without finding out first if I need you. All right?'

'Yes, sir,' I said, trying not to show too much of the idiotic delight I was feeling. But he knew. He was too old a hand not to. His eyes glimmered with understanding and friendliness and promise.

I telephoned to Joanna. 'How about dinner? I want to celebrate.'

'What?' she asked economically.

'A winner. A new job. All's right with the world,' I said.

'You sound as if you've been celebrating already.'

'No,' I said. 'Any drunkenness you can hear in my voice is due to being hit on the head by good luck.'

She laughed. 'All right then. Where?'

'Hennibert's,' I said. It was a small restaurant in St James's Street with a standard of cooking to match its address, and prices to match both.

'Oh yes,' said Joanna. 'Shall I come in my golden coach?'

'I mean it,' I said. 'I've earned forty pounds this week. I want to spend some of it. And besides, I'm hungry.'

'You won't get a table,' she said.

'It's booked.'

'I'm sold,' she said. 'I'll be there at eight.'

She came in a taxi, a compliment to me as she was a girl who liked walking. She wore a dress I had not seen before, a slender straight affair made of a firm, deep-blue material which moved with a faint shimmer when the light fell on it. Her springy dark hair curved neatly down on to the nape of her neck, and the slanting outward tapering lines she had drawn on her eyelids made her black eyes look bigger and deep set and mysterious. Every male head turned to look at her as we walked down the room: yet she was not pretty, not eye-catchingly glamorous, not even notably well dressed. She looked . . . I surprised myself with the word . . . intelligent.

We ate avocados with french dressing and *boeuf stroganoff* with spinach, and late crop strawberries and cream, and a mushroom and bacon and prune savoury. For me, after so many bird-sized meals, it was a feast. We took a long time eating and drank a bottle of wine, and sat over our coffee talking with the ease of a friendship which stretched back to childhood. Most of the time, after so much practice, I could keep my more uncousinly feelings for Joanna well concealed from her; and it was necessary to conceal them because I knew from past experience that if I even approached the subject of love she would begin to fidget and avoid my eyes, and would very soon find a good reason for leaving. If I wanted to enjoy her company, it had to be on her terms.

She seemed genuinely pleased about the James Axminster job. Even though racing didn't interest her, she saw clearly what it meant to me.

'It's like the day the musical director at the Handel Society picked me out of the choir to sing my first recitative. I felt like a pouter pigeon and so full of air that I thought I would need guy-ropes to keep my feet on the ground.'

'Heady stuff,' I agreed. My first elation had settled down to a warm cosy glow of satisfaction. I did not remember ever having felt so content.

I told her about the television programme.

'Tomorrow?' she said. 'Good, I think I'll be free to watch you. You don't do things by halves, do you?'

I grinned. 'This is just the start,' I said. I almost believed it.

We walked all the way back to Joanna's studio. It was a clear crisp night with the stars blazing coldly in the black sky. Depth upon depth of infinity. We stopped in the dark mews outside Joanna's door and looked up.

'They put things into proportion, don't they?' she said.

'Yes.' I wondered what it was that she needed to see in proportion. I looked at her. It was a mistake. The up-tilted face with starlight reflected in the shadowy eyes, the dark hair tousled again by our walk, the strong line of throat, the jut of breasts close to my arm, they swept me ruthlessly into the turmoil I had been suppressing all evening.

'Thank you for coming,' I said abruptly. 'Good night, Joanna.'

She said, surprised, 'Wouldn't you like some more coffee ... or something?'

Or something. Yes.

I said, 'I couldn't eat or drink another thing. Anyway ... there's Brian ...'

'Brian's in Manchester, on tour,' she said. But it was a statement of fact, not an invitation.

'Oh. Well, all the same, I think I'd better get some sleep,' I said.

'All right, then.' She was undisturbed. 'A lovely dinner, Rob. Thank you.' She put her hand for a moment on my shoulder in a friendly fashion and smiled good night. She put the key in her door and opened it and waved briefly to me as I turned and started back down the mews. She shut her door. I swore violently, aloud. It wasn't much relief. I looked up at the sky. The stars went on whizzing round in their courses, uncaring and cold.

CHAPTER FIVE

They gave me what in the Finn family was known as
F.I.P. treatment at the Universal Telecast Studios.
Fairly Important Person. It meant being met by
someone well enough up in the hierarchy of the
organization for it to be clear that trouble was being
taken, but not so high that he needed to be supported
by lieutenants.

My mother was a connoisseur of all the shades
between V.I.P. and F.I.P. and invariably noticed every
detail of the pains or lack of them taken to make her
feel comfortable. Her awareness had rubbed off on to
me at a very early age and the whole gambit caused me
a lot of quiet amusement when I grew up. Years of
being a U.I.P. (Unimportant Person) had only
sharpened my appreciation.

I went through the swinging glass doors into the
large echoing entrance hall and asked the girl at
the reception desk where I should go. She smiled
kindly. Would I sit down, she said, gesturing to a near-

by sofa. I sat. She spoke down the telephone, 'Mr Finn is here, Gordon.'

Within ten seconds a burly young man with freckles and a rising-young-executive, navy-blue, pin-striped suit advanced briskly from one of the corridors.

'Mr Finn?' he said expansively, holding out a hand protruding from a snowy, gold-linked shirt cuff.

'Yes,' I said, standing up and shaking hands.

'Glad to have you here. I am Gordon Kildare, Associate Producer. Maurice is up in the studio running over the last-minute details, so I suggest we go along and have a drink and a sandwich first.' He led the way down the corridor he had come from and we turned in through an open door into a small impersonal reception room. On the table stood bottles and glasses and four plates of fat freshly-cut and appetizing-looking sandwiches.

'What will you have?' he asked hospitably, his hands hovering over the bottles.

'Nothing, thank you,' I said.

He was not put out. 'Perhaps afterwards, then?' He poured some whisky into a glass, added soda and raised it to me, smiling. 'Good luck,' he said. 'Is this your first time on television?'

I nodded.

'The great thing is to be natural.' He picked up a sandwich with a pink filling and took a squelchy bite.

The door opened and two more men came in. Introduced to me as Dan something and Paul

69

something, they were a shade less carefully dressed than Gordon Kildare, to whom they deferred. They too dug into the sandwiches and filled their glasses, and wished me luck and told me to be natural.

Maurice Kemp-Lore strode briskly in with a couple of sports-jacketed assistants in tow.

'My dear chap,' he greeted me, shaking me warmly by the hand. 'Glad to see you're here in good time. Has Gordon been looking after you? That's right. Now, what are you drinking?'

'Nothing just now,' I said.

'Oh? Oh well, never mind. Perhaps afterwards? You got the list of questions all right?'

I nodded.

'Have you thought out some answers?'

'Yes,' I said.

'Good, good. That's fine,' he said.

Gordon handed him a well-filled glass and offered him the sandwiches. The assistants helped themselves. It dawned on me that the refreshments provided for the entertainment of visitors probably served all of them as their main evening meal.

Kemp-Lore looked at his watch. 'Our other guest is cutting it rather fine.' As he spoke, the telephone rang. Gordon answered it, listened briefly, said 'He's here, Maurice,' and opened the door.

Kemp-Lore went out first, followed by Gordon and either Dan or Paul, who looked very much alike. It was a more impressive welcoming committee than had been accorded me: I smiled to think of what my mother would have said.

A sports-jacketed assistant offered me sandwiches. 'No?' he said. 'Oh, well, a lot of people feel like that beforehand. You'll be very hungry afterwards.' He put two sandwiches carefully together and stretched open his mouth to bite them.

The voice of Kemp-Lore could be heard coming back along the corridor talking with someone who spoke in a harsh voice with a nasal twang. I wondered idly who the other guest would be and whether I knew him. At the doorway Kemp-Lore stood respectfully back to let his guest precede him into the room. My spirits sank. Paunch and horn-rims well to the fore, Mr John Ballerton allowed himself to be ushered in.

Kemp-Lore introduced all the television men to him. 'And Rob Finn, of course, you know?' he said.

Ballerton nodded coldly in my direction without meeting my eyes. Evidently it still rankled with him that I had seen him sicking up beside Art's body. Perhaps he knew that I had not kept it a secret from the other jockeys.

'It's time we went up to the studio, I think,' Kemp-Lore said, looking enquiringly at Gordon, who nodded.

We all filed out into the corridor, and as I passed the table I noticed the sandwich plates now held nothing but crumbs and a few straggly pieces of cress.

The smallish studio held a chaotic-looking tangle of cameras trailing their thick cables over the floor. To one side there was a shallow carpet-covered platform on which stood three low-slung chairs and a coffee table. A tray with three cups, cream jug and sugar basin shared the table with three empty balloon brandy glasses, a silver cigarette box and two large glass ash-trays.

Kemp-Lore took Ballerton and me towards this arrangement.

'We want to look as informal as possible,' he said pleasantly. 'As if we had just had dinner and were talking over coffee and brandy and cigars.'

He asked Ballerton to sit in the left-hand chair and me in the right, and then took his place between us. Set in front and slightly to one side stood a monitor set with a blank screen; and in a semicircle a battery of cameras converged their menacing black lenses in our direction.

Gordon and his assistants spent some time checking their lights, which dazed us with a dazzling intensity for a few moments, and then tested for sound while the three of us made stilted conversation over the empty cups. When he was satisfied, Gordon came over to us. 'You all need make-up,' he said. 'Maurice, you'll see to yours as usual? Then Mr Ballerton and Mr Finn, I'll show you where to go, if you will follow me?'

He led us to a small room off one corner of the studio. There were two girls in pink overalls and bright smiles.

'It won't take long,' they said, smoothing coloured

cream into our skins. 'Just a little darkener under the eyes... that's right. Now powder...' They patted the powder on with pads of cotton wool, carefully flicking off the excess. 'That's all.'

I looked in the mirror. The make-up softened and blurred both the outlines of the face and texture of the skin. I didn't much care for it.

'You'd look ill on television without it,' the girls assured us. 'You need make-up to look natural and healthy.'

Ballerton frowned and complained as one of them powdered the bald patch on his head. The girl insisted politely. 'It'll shine too much otherwise, you see,' she said, and went on patting his head with the cotton wool.

He caught me grinning at him and it clearly made him furious, raising a dark flush under the sun-tone make-up. There was no question of his ever sharing a rueful joke at his own expense, and I should have known it. I sighed to myself. This made twice that I had seen him at what he considered a disadvantage, and though I had not meant at all to antagonize him, it seemed that I had made a thorough job of it.

We went back into the studio and Kemp-Lore beckoned to us to take our places in the chairs on the platform.

'I'll just run through the order of the programme,' he said, 'so that you will know what to expect. After the introductory music I am going to talk to you first,

73

John, along the lines we discussed. After that, Rob will tell us what his sort of life entails. We have some film of a race you rode in, Rob, which we are using as an illustration, and I plan to fit that in fairly near the beginning of our talk. It will be thrown on to that screen over there.' He pointed.

'For the last few minutes, John will have a chance to comment on what you have said and we might have a final word or two from you. We'll see how it goes. Now, the great thing is to talk naturally. I've explained that too much rehearsal spoils the spontaneity of a programme like this, but it means that a lot of the success of the next quarter of an hour depends on you. I'm sure you will both do splendidly.' He finished his pep talk with a cheerful grin, and I did in fact feel confidence flowing into me from him.

One of the sports-jacketed assistants stepped on to the shallow platform with a coffee pot in one hand and a brandy bottle in the other. He poured hot black coffee into the three cups, and put the pot down on the tray. Then he uncorked the brandy and wet the bottom of the balloon glasses.

'No expense spared,' he said cheerfully. He produced three cigars from the breast pocket of the sports jacket and offered them to us. Ballerton accepted one and sniffed it and rolled it between his fingers, curving his bad-tempered mouth into what passed with him for a smile.

'Two minutes,' shouted a voice.

The spotlights flashed on, dazzling as before, blacking out everything in the studio. For a moment the monitor set showed a close-up of the coffee cups: then it went dark and the next picture on it was an animated cartoon advertising petrol. It was tuned now to what was actually being transmitted.

'Thirty seconds. Quiet please. Quiet please,' Gordon said.

A hush fell over the whole area. I glanced at the monitor set in front of us. It was busy with a silent advertisement for soap flakes. Dimly seen beyond the lights, Gordon stood with his hand raised. There was dead silence. Steam rose gently from the three coffee cups. Everyone waited. Kemp-Lore beside me arranged his features in the well-known smile, looking straight ahead at the round black lens of the camera. The smile stayed in position for ten seconds without wavering.

On the monitor set the superimposed horses galloped and faded. Gordon's hand swept down briskly. The camera in front of Kemp-Lore developed a shining red eye and he began to speak, pleasantly, intimately, straight into a million sitting-rooms.

'Good evening ... tonight I am going to introduce you to two people who are both deeply involved with National Hunt racing, but who look at it, so to speak, from opposite poles. First, here is Mr John Ballerton ...' He gave him a good build-up but overdid the importance. There were about forty-nine other members of the National Hunt Committee, including Kemp-Lore's own father, all at least as active and devoted as the fat man now basking in praise.

Skilfully guided by Kemp-Lore, he talked about his duties as one of the three stewards at a race meeting. It involved, he said, hearing both sides if there was an objection to a winner and awarding the race justly to the more deserving, and yes, summoning jockeys and trainers for minor infringements of the rules and fining them a fiver or a tenner a time.

I watched him on the monitor set. I had to admit he looked a solid, sober, responsible citizen with right on his side. The aggressive horn rims gave him, on the screen, a definite air of authority; also for the occasion his habitually sour expression had given way to a rather persuasive geniality. No one watching the performance Kemp-Lore coaxed out of him would have suspected him to be the bigoted, pompous bully we knew on the racecourse. I understood at last how he had come to be voted on to the National Hunt Committee.

Before I expected it, Kemp-Lore was turning round to me. I swallowed convulsively. He smiled at the camera.

'And now,' he said with the air of one producing a treat, 'here is Rob Finn. This is a young steeplechase jockey just scratching the surface of his career. Few of you will have heard of him. He has won no big races, nor ridden any well-known horses, and that is why I have invited him here tonight to meet you, to give us all a glimpse of what it is like to break into a highly competitive sport . . .'

The red light was burning on the camera pointing at me. I smiled at it faintly. My tongue stuck to the roof of my mouth.

'First,' he went on, 'here is a piece of film which shows Finn in action. He is the rider with the white cap, fourth from last.'

We watched on the monitor set. I was all too easy to pick out. It was one of the first races I ever rode in, and my inexperience showed sorely. During the few seconds the film lasted the white cap lost two places, and as an illustration of an unsuccessful jockey it could not have been bettered.

The film faded out and Kemp-Lore said, smiling, 'How did you set about starting to be a jockey, once you had decided on it?'

I said, 'I knew three farmers who owned and trained their own horses, and I asked them to let me try my hand in a race.'

'And they did?'

'Yes, in the end,' I agreed. I could have added, 'After I had promised to return the riding fees and not even ask for expenses'; but the method I had used to persuade a string of farmers to give me rides was strictly against the rules.

'Usually,' Kemp-Lore said, turning towards the camera which immediately glowed with its red eye, 'jumping jockeys either start as amateur steeplechase riders or as apprentices on the flat, but I understand that you did neither of these things, Rob?'

'No,' I said. 'I started too old to be an apprentice and couldn't be an amateur because I had earned my living riding horses.'

'As a stable lad?' He put it in the form of a question but from his intonation he clearly expected me to say yes. It was, after all by far the commonest background of jockeys riding as few races as I had been doing.

'No,' I said.

He was waiting for me to go on, his eyebrows a fraction raised in a tinge of surprise mingled with what looked like the beginning of apprehension. Well, I thought in amusement, you wouldn't listen when I said I was hardly typical, so if my answers are not what you expect, it's entirely your own fault.

I said, 'I was away from England for some years, wandering round the world, you know? Mainly in Australia and South America. Most of the time I got jobs as a stockman, but I spent a year in New South Wales working as a hand in a travelling rodeo. Ten seconds on the bucking bronc: that sort of thing.' I grinned.

'Oh.' The eyebrows rose another fraction, and there was a perceptible pause before he said, 'How very interesting.' He sounded as if he meant it. He went on, 'I wish we had more time to hear about your experiences, but I want to give viewers a picture of the economics of a jockey in your position . . . trying to make a living on a race or two a week. Now, your fee is ten guineas a time, that's right? . . .'

He took me at some length through my finances, which didn't sound too good when dissected into travelling expenses, valets' fees, replacement of kit, and so on. It emerged quite clearly that my net income over the last two years was less than I could have earned driving a delivery van, and that my future prospects were not demonstrably much better. I could almost feel the thought clicking into the viewers' heads that I was a fool.

Kemp-Lore turned deferentially to Ballerton. 'John, have you any comment to make on what we have been hearing from Rob?'

A trace of purely malicious pleasure crept into Ballerton's man-of-authority smile.

'All these young jockeys complain too much,' he stated in his harsh voice, ignoring the fact that I had not complained at all. 'If they aren't very good at their job they shouldn't expect to be highly paid. Racehorse owners don't want to waste their money and their horses' chances by putting up jockeys in whom they have no confidence. I speak as an owner myself, of course.'

'Eh . . . of course,' said Kemp-Lore. 'But surely every jockey has to make a start? And there must always be large numbers of jockeys who never quite reach the top grade, but who have a living to make, and families to support.'

'They'd be better off in a factory, earning a fair wage on a production line,' said Ballerton, with heavy, reasonable-sounding humour. 'If they can't endure the fact that they are unsuccessful without snivelling about how poor they are, they ought to get out of racing altogether. Not many of them do,' he added with an unkind chuckle, 'because they like wearing those bright silks. People turn to look at them as they go by, and it flatters their little egos.'

There was a gasp somewhere out in the dark studio at this ungentlemanly blow below the belt, and I saw out of the corner of my eye that the red spot on the camera pointing at me was glowing. What expression it had initially caught on my face I did not know, but I raised a smile for Mr Ballerton then, as sweet and cheerful and forgiving a smile as ever turned the other cheek. It was made easier by the certain knowledge that wearing bright shirts was if anything an embarrassment to me, not a gratification.

Kemp-Lore's head switched to me. 'And what do you say to that, Rob?'

I spoke truthfully, vehemently, and straight from the heart. 'Give me a horse and a race to ride it in, and I don't care if I wear silks or ... or ... pyjamas. I don't care if there's anyone watching or not. I don't care if I don't earn much money, or if I break my bones, or if I have to starve to keep my weight down. All I care about is racing . . . racing . . . and winning, if I can.'

There was a small silence.

'I can't explain it,' I said.

Both of them were staring at me. John Ballerton looked as if a squashed wasp had revived and stung him, and his earlier animosity settled and deepened into a scowl. And Kemp-Lore? There was an expression on his face that I could not read at all. There were only a few empty seconds before he turned smoothly back to his camera and slid the familiar smile into place, but I felt irrationally that something important had taken place in them. I found it oddly disturbing not to have the slightest clue to what it was.

Kemp-Lore launched into his usual review of the following week's racing, and was very soon closing the programme with the customary words, 'See you all next week at the same time . . .'

The image on the monitor faded on Kemp-Lore's smile and changed to another soap advertisement. The hot spotlight flicked off and my eyes began to get used to not being dazzled.

Gordon strode up beaming. 'A very good programme. It came over well. Just what they like, an argument with an edge to it. Well done, well done, Mr Ballerton, Mr Finn. Splendid.' He shook us both by the hand.

Kemp-Lore stood up and stretched and grinned around at us all. 'Well, John. Well, Rob. Thank you both very much.' He bent down, picked up my brandy glass and handed it to me. 'Drink it,' he said, 'you deserve it.' He smiled warmly. He crackled with released tension.

I smiled back and drank the brandy, and reflected again how superlative he was at his job. By encouraging Ballerton to needle me he had drawn from me, for the ears of a few million strangers, a more soul-baring statement than I would ever have made privately to a close friend.

A good deal of back-slapping followed, and more plates of sandwiches were dealt with downstairs in the reception room before I left the television building and went back to Kensington. In view of the approval which had been generously, if undeservedly, heaped upon Ballerton and me after the show, I wondered why it was that I felt more apprehensive than I had before I started.

CHAPTER SIX

Three weeks and a day after the broadcast, Pip
Pankhurst broke his leg. His horse, falling with him
and on him at the last hurdle of the second race on a
dreary, drizzly mid-November Saturday afternoon,
made a thorough job of putting the champion jockey
out of action for the bulk of the 'chasing season.

The first-aid men beside the hurdle were slow to
move him into the ambulance for the good reason that
a sharp arrow of shin bone was sticking out at a crazy
angle through a tear in the thin leather racing boot;
and they finally managed to lift him on to a stretcher,
one of them told me later, only because Pip slid off
into a dead faint.

From the stands I saw only the white flag waving,
the ambulance creeping down over the bumpy ground,
and the flat, ominously unmoving figure of Pip on the
grass. It would be untrue to say that I went down
the stairs to the weighing-room with a calm heart.
However sincere my pity for his plight might be, the

83

faint chance that I might take his place in the following race was playing hop, skip and jump with my pulse.

It was the big race of the day, the big race of the week, a three-mile chase with a substantial prize put up by a firm of brewers. It had attracted a good number of top horses and had been well discussed on the sports pages of all the day's papers. Pip's mount, which belonged to Lord Tirrold, was the rising star of the Axminster stable; a stringy six-year-old brown gelding with nothing much to recommend him at first sight, but intelligent, fast, and a battler. He had all the qualities of a world beater, and his best years lay ahead. At present he was still reckoned 'promising'. He was called Template.

Stifling hope is a hopeless business. As I went into the weighing-room I saw James Axminster talking to Pip's close friend, another leading jockey. The jockey shook his head, and across the room I watched his lips say, 'No, I can't.'

Axminster turned slowly round looking at faces. I stood still and waited. Gradually his head came round and he saw me. He looked at me steadily, pondering, unsmiling. Then his eyes were past me and focused on someone to my left. He came to a decision and walked briskly past me.

Well, what did I expect? I had ridden for him for only four weeks. Three winners. A dozen also-rans. During the past fortnight I had taken digs in the village near his stable and ridden out at exercise on his horses every morning; but I was still the new boy, the unknown, unsuccessful jockey of the television programme. I began to walk disconsolately over to the changing room door.

'Rob,' he said in my ear. 'Lord Tirrold says you can ride his horse. You'd better tell Pip's valet; he has the colours.'

I half-turned towards them. They stood together, the two tall men, looking at me appraisingly, knowing they were giving me the chance of a lifetime, but not sure that I was up to it.

'Yes, sir,' I said; and I went on into the changing-room, queerly steadied by having believed that I had been passed over.

I rode better than I had ever done before, but that was probably because Template was the best horse I had ever ridden. He was smooth and steely, and his rocketing spring over the first fence had me gasping; but I was ready for it at the second, and exulted in it at the third; and by the fourth I knew I had entered a new dimension of racing.

Neither Axminster nor Lord Tirrold had given me any orders in the paddock on how to shape the race. They had been too concerned about Pip, whom they had just briefly visited. The sight of his shattered leg had left them upset and preoccupied.

Axminster said only, 'Do the best you can, Rob,' and Lord Tirrold, unusually tactless for so diplomatic a man, said gloomily, 'I put a hundred on Template this morning. Oh, well, it's too late to cancel it, I suppose.' Then seeing my rueful amusement, added, 'I beg your pardon, Rob. I'm sure you'll do splendidly.' But he did not sound convinced.

As the pattern of the race shifted and changed, I concentrated solely on keeping Template lying in about fourth position in the field of twelve runners. To be farther back meant leaving him a lot to do at the end, and to be farther forward meant that one could not see how well or how badly everyone else was going. Template jumped himself into third place at the second last fence, and was still not under pressure. Coming towards the last I brought him to the outside, to give him a clear view, and urged him on. His stride immediately quickened. He took off so far in front of the fence that for a heart-breaking second I was sure he would land squarely on top of it, but I had underestimated his power. He landed yards out on the far side, collecting himself without faltering and surged ahead towards the winning post.

One of the two horses close in front had been passed in mid-air over the fence. There remained only a chestnut to be beaten. Only. Only the favourite, the choice of the critics, the public and the press. No disgrace, I fleetingly thought, to be beaten only by him.

I dug my knees into Template's sides and gave him two taps with the whip down his shoulder. He needed only this signal, I found, to put every ounce into getting to the front. He stretched his neck out and flattened his stride, and I knelt on his withers and squeezed him and moved with his rhythm, and kept my whip still for fear of disturbing him. He put his head in front of the chestnut's five strides from the winning post, and kept it there.

I was almost too exhausted to unbuckle the saddle. There was a cheer as we went into the unsaddling enclosure, and a lot of smiling faces, and some complimentary things were said, but I felt too weak and breathless to enjoy them. No race had ever before taken so much out of me. Nor given me so much, either.

Surprisingly Lord Tirrold and Axminster were almost subdued.

'That was all right, then,' said Axminster, the lower teeth glimmering in a smile.

'He's a wonderful horse,' I said fervently.

'Yes,' said Lord Tirrold, 'he is.' He patted the dark sweating neck.

Axminster said, 'Don't hang about then, Rob. Go and weigh in. You haven't any time to waste. You're riding in the next race. And the one after.'

I stared at him.

'Well, what did you expect?' he said. 'Pip's obviously going to be unfit for months. I took you on to ride second to him, and you will stand in for him until he comes back.'

*

Tick-Tock said, 'Some people would climb out of a septic tank smelling of lavender.'

He was waiting for me to change at the end of the afternoon.

'Six weeks ago you were scrounging rides. Then you get yourself on television as a failure and make it obvious you aren't one. Sunday newspapers write columns about you and your version of the creed gets a splash in *The Times* as well. Now you do the understudy-into-star routine, and all that jazz. And properly too. Three winners in one afternoon. What a nerve.'

I grinned at him. 'What goes up must come down. You can pick up the pieces later on.'

I tied my tie and brushed my hair, and looked in the mirror at the fatuous smile I could not remove from my face. Days like this don't happen very often, I thought.

'Let's go and see Pip,' I said abruptly, turning round.

'Okay,' he agreed.

We asked the first-aid men where Pip had been taken, and as they were leaving in any case they gave us a lift to the hospital in the ambulance. It was not until they told us that we realized how seriously the leg was broken.

We saw Pip only for a few moments. He lay in a cubicle in the casualty department, a cradle over his leg and blankets up to his chin. A brisk nurse told us he was going to the operating theatre within minutes and not to disturb the patient, as he had been given his pre-med. 'But you can say hello,' she said, 'as you've come.'

Hello was just about all we did say. Pip looked terribly pale and his eyes were fuzzy, but he said weakly, 'Who won the big race?'

'Template,' I said, almost apologetically.

'You?'

I nodded. He smiled faintly. 'You'll ride the lot now, then.'

'I'll keep them warm for you,' I said. 'You won't be long.'

'Three bloody months.' He shut his eyes. 'Three bloody months.'

The nurse came back with a stretcher trolley and two khaki-overalled porters, and asked us to leave. We waited outside in the hall, and saw them trundle Pip off towards the open lift.

'He'll be four months at least with a leg like that,' said Tick-Tock. 'He might just be ready for Cheltenham in March. Just in time to take back all the horses and do you out of a chance in the Champion Hurdle and the Gold Cup.'

'It can't be helped,' I said. 'It's only fair. And anything can happen before then.'

I think Axminster had trouble persuading some of his

owners that I was capable of taking Pip's place, because I didn't ride all of the stable's horses, not at first. But gradually as the weeks went by and I seemed to make no unforgivable bloomers, fewer and fewer other jockeys were engaged. I became used to seeing my name continually in the number boards, to riding three or four races a day, to going back to my digs contentedly tired in body and mind and waking the next morning with energy and eagerness. In some ways, I even became used to winning. It was no longer a rarity for me to be led into the first's enclosure, or to talk to delighted owners, or to see my picture in the sporting papers.

I began earning a good deal of money, but I spent very little of it. There was always the knowledge, hovering in the background, that my prosperity was temporary. Pip's leg was mending. Tick-Tock and I decided, however, to share the cost of buying a car. It was a second-hand cream-coloured Mini-Cooper which did forty miles to the gallon on a long run and could shift along at a steady seventy on the flat, and a friend of Tick-Tock's who kept a garage had recommended it to him as a bargain.

'All we want now are some leopard-skin seat covers and a couple of blondes in the back,' said Tick-Tock, as we dusted the small vehicle parked outside my digs, 'and we'll look like one of those gracious living advertisements in the *Tatler*.' He lifted up the bonnet and took at least his tenth look at the engine. 'A beautiful job of design,' he said fondly.

Gracious living, good design or not, the little car smoothed our paths considerably, and within a fortnight I could not imagine how we had ever managed without it. Tick-Tock kept it where he lived, seven miles away, near the stable he rode for, and came to collect me whenever Axminster himself was not taking me to meetings in his own car. Race trains came and went without any further support from either of us as we whizzed homewards through the black December afternoons in our cosy box on wheels.

While the Gods heaped good fortune on my head, others fared badly.

Grant had offered neither explanation nor apology for hitting me on the nose. He had not, in fact, spoken one word to me since that day, but, as at the same time he had also stopped borrowing my kit, I was not sure that I minded. He withdrew more and more into himself. The inner volcano of violence showed itself only in the stiffness of his body and the tightness of his lips, which seemed always to be compressed in fury. He loathed to be touched, even accidentally, and would swing round threateningly if anyone bumped into him in the changing-room. With my peg at most meetings still next to his I had knocked into him several times, for however hard I tried it was impossible in those cramped quarters not to, and the glare he gave me each time was frankly murderous.

It was not only to me that he had stopped speaking. He no longer said much at all. The trainers and owners who still employed him could get him neither to discuss a race beforehand nor explain what had happened afterwards. He listened to his orders in silence and left the trainer to draw his own conclusions through his race-glasses about how the horse had run. When he did speak, his remarks were laden with such a burden of obscenity that even the hardened inmates of the changing-room shifted uncomfortably.

Oddly enough Grant's riding skill had not degenerated with his character. He rode the same rough, tough race as always; but he had, we knew, begun to let out his anger on his mounts, and twice during November he was called before the stewards for 'excessive use of the whip'. The horses in question had each come in from their races with raw red weals on their flanks.

The Oldfield volcano erupted, as far as I was concerned, one cold afternoon in the jockeys' and trainers' car park at Warwick. I was late leaving the meeting as I had won the last race and had been taken off to the bar afterwards by the elated owner, one of my farmer friends. Tick-Tock had gone to a different meeting, and I had the car. By the time I got there the park was empty except for the Mini-Cooper and another car which was standing almost next to it, and two or three cars further on down the row.

I went towards the Mini still smiling to myself with

the pleasure of this latest win, and I did not see Grant until I was quite close to him. I was approaching the cars from behind, with Grant's on the right of mine. His near hind wheel lay on the grass, surrounded by a collection of implements spilling out of a holdall tool bag. A jack held up the bare axle of his black saloon and he was kneeling beside it with the spare wheel in his hand.

He saw me coming, and he saw me smiling, and he thought I was laughing at him for having a puncture. I could actually see the uncontrollable fury rise in his face. He got to his feet and stood rigidly, his thickset body hunched with belligerence, the strong shoulders bunching under his coat, his arms hanging down. Then he bent forward and from among the mess of tools picked up a tyre lever. He swished it through the air, his eyes on me.

'I'll help you with your puncture, if you like,' I said mildly.

For answer he took a step sideways, swung his arm in a sort of backwards chop, and smashed the tyre lever through the back window of the Mini-Cooper. The glass crashed and tinkled into the car, leaving only a fringe of jagged peaks round the frame.

Tick-Tock and I had had the car barely three weeks. My own anger rose quick and hot and I took a step towards Grant to save my most precious possession from further damage. He turned to face me squarely and lifted the tyre lever again.

'Put it down,' I said, reasonably, standing still. We were now about four feet apart. He told me to do something which was biologically impossible.

'Don't be an ass, Grant,' I said. 'Put that thing down and let's get on with changing your tyre.'

'You—' he said, 'you took my job.'

'No,' I said. It was pointless to add more, not least because if he was going to try to hit me I wanted to have all my concentration focused on what he was doing, not on what I was saying.

His eyes were red-rimmed above the high cheek bones. The big nostrils flared open like black pits. With his wild face, his bursting anger, and the upheld quivering tyre lever, he was a pretty frightening sight.

He slashed forward and downward at my head.

I think that at that moment he must have been truly insane, for had the blow connected he would surely have killed me, and he couldn't have hoped to get away with it with his car standing there with the wheel off. He was beyond thought.

I saw his arm go up a fraction before it came down and it gave me time to duck sideways. The lever whistled past my right ear. His arm returned in a backhand, again aiming at my head. I ducked again underneath it, and this time, as his arm swung wide and his body lay open to me, I stepped close and hit him hard with my fist just below his breast bone. He grunted as the wind rushed out of his lungs, and the arm with the tyre lever dropped and his head came forward. I took a half pace to the right and hit him on the side of the neck with the edge of my hand.

He went down on his hands and knees, and then weakly sprawled on the grass. I took the tyre lever from his slack fingers and put it with all the other tools into the holdall, and shut the whole thing into the boot of his car.

It was getting very cold and the early dusk was turning colours to black and grey. I squatted beside Grant. He was hovering on the edge of consciousness, breathing heavily and moaning slightly.

I said conversationally, close to his ear, 'Grant, why did you get the sack from Axminster?'

He mumbled something I could not hear. I repeated my question. He said nothing. I sighed and stood up. It had been only a faint chance, after all.

Then he said distinctly, 'He said I passed on the message.'

'What message?'

'Passed on the message,' he said, less clearly. I bent down and asked him again, 'What message?' But although his lips moved he said nothing more.

I decided that in spite of everything I could not just drive off and leave him lying there in the cold. I took out the tools again, and sorting out the brace, put the spare wheel on and tightened up the nuts. Then I pumped-up the tyre, let the jack down and slung it with the punctured wheel into the boot on top of the tools.

Grant was still not properly conscious. I knew I hadn't hit him hard enough to account for such a long semi-waking state, and it occurred to me that perhaps his disturbed brain was finding this a helpful way to dodge reality. I bent down and shook his shoulder and called his name. He opened his eyes. For a split second it seemed as though the old Grant smiled out of them, and then the resentment and bitterness flooded back as he remembered what had happened. I helped him sit up, and propped him against his car. He looked desperately tired, utterly worn out.

'O God,' he said, 'O God.' It sounded like a true prayer, and it came from lips which usually blasphemed without thought.

'If you went to see a psychiatrist,' I said gently, 'you could get some help.'

He didn't answer; but neither did he resist when I helped him into the passenger seat of the Mini-Cooper. He was in no state to drive his own car, and there was no one else about to look after him. I asked him where he lived, and he told me. His car was safe enough where it was, and I remarked that he could fetch it on the following day. He made no reply.

Luckily he lived only thirty miles away, and I drew up where he told me outside a semi-detached featureless house on the outskirts of a small country town. There were no lights in the windows.

'Isn't your wife in?' I asked.

'She left me,' he said absently. Then his jaw tensed

and he said, 'Mind your own — business.' He jerked
the door open and climbed out and slammed it noisily.
He shouted, 'Take your bloody do-gooding off and —
it. I don't want your help, you — '. He appeared to be
back to his usual frame of mind, which was a pity, but
there didn't seem to be any point in staying to hear
more so I let in the clutch and drove off: but I had
gone only half a mile down the road when I reluctantly
came to the conclusion that he shouldn't be left alone
in an empty house.

I was at that point in the centre of the little town
whose brightly lit shops were closing their doors for
the day, and I stopped and asked an elderly woman
with a shopping basket where I could find a doctor.
She directed me to a large house in a quiet side street,
and I parked outside and rang the door bell.

A pretty girl appeared and said, 'Surgery at six,'
and began to close the door again.

'If the doctor is in, please let me speak to him,' I
said quickly, 'it's not a case for the surgery.'

'Well, all right,' she said and went away. Children's
voices sounded noisily somewhere in the house.
Presently, a youngish, chubby, capable-looking man
appeared, munching at a piece of cream-filled
chocolate cake and wearing the resigned, enquiring
expression of a doctor called to duty during his free
time.

'Are you by any chance Grant Oldfield's doctor?' I

asked. If he weren't, I thought, he could tell me where else to go.

But he said at once, 'Yes, I am. Has he had another fall?'

'Not exactly,' I said, 'but could you please come and take a look at him?'

'Now?'

'Yes, please,' I said. 'He ... er ... he was knocked out at the races.'

'Half a mo,' he said and went back to the house, reappearing with his medical bag and another piece of cake. 'Can you run me down there? Save me getting my car out again for those few yards.'

We went out to the Mini-Cooper and as soon as he sat in it he made a remark about the broken window, not unreasonably, since gusts of December wind blowing through it were freezing our necks. I told him that Grant had smashed it and explained how I had come to bring him home.

He listened in silence, licking the cream as it oozed out of the side of the cake. Then he said, 'Why did he attack you?'

'He seems to believe I took his job.'

'And did you?'

'No,' I said. 'He lost it months before it was offered to me.'

'Are you a jockey too, then?' he asked, looking at me curiously, and I nodded and told him my name. He said his was Parnell. I started the car and drove the few hundred yards back to Grant's house. It was still in complete darkness.

'I left him here not ten minutes ago,' I said as we went up the path to the front door. The small front garden was ragged and uncared for, with rotting dead leaves and mournful grass-grown flower beds dimly visible in the light from the street lamp. We rang the bell. It sounded shrilly in the house, but produced no other results. We rang again. The doctor finished his cake and licked his fingers.

There was a faint rustle in the darkness of the patch of garden. The doctor unclipped from his breast pocket the pen-shaped torch he normally used for peering into eyes and down throats, and directed its tiny beam round the bordering privet hedge. It revealed first some pathetic rose bushes choked with last summer's unmown grass; but in the corner where the hedge dividing the garden from the next door one met the hedge bordering the road, the pin point of light steadied on the hunched shape of a man.

We went over to him. He was sitting on the ground, huddling back into the hedge, with his knees drawn up to his chin and his head resting on his folded arms.

'Come along old chap,' said the doctor encouragingly, and half-helped, half-pulled him to his feet. He felt in Grant's pockets, found a bunch of keys, and handed them to me. I went over and unlocked the front door and turned on the lights in the hall. The doctor guided Grant through the hall and into the first room we came to, which happened to be a dining-room. Everything in it was covered with a thick layer of dust.

Grant collapsed in a heap on a dining chair and laid his head down on the dirty table. The doctor examined him, feeling his pulse, lifting up his eyelid and running both hands round the thick neck and the base of the skull. Grant moved irritably when Parnell's fingers touched the place where I had hit him and he said crossly, 'Go away, go away.'

Parnell stepped back a pace and sucked his teeth. 'There's nothing physically wrong with him as far as I can see, except for what is going to be a stiff neck. We'd better get him into bed and I'll give him something to keep him quiet, and in the morning I'll arrange for him to see someone who can sort out his troubles for him. You'd better give me a ring during the evening if there's any change in his condition.'

'I?' I said. 'I'm not staying here all evening...'

'Oh yes, I think so, don't you?' he said cheerfully, his eyes shining sardonically in his round face. 'Who else? All night too, if you don't mind. After all, you hit him.'

'Yes, but,' I protested, 'that's not what's the matter with him.'

'Never mind. You cared enough to bring him home and fetch me. Be a good chap and finish the job. I do really think someone ought to stay here all night... someone strong enough to deal with him in a crisis.

It's not a job for elderly female relatives, even if we could rake one up so late in the day.'

Put like that, it was difficult to refuse. We took Grant upstairs, balancing his thick-set body between us as he stumbled up the treads. His bedroom was filthy. Dirty tangled sheets and blankets were piled in heaps on the unmade bed, dust lay thick on every surface, and soiled clothes were scattered over the floor and hung sordidly over chairs. The whole room smelled of sour sweat.

'We'd better put him somewhere else,' I said, switching on lights and opening all the other doors on the small landing. One door led into a bathroom whose squalor defied description. Another opened on to a linen cupboard which still contained a few sheets in a neat pile, and the last revealed an empty bedroom with bright pink rosebuds on the walls. Grant stood blinking on the landing while I fetched some sheets and made up the bed for him. There were no clean pyjamas. Doctor Parnell undressed Grant as far as his underpants and socks and made him get into the fresh bed. Then he went downstairs and returned with a glass of water, wearing so disgusted an expression that I knew without being told what state the kitchen must be in.

Opening his case, he shook two capsules on to his hand and told Grant to swallow them, which he docilely did. Grant at this time seemed as if he were sleep-walking; he was only a shell, his personality a blank. It was disturbing, but on the other hand it made the business of putting him to bed much easier than it might have been.

Parnell looked at his watch. 'I'm late for surgery,' he said as Grant lay back on his pillow and shut his eyes. 'Those pills ought to keep him quiet for a bit. Give him two more when he wakes up.' He handed me a small bottle. 'You know where to find me if you want me,' he added with a callous grin. 'Have a good night.'

I spent a miserable evening and dined off a pint of milk I found on the back doorstep. Nothing else in the stinking kitchen was any longer edible. There were no books and no radio to be found, and to pass the hours I made an effort to clean up some of the mess, but what that dreadful house really needed was a breezy spring day, lashings of disinfectant, and an army of strong-minded charwomen.

Several times I went softly in to see how Grant was doing, but he slept peacefully, flat on his back, until midnight. I found him then with his eyes open, but when I went close to him there was no recognition in them. He was still in a withdrawn blank state and he obediently, without a word, swallowed the capsules when I offered them to him. I waited until his eyes had closed again, then I locked his door and went downstairs and eventually fell uneasily asleep myself, wrapped in a travelling rug on a too short sofa. There was no sound from Grant all night, and when I went up to him at six in the morning he was still sleeping quietly.

Dr Parnell at least had the decency to release me at an early hour, arriving with a middle-aged male nurse at 7.30 in the freezing dawn. He had also brought a basket packed by his wife, containing eggs, bacon, bread, milk, and coffee, and from his medical bag he produced a powerful battery razor.

'All mod. cons,' he said cheerfully, his round face beaming.

So I went back to the races washed, shaved and fed. But thinking of the husk of a man I left behind me, not in a happy frame of mind.

CHAPTER SEVEN

'The trouble is, there's such a shortage of jockeys just now,' said James Axminster.

We were on our way to Sandown, discussing whom he should engage to ride for him the following week when he would be sending horses to two different places on the same day.

'You'd almost think there was a hoodoo on the whole tribe,' he said, expertly swinging his large car between a wobbly girl cyclist and an oncoming pantechnicon. 'Art shot himself, Pip's broken his leg, Grant's had a breakdown. Two or three others are out with more ordinary things like busted collar bones, and at least four quite useful chaps took that wretched Ballerton's misguided advice and are now churning out car bodies on assembly lines. There's Peter Cloony... but I've heard he's very unreliable and might not turn up in time; and Danny Higgs bets too much, they say, and Ingersoll doesn't always try, so I've been told...'

He slowed down while a mother pushed a

perambulator and three small children untidily across the road in front of us, and went on talking. 'Every time I think I've found a good up-and-coming jockey I seem to hear something to his disadvantage. With you, it was that film, the one they showed on that television programme. It was shocking, wasn't it? I watched it and thought, my God, what have I done, asking this clod to ride for me, however will I explain it away to the owners.' He grinned. 'I was on the point of ringing them all up and assuring them you'd not be on their horses after all. Luckily for you I remembered the way you had already ridden for me and I watched the rest of the programme first, and when it had finished I had changed my mind. I had even begun to think I had perhaps struck oil in annexing you. Nothing that has happened since,' he glanced at me sideways, smiling, 'has led me to alter that opinion.'

I smiled back. In the weeks since Pip broke his leg I had come to know him well, and liked him better with every day that passed. Not only was he a superb craftsman at his job and a tireless worker, but he was reliable in other ways. He was never moody: one did not have to approach him circumspectly every time to see if he were in a good or bad humour because he was always the same, neither boisterous nor irritable, just reasonable and receptive. He said directly what he thought, so that one never had to search for innuendoes or suspect hidden sarcasm and it made any relationship with him stable and free from worry. He was, on the other hand, in many ways thoroughly selfish. Unless it were a strictly business matter, his own comfort and convenience came first, second and third, and he would do a favour for someone else only if it caused him absolutely no personal sacrifice of time or effort. Even this was often a blessing to his stable lads since it was typical of him, if the occasion arose, to give them a generous travelling allowance out of his own pocket to visit their homes, rather than go five miles out of his way to drop them on their doorsteps.

He had seemed from the first to be as satisfied with my company as I was with his, and had quite soon told me to drop the 'sir' and stick to 'James'. Later the same week as he drove us back from Birmingham races, we passed some brightly lit posters advertising a concert which was to be held there that evening.

'Conductor, Sir Trelawny Finn,' he read aloud, the enormous lettering catching his eye. 'No relation, I suppose,' he said jokingly.

'Well, yes, as a matter of fact, he's my uncle,' I said.

There was a dead silence. Then he said, 'And Caspar Finn?'

'My father.' A pause.

'Anyone else?'

'Dame Olivia Cottin is my mother,' I said, matter-of-factly.

'Good God,' he said explosively.

I grinned.

'You keep it very quiet,' he said.

'It's really the other way round,' I said cheerfully. 'They like to keep me quiet. A jockey in the family is a disgrace to them, you see. It embarrasses them. They don't like the connexion to be noticed.

'All the same,' he said thoughtfully, 'it explains quite a lot about you that I had begun to wonder about. Where you got that air of confidence from . . . and why you've said so little about yourself.'

I said, smiling, 'I'd be very glad . . . James . . . if you'd not let my parentage loose in the weighing-room, as a favour to them.'

He had said he would not, and he had kept his word, but he had accepted me more firmly as a friend from then on. So when he ran through the reported shortcomings of Peter Cloony, Danny Higgs and Tick-Tock, it was with some confidence that I said, 'You seem to have heard a great many rumours. Do you know all these things for a fact?'

'For a fact?' he repeated, surprised. 'Well, Peter Cloony definitely missed two races a few weeks back because he was late. That's a fact.'

I told him about Peter's atrocious luck in twice finding a vehicle stuck across the mouth of the narrow lane from his village to the main road. 'As far as I know,' I said, 'he hasn't been late since then. His reputation for lateness seems to be built mainly on those two days.'

'I've heard several times that he can't be trusted to turn up,' said James obstinately.

107

'Who from?' I asked curiously.

'Oh, I don't know. Corin Kellar for one. And of course Johnson who employs him. Ballerton too, though it's against my better judgement to pay too much attention to what he says. It's common knowledge though.'

'How about Danny Higgs, then?' I said. Danny was an irrepressible cockney, tiny in size, but ferociously brave.

'He bets too heavily,' James said positively.

'Who says so?' I asked. I knew Danny broke the regulations by backing horses, but from what he said in the changing-room, it was only in amounts of five or ten pounds, which would cause few trainers to look askance at him.

'Who says? I... er... Corin,' he finished lamely. 'Corin, come to think of it, has told me so several times. He says he never puts him up because of it.'

'And Tick-Tock?' I said. 'Who says Ingersoll doesn't always try?'

He didn't answer at once. Then he said, 'Why shouldn't I believe what Corin says? He has no axe to grind. He's an excellent trainer, but he depends as we all do on securing good jockeys. He certainly wouldn't deny himself the use of people like Cloony or Higgs if he didn't have a good reason.'

I thought for a few moments, and then said, 'I know it's really none of my business, but would you mind very much telling me why you dropped Grant

Oldfield? He told me himself that it was something to do with a message, but he wouldn't explain what.' I refrained from mentioning that he had been semi-conscious at the time.

'A message? Oh yes, he passed on the message, I couldn't have that.'

I still looked mystified. Axminster squeezed through the traffic lights on the amber and glanced sideways at me.

'The message,' he said impatiently, 'you know, the news. He was passing on the news. If we had a fancied runner he would tip off a professional backer. The owner of the horse didn't get good odds to his money because the professional was there before him and spoiled the market. Three of my owners were very angry about it – no fun for them having to take two or three to one when they expected sixes or sevens. So Grant had to go. It was a pity; he was a strong jockey, just what I needed.'

'How did you discover it was Grant passing on the information?'

'Maurice Kemp-Lore found out while he was working on one of those programmes of his. Something to do with how professional backers work, I think it was, and he found out about Grant more or less by accident. He told me very apologetically, and just said it would be wiser not to let Grant know too much. But you can't work properly with a jockey and keep secrets from him, it's a hopeless set-up.'

'What did Grant say when you sacked him?' I asked.

'He denied the whole thing very indignantly. But of course he would. No jockey would ever confess to selling information if he wanted another trainer to take him on.'

'Did you talk to the professional backer in question?' I asked.

'Yes I did, as a matter of fact,' he said. 'I didn't want to believe it, you see. But it was open and shut. I had to press him a bit, because it didn't reflect well on him, but Lubbock, the professional, did admit that Grant had been tipping him off over the telephone, and that he had been paying him ever since he had started to ride for me.'

It seemed conclusive enough, but I had an elusive feeling that I had missed something, somewhere.

I changed the subject. 'Going back to Art,' I said, 'why was he always having rows with Corin?'

'I don't really know,' James said reflectively. 'I heard Corin say once or twice that Art didn't ride to orders. Perhaps it was that.' He neatly passed two slow lorries on a round-about, and glanced at me again. 'What are you getting at?'

'It seems to me sometimes that there is too much of a pattern,' I said. 'Too many jockeys are affected by rumours. You said yourself that there seems to be a hoodoo on the whole tribe.'

'I didn't mean it seriously,' he protested. 'You're

imagining things. And as for rumours, what rumour made Art kill himself or broke Pip's leg, or made Grant sell information? Rumour didn't make Cloony late either.'

'Danny Higgs doesn't bet heavily,' I said, feeling I was fighting a rearguard action, 'and Ingersoll rides as honestly as anyone.'

'You can't know about Higgs,' he pointed out, 'and Ingersoll, let me remind you, was called in before the stewards last week for easing his mount out of third place. John Ballerton owned the horse and he was very annoyed about it, he told me so himself.'

I sighed. Tick-Tock's version was that since Corin had told him not to overwork the horse, which was not fully fit, he had decided that he ought not to drive the horse too hard just for the sake of finishing third. Better to save the horse's energy for winning next time, he had thought, adopting a view commonly held and acted on by at least half the jockeys and trainers engaged in the sport: but owners and members of the public who had backed the horse for a place were liable to disagree. After the enquiry, changing with the wind as usual, Corin had been heard condemning Tick-Tock for his action.

'I may be quite wrong about it all,' I said slowly, 'I hope so. Only . . .'

'Only?' he prompted as I paused.

'Only,' I finished lightly, 'if you ever hear any rumours about me, will you remember what I think . . .

and make utterly sure they're true before you believe them?'

'All right,' he said, humouring me. 'I think it's nonsense, but all right, I'll agree to that.' He drove in silence for a while, and then said with an impatient shake of his big head, 'No one stands to gain anything by trying to ruin jockeys. It's nonsense. Pointless.'

'I know,' I said. 'Pointless.'

We changed the subject.

Christmas came, and during the week before it, when there was no racing, I spent several days in Kensington. My parents greeted me with their usual friendly detachment and left me to my own devices. They were both preoccupied with crowded Christmas schedules, and my mother also spent each morning working at her piano on a new concerto which was to have its first performance in the New Year. She started daily at seven punctually, and played with short interruptions for coffee and thought until twelve-thirty. I awoke as so often during my life to the sound of warming up chromatics and wrist loosening arpeggios, and lay lazily in bed listening to her pick her way phrase by phrase through a dissonant modern score, repeating and repeating each section until she was satisfied she knew it, until the notes flowed easily in their intended order.

I could picture her exactly, dressed for work in a

cashmere sweater and ski pants, sitting upright on her special stool, with her head thrust forward as if to hear more from the piano than the notes themselves. She was digging the bones out of the piece, and I knew better than to interrupt her. Digging the bones, the essence, the composer's ultimate intention: and when she had these things firmly in her mind, she would begin the process of clothing them with her own interpretations, sharpening the contrasts of mood and tone, until the finished conception emerged clear and shining and memorable.

My mother might not have been a comforting refuge in my childhood nor take much loving interest in me now I was a man, but she had by her example shown me many qualities to admire and value. Professionalism, for instance; a tough-minded singleness of purpose; a refusal to be content with a low standard when a higher one could be achieved merely by working. I had become self-reliant young and thoroughly as a result of her rejection of motherhood, and because I saw the grind behind the gloss of her public performances, I grew up not expecting life's plums to be tossed into my lap without any effort from me. What mother could teach her son more?

Joanna's time was tangled inextricably with several performances in different places of the Christmas Oratorio. I managed to hook her only for one chilly morning's walk in the Park, which was not a success from my point of view since Bach easily shoved me into second place for her attention. She hummed bits of the Oratorio continuously from the Albert Gate to the Serpentine, and from the Serpentine to Bayswater Road. There I put her into a taxi and gave her a Christmassy lunch at the Savoy, where she appeared to restrain herself with difficulty from bursting into full song, as the acoustics in the entrance hall appealed to her. I couldn't decide whether or not she was being irritating on purpose, and if she was, why?

She was definitely a great deal less serene than usual, and there was a sort of brittleness in her manner which I didn't like and couldn't understand, until when we were half-way through some excellent mince pies it belatedly occurred to me that she might be unhappy. Unhappiness was not a state I had seen her in before, so I couldn't be sure. I waited until the coffee came, and then said, casually, 'What's up, Joanna?'

She looked at me, then she looked round the room, then at me again, then at her coffee.

Finally she said, 'Brian wants me to marry him.'

It wasn't what I expected, and it hurt. I found myself looking down at my own coffee: black and bitter, very appropriate, I thought.

'I don't know what to do,' she said. 'I was content as we were. Now I'm unsettled. Brian keeps talking about "living in sin" and "regularizing the position". He goes to church a lot now, and he can't reconcile our relationship with his religion. I never thought of it as sinful, just as enjoyable and fruitful and . . . and comfortable. He is talking about buying a house and settling down, and sees me as the complete housewife, cleaning, mending, cooking, and so on. I'm not that sort of person. The thought appals me. If I marry him, I know I'll be miserable . . .' Her voice trailed off.

'And if you don't marry him?' I asked.

'I'll be miserable then, too, because he refuses to go on as we are. We're not easy together any more. We nearly have rows. He says it's irresponsible and childish not to want to marry at my age, and I say I'll gladly marry him if we live as we do now, with him coming and going from the studio when he likes, and me free to work and come and go as I please too. But he doesn't want that. He wants to be respectable and conventional and . . . and stuffy.' The last word came out explosively, steeped in contempt. There was a pause while she stirred her coffee vigorously. There was no sugar in it. I watched the nervous gesture, the long strong fingers with the pink varnished nails gripping the spoon too hard.

'How much do you love him?' I asked painfully.

'I don't know,' she said unhappily. 'I don't know any more what love is.' She looked straight across the little table. 'If it means that I want to spend my life attending to his creature comforts, then I don't love him. If it means being happy in bed, then I do.'

She saw the movement in my face, and said

abruptly, 'Oh hell . . . Rob, I'm sorry. It's so long since you said anything . . . I thought you didn't still . . .'

'Never mind,' I said. 'It can't be helped.'

'What . . . what do you think I should do?' she said after a pause, still fiddling with the coffee spoon.

'It's quite clear,' I said positively, 'that you should not marry Brian if you can't bear the prospect of the life he intends to lead. It wouldn't work for either of you.'

'So?' she said, in a small voice.

But I shook my head. The rest she would have to resolve for herself. No advice I could give her would be unbiased, and she must have known it.

She left presently to go to a rehearsal, and I paid the bill and wandered out into the festive streets. I bought some presents for my family on the way, walking slowly back to the flat. The sort of marriage which Joanna had offered Brian, and which he had spurned, was what I most wanted in the world. Why, I wondered disconsolately, was life so ruddy unfair.

On Boxing Day Template won the King 'Chase, one of the ten top races of the year. It put him conclusively into the star class and it didn't do me any harm either.

The race had been televised, and afterwards, as was his custom, Maurice Kemp-Lore interviewed me as the winning jockey before the cameras. Towards the end of the brief talk he invited me to say hullo directly to

Pip, who, he explained to viewers, was watching at home. I had seen Pip only a week or two earlier and had discussed big-race tactics with him, but I obligingly greeted him and said I hoped his leg was mending well. Kemp-Lore smilingly added, 'We all wish you a speedy recovery, Pip,' and the interview was over.

On the following day the sporting press was complimentary about the race, and a number of trainers I had not yet ridden for offered me mounts. I began to feel at last as though I were being accepted as a jockey in my own right, and not principally as a substitute for Pip. It even seemed likely that when Pip returned to his job I would not fade back into the wilderness, for two of the new trainers said they would put me up on their horses as often as I was free.

I had, of course, my share of falls during this period, for however fortunate I was I couldn't beat the law of averages: but no damage was done except for a few bruises here and there, and none of them was bad enough to stop me riding.

The worst fall from the spectators' point of view happened one Saturday afternoon in January, when the hurdler I was riding tripped over the flight of hurdles nearest to the grandstand and flung me off on to my head. I woke up dizzily as the first-aid men lifted me into the ambulance on a stretcher, and for a moment or two could not remember where I was.

James's face, looming over me, as they carried me

into the first-aid room, brought me back to earth with a click, and I asked him if his horse was all right.

'Yes,' he said, 'how about you?'

'Nothing broken,' I assured him, having explored my limbs rather drunkenly during the short trip back in the ambulance.

'He rolled on you,' he said.

'I'm not surprised.' I grinned up at him. 'I feel a bit squashed, come to think of it.'

I lay for a while on a bed in the first-aid room, but there was nothing wrong with me that a good sleep wouldn't cure, and at the end of the afternoon I went back to Berkshire with James as expected.

'Are you all right?' he asked once, on the way.

'Yes,' I said cheerfully. 'Fine.' Actually I felt dizzy now and then, and also shivery and unsettled, but concealing one's true state of health from trainers was an occupational habit, and I knew I would be fit again to ride on Monday.

The only person who was openly annoyed at the run of good luck I had had was John Ballerton, and I had caught him several times in the parade ring staring tight-lipped at me with a patent and most unstewardly animosity.

Since the day of our joint broadcast we had exchanged the fewest possible words, but I had heard from Corin, who repeated it to me with sly relish, that Ballerton had said loudly to him and Maurice Kemp-Lore in the members' bar at Kempton, 'Finn isn't worth all the fuss that's being made of him. He'll come down just as quickly as he's gone up, you'll see. And I for one won't weep about it.'

In view of this it was astonishing that on the day after my fall I should be offered a ride on one of his horses. At first I refused to take Corin seriously. His telephone call woke me on the Sunday morning, and I was inclined to think the concussion had returned.

'If it were a choice between me and a sack of potatoes,' I said sleepily, 'he'd choose the potatoes.'

'No, seriously Rob, he wants you to ride Shantytown at Dunstable tomorrow.' Corin's voice held no trace of humour. 'I must say, I don't really understand why, as he's been so set against you before. But he was quite definite on the telephone, not five minutes ago. Perhaps it's an olive branch.'

And perhaps not, I thought. My first instinct was to refuse to ride the horse, but I couldn't think of a reasonable excuse, as Corin had found out I was free for the race before he told me whose the horse was. A point-blank excuseless refusal was, while possible, a senseless course. It would give Ballerton a genuine grievance against me, and if he sincerely wanted to smooth over his hostility, which I doubted, I should only deepen it by spurning his offer.

Shantytown was no Template. Far, far from it. His uncertain temper and unreliable jumping were described to me in unreassuring terms by Tick-Tock on the way to Dunstable the following morning.

'A right one,' he said, putting his foot down on the Mini-Cooper's accelerator. 'A knacker's delight. Dog-meat on the hoof.'

'His form's not bad,' I protested mildly, having looked it up the previous day.

'Hmph. Any time he's won or been placed it's because he's dragged his jockey's arms out of the sockets by a blast-off start and kept right on going. Hang on and hope, that's how to ride him when he's in that mood. His mouth is as hard as Gibraltar. In fact I cannot,' finished Tick-Tock with satiric formality, 'I cannot instantly recall any horse who is less receptive of his jockey's ideas.'

There was no bitterness in his voice, but we were both aware that a few weeks ago riding Shantytown would have been his doubtful pleasure, not mine. Since his parade before the stewards for not pushing his horse all out into third place, had had been ignored by Corin Kellar. It was the sort of injustice typical of Corin, to sack a man who ran into trouble looking after his interests, and it had done nothing to lay the unfair rumour that Tick-Tock was a habitual non-trier.

Apart from abruptly lessening the number of races he rode in, the rumour had had little effect on Tick-Tock himself. He shrugged his shoulders, and with a determined look on his angular young face stated, 'They'll change their minds again in time. I'll mash every horse I ride into a pulp. I'll do my nut on every hopeless hack. No one henceforth will see me finish eighth when by bashing the beast I could be sixth.'

I had smiled to hear these fighting words from one whose chief asset was his lightness of touch, but was relieved, too, that he was intact in spirits. No suicides, no mental breakdowns for him.

Shantytown, when it came to the race, was not what I had been led to expect. The damp raw January afternoon had drawn only a small crowd of stalwarts to watch a second-class programme at a minor meeting, and as I watched the big chestnut plod round the parade ring I thought how well he matched the circumstances. Uninspiring.

But far from pulling my arms out of their sockets, Shantytown seemed to me to be in danger of falling asleep. The start caught him flat-footed, so little interest was he taking in it, and I had to boot him into the first fence. He rose to it fairly well, but was slow in his recovery, and it was the same at every jump. It was puzzling, after what Tick-Tock had said, but horses do have their off-days for no discernible reason, and I could only suppose that this was one of them.

We trailed round the entire three miles in the rear of the field, and finished ingloriously last. All my efforts to get him to quicken up the straight met with no response. Shantytown hadn't taken hold of his bit from the beginning and at the end he seemed to be dead beat.

A hostile reception met us on our return. John

Ballerton, with whom I had exchanged coldly polite 'Good afternoons' in the parade ring before the race, now glowered like a July thunderstorm. Corin, standing on one leg and wearing an anxious, placatory expression, was obviously going to use me as the scapegoat for the horse's failure, to save his face as its trainer. That was always one of the hazards to be run in riding Corin's horses.

'What the hell do you think you were doing?' Ballerton said aggressively, as I slid off on to the ground and begun to unbuckle the saddle girths.

'I'm sorry, sir,' I said. 'He wouldn't go any faster.'

'Don't talk such bloody rubbish,' he said, 'he always goes faster than that. I've never seen a more disgusting display of incompetence . . . you couldn't ride in a cart with a pig net over it. If you ask me, the horse wasn't given a chance. You missed the start and couldn't be bothered to make it up.'

'I did say,' said Corin to me reproachfully, 'not to let him run away with you, and to keep tucked in behind for the first two miles. But I do think you carried my orders a bit too far . . .'

'A bit too far!' interrupted Ballerton furiously. 'Were you afraid to let him go, or something? If you can't manage to ride a decent race on a horse which pulls, why the hell do you try to. Why not say straight out that you can't? Save us all a lot of time and money.'

I said, 'The horse didn't pull. There was no life in him.'

'Kellar,' Ballerton was nearly shouting. 'Is my horse a puller or is he not?'

'He is,' said Corin, not meeting my eyes.

'And you told me he was fit. On his toes.'

'Yes,' said Corin. 'I thought he'd win.'

They looked at me accusingly. Corin must have known that the horse had run listlessly because he had seen the race with experienced eyes, but he was not going to admit it. If I had to ride often for Corin, I thought wryly, I would soon have as many rows with him as Art had had.

Ballerton narrowed his eyes and said to me, 'I asked you to ride Shantytown against my better judgement and only because Maurice Kemp-Lore insisted I had been misjudging you and that you were really a reliable man who would ride a genuine race. Well, I'm going to tell him he is wrong. Very wrong. You'll never ride another horse of mine, I promise you that.'

He turned on his heel and stalked off, followed by Corin. My chief feeling, as I went back to the weighing-room, was of irritation that I hadn't relied on instinct and refused to ride for him in the first place.

By the end of the afternoon the puzzlement I had felt over Shantytown's dead running had changed to a vague uneasiness, for neither of the other two horses I rode afterwards did anything like as well as had been

123

expected. Both were well backed, and both finished nearly last, and although their owners were a great deal nicer about it than Ballerton had been, their disappointment was obvious.

On the following day, still at Dunstable, the run of flops continued. I had been booked for three horses, and they all ran badly. I spent the whole depressing afternoon apologetically explaining to owner after owner that I had not been able to make their horse go faster. The third horse, in fact, went so badly that I had to pull him up half-way round. He was a slow jumper on the best of days, but on that particular one he took so long putting himself right and so long starting off again when he landed, that the rest of the field were a whole fence ahead by the time we had gone a mile. It was hopeless. When I reined him in he slowed from a reluctant gallop to a walk in a couple of strides, sure sign of a very tired horse. I thought as he was trained by a farmer-owner who might not know better, that he must have been given too stiff a training gallop on the previous day, but the farmer said he was sure he had not.

Runs of bad luck are commoner in racing than good ones, and the fact that six of my mounts in a row had made a showing far below their usual capabilities would not have attracted much notice had it not been for John Ballerton.

I changed into street clothes after the fifth race and strolled out of the weighing-room to find him standing close by with a small circle of cronies. All the heads turned towards me with that sideways, assessing look which meant they had been talking about me, and Ballerton said something forceful to them, of which the word 'disgrace' floated across clearly.

Jockeys being as accustomed as politicians to abuse I gave no sign of having heard what had obviously been intended for my ears, and walked casually off to the stands to watch the last race; but I did wonder how long and how maliciously Ballerton would hold Shantytown's failure against me, and what effect his complaints would have on the number of horses I was asked to ride. He was not a man to keep his grudges to himself, and as a National Hunt Committee member he was not without influence either.

Up on the stands Maurice Kemp-Lore came across to talk to me. We had met briefly on racecourses several times now, and were on superficially friendly terms, but in spite of his charm, or perhaps because it sometimes seemed too polished, I felt his friendship came strictly into the professional, 'might be useful' category. I did not believe that he liked me for my own sake.

He smiled vividly, the charm turned on to full wattage, his slim figure radiating health and confidence and his blue eyes achieving the near impossible of twinkling on a grey January afternoon. I smiled back automatically: one couldn't help it. All his impressive success stemmed from the instantaneous, irresistible feeling of well-being he inspired in whomever he talked to, and there was no one from the Senior Steward downwards who did not enjoy his company, even if, like me, one suspected his unfailing motive was the gathering of material for his programme.

'What bad luck, Rob,' he said cheerfully. 'I hear the good word I put in for you with John Ballerton has gone awry.'

'You can say that again,' I agreed. 'But thanks for trying anyway.'

The blue eyes glimmered. 'Anything to help,' he said.

I could hear distinctly a faint high-pitched wheeze as he drew breath into his lungs, and I realized it was the first time I had encountered him in an asthmatic attack. I was vaguely sorry for him.

The horses for the sixth race cantered past, going down to the start.

'Are James's plans fixed for the Midwinter Cup?' he asked casually, his eyes on the horses. I smiled. But he had his job to do, I supposed, and there was no harm in telling him.

'Template runs, all being well,' I said.

'And you ride him?'

'Yes,' I agreed.

'How is Pip getting along?' he asked, wheezing quietly.

'They think his leg is mending well, but he is still in plaster,' I said. 'It comes off next week, I believe, and he might be ready for Cheltenham, but of course he won't be fit for the Midwinter.'

The race in question was a richly endowed new event at Ascot, introduced to provide a high spot in mid-February, and nicely timed to give three full weeks for recovery and retuning before the Cheltenham Gold Cup. It lay almost a month ahead, on that day at Dunstable, and I was looking forward to it particularly as it seemed possible that it would be my last chance on Template. Pip would do his very best to be fit to ride him in the Gold Cup, and so would I have done in his place.

'What chance do you give Template in the Midwinter?' Maurice asked, watching the start through his race glasses.

'Oh, I hope he'll win,' I said, grinning. 'You can quote me.'

'I probably will,' he agreed, grinning back. We watched the race together, and such was the effect of his personality that I left Dunstable quite cheerfully, the dismal two days' results temporarily forgotten.

CHAPTER EIGHT

It was a false security. My charmed run of good luck had ended with a vengeance, and Dunstable proved to be only the fringe of the whirlpool. During the next two weeks I rode seventeen horses. Fifteen of them finished in the rear of the field, and in only two cases was this a fair result.

I couldn't understand it. As far as I knew there was no difference in my riding, and it was unbelievable that my mounts should all lose their form simultaneously. I began to worry about it, and that didn't help, as I could feel my confidence oozing away as each disturbing and embarrassing day passed.

There was one grey mare I particularly liked riding because of the speed of her reactions: she often seemed to know what I intended to do a split second before I gave her signals, rather as if she had sized up the situation as quickly as I had and was already taking independent action. She was sweet tempered and silken mouthed, and jumped magnificently. I liked her owner too, a short jolly farmer with a thick Norfolk accent, and while we watched her walk round the parade ring before her race he commiserated with me on my bad luck and said, 'Never mind, lad. The mare will put you right. She'll not fail you. You'll do all right on her, never fear.'

I went out smiling to the race because I too believed I would do all right on her. But that week she might have been another horse. Same colour, same size, same pretty head. But no zip. It was like driving a car with four flat tyres.

The jolly farmer looked less jolly and more pensive when I brought her back.

'She's not been last ever before, lad,' he said reproachfully.

We looked her over, but there was nothing wrong with her that we could see, and she wasn't even blowing very hard.

'I could get her heart tested I suppose,' the farmer said doubtfully. 'Are you sure you gave her her head, lad?'

'Yes,' I said. 'But she had no enthusiasm at all today.'

The farmer shook his head, doleful and puzzled.

One of the horses I rode belonged to a tall sharp-faced woman who knew a great deal about racing and had no sympathy with bunglers. She laid straight into me with her tongue after I had eased her ultra-expensive new gelding from last into second last place only feet from the winning post.

'I suppose you realize,' she said in a loud, hard voice, unashamedly listened to by a large group of racegoers, 'that in the last five minutes you have succeeded both in halving the value of my horse and making me look a fool for having paid a fortune for him.'

I apologized. I suggested possibly that her animal needed a little time.

'Time?' she repeated angrily. 'For what? For you to wake up? You speak as if it were my judgement that is at fault, not yours. You lay far too far out of your ground. You should have taken closer order from the beginning...' Her acid lecture went on and on and on, and I looked at the fine head of her glossy black high-bred gelding and admitted to myself that he was probably a great deal better than he had appeared.

One Wednesday was the big day for a ten-year-old schoolboy with sparkly brown eyes and a con-spiratorial grin. His wealthy eccentric grandmother, having discovered that there was no minimum age laid down for racehorse owners, had given Hugo a colossal chestnut 'chaser twice his height, and was considerate enough to foot the training bills as well.

I had become firm friends with Hugo. Knowing that I saw his horse most mornings at James's, he used to send me tiny parcels containing lumps of sugar filched from the dining table at his prep. school, which I conscientiously passed on to their intended destination: and I used to write back to Hugo, giving him quite detailed accounts of how his giant pet was progressing.

On that Wednesday Hugo had not only begged a day off from school to see his horse run, but had brought three friends with him. The four of them stood with me and James in the parade ring, Hugo's mother being the rare sort who liked her son to enjoy his limelight alone. As I had walked down from the weighing-room she had smiled broadly to me from her station on the rails.

The four little boys were earnest and excited, and James and I had great fun with them before the race, treating them with seriousness and as man-to-man, which they obviously appreciated. This time, I promised myself, this time, for Hugo, I will win. I must.

But the big chestnut jumped very clumsily that day. On the far side of nearly every fence he ducked his head, and once, to prevent myself being hauled over in a somersault, I had to stretch forward down his neck with one hand only, leaving go of the reins entirely with the other. The free arm, swinging up sideways, helped to bring my weight far enough back to keep me in the saddle, but the gesture known as 'calling a cab' was not going to earn me any bonus points with James, who had denounced it often as the style of 'bad, tired, scared or unfit amateurs'.

Hugo's little face was pink when I dismounted, and the three friends glumly shuffled their feet behind him. With them as witnesses there would be no chance of

Hugo smoothing over the disaster with the rest of his schoolmates.

'I'm very sorry, Hugo,' I said sincerely, apologizing for everything – myself, the horse, the race, and the miserliness of fate.

He answered with a stoicism which would have been a lesson to many of his seniors. 'I expect it was an off day,' he said kindly. 'And anyway, someone always has to be last. That's what Daddy said when I came bottom in History.' He looked at the chestnut forgivingly, and said to me, 'I expect he's keen really, don't you?'

'Yes,' I agreed. 'Keen, very.'

'Well,' said Hugo, turning bravely to his friends. 'That's that, then. We might as well have tea.'

Failures like these were too numerous to escape anyone's attention, but as the days passed I noticed a change in the way people spoke to me. One or two, and Corin in particular, showed something like contempt. Others looked uncomfortable, others sympathetic, others pitying. Heads turned towards me wherever I went, and I could almost feel the wave of gossip I left in my wake. I didn't know exactly what they were saying, so I asked Tick-Tock.

'Pay no attention,' he said. 'Ride a couple of winners and they'll be throwing the laurel wreaths again, and back-pedalling on everything they're saying now. It's badpatchville, chum, that's all.'

And that was all I could get out of him.

One Thursday evening James telephoned to my digs and asked me to go up to his house. I walked up in the dark, rather miserably wondering whether he, like two other trainers that day, was going to find an excuse for putting someone else up on his horses. I couldn't blame him. Owners could make it impossible for him to continue with a jockey so thoroughly in the doldrums.

James called me into his office, a square room joining his house to the stable yard. Its walls were covered with racing photographs, bookshelves, a long row of racing colours on clothes hangers, and filing cabinets. A huge roll-top desk stood in front of the window, which looked out on to the yard. There were three broken-springed armchairs with faded chintz covers, a decrepit Turkish carpet on the floor, and a red-hot coal fire in the grate. I had spent a good many hours there in the past three months, discussing past performances and future plans.

James waited for me and stood aside to let me go in first. He followed me in and shut the door, and faced me almost aggressively across the familiar room.

'I hear,' he said without preamble, 'that you have lost your nerve.'

The room was very still. The fire crackled slightly. A horse in a near-by loose box banged the floor with his hoof. I stared at James, and he stared straight back, gravely.

I didn't answer. The silence lengthened. It was not

a surprise. I had guessed what was being said about me when Tick-Tock had refused to tell me what it was.

'No one is to blame for losing his nerve,' James said non-committally. 'But a trainer cannot continue to employ someone to whom it has happened.'

I still said nothing.

He waited a few seconds, and went on, 'You have been showing the classic symptoms ... trailing round nearly last, pulling up for no clear reason, never going fast enough to keep warm, and calling a cab. Keeping at the back out of trouble, that's what you've been doing.'

I thought about it, rather numbly.

'A few weeks ago,' he said, 'I promised you that if I heard any rumours about you I would make sure they were true before I believed them. Do you remember?'

I nodded.

'I heard this rumour last Saturday,' he said. 'Several people sympathized with me because my jockey had lost his nerve. I didn't believe it. I have watched you closely ever since.'

I waited dumbly for the axe. During the week I had been last five times out of seven.

He walked abruptly over to an armchair by the fire and sat down heavily.

Irritably he said, 'Oh sit down, Rob. Don't just stand there like a stricken ox, saying nothing.'

I sat down and looked at the fire.

'I expected you to deny it,' he said in a tired voice. 'Is it true, then?'

'No,' I said.

'Is that all you've got to say? It isn't enough. What has happened to you? You owe me an explanation.'

I owed him much more than an explanation.

'I can't explain,' I said despairingly. 'Every horse I've ridden in the last three weeks seems to have had its feet dipped in treacle. The difference is in the horses ... I am the same.' It sounded futile and incredible, even to me.

'You have certainly lost your touch,' he said slowly. 'Perhaps Ballerton is right ...'

'Ballerton?' I said sharply.

'He's always said you were not as good as you were made out to be, and that I'd pushed you too fast ... given you a top job when you weren't ready for it. Today he has been going round smugly saying "I told you so." He can't leave the subject alone, he's so pleased.'

'I'm sorry, James,' I said.

'Are you ill, or something?' he asked exasperatedly.

'No,' I said.

'They say the fall you had three weeks ago was what frightened you – the day you got knocked out and your horse rolled on you. But you were all right going home, weren't you? I remember you being a bit sore, but you didn't seem in the least scared of falling again.'

'I didn't give that fall another thought,' I said.

'Then why, Rob, why?'

But I shook my head. I didn't know why.

He stood up and opened a cupboard which contained bottles and glasses, poured out two whiskies, and handed one to me.

'I can't convince myself yet that you've lost your nerve,' he said. 'Remembering the way you rode Template on Boxing Day, only a month ago, it seems impossible. No one could change so fundamentally in so short a time. Before I took you on, wasn't it your stock in trade to ride all the rough and dangerous horses that trainers didn't want to risk their best jockeys on? That's why I first engaged you, I remember it clearly. And all those years you spent in wherever it was as a stockman, and that spell in a rodeo ... you aren't the sort of man to lose his nerve suddenly and for nothing, and especially not when you're in the middle of a most spectacularly successful season.'

I smiled for almost the first time that day, realizing how deeply I wanted him not to lose faith in me.

I said, 'I feel as if I'm fighting a fog. I tried everything I knew today to get those horses to go faster, but they were all half-dead. Or I was. I don't know ... it's a pretty ghastly mess.'

'I'm afraid it is,' he said gloomily. 'And I'm having owner trouble about it, as you can imagine. All the original doubters are doubting again. I can't reassure

them ... it's like a Stock Exchange crash; catching.
And you're the bad stock that's being jettisoned.'

'What rides can I still expect?' I said.

He sighed. 'I don't exactly know. You can have all
the Broome runners because he's on a cruise in the
Mediterranean and won't hear the rumours for a while.
And my two as well; they both run next week. For the
rest, we'll have to wait and see.'

I could hardly bring myself to say it, but I had to
know.

'How about Template?' I asked.

He looked at me steadily. 'I haven't heard from
George Tirrold,' he said. 'I think he will agree that he
can't chuck you out after you've won so many races
for him. He is not easily stampeded, there's that to
hope for, and it was he who drew my attention to you
in the first place. Unless something worse happens,' he
finished judiciously, 'I think you can still count on
riding Template in the Midwinter a week on Saturday.
But if you bring him in last in that ... it will be the
end.'

I stood up and drained the whisky.

'I'll win that race,' I said, 'whatever the cost, I'll
win it.'

We went silently together to the races the following
day, but when we arrived I discovered that two of my
three prospective mounts were mine no longer. I had

been, in the expressive phrase, jocked off. The owners, the trainer in question brusquely explained, thought they would have no chance of winning if they put me up as planned. Very sorry and all that, he said, but no dice.

I stood on the stands and watched both the horses run well: one of them won, and the other finished a close third. I ignored as best I could the speculative, sideways glances from all the other jockeys, trainers and pressmen standing near me. If they wanted to see how I was taking it, that was their affair; just as it was mine if I wanted to conceal from them the inescapable bitterness of these two results.

I went out to ride James's runner in the fourth race absolutely determined to win. The horse was capable of it on his day, and I knew him to be a competent jumper and a willing battler in a close finish.

We came last.

All the way round I could barely keep him in touch with the rest of the field. In the end he cantered slowly past the winning post with his head down in tiredness, and mine down too, in defeat and humiliation. I felt ill.

It was an effort to go back and face the music. I felt more like driving the Mini-Cooper at top speed into a nice solid tree.

The freckle-faced lad who looked after the horse deliberately did not glance at me when he took hold of the reins in the paddock. He usually greeted me with a beaming smile. I slid off the horse. The owner and James stood there, their faces blank. No one said anything. There was nothing to say. Finally, without a word, the owner shrugged his shoulders and turned on his heel, and walked off.

I took my saddle off the horse and the lad led him away.

James said, 'It can't go on, Rob.'

I knew it.

He said, 'I'm sorry. I'm very sorry. I'll have to get someone else to ride my horses tomorrow.'

I nodded.

He gave me a searching look in which puzzlement and doubt were tinged for the first time with pity. I found it unbearable.

'I think I'll go to Kensington tonight after the races,' I said, trying to speak evenly. 'Instead of coming back with you.'

'Very well,' he said, obviously relieved at not having to face an embarrassing return journey. 'I really am sorry, Rob.'

'Yes,' I said. 'I know.'

I took my saddle back to the weighing-room, acutely aware of the glances which followed me. The conversation in the changing-room died into an embarrassed silence when I walked in. I went over to my peg and put the saddle on the bench, and began to take off my colours. I looked at the circle of faces turned towards me, reading on some curiosity, on some hostility, on some sympathy, and on one or two, pleasure. No contempt: they would leave that to people who didn't ride, to the people who didn't know at first hand how formidable a big fence can look to a jockey on a bad horse. In the changing-room there was too much consciousness in their minds of 'there but for the grace of God go I,' for them to feel contempt.

They began to talk again, but not much to me. I guessed they didn't know what to say. Nor did I.

I felt neither more nor less courageous than I had done all my life. It was surely impossible, I thought confusedly, to be subconsciously afraid, to keep out of trouble and yet think one was as willing as ever to accept risks. Three weeks earlier, I would have laughed at the idea. But the shattering fact remained that none of the twenty-eight horses I had ridden since I had been knocked out in that fall had made any show at all. They were trained by several different trainers and owned by different owners: all they had had in common was me. There were too many of them for it to be a coincidence, especially as those I had been removed from had done well.

Round and round in a jumble went the profitless thoughts, the hopeless statistics, the feeling that the sky had fallen. I put on my street clothes and brushed my hair, and was surprised to see in the mirror that I looked the same as usual.

I went outside on to the steps outside the weighing-room and heard the normal chatter which my presence had muffled in the changing-room break out cheerfully again as soon as I was gone. No one outside either seemed very anxious to talk to me: no one, that is, except a weedy little ferret of a man, who worked, I knew, for one of the minor sporting papers.

He was standing with John Ballerton, but when he caught sight of me he came directly over.

'Oh, Finn,' he said, taking a notebook and pencil out of his pocket and looking at me with a sly, malicious smile. 'May I have a list of the horses you are riding tomorrow? And next week?'

I looked across at Ballerton. There was a smirk of triumph on his heavy face. I took a great grip on my rising temper and spoke mildly to the pressman.

'Ask Mr Axminster,' I said. He looked disappointed, but he didn't know how close he had come to feeling my fist in his face. I had just enough sense to know that letting fly at him would be the worst thing I could do.

I strode away from him, seething with rage; but the day had not done with me, even yet. Corin, crossing my path purposefully, stopped me and said, 'I suppose you've seen this?' He held out a copy of the paper for which the ferrety little man wrote.

'No,' I said. 'And I don't want to.'

Corin smiled thinly, enjoying himself. 'I think you ought to sue them. Everyone thinks so. You'll have to sue them when you've read it. You can't ignore it, or everyone will think . . .'

'Everyone can think what they damn well please,' I said roughly, trying to walk on.

'Read it,' insisted Corin, thrusting the paper in front of my eyes. 'Everyone else has.'

It needed only a half glance to see the headline. There was no missing it. In bold type it said, 'Nerve Lost.'

Against my will I began to read.

'Nerve, depending on how it takes you, is either fear overcome by an effort of will, or a total lack of imagination. If you ride steeplechasing it doesn't matter which sort you have, as long as you have one of them.

'Does anyone understand why one man is brave and another is not? Or why a person can be brave at one time and cowardly at another?

'Maybe it is all a matter of hormones! Maybe a bang on the head can destroy the chemical make-up which produces courage. Who knows? Who knows?

'The crumbling of a jumping jockey's nerve is a pathetic sight, as every recent racegoer will realize. But while one may extend sympathy to a man for a state which he cannot help, one must at the same time ask whether he is doing the right thing if he continues to seek and accept rides in races.

'The public deserves a fair run for its money. If a jockey can't give it to them because he is afraid

142

of hurting himself, he is taking fees under false pretences.

'But it is only a matter of time, of course, before owners and trainers withdraw their custom from such a man and, by forcing him into retirement, protect the betting public from wasting any more of its money.

'And a good thing too!'

I gave the paper back to Corin and tried to loosen the clamped tension of my jaw muscles.

'I can't sue them,' I said. 'They don't mention my name.'

He didn't look surprised, and I realized sharply that he had known it all along. He had wanted only the pleasure of watching me read, and there was still about his eyes a remnant of a very nasty smile.

'What did I ever do to you, Corin,' I asked, 'to make you feel the way you do?'

He looked taken aback, and said weakly, 'Er . . . nothing . . .'

'Then I'm sorry for you,' I said stonily. 'I'm sorry for your spiteful, mean, cowardly little soul . . .'

'Cowardly!' he exclaimed, stung and flushing. 'Who are you to call anyone else cowardly? That's a laugh, that really is. Just wait till they hear this. Just wait till I tell . . .'

But I didn't wait. I had had far, far more than enough. I went back to Kensington in as deep and terrible a mood of despair as I ever hope to have to live through.

There was no one in the flat, and for once it was spotlessly tidy. The family, I concluded, were away. The kitchen confirmed it. There was no food or milk in the refrigerator, no bread in the bin, no fruit in the basket.

Back in the silent sitting-room I took a nearly full whisky bottle out of the cupboard and lay down full length on the sofa. I uncorked the bottle and took two large gulps. The neat spirit bit into my gums and scorched down to my empty stomach. I put the cork in the bottle and the bottle on the floor beside me. What is the point of getting drunk, I thought: I'd only feel worse in the morning. I could stay drunk for several days perhaps, but it wouldn't do any good in the end. Nothing would do any good. Everything was finished. Everything was busted and gone.

I spent a long time looking at my hands. Hands. The touch they had for horses had earned me my living all my adult life. They looked the same as always. They were the same, I thought desperately. Nerves and muscles, strength and sensitivity, nothing was changed. But the memory of the last twenty-eight horses I had ridden denied it: heavy, cumbersome and unre-sponsive.

I knew no other skill but riding, nor had ever wanted any. I felt more than whole on horseback: I felt extended. Four extra limbs and a second brain.

More speed, more strength, more courage . . . I winced at the word . . . and quicker reactions. A saddle was to me as the sea to a fish, natural and easy. Home. And a racing saddle? I drew in a breath, shivering. For a racing saddle, I thought bleakly, I am not sufficient.

It wasn't enough after all to *want* to race as well as anybody, one had to have the talent and the staying power as well; and I was face to face with the conviction that I was not good enough, that I was never going to be good enough, to take firm hold of the position which had been so nearly in my grasp. I had thought myself capable of seizing the incredible opportunity I had been given. The mess I had made of it, the weak, degrading retreat from the brink of success, was tearing to shreds all I had known or believed about myself.

I picked up the whisky bottle and held it on my chest. It was all the company I had, and it offered sleep, at least. But I suppose old habits cling hard: I held the bottle to my chest like a life-jacket to a drowning man and knew I wouldn't pull the cork out again. Not for a while. Not that night, anyway.

And what of the future? I could return during the next week and race on one or two of James's horses, if he would still let me, and perhaps even on Template in the Midwinter. But I no longer either expected or hoped to do well, and I could feel myself shrink at the prospect of going back to a racecourse to face all those stares and insults again. Better to start a new life at once, perhaps. But a new life doing what?

It couldn't be the old life. Being a stockman might have suited me at twenty, but it was not what I would want at thirty, nor at forty, nor fifty. And whatever I did, wherever I went now, I would drag around with me the knowledge that I had totally failed at what I had tried hardest to do.

After a long time I stood up and put the bottle back into the cupboard.

It was then a good twenty-six hours since I had eaten, and despite everything my stomach was beginning its squeezing routine. On a second inspection the kitchen revealed only some assorted tins of *escargots*, cheese straws and *marrons glacés*; so I went out and along the streets until I came to a decent-looking pub where I was sure I was not known by sight. I didn't want to have to talk.

I ordered ham sandwiches and a glass of beer, but when it came the thick new white bread stuck tastelessly in my mouth and my throat kept closing convulsively against all attempts to swallow. This can't go on, I thought. I've got to eat. If I can't get drunk and I can't have Joanna and I can't ... I can't be a jockey any more ... at least I can eat now as much as I like, without worrying about gaining a pound or two ... but after ten minutes trying I had swallowed only two mouthfuls, and I couldn't manage another bite.

The fact that it was Friday had meant nothing to me all evening, and the approach of 9 o'clock went unnoticed. But just when I pushed away the sandwiches and was eyeing the beer with the beginnings of nausea, someone turned up the volume of the television set which stood at one end of the bar, and the opening bars of the 'Galloping Major' suddenly blared out across the tinkling glasses and the buzzing voices. A large bunch of devotees who had settled themselves with full pint pots in front of the set made shooshing noises to those nearest to them, and by the time Maurice Kemp-Lore's tidy features materialized there was a more or less attentive audience to receive him. My little glass-topped table was as far as it could be from the door, so that it was more because leaving meant weaving my way through the sprawling silent crowd, than from a positive desire to watch, that I stayed where I was.

'Good evening,' Maurice said, the spellbinding smile in place. 'This evening we are going to talk about handicapping, and I have here to meet you two well-informed men who look at weights and measures from opposing angles. The first is Mr Charles Jenkinson, who has been an official handicapper for several years.' Mr Jenkinson's self-conscious face appeared briefly on the screen. 'And the other is the well-known trainer, Corin Kellar.'

Corin's thin face glowed with satisfaction. We'll never hear the last of this, I thought; and then with a stab remembered that I wouldn't be there to hear any of it anyway.

'Mr Jenkinson,' said Maurice, 'will explain how he builds a handicap. And Mr Kellar will tell you how he tries to avoid having his horses defeated by their weights. The battle between handicappers and trainers is none the less fierce for being conducted in gentlemanly and largely uncomplaining reticence, and perhaps tonight you will capture a whiff of that unrelenting struggle.' He smiled engagingly. 'A handicapper's pinnacle of success is for every single runner in a race to pass the winning post in a straight line abreast – a multiple dead-heat – since it is his aim to give each horse an exactly equal chance. It never actually happens, but handicappers dream about it in their softer moments.' He grinned sideways in a friendly fashion towards his guest, and when Mr Jenkinson appeared on the screen one could almost see the self-confidence begin to flow in him as he started to talk about his job.

I listened with only half my mind, the rest being submerged in persistent misery, and Corin had been speaking for some moments before I paid much attention to him. He was being of necessity less than frank, since the bald truth would have lost him his licence very smartly. In practice he felt no qualms at all when giving his jockey orders to start at the back and stay there, but in theory, I was sardonically amused to see, he was righteously on the side of the angels.

'Horses from my stable are always doing their best to win,' he said, lying without a tremor.

'But surely you don't insist on them being ridden hard at the end when they've no chance at all?' said Maurice, reasonably.

'As hard as necessary, yes,' Corin asserted. 'I hate to see jockeys easing up too soon, even if they are beaten. I dismissed a jockey a short while ago for not riding hard enough at the end. He could have come third if he had ridden the horse out...' his voice droned on, pious and petulant, and I thought of Tick-Tock, thrown to the stewards for obeying his orders too conscientiously and now having trouble getting other trainers to trust him. I thought of Art, nagged and contradicted and driven to death; and the active dislike I already felt for Corin Kellar sharpened in that dim pub corner into hatred.

Maurice dragged him back to handicapping and finally wrung from him a grudging admission that from the point of view of the weight he would be allotted in future, it was better for a horse to win by one length than by ten. Maurice would have done better, I thought, to have chosen almost anyone else to show how to dodge the handicapper; or perhaps he did not know Corin well enough to expect him hypocritically to deny in public what he had said in private. Every jockey who had ridden the Kellar horses had learned it the hard way.

'One is always in the hands of one's jockey,' Corin was saying.

'Go on,' said Maurice encouragingly, leaning forward. A light somewhere in the studio lent his eyes a momentary shimmer as he moved. Corin said, 'You can slave away for weeks preparing a horse for a race and then a jockey can undo it all with one stupid mistake.'

'It does the handicap good though,' Maurice interrupted, laughing. The pub audience laughed too.

'Well . . .' agreed Corin, nonplussed.

'If you look at it that way,' Maurice continued, 'there is always some compensation for a jockey not getting the most out of a horse. Whatever the reason, trivial, like a mistake, or more serious, like a failure of resolution at a crucial point . . .'

'No guts, you mean?' said Corin flatly. 'I'd say that that would be as obvious to a handicapper as to everyone else, and that he'd take it into account. There's a case in point now . . .' he hesitated, but Maurice did not try to stop him, so he went on more boldly, 'a case now where everything a certain jockey rides goes round at the back of the field. He is afraid of falling, you see. Well, you can't tell me any handicapper thinks those particular horses are not as good as they were. Of course they are. It's just the rider who's going downhill.'

I could feel the blood rush to my head and begin

to pulse there. I leaned my elbows on the table and bit my knuckle. Hard.

The voices went on inexorably.

Maurice said, 'What are your views on that, Mr Jenkinson?'

And the handicapper, looking embarrassed, murmured that 'Of course ... er ... in certain circumstances, one would ... er ... overlook the occasional result.'

'Occasional!' said Corin. 'I wouldn't call nearly thirty races in a row occasional. Are you going to overlook them all?'

'I can't answer that,' protested Jenkinson.

'What do you usually do in these cases?' Maurice asked.

'I ... that is ... they aren't usually as blatant as this. I may have to consult ... er, others, before coming to a decision. But it really isn't a thing I can discuss here.'

'Where better?' said Maurice persuasively. 'We all know that this poor chap took a toss three weeks ago and has ridden ... er ... ineffectively ... ever since. Surely you'd have to take that into account when you are handicapping those horses?'

While the cameras focused on Jenkinson hesitating over his answer Corin's voice said, 'I'll be interested to know what you decide. One of those horses was mine, you know. It was a shocking exhibition. Finn won't be riding for me again, or for anyone else either, I shouldn't wonder.'

Jenkinson said uneasily, 'I don't think we should mention names,' and Maurice cut in quickly, saying, 'No, no. I agree. Better not.' But the damage was done.

'Well, thank you both very much for giving us your time this evening. I am sorry to say we have come nearly to the end once again . . .' He slid expertly into his minute of chit-chat and his closing sentences, but I was no longer listening, Between them he and Corin had hammered in the nails on the ruins of my brief career, and watching them at it on the glaring little screen had given me a blinding headache.

I stood up stiffly as the chatter broke out again in the crowded pub and threaded my way a little unsteadily to the door. The bunch of racing enthusiasts were downing their pints and I caught a scrap of their conversation as I squeezed around them.

'Laid it on a bit thick, I thought,' one of them said.

'Not thick enough,' contradicted another. 'I lost a quid on Finn on Tuesday. He deserves all he gets, if you ask me, the windy b—.'

I stumbled out into the street, breathing in great gulps of cold air and making a conscious effort to stand up straight. It was no use sitting down and weeping in the gutter, which would have been easy enough to do. I walked slowly back to the dark, empty flat, and without switching on any lights lay down fully dressed on my bed.

The glow from the street below dimly lit the small room, the window frame throwing an angular distorted shadow on the ceiling. My head throbbed. I remembered lying there like that before, the day Grant's fist pulped my nose. I remembered pitying him, and pitying Art. It had been so easy. I groaned aloud, and the sound shocked me.

It was a long way down from my window to the street. Five storeys. A long, quick way down. I thought about it.

There was a chiming clock in the flat below ours, counting away the quarter-hours, and in the quiet house I could hear it clearly. It struck ten, eleven, twelve, one, two.

The window threw its shadow steadily on the ceiling. I stared up at it. Five storeys down. But however bad things were I couldn't take that way, either. It wasn't for me. I shut my eyes and lay still, and finally after the long despairing hours drifted into an exhausted, uneasy, dream-filled sleep.

I woke less than two hours later, and heard the clock strike four. My headache had gone, and my mind felt as clear and sharp as the starry sky outside: washed and shining. It was like coming out of a thick fog into sunshine. Like coolness after fever. Like being re-born.

Somewhere between sleeping and waking I found I had regained myself, come back to the life-saving certainty that I was the person I thought I was, and not the cracked-up mess that everyone else believed.

And that being so, I thought in puzzlement, there must be some other explanation of my troubles. All – *all* I had to do was find it. Looking back unsympathetically on the appalling desolation in which I had so recently allowed myself to flounder, I began at last, at long last, to use my brain.

Half an hour later it was clear that my stomach was awake too, and it was so insistent to be filled that I couldn't concentrate. I got up and fetched the tins of cheese straws and *marrons glacés* from the kitchen, but not the snails. How hungry would one have to be, I wondered idly, to face those molluscs cold and butterless at five o'clock in the morning?

I opened the tins and lay down again, and crunched up all the cheese straws while I thought, and peeled and chewed half of the syrupy weight-producing chestnuts. My stomach quietened like a dragon fed its daily maiden, and outside the stars faded into the wan London dawn.

In the morning I took the advice I had given to Grant, and went to see a psychiatrist.

CHAPTER NINE

I had known the psychiatrist all my life as he was a friend of my father, and, I hoped, I knew him well enough to ring him up for help on a morning which he always reserved for golf. At eight o'clock I telephoned to his house in Wimpole Street where he lived in a flat above his consulting rooms.

He asked after my father. He sounded in a hurry.

'Can I come and see you, sir?' I said.

'Now? No. Saturday. Golf,' he said economically.

'Please . . . it won't take long.'

There was a brief pause.

'Urgent?' A professional note to his question.

'Yes,' I said.

'Come at once, then. I'm due at Wentworth at ten.'

'I haven't shaved . . .' I said, catching sight of myself in the looking-glass and realizing what a wreck I looked.

'Do you want to shave, or do you want to talk?' he said, exasperated.

'Talk,' I said.

'Then arrive,' he said, and put down his receiver.

I took a taxi, and he opened the door to me with a corner of toast and marmalade in his hand. The eminent Mr Claudius Mellit, whose patients usually saw him in striped trousers and black jacket, was sensibly attired for winter golf in waterproof trousers and a comfortably sloppy Norwegian sweater. He gave me a piercing preliminary glance and gestured, 'Upstairs.'

I followed him up. He finished his breakfast on the way. We went into his dining-room, where he gave me a seat at the oval mahogany table and some lukewarm coffee in a gold-rimmed cup.

'Now,' he said, sitting down opposite me.

'Suppose . . .' I began, and stopped. It didn't seem so easy, now that I was there. What had seemed obvious and manifest at five in the morning was now tinged with doubt. The dawn hours had shown me a pattern I believed in, but in the full light of day I felt sure it was going to sound preposterous.

'Look,' he said, 'if you really need help my golf can go hang. When I said on the telephone that I was in a hurry I hadn't seen the state you are in . . . and if you will excuse my saying so, your suit looks as if you had slept in it?'

'Well, yes, I did,' I said, surprised.

'Relax then, and tell me all.' He grinned, a big bear of a man, fifty years old and formidably wise.

'I'm sorry I look so untidy and unshaven,' I began.

'And sunken-eyed and hollow-cheeked,' he murmured, smiling.

'But I don't feel as bad as I suppose I look. Not any more. I won't keep you away from your golf if you'll just tell me . . .'

'Yes?' he waited for me calmly.

'Suppose I had a sister,' I said, 'who was as good a musician as Mother and Father, and I was the only one in the entire family to lack their talent – as you know I am – and I felt they despised me for lacking it, how would you expect me to act?'

'They don't despise you,' he protested.

'No . . . but if they did, would there be any way in which I could persuade them – and myself – that I had a very good excuse for not being a musician?'

'Oh, yes,' he said instantly, 'I'd expect you to do exactly what you have done. Find something you can do, and pursue it fanatically until in your own sphere you reach the standard of your family in theirs.'

I felt as if I'd been hit in the solar plexus. So simple an explanation of my compulsion to race had never occurred to me.

'That . . . that isn't what I meant,' I said helplessly. 'But when I come to think of it, I see it is true.' I paused. 'What I really meant to ask was, could I, when I was growing up, have developed a physical infirmity to explain away my failure? Paralysis, for instance, so that I simply couldn't play a violin or a piano or any musical instrument? An apparently honourable way out?'

He looked at me for a few moments, unsmiling and intent.

'If you were a certain type of person, yes, it's possible. But not in your case. You had better stop waltzing round it and ask me your question straight out. The real question. I am very well accustomed to hypothetical questions ... I meet them every day ... but if you want a trustable answer you'll have to ask the real question.'

'There are two,' I said. I still hesitated. So very much, my whole life, depended on his answers. He waited patiently.

I said at last, 'Could a boy whose family were all terrific cross-country riders develop asthma to hide the fact that he was afraid of horses?' My mouth was dry.

He didn't answer at once. He said, 'What is the other question?'

'Could that boy, as a man, develop such a loathing for steeplechase jockeys that he would try to smash their careers? Even if, as you said, he had found something else which he could do extremely well?'

'I suppose this man has that sister you mentioned?'

'Yes,' I said. 'She is getting to be the best girl point-to-point rider for a generation.'

He slouched back in his chair.

'It obviously matters so desperately to you, Robert, that I can't give you an answer without knowing more

158

about it. I'm not giving you a couple of casual yeses and find afterwards I've let you stir up disastrous trouble for all sorts of people. You must tell me why you ask these questions.'

'But your golf,' I said.

'I'll go later,' he said calmly. 'Talk.'

So I talked. I told him what had happened to Art, and to Grant, and to Peter Cloony, and Tick-Tock, and myself.

I told him about Maurice Kemp-Lore. 'He comes from a family who ride as soon as walk, and he's the right build for steeplechasing. But horses give him asthma, and that, everyone knows, is why he doesn't race himself. Well . . . it's a good reason, isn't it? Of course there are asthmatics who do ride – asthma doesn't stop people who think that racing is worth the wheezing – but no one would dream of blaming a man who didn't.'

I paused, but as he made no comment, I went on, 'You can't help being drawn to him. You can't imagine the spell of his personality unless you've felt it. You can see people wake up and sparkle when he speaks to them. He has the ear of everyone from the stewards down . . . and I think he uses his influence to sow seeds of doubt about jockeys' characters.'

'Go on,' Claudius said, his face showing nothing.

'The men who seem to be especially under his spell are Corin Kellar, a trainer, and John Ballerton, a member of the ruling body. Neither of them ever has

159

a good word to say for jockeys. I think Kemp-Lore picked them out as friends solely because they had the right sort of mean-mindedness for broadcasting every damaging opinion he insinuated into their heads. I think all the ruinous rumours start with Kemp-Lore, and that even the substance behind the rumours is mostly his work. Why isn't he content with having so much? The jockeys he is hurting like him and are pleased when he talks to them. Why does he need to destroy them?'

He said, 'If this were a hypothetical case I would tell you that such a man could both hate and envy his father – and his sister – and have felt both these emotions from early childhood. But because he knows these feelings are wrong he represses them, and the aggression is unfortunately transferred on to people who show the same qualities and abilities that he hates in his father. Such individuals can be helped. They can be understood, and treated, and forgiven.'

'I can't forgive him,' I said. 'And I'm going to stop him.'

He considered me. 'You must make sure of your facts,' he said, stroking his thumbnail down his upper lip. 'At present you are just guessing. And as I've had no opportunity to talk to him you'll get no more from me than an admission that your suspicions of Kemp-Lore are *possibly* correct. Not even probably correct. He is a public figure of some standing. You are making a very serious accusation. You need cast-iron facts.

Until you have them, there is always the chance that you have interpreted what has happened to you as malice from outside in order to explain away your own inner failure. Asthma of the mind, in fact.'

'Don't psychologists ever take a simple view?' I said, sighing.

He shook his head. 'Few things are simple.'

'I'll get the facts. Starting today,' I said. I stood up. 'Thank you for seeing me, and being so patient, and I'm sincerely sorry about your golf.'

'I won't be very late,' he reassured me, ambling down the stairs and opening his front door. On the doorstep shaking hands, he said as if making up his mind, 'Be careful, Robert. Go gently. If you are right about Kemp-Lore, and it is just possible that you are, you must deal with him thoughtfully. Persuade him to ask for treatment. Don't drive him too hard. His sanity may be in your hands.'

I said flatly, 'I can't look at it from your point of view. I don't think of Kemp-Lore as ill, but as wicked.'

'Where illness ends and crime begins . . .' he shrugged. 'It has been debated for centuries, and no two people agree. But take care, take care.' He turned to go in. 'Remember me to your parents.' He smiled, and shut the door.

Round a couple of corners, first during a luxurious shave in a fresh-smelling barber's and second over a triple order of eggs and bacon in the café next door, I bent my mind to the problem of how the cast-iron facts were to be dug up. On reflection, there seemed to be precious few of them to work on, and in the digging, to start with at least, I was going to come up against the barrier of pity and contempt which my recent performances had raised. Nasty medicine; but if I wanted a cure, I'd have to take it.

Using the café's telephone, I rang up Tick-Tock.

'Are you riding this afternoon?' I asked.

He said, 'Do me a favour, pal. No unkind questions so early in the day. In a word – negative.' A pause. 'And you?' Innocently, too innocently.

'You're a bastard,' I said.

'So my best friends tell me.'

'I want the car,' I said.

'Not if you're thinking of driving it over Beachy Head.'

'I'm not,' I said.

'Well, I'm relieved to hear it. But if you change your mind, let me know and I'll join you.' His voice was light and mocking; the desperate truth underneath needed no stating.

'I want to call at some stables,' I began.

'Whose?' he interrupted.

'Several people's . . . about six altogether, I think, apart from Axminster's. And Kellar's. I'll have to go there as well.'

'You've got a nerve,' said Tick-Tock.

'Thank you,' I said. 'You're about the only person in the country who thinks so.'

'Damn it . . . I didn't mean . . .'

I grinned into the telephone. 'Save it. Where's the car now?'

'Outside the window.'

'I'll come down to Newbury by train and pick it up, if you'll meet me at the station,' I said.

'It's no use going to any stables today,' he said. 'The trainers will all be at the races.'

'Yes, I sincerely hope so,' I agreed.

'What are you up to?' he asked suspiciously.

'Retrieving the fallen fortunes of the House of Finn,' I said. 'I'll catch the 10.10. You meet it. O.K.?' And I put the receiver down, hearing and ignoring, a protesting 'Hey' before I cut him off.

But when I stepped off the train at Newbury he was waiting, dressed in a dandyish waisted riding jacket of almost eighteenth-century length on top of some unbelievably narrow cavalry cord trousers. He enjoyed his moment ironically while I looked him up and down.

'Where's the cravat, the ruffles and the sword?' I asked.

He said, 'You don't get the message. I'm tomorrow's man. My sword will be a do-it-yourself instant anti-radiation kit. You must fit your defence to the danger you meet . . .' He grinned.

Young Tick-Tock, I reflected, not for the first time, took an uncompromisingly realistic view of the world.

He opened the car door and settled himself behind the wheel.

'Where to?' he said.

'You're not coming,' I said.

'I certainly am. This car is half mine. Where it goes, I go.' He was clearly determined. 'Where to?'

'Well...' I got in beside him, fished out of my pocket a list I had made on the train, and showed it to him. 'These are the stables I want to go to. I've tried to arrange them in order so that there isn't too much back-tracking, but even so it means a lot of driving.'

'Phew,' he said. 'There's a lot of them. Hampshire, Sussex, Kent, Oxford, Leicester, and Yorkshire ... how long will you be staying in each place? We'll never cover this lot in one day. Especially as you look tired already.'

I glanced at him, but he was looking down at the paper. It was true that I felt tired, but disconcerting that it should be so obvious. I had thought that the shave and breakfast and the return of self-confidence would have wiped away the ravages of the previous day and night.

'You needn't come,' I began.

'We've been through all that,' he interrupted. 'We'll start by going to your digs and mine for overnight things, and then make for Kent. And on the way you can tell me why we're going.' He calmly let in the clutch and drove off; and truth to tell I was very glad of his company.

We collected our things, and Tick-Tock pointed the

Mini-Cooper's blunt nose towards the first stable on the list, Corin Kellar's, in Hampshire.

'Now,' he said. 'The works.'

'No,' I said. 'I'm not going to tell you why we're going. Listen and watch, and then you tell me.'

'You're a cagey blighter,' he said, without arguing. He added, 'I suppose you've taken into account all that about saps rushing in where angels wouldn't plonk their holy feet? I mean, to put it mildly, we are neither of us in the red carpet bracket just now. Strictly doomsville, us.'

'You are so right,' I said, smiling.

Tick-Tock turned his head and gave me a surprised stare.

'Keep your eyes on the road,' I said mildly.

'I'll never know you,' he said. 'I'd have thought you'd take it very hard ... what has happened ... but since I picked you up at the station I've felt more cheerful than I have for weeks.' His foot went down on the accelerator and he began to whistle.

We arrived at Corin's extensive, well-groomed stable while the lads were doing up the horses after the second morning exercise. Arthur, the head lad, was crossing the yard with a bucket of oats when we climbed out of the little car, and the crinkling smile with which he usually greeted me got half-way to his eyes before he remembered. I saw the embarrassment take over and the welcome fade away.

'The guvnor isn't here,' he said awkwardly. 'He's gone to the races.'

'I know,' I said. 'Can I speak to Davey?'

Davey was the lad who looked after Shantytown.

'I suppose so,' said Arthur doubtfully, 'but you won't make no trouble?'

'No,' I said. 'No trouble. Where is he?'

'Fourth box from the end over that side,' he said, pointing. Tick-Tock and I walked over, and found Davey tossing and tidying the straw bed round a big chestnut, Shantytown. We leaned over the bottom half of the door, and watched Davey's expression too change from warmth to disgust. He was a short, tough, sixteen-year-old boy with flaming red hair and an intolerant mouth. He turned his back on us and ran his hand down the horse's neck. Then he spat into the straw. Tick-Tock took a sharp breath and his hands clenched into fists.

I said quickly, 'Davey, there's a quid for you if you feel like talking a bit.'

'What about?' he said, without turning round.

'About the day I rode Shantytown at Dunstable,' I said. 'Three weeks ago. Do you remember?'

'I'll say I remember,' he said offensively.

I ignored his tone. 'Well, tell me what happened from the moment you arrived on the course until I got up on Shantytown in the parade ring.'

'What the hell do you mean?' he said, wheeling

round and coming over to the door. 'Nothing happened. What should happen?'

I took a pound note out of my wallet and gave it to him. He looked at it for a second or two, then shrugged, and thrust it into his pocket.

'Start when you set off from here. Don't leave anything out,' I said.

'Are you off your nut?' he said.

'No,' I said, 'and I want my quid's worth.'

He shrugged again, but said, 'We went in the horse box from here to Dunstable, and . . .'

'Did you stop on the way?' I asked.

'Yes, Joe's Caff, same as always when we go to Dunstable.'

'Did you see anyone there you knew?'

'Well . . . Joe, and the girl who pours out the char.'

'No one you wouldn't expect?' I pressed.

'No, of course not. Like I said, we got to the course and unloaded the horses, two of them, in the stables there, and went and got another cuppa and a wad in the canteen, and then I went round the bookies, like, and put ten bob on Bloggs in the first, and went up on the stands and watched it get stuffed . . . sodding animal didn't try a yard . . . and then I went back to the stables and got Shantytown and put on his paddock clothing and led him out into the paddock . . .' His voice was bored as he recited the everyday racing routine of his job.

'Could anyone have given Shantytown anything to

eat or drink in the stables, say a bucket of water just before the race?' I asked.

'Don't be so ruddy stupid. Of course not. Who ever heard of giving a horse anything to eat or drink before a race? A mouthful of water, I dare say, a couple of hours beforehand, but a bucketful ...' The scorn in his voice suddenly changed to anger. 'Here, you're not suggesting I gave him a drink, are you? Oh no, mate, you're not putting the blame on me for the balls you made of it.'

'No,' I said, 'no, Davey. Calm down. How tight is the security on the Dunstable stables? Would anyone but a lad or a trainer get in there?'

'No,' he said, more moderately, 'it's as tight as a drum. The last gateman got sacked for letting an owner in alone without a trainer, and the new man's as pernickety as they come.'

'Go on, then,' I said. 'We've got you as far as the paddock.'

'Well, I walked the horse round the assembly ring for a bit, waiting for the guvnor to bring the saddle up from the weighing-room ...' He smiled suddenly, as at some pleasant memory '... and then when he came I took Shanty into one of the saddling boxes and the guvnor saddled up, and then I took Shanty down into the parade ring and walked him round until they called me over and you got up on him.' He stopped. 'I can't see what you wanted to hear all that for.'

'What happened while you were walking round the assembly ring?' I asked. 'Something you enjoyed? Something you smile about when you remember it?'

He sniffed. 'It's nothing you'd want to know.'

I said, 'The quid was for telling everything.'

'Oh, very well then, but it's nothing to do with racing. It was that chap on the telly, Maurice Kemp-Lore, he came over and spoke to me and admired the horse. He said he was a friend of the owner, old man Ballerton. He patted Shanty and gave him a couple of sugar knobs, which I wasn't too keen on, mind, but you can't be narky with a chap like him, somehow, and he asked me what his chances were, and I said pretty good ... more fool me ... and then he went away again. That's all. I told you it wasn't anything to do with racing.'

'No,' I said. 'Well, never mind. Thanks for trying.'

I straightened up and turned away from the door, and Tick-Tock had taken a step or two towards the car when Davey said under his breath behind me, 'Trying ... you two could both do a bit more of that yourselves, if you ask me.' But Tick-Tock fortunately didn't hear, and we folded ourselves back into the Mini-Cooper and drove unmourned out of the yard.

Tick-Tock exploded. 'Anyone would think you'd killed your mother and robbed your grandmother, the way they look at you. Losing your nerve isn't a crime.'

'Unless you can put up with a few harmless sneers you'd better get out at the next railway station,' I said cheerfully, having blessedly discovered in the last half-hour that they no longer hurt. 'And I haven't lost my nerve. Not yet, anyway.'

He opened his mouth and shut it again and flicked a glance at me, and drove another twenty miles without speaking.

We reached the next yard on my list shortly before one o'clock, and disturbed the well-to-do farmer, who trained his own horses, just as he was about to sit down to his lunch. When he opened the door to us a warm smell of stew and cabbage edged past him, and we could hear a clatter of saucepans in the kitchen. I had ridden several winners for him in the past two years before disgracing his best horse the previous week, and after he had got over the unpleasant shock of finding me on his doorstep, he asked us, in a friendly enough fashion, to go in for a drink. But I thanked him and refused, and asked where I could find the lad who looked after the horse in question. He came out to the gate with us and pointed to a house down the road.

We winkled the lad out of his digs and into the car, where I gave him a pound and invited him to describe in detail what had happened on the day I had ridden his horse. He was older, less intelligent and less truculent than Davey, but not much more willing. He didn't see no sense in it, he didn't. He said so, several times. Eventually I got him started, and then there was no stopping him. Detail I had asked for, and detail I got, solidly, for close on half an hour.

Sandwiched between stripping off the paddock clothing and buckling up the saddle came the news that Maurice Kemp-Lore had lounged into the saddling box, said some complimentary things to the farmer-owner about his horse, meanwhile feeding the animal some lumps of sugar, and had drifted away again leaving behind him the usual feeling of friendliness and pleasure.

'A proper corker, ain't he?' was how the lad put it.

I waited until he had reached the point when the farmer had given me a leg up on the horse, and then stopped him and thanked him for his efforts. We left him muttering that we were welcome, but he still didn't see the point.

'How odd,' said Tick-Tock pensively as we sped along the road to the next stable, eighty miles away. 'How odd that Maurice Kemp-Lore . . .' but he didn't finish the sentence; and nor did I.

Two hours later, in Kent, we listened, for another pound, to a gaunt boy of twenty telling us what a smashing fellow that Maurice Kemp-Lore was, how interested he'd been in the horse, how kind to give him some sugar, though it wasn't really allowed in his stables, but how could you tell a man like that not to, when he was being so friendly? The lad also treated us with a rather offensive superiority, but even Tick-Tock by now had become too interested to care.

171

'He drugged them,' he said flatly, after a long silence, turning on to the Maidstone by-pass. 'He drugged them to make it look as if you couldn't ride them ... to make everyone believe you'd lost your nerve.'

'Yes,' I agreed.

'But it's impossible,' he protested vehemently. 'Why on earth should he? It can't be right. It must be a coincidence that he gave sugar to three horses you rode.'

'Maybe. We'll see,' I said.

And we did see. We went to the stables of every horse (other than James's) that I had ridden since Shantytown, talking to every lad concerned. And in every single case we heard that Maurice Kemp-Lore had made the lad's afternoon memorable (before I had blighted it) by admiring the way the lad had looked after his horse, and by offering those tempting lumps of sugar. It took us the whole of Saturday, and all Sunday morning, and we finished the last stable on my list on the edge of the Yorkshire moors at two o'clock in the afternoon. Only because I wanted my facts to be as cast-iron as possible had we gone so far north. Tick-Tock had become convinced in Northampton-shire.

I drove us back to our respective digs in Berkshire, and the following morning, Monday, I walked up to the Axminster stables to see James.

He had just come in from supervising the morning

172

exercise, and the cold downland air had numbed his toes and fingers.

'Come into the office,' he said when he saw me waiting. His tone was neutral, but his protruding lower jaw was unrelenting. I followed him in, and he turned on an electric heater to warm his hands.

'I can't give you much to ride,' he said, with his back to me. 'All the owners have cried off, except one. You'd better look at this; it came this morning.' He stretched out his hand, picked up a paper from his desk, and held it out to me.

I took it. It was a letter from Lord Tirrold. It said,

'Dear James,
Since our telephone conversation I have been thinking over our decision to replace Finn on Template next Saturday, and I now consider that we should reverse this and allow him to ride as originally planned. It is, I confess, at least as much for our sake as for his, since I do not want it said that I hurried to throw him out at the first possible moment, showing heartless ingratitude after his many wins on my horses. I am prepared for the disappointment of not winning the Midwinter and I apologize to you for robbing you of the chance of adding this prize to your total, but I would rather lose the race than the respect of the racing fraternity.
Yours ever, George.'

I put the letter back on the desk.

'He doesn't need to worry,' I said thickly. 'Template will win.'

'Do you mean you aren't going to ride it?' said James, turning round quickly. There was a damaging note of eagerness in his voice, and he saw that I had heard it. 'I . . . I mean . . .' he tailed off.

'James,' I said, sitting down unasked in one of the battered armchairs. 'There are a few things I'd like you to know. First, however bad it looks, and whatever you believe, I have not lost my nerve. Second, every single horse I have ridden since that fall three weeks ago has been doped. Not enough to be very noticeable, just enough to make it run like a slug. Third, the dope has been given to all the horses on sugar lumps. I should think it was some form of sleeping draught, but I've no way of knowing for sure.' I stopped abruptly.

James stood looking at me with his mouth open, the prominent lower teeth bared to the gums as his lip dropped in shocked disbelief.

I said, 'Before you conclude that I am out of my mind, do me the favour of calling in one of the lads, and listening to what he has to say.'

James shut his mouth with a snap. 'Which lad?'

'It doesn't really matter. Any of them whose horse I have ridden in the last three weeks.'

He paused dubiously, but finally went to the door and shouted for someone to find Eddie, the lad who looked after Hugo's big chestnut. In less than a minute the boy arrived, out of breath, and with his curly hair sticking up in an uncombed halo.

James gave me no chance to do the questioning. He said brusquely to Eddie, 'When did you last talk to Rob?'

The boy looked scared and began to stutter, 'N-not since l-l-last week.'

'Since last Friday?' That was the day James himself had last seen me.

'No sir.'

'Very well, then. You remember the big chestnut running badly last Wednesday week?'

'Yes sir.' Eddie treated me to a scornful glance.

'Did anyone give the chestnut a lump of sugar before the race?' There was now only interest to be heard in James's voice: the severity was masked.

'Yes sir,' said Eddie eagerly. The familiar remembering smile appeared on his grubby face, and I breathed an inward sigh of bottomless relief.

'Who was it?'

'Maurice Kemp-Lore, sir. He said how splendidly I looked after my horses, sir. He was leaning over the rails of the assembly ring and he spoke to me as I was going past. So I stopped, and he was ever so nice. He gave the chestnut some sugar, sir, but I didn't think it would matter as Mr Hugo is always sending sugar for him anyway.'

'Thank you, Eddie,' said James, rather faintly. 'No matter about the sugar . . . run along, now.'

Eddie went. James looked at me blankly. The loud clock ticked.

Presently I said, 'I've spent the last two days talking to the lads of all the horses I've ridden for other stables since I had that fall. Every one of them told me that Maurice Kemp-Lore gave the horse some lumps of sugar before I rode it. Ingersoll came with me. He heard them too. You've only to ask him if you can't believe it from me.'

'Maurice never goes near horses at the races,' James protested, 'or anywhere else for that matter.'

'That's precisely what helped me to understand what was happening,' I said. 'I talked to Kemp-Lore on the stands at Dunstable just after Shantytown and two other horses had run hopelessly for me, and he was wheezing quite audibly. He had asthma. Which meant that he had recently been very close to horses. I didn't give it a thought at the time, but it means a packet to me now.'

'But Maurice . . .' he repeated, unbelievingly. 'It's just not possible.'

'It is, however, possible,' I said, more coldly than I had any right to, having believed it myself for twelve awful hours, 'for me to fall apart from a small spot of concussion?'

'I don't know what to think,' he said uncomfortably. There was a pause. There were two things I wanted

James to do to help me: but in view of his ingrained
disinclination to do favours for anyone, I did not think
my requests would be very enthusiastically received.
However, if I didn't ask, I wouldn't get.

I said slowly, persuasively, as if the thought had just
occurred to me, 'Let me ride a horse for you ... one
of your own, if the owners won't have me ... and see
for yourself if Kemp-Lore tries to give it sugar.
Perhaps you could stick with the horse yourself, all
the time? And if he comes up with his sugar lumps,
maybe you could manage to knock them out of his
hand before the horse eats them. Perhaps you could
pick them up yourself and put them in your pocket,
and give the horse some sugar lumps of your own
instead? Then we would see how the horse runs.'

It was too much trouble; his face showed it. He
said, 'That's too fantastic. I can't do things like that.'

'It's simple,' I said mildly, 'you've only to bump his
arm.'

'No,' he said, but not obstinately. A hopeful no, to
my ears. I didn't press him, knowing from experience
that he would irrevocably stick in his toes if urged too
vehemently to do anything he did not want to.

I said instead, 'Aren't you friendly with that man
who arranges the regular dope tests at the races?' One
or two spot checks were taken at every meeting,
mainly to deter trainers of doubtful reputation from
pepping-up or slowing-down their horses with drugs.
At the beginning of each afternoon the stewards

decided which horses to test – for example, the winner of the second race, and the favourite in the fourth race (especially if he was beaten). No one, not even the stewards, always knew in advance exactly which horses would have their saliva taken, and the value of the whole system lay in this uncertainty.

James followed my thoughts. 'You mean, will I ask him if any of the horses you have ridden since your fall have been tested for dope in the normal course of events?'

'Yes,' I agreed. 'Could you possibly do that?'

'Yes, I'll do that,' he said. 'I will ring him up. But if any of them have been tested and proved negative, you do realize that it will dispose of your wild accusations absolutely?'

'I do,' I agreed. 'Actually, I've ridden so many beaten favourites that I can't think why such systematic doping has not already been discovered.'

'You really do believe it, don't you?' said James, wonderingly.

'Yes,' I said, getting up and going to the door. 'Yes, I believe it. And so will you, James.'

But he shook his head, and I left him staring frozen-faced out of the window, the incredible nature of what I had said to him still losing the battle against his own personal knowledge of Kemp-Lore. James liked the man.

CHAPTER TEN

Late that Monday evening James rang me up at my digs and told me that I could ride his own horse, Turniptop, which was due to run in the novice 'chase at Stratford-on-Avon on the following Thursday. I began to thank him, but he interrupted, 'I'm doing you no favour. You know it won't win. He's never been over fences, only hurdles, and all I want is for you to give him an easy race round, getting used to the bigger obstacles. All right?'

'Yes,' I said. 'All right.' And he rang off. There was no mention of whether he would or would not contemplate juggling with sugar knobs.

I was tired. I had spent the whole day driving to Devon and back to visit Art Mathews's beautiful widow, the ice maiden. A fruitless journey. She had been as chilly as ever. Widowhood had warmed her no more than wifehood had done. Blonde, well-bred and cold, she had answered my questions calmly and incuriously and with a complete lack of interest. Art had been dead four months. She spoke of him as though she could hardly remember what he had looked like. No, she did not know exactly why Art had quarrelled so continuously with Corin. No, she did not know why Art had thought fit to shoot himself. No, Art had not got on well with Mr John Ballerton, but she did not know why. Yes, Art had once appeared on television on *Turf Talk*. It had not been a success, she said, the shadow of an old grievance sharpening her voice. Art had been made to look a fool. Art, whose meticulous sense of honour and order had earned him only respect on the racecourse, had been made to look a cantankerous, mean-minded fool. No, she could not remember exactly how it had been done, but she did remember, only too well, the effect it had had on her own family and friends. They had, it appeared, loudly pitied her on her choice of husband.

But I, listening to her, inwardly pitied poor dead Art on his choice of wife.

On the following day, Tuesday, I again appropriated the Mini-Cooper, much to Tick-Tock's disgust. This time I went towards Cheltenham, and called at Peter Cloony's neat, new bungalow, turning down the narrow, winding lane from the high main road to the village in the hollow.

Peter's wife opened the door to me and asked me in with a strained smile. She no longer looked happy and rosily content. She was too thin, and her hair hung straight and wispy round her neck. It was very nearly as cold inside the house as it was outside, and she wore some tattered fur boots, thick stockings, bulky clothes, and gloves. With no lipstick and no life in her eyes, she was almost unrecognizable as the loving girl who had put me up for the night four months ago.

'Come in,' she said, 'but I'm afraid Peter isn't here. He was given a lift to Birmingham races... perhaps he'll get a spare ride...' She spoke without hope.

'Of course he will,' I said. 'He's a good jockey.'

'The trainers don't seem to think so,' she said despairingly. 'Ever since he lost his regular job, he's barely had one ride a week. We can't live on it, how could we? If things don't change very soon, he's going to give up racing and try something else. But he only cares for horses and racing... it will break his heart if he has to leave it.'

She had taken me into the sitting-room. It was as bare as before. Barer. The rented television set had gone. In its place stood a baby's cot, a wickerwork basket affair on a metal stand. I went over and looked down at the tiny baby, only a small bump under the mound of blankets. He was asleep. I made admiring remarks about what I could see of him, and his mother's face momentarily livened up with pleasure.

She insisted on making us a cup of tea, and I had to wait until the question of no milk, no sugar, no biscuits had all been settled before asking her what I really wanted to know.

I said, 'That Jaguar – the one which blocked the lane and made Peter late – who did it belong to?'

'We don't know,' she said. 'It was very odd. No one came to move it away and it stayed across the lane all that morning. In the end the police arranged for it to be towed away. I know Peter asked the police who owned it, because he wanted to tell the man just what his filthy Jaguar had cost him, but they said they hadn't yet traced him.'

'You don't happen to know where the Jaguar is now?' I asked.

'I don't know if it is still there,' she said, 'but it used to be outside the big garage beside Timberley Station. They're the only garage round here with a breakdown truck, and they were the ones who towed it away.'

I thanked her and stood up, and she came out to the car with me to say goodbye. I had spent some time going through the form book adding up the number of races Peter had ridden during the past few weeks, and I knew how little he had earned. I had brought with me a big box of groceries, butter, eggs, cheese and so on, and a stack of tins, and also a string of plastic ducks for the baby. This collection I carried back into the bungalow and dumped on the kitchen table, ignoring her surprised protest as she followed me in.

I grinned. 'They are too heavy to take back. You'll have to make the best of it.'

She began to cry.

'Cheer up,' I said, 'things will get better soon. But

meanwhile, don't you think the bungalow is too cold for a baby? I read somewhere that some babies die every winter from breathing freezing air, even though they may be as warmly wrapped up as yours is.'

She looked at me aghast, tears trickling down her cheeks.

'You ought to heat that room a little, and especially keep it warm all night too, if he sleeps in there,' I said.

'But I can't,' she said jerkily, 'the payments on the bungalow take nearly all we have . . . we can't afford a fire, except just in the evenings. Is it really true about babies dying?'

She was frightened.

'Yes, quite true,' I said. I took a sealed envelope out of my pocket and gave it to her. 'This is a present for the baby. Warmth. It's not a fortune, but it will pay your electricity bills for a while, and buy some coal if you want it. There's likely to be a lot of cold weather coming, so you must promise to spend most of it on keeping warm.'

'I promise,' she said faintly.

'Good.' I smiled at her as she wiped her eyes, and I went back to the car and drove away up the lane.

The garage at Timberley Station was a modernized affair with the front all snowy plaster and the back, when I walked round there, of badly pointed cheap brickwork. The elderly abandoned Jaguar stood there, tucked away between the burnt-out remains of a Standard 8 and a pile of old tyres. I went back to the front of the garage to talk to the man in charge, and I asked him if I could buy the car.

'Sorry, sir, no can do,' he said breezily. He was a dapper thirtyish man with no oil on his hands.

'Why not?' I said. 'It doesn't look good for anything but the scrap heap.'

'I can't sell it to you because I don't know who it belongs to,' he said regretfully, 'but,' he brightened, 'it's been here so long now that it might be mine after all ... like unclaimed lost property. I'll ask the police.'

With a bit of prompting he told me all about the Jaguar being stuck across the lane and how his firm had fetched it.

I said, 'But someone must have seen the driver after he left the car?'

'The police think he must have got a lift, and then decided the car wasn't worth coming back for. But it's in good enough order. And it wasn't hot ... stolen, I mean.'

'What's it worth?' I asked.

'To you, sir,' he smiled glossily, 'I'd have let it go for a hundred pounds.'

A hundred. I parted from him and strolled out on to the forecourt. Was it worth a hundred to Kemp-Lore I wondered, to ruin Peter Cloony? Was his obsessive hatred of jockeys so fierce? But then a hundred to Kemp-Lore, I reflected, was probably a lot less than a hundred to me.

Timberley railway station (six stopping trains a day

and twenty-two expresses) lay on my left. I stood and considered it. The station was nearly four miles from the top of the lane leading to Peter's village; say an hour's quick walk. Peter had found the Jaguar across the lane at eleven o'clock, and it had to have been jammed in position only seconds before he came up the hill, as his had been the first car to be obstructed. I had a vivid mental picture of Kemp-Lore parked in the gateway where the lane began to curve downwards, watching Peter's house through binoculars, seeing him go out and get into his car and start on his way to the races. There wouldn't have been much time to force the Jaguar into position, lock its door and disappear before Peter got there. Not much time: but enough.

And then? The one tremendous disadvantage Kemp-Lore had to overcome, I thought, was his own fame. His face was so well known to almost the entire British population that he could not hope to move about the country inconspicuously, and wherever he went he would be noticed and remembered. Surely, I thought, in this sparsely populated area, it should be possible to find someone who had seen him.

As I was there anyway, I started with the station. Outside, I looked up the times of the stopping trains. There was, I found, a down train at twelve-thirty but no up train until five o'clock. The only other trains ran early in the morning and later in the evening. The booking office was shut. I found the clerk-ticket-collector-porter nodding over a hot stove and a racing

185

paper in the parcels office. A large basket of hens squawked noisily in a corner as I walked in, and he woke with a jerk and told me the next train was due in one hour and ten minutes.

I got him talking via the racing news, but there was nothing to learn. Maurice Kemp-Lore had never (more's the pity he said) caught a train at Timberley. If it had happened when he was off-duty, he'd have heard about it all right. And yes, he said, he'd been on duty the day they'd fetched the Jaguar down to the garage. Disgusting that. Shouldn't be allowed, people being rich enough to chuck their old cars in the ditch like cigarette ends.

I asked him if the station had been busy that day: if there had been a lot of passengers catching the midday train.

'A lot of passengers?' he repeated scornfully. 'Never more than three or four, excepting Cheltenham race days . . .'

'I was just wondering,' I said idly, 'whether the chap who left his Jaguar behind could have caught a train from here that morning?'

'Not from here, he didn't,' the railway man said positively. 'Because, same as usual, all the people who caught the train were ladies.'

'Ladies?'

'Yeh, women. Shopping in Cheltenham. We haven't had a man catch the midday – excepting race days of course – since young Simpkins from the garage got sent home with chickenpox last summer. Bit of a joke it is round here, see, the midday.'

I gave him a hot tip for Birmingham that afternoon (which won, I was glad to see later) and left him busily putting a call through to his bookmaker on the government's telephone bill.

Timberley village pub, nearly empty, had never been stirred, they told me regretfully, by the flashing presence of Maurice Kemp-Lore.

The two transport cafés along the main road hadn't heard of any of their chaps giving him a lift.

None of the garages within ten miles had seen him ever.

The local taxi service had never driven him. He had never caught a bus on the country route.

It wasn't hard at each place to work conversation round to Kemp-Lore, but it was never quick. By the time a friendly bus conductor had told me, over a cigarette at the Cheltenham terminus, that none of his mates had ever had such a famous man on board because they'd never have kept quiet about it (look how Bill went on for days and days when Dennis Compton took a tenpenny single), it was seven o'clock in the evening.

If I hadn't been so utterly, unreasonably sure that it was Kemp-Lore who had abandoned the Jaguar, I would have admitted that if no one had seen him, then he hadn't been there. As it was, I was depressed by the failure of my search, but not convinced that there was nothing to search for.

The army tank carrier that had blocked Peter's and my way to Cheltenham was there accidentally: that much was clear. But Peter had got into such trouble for being late that a weapon was put straight into the hand of his enemy. He had only to make Peter late again, and to spread his little rumours, and the deed was done. No confidence, no rides, no career for Cloony.

I found I still hoped by perseverance to dig something up, so I booked a room in a hotel in Cheltenham, and spent the evening in a cinema to take my mind off food. On the telephone Tick-Tock sounded more resigned than angry to hear that he would be car-less yet again. He asked how I was getting on, and when I reported no progress, he said, 'If you're right about our friend, he's as sly and cunning as all get out. You won't find his tracks too easily.'

Without much hope I went down in the morning to the Cheltenham railway station and sorted out, after a little difficulty with old time-sheets and the passing of a pound note, the man who had collected the tickets from the passengers on the stopping train from Timberley on the day the Jaguar was abandoned.

He was willing enough, but he too had never seen Kemp-Lore, except on television; though he hesitated while he said so.

'What is it?' I asked.

'Well, sir, I've never seen him, but I think I've seen his sister.'

'What was she like?' I asked.

'Very like him, of course, sir, or I wouldn't have known who she was. And she had riding clothes on. You know – jodhpurs, I think they're called. And a scarf over her head. Pretty she looked, very pretty. I couldn't think who she was for a bit, and then it came to me, afterwards like. I didn't talk to her, see? I just took her ticket when she went through the barrier, that's all. I remember taking her ticket.'

'When was it that you saw her?' I asked.

'Oh, I couldn't say. I don't rightly know when it was. Before Christmas though, some time before Christmas, I'm certain of that.'

He flipped the pound I gave him expertly into an inner pocket. 'Thank you, sir, thank you indeed,' he said.

I dressed and shaved with particular care on the Thursday morning as, I supposed, a sort of barrier against the reception I knew I was going to meet. It was six days since I had been racing, six days in which my shortcomings and the shreds of my riding reputation would have been brought up, pawed over and discarded. Life moved fast in the changing-room;

today was important, tomorrow more so; but yesterday was dead. I belonged to yesterday. I was ancient news.

Even my valet was surprised to see me, although I had written to say I was coming.

'You are riding today then?' he said. 'I was wondering if you wanted to sell your saddle . . . there's a boy just starting who needs one.'

'I'll keep it a bit longer,' I said. 'I'm riding Turniptop in the fourth. Mr Axminster's colours.'

It was a strange day. As I no longer felt that I deserved the pitying glances to which I was treated, I found that they had, to a great extent, ceased to trouble me, and I even watched with fair equanimity the success of two of my ex-mounts in the first two races. The only thing I worried about was whether or not James would have both sugar lumps in his pocket and willingness in his heart.

He was so busy with his other runners that I did not exchange more than a few words with him during the first part of the afternoon, and when I went out into the parade ring to join him for Turniptop's race, he was standing alone, thoughtfully gazing into the distance.

'Maurice Kemp-Lore's here,' he said abruptly.

'Yes, I know,' I said. 'I saw him.'

'He has given sugar to several horses already.'

'What?' I exclaimed.

'I have asked quite a few people . . . Maurice has been feeding sugar to any number of horses during the past few weeks, not only to the ones you have ridden.'

'Oh,' I said weakly. Cunning as all get out, Tick-Tock had said.

'None of the horses you rode were picked for the regulation dope test,' said James, 'but some of the other horses Maurice gave sugar to were tested. All negative.'

'He only gave doped sugar to my mounts. The rest were camouflage, and he was damn lucky that the horses I rode weren't tested,' I said. It sounded improbable, but I was sure of it.

James shook his head.

'Did you . . . ?' I began without much hope. 'Did he . . . Kemp-Lore . . . try to give Turniptop any sugar?'

James compressed his lips and stared into the middle distance. I positively held my breath.

'He did come into the saddling box,' he said grudgingly. 'He admired the horse's coat.'

Turniptop ambled past glowing with good health, but before James could say any more one of the stewards came over to talk to him, and I had no chance to find out about the sugar before it was time to mount and go out for the race.

I knew by the second fence that whether Kemp-Lore had fed him sugar or not, Turniptop was not doped. The leaden sluggishness which had afflicted my last twenty-eight mounts and which I had been forced to believe was due to my own deficiency had lifted like a spent thundercloud.

Turniptop leapt and sprang and surged, pulling like a train and doing his damnedest to run away with me. I could have shouted aloud with relief. He was an untidy jumper with more enthusiasm than judgement, a style which had brought him no especial grief over hurdles; but now, in his first steeplechase, he showed signs of treating fences with the same disrespect. It wouldn't really do; there's a world of difference between a single-thickness, easily knocked-down hurdle and a three-foot-wide fence, solidly built of birch twigs, particularly when an open ditch lies in front of it. But Turniptop did not want to be steadied. He was eager. He was rash.

With things as they were, and with James to be convinced, I must admit that my mood matched Turniptop's exactly. We infected each other with recklessness. We took some indefensible risks, and we got away with them.

I kept him continually on the rails, squeezing forward into tiny openings and letting him take all the bumps that came his way. When he met a fence dead right he gained lengths over it, and when he met one wrong he scrambled through and found a foot to land on somehow. It was more like a roller-coaster ride than the sensible, well-judged race James had indicated, but it taught the tough-minded Turniptop just as much about getting himself out of trouble as going round quietly on the outside would have done.

Coming into the second-to-last fence, I was afraid we would win. Afraid, because I knew James wanted to sell the horse and if he had already won a novice 'chase he would not be as valuable as if he had not. An apparent paradox: but Turniptop, young and still green, showed great promise. Too early a win would disqualify him from entering a string of good novice 'chases in the following season.

It would be far, far better, I knew, to come second. To have shown what he could do but not actually to have won would have put hundreds on his value. But we had run too fierce a race, and at the second-last the disaster of winning seemed unavoidable. There was only one other tiring horse alongside, and I could hear no others on my tail.

Turniptop rose, or rather fell to the occasion. In spite of my urging him to put in another stride, he took off far too soon and landed with his hind feet tangled hopelessly in the birch. His forelegs buckled under the strain and he went down on to his knees, with my chin resting on his right ear and my hands touching each other round his throat. Even then his indomitable sense of balance rescued him, and he staggered back on to his feet with a terrific upthrust of his shoulders, tipping me back into the saddle, and, tossing his head as if in disgust, he set off again towards the winning-post. The horse which had been alongside was now safely ahead, and two that had been behind me had jumped past, so that we came into the last fence in fourth position.

I had lost my irons in the débâcle and couldn't get my feet into them again in time to jump, so we went over the last with them dangling and clanking in the air. I collected him together and squeezed with my legs, and Turniptop, game to the end, accelerated past two of the horses ahead and flashed into second place four strides from the post.

James waited for me to dismount in the unsaddling enclosure with a face from which all expression had studiously been wiped. Poker-faced to match, I slid from the saddle.

'Don't ever ride a race like that for me again,' he said.

'No,' I agreed. I undid the girth buckles and took my saddle over my arm, and at last looked into his eyes.

They gleamed, narrowed and inscrutable. He said, 'You proved your point. But you could have killed my horse doing it.'

I said nothing.

'And yourself,' he added, implying that that was less important.

I shook my head, smiling faintly. 'Not a chance,' I said.

'H'm.' He gave me a hard stare. 'You'd better come up to the stable this evening,' he said. 'We can't talk about ... what we have to talk about ... here. There are too many people about.'

As if to punctuate this remark the owner of the winner leant over the dividing rails to admire Turniptop and I had to loop up the girths and go and weigh in, still without knowing exactly what had happened in the saddling box before the race.

Tick-Tock was standing by my peg in the changing-room, one smoothly shod foot up on the bench and the Tyrolean hat pushed back on his head.

'Before you ride like that again, you might make a will leaving me your half of the car,' he said. 'It would solve so many legal complications.'

'Oh, shut up,' I said, peeling off first the crimson and white sweater, James's colours, and then the thin brown jersey underneath. I took a towel from the valet and went along to the wash-basin.

'A lot of people,' said Tick-Tock in a loud voice across the room, 'are going to have a fine old time eating their words, and I hope it gives them indigestion.' He followed me along and watched me wash, leaning languidly against the wall. 'I suppose you realize that your exploits this afternoon were clearly visible to several million assorted housewives, invalids, babes in arms, and people hanging about on the pavement outside electric shops?'

'What?' I exclaimed.

'It's a fact. Didn't you really know? The last three races are filling up the spare time between *Sex for*

Sixth Forms and *Goggle with Granny.* Universal T. C.
Maurice's lot. I wonder,' he finished more soberly,
'what he'll do when he knows you've rumbled the
sugar bit?'

'He may not know,' I said, towelling my chest and
shoulders. 'He may think it was accidental . . . I haven't
heard yet from James what happened before the race.'

'Anyway,' said Tick-Tock confidently, 'his campaign
against you is over. He won't risk going on with it
after today.'

I agreed with him. It just shows how little either of
us understood about obsession.

James was waiting for me in the office, busy with
papers at his big desk. The fire blazed hotly and the
light winked on the glasses standing ready beside
the whisky bottle.

He stopped writing when I went in, and got up and
poured our drinks, and stood towering above me as I
sat in the battered armchair by the fire. His strong
heavy face looked worried.

'I apologize,' he said abruptly.

'Don't,' I said. 'No need.'

'I very nearly let Maurice give Turniptop that
damned sugar,' he said. 'I couldn't believe him capable
of a scheme as fantastic as doping every horse you
ride. I mean, it's . . . it's ridiculous.'

'What happened in the saddling box?' I asked.

He took a sip from his glass. 'I gave Sid instructions that no one, absolutely no one, however important they were, was to give Turniptop anything to eat or drink before the race. When I reached the box with your saddle, Maurice was in the box next door and I watched him giving the horse there some sugar. Sid said no one had given Turniptop anything.' He paused and drank again. 'I put on your number cloth, weight pad and saddle, and began to do up the girths. Maurice came round the partition from the next box and said hello. That infectious smile of his ... I found myself smiling back and thinking you were mad. He was wheezing a bit with asthma ... and he put his hand in his pocket and brought out three lumps of sugar. He did it naturally, casually, and held them out to Turniptop. I had my hands full of girths and I thought you were wrong ... but ... I don't know ... there was something in the way he was standing, with his arm stretched out rather stiffly and the sugar flat on the palm of his hand, that didn't look right. People who are fond of horses stroke their muzzles when they give them sugar, they don't stand as far away as possible. And if Maurice wasn't fond of horses, why was he giving them sugar? Anyway, I did decide suddenly that there would be no harm done if Turniptop didn't eat that sugar, so I dropped the girths and pretended to trip, and grabbed Maurice's arm to steady myself. The sugar fell off his hand on to the straw on the ground and I stepped on it as if by accident while I was recovering my balance.'

'What did he say?' I asked, fascinated.

'Nothing,' said James. 'I apologized for bumping into him, but he didn't answer. Just for a second he looked absolutely furious. Then he smiled again, and . . .' James's eyes glinted, '. . . he said how much he admired me for giving poor Finn this one last chance.'

'Dear of him,' I murmured.

'I told him it wasn't exactly your last chance. I said you would be riding Template on Saturday as well. He just said "Oh really?", and wished me luck and walked away.'

'So the sugar was crunched up and swept out with the dirty straw,' I said.

'Yes,' he agreed.

'Nothing to analyse. No evidence.' A nuisance.

'If I hadn't stepped on it, Maurice could have picked it up and offered it to Turniptop again. I hadn't taken any sugar with me . . . I hadn't any lumps to substitute . . . I didn't believe I would need them.'

He hadn't intended to bother, I knew. But he had bothered. I would never stop feeling grateful.

We drank our whisky. James said suddenly, 'Why? I don't understand why he should have gone to such lengths to discredit you. What has he got against you?'

'I am a jockey, and he is not,' I said flatly. 'That's all.' I told about my visit to Claudius Mellit and the answers he had given me. I said, 'It's no coincidence that you and most other trainers have had trouble finding and keeping a jockey. You've all been swayed by Kemp-Lore, either by him directly, or through those two shadows of his, Ballerton and Corin Kellar, who soak up his poison like sponges and drip it out into every receptive ear. They've said it all to you. You repeated it to me yourself, not so long ago. Peter Cloony is always late, Tick-Tock doesn't try, Danny Higgs bets too heavily, Grant sold information, Finn has lost his nerve . . .'

He stared at me, appalled. I said, 'You believed it all, James, didn't you? Even you? And so did everyone else. Why shouldn't they, with so much evident foundation for the rumours? It doesn't take much for an owner or a trainer to lose confidence in a jockey. The thought has only to be insinuated, however fleetingly, that a jockey is habitually late, or dishonest, or afraid, and very soon, very soon indeed, he is on his way out . . . Art. Art killed himself because Corin sacked him. Grant had a mental breakdown. Peter Cloony is so broke his wife was starving herself in a freezing cold house. Tick-Tock makes jokes like Pagliacci . . .'

'And you?' asked James.

'I? Well . . . I haven't exactly enjoyed the last three weeks.'

'No,' he said, as if thinking about it from my point of view for the first time. 'No, I don't suppose you have.'

'It's been so calculated, this destruction of jockeys,' I said. 'Every week in *Turf Talk*, looking back on it, there has been some damaging reference to one jockey or another. When he had me on the programme he introduced me as an unsuccessful rider, and he meant me to stay that way. Do you remember that ghastly bit of film he showed of me? You'd never have taken me on if you'd seen that before I'd ridden for you, would you?'

He shook his head, very troubled.

I went on, 'On every possible occasion – when Template won the King 'Chase for instance – he has reminded everyone watching on television that I am only substituting for Pip, and that I'll be out on my ear as soon as that broken leg is strong again. Fair enough, it's Pip's job and he should have it back, but that patronizing note in Kemp-Lore's voice was calculated to make everyone take it for granted that my brief spell in the limelight was thoroughly undeserved. I dare say it was, too. But I think a lot of your owners would have been readier to trust your judgement in engaging me, and less quick to chuck me overboard at the first sign of trouble, if it hadn't been for the continual deflating pin-pricks Kemp-Lore had dealt out all round. And last Friday . . .' I tried, not too successfully, to keep my voice evenly conversational. 'Last Friday he led Corin and that handicapper on until they said straight out that I was finished. Were you watching?'

James nodded, and poured us another drink.

'It's a matter for the National Hunt Committee,' he said firmly.

'No,' I said. 'His father is a member of it.'

James gasped sharply. 'I had forgotten . . .'

I said, 'The whole Committee's a stronghold of pro-Kemp-Lore feeling. They're all sold on Maurice. Most of them wear the same old school tie,' I grinned. James wore it too. 'I would be very glad if you would say nothing to any of them, just yet. They would take even more convincing than you did, and there aren't any facts that Kemp-Lore couldn't explain away. But I'm digging.' I drank. 'The day will come.'

'You sound unexpectedly cheerful,' he said.

'O God, James.' I stood up abruptly. 'I wanted to kill myself last week. I'm glad I didn't. It makes me cheerful.'

He looked so startled that I relaxed and laughed, and put down my glass. 'Never mind,' I said, 'but you must understand I don't think the National Hunt Committee meets the case at the moment. Too gentlemanly. I favour something more in the biter-bit line for dear Maurice.'

But I had as yet no useful plan, and dear Maurice still had his teeth, and they were sharp.

CHAPTER ELEVEN

Although neither Tick-Tock nor I had any rides the next day I pinched the car from him to go to the meeting at Ascot, and walked round the course to get the feel of the turf. There was a bitterly cold northeast wind blowing across the heath and the ground was hard with a touch of frost in the more exposed patches. It had been a surprisingly mild winter so far, but the high clear sky spoke ominously of ice to come. One more day, that was all I asked; only one more day. But prodding the earth on the landing side of the water jump with my heel I felt it jar instead of give.

I finished the circuit, planning the race in my mind as I went. If the ground remained firm it would be a fast run affair, but that suited Template well, especially with top weight to carry. Lugging packets of lead around in the mud was not what his lean streamlined frame was best fitted for.

Outside the weighing-room Peter Cloony stopped me. His face was white and thin and mournful, and lines were developing on his forehead.

'I'll pay you back,' he said, almost belligerently. He seemed prepared to argue about it.

'All right. One day. No hurry,' I said mildly.

'You shouldn't have gone behind my back and given my wife that money and the food. I wanted to send it back at once but she won't let me. We don't need charity. I don't approve of it.'

'You're a fool, Peter,' I said. 'Your wife was right to accept what I gave her, and I'd have thought her a stubborn ass if she hadn't. And you'd better get used to the idea: a box of groceries will be delivered to your house every week until you're earning a decent screw again.'

'No,' he almost shouted, 'I won't have it.'

'I don't see why your wife and baby should suffer because of your misplaced pride,' I said. 'But if it will ease your conscience, I'll tell you why I'm doing it. You'll never get much work as long as you go around with that hang-dog expression. Looking weak and miserable isn't going to persuade anybody to employ you. You need to cheer up, get fit again, and prove you're worth having. Well – all I'm doing is removing one of your worries so that you can think a bit more about racing and bit less about your cold house and empty larder. So now you can get on with it . . . it's all up to you. And don't ever even risk being late.'

I walked off and left Peter standing with his mouth open and his eyebrows half-way to his hair.

What Kemp-Lore had pulled down, I could try to

rebuild, I thought. When I had arrived I had seen him in the distance, talking animatedly to one of the stewards, who was laughing. Slim, vital and wholesome-looking, he seemed to attract the light of the day on to his fair head.

In the weighing-room after the fourth race I was handed a telegram. It said, 'Pick me up White Bear, Uxbridge, 6.30 p.m. Important, Ingersoll.' I felt like cursing Tick-Tock soundly because Uxbridge was in the opposite direction from home. But the car was half his, after all, and I'd had more than my fair share of it during the past week.

The afternoon dragged. I hated having to watch, hated it even more after my reassuring ride on Turniptop, but I tried to take my own advice to Peter and look cheerful: and I was rewarded, as time went on, with a definite thawing of the cold shoulder. It made life much easier not finding everyone still too embarrassed to speak to me; but I was also in no doubt that most final judgements were being reserved until after Template's race. I didn't mind that. I was confident that he was the fastest 'chaser in training and I had James's promise that he would be guarded every second against being doped.

I dawdled after racing ended, with two hours to kill before turning up at Uxbridge to collect Tick-Tock. I watched the men from Universal Telecast erecting their scaffolding towers, ready to televise the Midwinter the next day, and recognized a man directing them as Gordon Kildare, still in navy-blue pinstripe suiting and still looking like a rising young executive who knew the score. He passed by me with the practised half smile which from a man of his sort always means that he doesn't know who he's smiling at, but smiles all the same in case he should later find out it was someone important. However he had only gone two steps past me when he turned and came back.

'We've had you on the programme,' he said pleasantly. 'No don't tell me...' His brow furrowed; then he snapped his fingers. 'Finn, that's it, Finn.' But his smile at the triumph of his memory began ludicrously to slip and I knew he was also remembering what had been said about me on his programme a week ago.

'Yes, Finn,' I said, taking no notice. 'All set for tomorrow?'

'Eh, oh, yes. Busy day. Well now, I'm sorry to have to rush off but you know how it is... we've got the programme to put out tonight and I'm due back in the studios. Maurice went ages ago.'

He looked at his watch, gave me a noncommittal smile, and gracefully retreated.

I watched him drive off in the latest streamlined Ford, picturing the studio he was going to; the ranks of cameras, the dazzling lights, the plates of sandwiches; they would all be the same. And who, I wondered, who was to be Kemp-Lore's victim this evening? For whom was the chopper poised, the false charm ready?

There was so little I could do against him. Pick up some of the pieces, start some counter rumours? Try to undermine his influence? All that, yes. But I didn't have his sparkle, nor his prestige, nor yet his ruthlessness. I thrust my hands into my pockets, went out to the Mini-Cooper, and drove off to fetch Tick-Tock.

Mine was only the second car in the dark park beside the White Bear. It was one of those disappointing pubs built of tidy pinkish bricks with cold lighting inside and no atmosphere. The saloon bar was empty. The public bar held only a droopy-moustached old man pursing his lips to the evening's first half-pint. I went back to the saloon bar and ordered a whisky. No Tick-Tock. I looked at my watch. Twenty to seven.

The green plastic seats round the walls were so inhospitable that I didn't wonder the pub was empty. The dark-green curtains didn't help. Nor the fluorescent strip-lights on the ceiling.

I looked at my watch again.

'Are you by any chance waiting for someone, sir?' asked the characterless barman.

'Yes, I am,' I said.

'You wouldn't be a Mr Finn?'

'Yes.'

'Then I've a message for you, sir. A Mr Ingersoll

telephoned just now and said he couldn't get here to meet you, sir, and he was very sorry but could you go and pick him up from the station at six fifty-five. The station is just down the road, first turning left and straight on for half a mile.'

Finishing my drink, I thanked the barman and went out to the car. I climbed into the driving seat and stretched my hand out to turn on the lights and the ignition. I stretched out my hand ... but I didn't reach the lights.

My neck was gripped violently from behind.

There was movement then in the back of the car as the arms shifted to get a better leverage, a rustling of clothes and the scrape of shoe across the thin carpet.

I flung up my hands and clawed but I couldn't reach the face of whoever was behind me, and my nails were useless against his gloves. Thick leather gloves. The fingers inside them were strong, and what was worse, they knew exactly where to dig in and press, each side of the neck, just above the collarbone, where the carotid arteries branched upwards. Pressure on one carotid, I remembered wildly from some distant first-aid course, stops arterial bleeding from the head ... but pressure on both at once blocked all blood supplies to the brain.

I hadn't a chance. My struggles were hampered by the steering wheel and gained me nothing. In the few seconds before a roaring blackness took me off, I had time for only two more thoughts. First that I should have known that Tick-Tock would never meet me in a dreary pub like that. Secondly, angrily, that I was dead.

I couldn't have been out very long, but it was long enough. When consciousness slowly and fuzzily returned, I found I could open neither my eyes nor my mouth. Both were covered with sticking plaster. My wrists were tied together, and my ankles, when I tried to move them, would only part a foot or two: they were hobbled together, like a gipsy's pony.

I was lying on my side, awkwardly doubled up, on the floor in the back of a car which, from the size and smell and feel, I knew to be the Mini-Cooper. It was very cold, and after a while I realized that this was because I was no longer wearing a jacket or an overcoat. My shirt-sleeved arms were dragged forward between the two front seats so that I couldn't reach the sticking plaster to rip it off, and I was extremely, horribly uncomfortable. I tried once with all my strength to free my arms, lifting and jerking at the same time, but they were securely fastened, and a fist – I supposed – crashed down on them so brutally that I didn't attempt it again. I couldn't see who was driving, and driving fast, but I didn't need to. There was only one person in the world who could have set such a trap; complicated but effective, like the Jaguar in the lane. Only one person who had any reason to abduct me, however mad that reason might be. I had no illusions. Maurice Kemp-Lore did not intend that I should win the Midwinter Cup, and was taking steps to prevent it.

Did he know, I wondered helplessly, that it was no accident that Turniptop had not eaten the doped sugar? Did he guess that I knew all about his anti-jockey activities? Had he heard about my trek round the stables or my enquiries about the Jaguar? If he did know these things, what was he going to do with me? To this last rather bleak question I was in no hurry to discover the answer.

When the journey had been going for some time, the car swung suddenly to the left and bumped on to an unevenly surfaced side road, increasing my discomfort. After a while it slowed, turned again, and rolled to a stop.

Kemp-Lore got out of the car, tipped forward the driver's seat, and tugged me out after him by the wrists. I couldn't get my feet under me because of the hobble, and I fell out on to the back of my shoulders. The ground was hard and gravelly. My shirt tore, and the sharp stones scraped into my skin.

He pulled me to my feet, and I stood there swaying, blinded by the plaster on my eyes and unable to run even if I could have wrenched myself from his grasp. He had some sort of lead fixed to my tied wrists, and he began to pull me forward by it. The ground was uneven and the rope joining my ankles was very short. I kept stumbling, and twice fell down.

It was very unpleasant, falling when I couldn't see, but I managed somehow to twist before hitting the ground, landing on my shoulders instead of my face. Always he pulled my hands so far in front of me that I couldn't reach the sticking plaster: the second time I fell I made a great effort to get it off, but he wrenched my arms roughly over my head and dragged me along the ground on my back for a long way. I very painfully lost a good deal more skin.

At length he paused and let me stand up again. He still didn't speak. Not a word. And I couldn't. There was only the sound of our footsteps on the stony ground and the faint sigh of the sharp north-easter in some near-by trees. My tattered shirt was no shield against that wind, and I began to shiver.

He stopped, and there was the sound of a door being opened, and I was tugged in. This time there was a step up, as I realized a fraction too late to prevent myself falling again. I hadn't time to twist, either. I fell flat on my stomach, elbows and chest. It knocked the wind out of me and made me dizzy.

It was a wooden floor, I thought, with my cheek on it. It smelled strongly of dust, and faintly of horses. He pulled me to my feet again and I felt my wrists being hauled upwards and fastened to something just above my head. When he had finished and stepped away I explored with my fingers to find out what it was; and as soon as I felt the smooth metal hooks, I knew exactly the sort of place I was in.

It was a tack-room. Every stable has one. It is the place where the saddles and bridles are kept, along with all the brushes and straps and bandages and rugs that horses need. From the ceiling of every tack-room hangs a harness hook, a gadget something like a three-pronged anchor, which is used for hanging bridles on while they are being cleaned. There were no bridles hanging from these particular hooks. Only me. I was securely fastened at the point where they branched off their stem.

Most tack-rooms are warm, heated by a stove which dries damp rugs and prevents leather getting mildewed. This tack-room was very cold indeed, and in the air the ingrained smells of leather and saddle soap were overlaid by a dead sort of mustiness. It was an unused room: an empty room. The silence took on a new meaning. There were no horses moving in the boxes. It was an empty stable. I shivered from something more than cold.

I heard him step out into the gritty yard, and presently there was a familiar rattle of bolts and the clang of a stable door being opened. After a few seconds it was shut again, and another one was opened. This again was shut, and another opened. He went on down the row, opening six doors. I thought he must be looking for something, and numbly wondered what it was, and began to hope very much that he wouldn't find it.

After the sixth stable door shut he was gone for

211

some time, and I couldn't hear what he was doing. But the car had not been started, so I knew he must still be there. I could make no impression at all on the strands of rope twined round my wrists. They were narrow and slippery to touch, and felt like nylon, and I couldn't even find a knot, much less undo one.

Eventually he came back, and dumped down outside the door something that clattered. A bucket.

He stepped into the room and walked softly on the wooden floor. He stopped in front of me. It was very quiet everywhere. I could hear a new sound, the high, faint asthmatic wheeze of the air going into his lungs. Even an empty stable, it seemed, could start him off.

Nothing happened for a while. He walked all round me, slowly, and stopped again. Walked and stopped. Making up his mind, I thought. But to do what?

He touched me once, dragging his gloved hand across my raw shoulders. I flinched, and his breath hissed sharply. He began to cough, the dry difficult asthmatic's cough. And may you choke, I thought.

He went outside, still coughing, and picked up the bucket and walked away across the yard. I heard the bucket clatter down and a tap being turned on. The water splashed into the bucket, echoing in the stillness.

Jack and Jill went up the hill, said my brain ridiculously, to fetch a pail of water. Jack fell down and broke his crown and Jill threw the water all over him.

Oh no, I thought, oh no, I'm so cold already. Part of my mind said I wouldn't mind what he did to me if only he'd let me go in time to ride Template, and the rest said don't be a fool, that's the whole point, he won't let you go, and anyway if you do get away you'll be so cold and stiff after this you won't be able to ride a donkey.

He turned off the tap and came back across the yard, the water splashing slightly as he walked. He brought the bucket with him into the tack-room and stopped behind me. The handle of the bucket clanked. I ground my teeth and took a deep breath, and waited.

He threw the water. It hit me squarely between the shoulder blades and soaked me from head to foot. It was bitterly, icy cold, and it stung like murder on the skinned patches.

After a short pause he went across the yard again and refilled the bucket. I thought I was almost past caring about that. You can't be wetter than wet and you can't be colder than freezing. And my arms, with being hauled up higher than my head, were already beginning to feel heavy and to ache. I began to worry less about the immediate future, and more about how long he intended to leave me where I was.

He came back with the bucket, and this time he threw the water in my face. I had been wrong about not caring. It was at least as bad as the first time, mostly because too much of it went up my nose. Couldn't he see, I thought desperately, that he was

213

drowning me. My chest hurt. I couldn't get my breath. Surely he'd pull the plaster off my mouth, surely ... surely ...

He didn't.

By the time a reasonable amount of air was finding its way into my heaving lungs he was across the yard again, with more water splashing into the bucket. In due course he turned the tap off, and his feet began once more to crunch methodically in my direction. Up the step and across the wooden floor. There wasn't anything I could do to stop him. My thoughts were unprintable.

He came round in front of me again. I twisted my face sideways and buried my nose against my upper arm. He poured the whole arctic bucketful over my head. After this, I thought, I am going to have more sympathy for those clowns in circuses. I hoped the poor blighters used warm water, anyway.

It seemed that he now thought that I was wet enough. In any case he dumped the bucket down outside the door instead of going to fill it again, and came back and stood close beside me. His asthma was worse.

He put his hand in my hair and pulled my head back, and spoke for the first time.

He said in a low voice, with obvious satisfaction, 'That should fix *you*.'

He let go of my hair and went out of the room, and I heard him walk away across the yard. His footsteps faded into the distance and after a while there was the distant slam of the Mini-Cooper's door. The engine started, the car drove off, and soon I could hear it no more.

It wasn't very funny being abandoned in a trussed condition soaking wet on a cold night. I knew he wouldn't be back for hours, because it was Friday. From eight o'clock until at least nine-thirty he would be occupied with his programme; and I wondered in passing what effect his recent capers would have on his performance.

One thing was clear, I could not meekly stand still and wait to be released. The first necessity was obviously to get some of the sticking plaster off. I thought that as it was wet it would come away fairly easily, but it was very adhesive, and after a good deal of rubbing my mouth against my arm, I only succeeded in peeling back one corner of it. It was enough to let in a precious extra trickle of air, but no good for shouting for help.

The cold was a serious problem. My wet trousers clung clammily to my legs, my shoes were full of water, and my shirt, what was left of it, was plastered against my arms and chest. Already my fingers were completely numb, and my feet were going through the stage that precedes loss of feeling. He had left the door open on purpose, I knew, and although the biting wind was not blowing straight in there were enough eddies swirling off the walls outside for me to be in a considerable draught. I shivered from head to foot.

Harness hooks. I considered their anatomy. A stem with three upward-curving branches at the bottom. At the top, a ring, and attached to the ring, a chain. The length of chain depended on the height of the ceiling. At the top of the chain, a staple driven into a beam. As the whole thing was solidly constructed to resist years of vigorous stablemen putting their weight on bridles while they cleaned them, it was absolutely hopeless to try and tug it straight out of the ceiling.

I had seen harness hooks which were only hitched on to their chains and would detach easily if lifted instead of being pulled down, but after some fruitless and tiring manoeuvring I knew the one I was fixed to was not so obliging.

But somewhere, I thought, there must be a weak link. Literally a weak link. When they were bought, harness hooks didn't have chains on. Chain was cut to the length needed and added when the hook was installed in the tack-room. Therefore, somewhere there was a join.

The bottom curve of the hooks brushed my hair, and my wrists were tied some three inches above that. It gave me very little leverage, but it was the only hope I had. I started pivoting, leaning my forearms on the hooks and twisting the chain, putting a strain on it and hearing the links rub hollowly together. In two and a half full turns, as near as I could judge, it locked solid. If I could turn it further, the weak link would snap.

The theory was simple. Putting it into operation was different. For one thing, twisting the chain had shortened it, so that my arms were stretched higher above my head and gave me less leverage than ever. And for another, they had begun to ache in earnest.

I pressed round as hard as I could. Nothing happened. I unwound the chain a fraction, and forcefully jerked it tight again. The jolt ran right down my body and threw me off my feet.

I stumbled miserably upright again, and with my legs braced, repeated the process. This time the jolt shook only the top part of my body. I did it again. The chain didn't break.

After that, as a respite from rattling my arms in their sockets, I got back to work on the sticking plaster and a while later dislodged it entirely. It meant that at last I could open my mouth and yell.

I yelled.

No one came. My voice echoed round the tack-room and sounded loud in my ears, but I feared that outside the wind would sweep it away. I shouted, on and off, for a long while. No results.

It was at this point, perhaps an hour after Kemp-Lore had gone, that I became both very frightened and very angry.

I was frightened for my hands, which I could no longer feel. I was now not only shivering but shuddering with cold, and the blood supply to my hands was having, to put it literally, an uphill job; and with the weight of my aching arms to support, the rope tying my wrists was viciously tight.

The dismal fact had to be faced that if I had to stay where I was all night my hands might be dead in the morning. My imagination trotted on unasked with scarifying pictures. Dead. Gangrenous. Amputated.

He can't have meant that, I thought suddenly. Surely he hadn't meant that all along. No one could be so savagely cruel. I remembered the satisfaction in his voice. 'That will fix *you*,' he said. But I'd thought he meant for the next day only. Not for life.

Being angry gave me both strength and resolution. I would not, I absolutely would not let him get away with it. The chain had got to be broken.

I wound it up tight again and jerked. It took my breath away. I told myself not to be a baby. I loosened and jerked, loosened and jerked, pushing against the hooks, trying to twist them round with all my strength. The chain rattled, and held.

I started doing it rhythmically. Six jerks and a rest. Six jerks and a rest. On and on, six jerks and a rest, until I was sobbing.

At least, I thought, with a last flicker of humour, the exercise is making me warmer. But it was little consolation for the cracking pain in my arms and shoulders, or the red-hot pincers which seemed to have attached themselves to the back of my neck, or the bite of the rope into my wrists as the friction rubbed away the skin.

Six jerks and a rest. Six jerks and a rest. The rests got longer. Anyone who has tried crying with sticking plaster over his eyes will know that the tears run down inside the nose. When I sniffed, they came into my mouth. Salty. I got tired of the taste.

Six jerks and a rest. I wouldn't stop. I refused to stop. Six jerks. Rest. Six. Rest.

After a while I unwound the chain by turning round and round where I stood and wound it up again in the opposite direction. I thought that jolting it the other way might both snap it more quickly and be easier on my protesting muscles; but I was wrong on both counts. Eventually, I wound back again.

Time passed. Because I couldn't see I became giddy as I grew tired. I began to sway and buckle at the knees if I didn't concentrate, and neither of these things did my arms any good.

Why – jerk – wouldn't – jerk – the ruddy chain – jerk – jerk – break. I wasn't going to admit it was too much for me without struggling to the end, though the disgusting temptation gradually grew to give up the excruciating wrenching and just hang and faint away and get some peace. A temporary, deceptive, useless, dangerous peace.

I went on jerking for what seemed like hours, sometimes sobbing, sometimes cursing, sometimes maybe praying as well.

I was quite unprepared for it when it happened. One minute I was screwing up the dregs of willpower for another series of jerks, and the next, after a convulsive, despairing heave, I was collapsing in a tumbled heap on the floor with the harness hook clattering down on top of me, still tied to my wrists.

For a moment or two I could hardly believe it. My head was whirling, all sense of direction gone. But the floor was hard beneath my body, dusty smelling and real, damp and reassuring.

After a while, when my head cleared, I rolled into a kneeling position so that the blood was flowing down my arms at last, and put my hands between my thighs to try to warm them. They felt like lumps of frozen meat, with no sensation and no movement. The rope round my wrists didn't cut so much now that it had no weight to support, and there was room for the blood to get back into my hands, I thought, if only it would.

The unimaginable relief of having my arms down made me forget for some time how cold I was, and how wet, and how far still from getting warm and dry. I felt almost cheerful, as if I had won a major battle; and indeed, looking back on it, I know I had.

CHAPTER TWELVE

Kneeling very soon became uncomfortable, so I shuffled across the floor until I came to a wall, and sat with the bottom of my spine propped against it and my knees bent up.

The plaster on my eyes was still stuck tight. I tried to scrape it off by rubbing it against the rope on my wrists, but made no headway. The hooks hindered me and bumped into my face, and in the end I gave it up and concentrated again on warming my hands, alternately cradling them between my thighs and thumping them against my knees to restore the circulation.

After a time I found I could move my fingers. I still couldn't feel them at all, but movement was a tremendous step forward, and I remember smiling about it for at least ten minutes.

I put my hands up to my face and tried to scrape the plaster off with my thumbnail. My thumb slid across my cheek, checked on the edge of the plaster and, when I pushed from the elbow, bent uselessly and slithered away. I tried again. It had to be done, because until I could see where I was going I couldn't leave the tack-room. It was colder outside, and my ankles were still hobbled, and wandering about blind in those conditions did not appeal to me a bit.

I bent my head down and put my right thumb in my mouth, to warm it. Every few minutes I tested the results on the edge of the plaster and at least got to the stage where the thumb would push without bending. I only needed to prise a corner up, but even that took a long time. Eventually, however, my nail had pushed a flap unstuck which was big enough for me to grip between my wrists, and with several false starts and a fair selection of oaths, I managed in the end to pull the obstinate thing off.

Dazzling moonlight poured through the open door and through a window beside it. I was sitting against the end wall with the door away on my left. Above my head and all round the room there were empty wooden supports for saddles and bridles, and bare shelves and a cupboard on the wall facing me. An efficient-looking stove occupied the corner on my right, with a few dead cinders still scattered on the ground beside it.

From the centre of the ceiling, pale in the moonlight, hung twenty inches of sturdy galvanized chain.

I looked down at my hands. The harness hook glinted with reflected light. No wonder it had been so difficult to break. I thought. The chain and the hook were almost new. Not the dark, old, rusty things I had been imagining all along. I swallowed, really shattered. It was just as well I hadn't known.

My hands themselves, including the thumb I had tried to warm, were white. Almost as white as my shirt-sleeves. Almost as white as the nylon rope which wound round the hooks. Only my wrists were dark.

I stretched my feet out. More white nylon rope ran from one ankle to the other, about fifteen inches of it.

My fingers wouldn't undo the knots. My pockets had been emptied; no knife, no matches. There was nothing in the tack-room to cut with. I stood up stiffly, leaning against the wall, and slowly, carefully, shuffled over to the door. My foot kicked against something, and I looked down. On the edge of a patch of moonlight lay the broken link. It was a grotesquely buckled piece of silvery metal. It had given me a lot of trouble.

I went on to the door and negotiated the step. The bucket stood there, dully grey. I looked round the moonlit L-shaped yard. Four boxes stretched away to my right, and at right-angles to them there were two more, on the short arm of the L. Over there too, was the tap; and beside the tap, on the ground, an object I was very glad to see. A boot-scraper made of a thin metal plate bedded in concrete.

With small careful steps I made my way to it across

the hard-packed gravel, the cutting wind ripping the last remnants of warmth from my body.

Leaning against the wall, and with one foot on the ground, I stretched the rope tautly over the boot-scraper and began to rub it to and fro, using the other foot as a pendulum. The blade of the scraper was far from sharp and the rope was new, and it took a long time to fray it through, but it parted in the end. I knelt down and tried to do the same with the strands round my wrists, but the harness hook kept getting in the way again and I couldn't get anything like the same purchase. I stood up wearily. It looked as though I'd have to lug that tiresome piece of ironmongery around with me a while longer.

Being able to move my legs, however, gave me a marvellous sense of freedom. Stiffly, shaking with cold, I walked out of the yard round to the house looming darkly behind it. There were no lights, and looking closer I found the downstairs windows were all shuttered. It was as empty as the stable; an unwelcome but not unexpected discovery.

I walked a bit unsteadily on past the house and down the drive. It was a long drive with no lodge at the gate, only an estate agent's board announcing that this desirable country gentleman's residence was for sale, together with some excellent modern stabling, forty acres of arable land and an apple orchard.

A country lane ran past the end of the drive giving no indication as to which way lay civilization. I tried to remember from which direction the Mini-Cooper had come, but I couldn't. It seemed a very long time ago. I glanced automatically at my left wrist but there was only rope there, no watch. Since it had to be one thing or the other, I turned right. It was a deserted road with open fields on the far sides of its low hedges. No cars passed, and nowhere could I see a light. Cursing the wind and aching all over, I stumbled on, hanging on to the fact that if I went far enough I was bound to come to a house in the end.

What I came to first was not a house but something much better. A telephone box. It stood alone, brightly lit inside, square and beckoning, on the corner where the lane turned into a more main road, and it solved the embarrassing problem of presenting myself at some stranger's door looking like a scarecrow and having to explain how I had got into such a state.

There were a lot of people I could have called. Police, Ambulance or the Fire Brigade for a start; but by the time I had forced my still nearly useless hands to pull the door open far enough for me to get my foot in, I had had time to think. Once I called in authority in any form there would be unending questions to answer and statements to make and like as not I'd end up for the night in the local cottage hospital. I hated being in hospitals.

Also, although I felt so bone cold, it was not, I thought, actually freezing. The puddles at the side of the road had no ice on them. They would be racing at

Ascot the next day. Template would turn up for the Midwinter, and James didn't know his jockey was wandering around unfit to ride.

Unfit... Between seeing the telephone box and clumsily picking up the receiver I came to the conclusion that the only satisfactory way to cheat Kemp-Lore of his victory was to go and ride the race, and win it if I could, and pretend that tonight's misfortunes had not happened. He had had things his own way for far too long. He was not, he was positively not, I vowed, going to get the better of me any more.

I dialled O with an effort, gave the operator my credit card number, and asked to be connected to the one person in the world who would give me the help I needed, and keep quiet about it afterwards, and not try to argue me out of what I intended to do.

Her voice sounded sleepy. She said, 'Hello?'

'Joanna ... are you busy?' I asked.

'Busy? At this hour?' she said. 'Is that you, Rob?'

'Yes,' I said.

'Well, go back to bed and ring me in the morning,' she said. 'I was asleep. Don't you know what time it is?' I heard her yawn.

'No,' I said.

'Well, it's ... er ... twenty to one. Good night.'

'Joanna, don't go,' I said urgently. 'I need your help. I really do. Please, don't ring off.'

'What's the matter?' She yawned again.

'I ... I ... Joanna, come and help me. Please.'

There was a little silence and she said in a more awake voice, 'You've never said "please" like that to me before. Not for anything.'

'Will you come?'

'Where to?'

'I don't really know,' I said despairingly. 'I'm in a telephone box on a country road miles from anywhere. The telephone exchange is Hampden Row.' I spelled it out for her. 'I don't think it's very far from London, and somewhere on the West, probably.'

'You can't come back on your own?' she asked.

'No,' I said. 'I've no money and my clothes are wet.'

'Oh.' A pause. 'All right, then. I'll find out where you are and come in a taxi. Anything else?'

'Bring a sweater,' I said. 'I'm cold. And some dry socks, if you have any. And some gloves. Don't forget the gloves. And a pair of scissors.'

'Sweater, socks, gloves, scissors. O.K. You'll have to wait while I get dressed again, but I'll come as soon as I can. Stay by the telephone box.'

'Yes,' I said.

'I'll hurry, don't worry,' she said. 'Good-bye.'

'Good-bye . . .' I fumbled the receiver back on to its rest. However quick she was, she wouldn't arrive for an hour. Well, what was one more hour after so many? I had had no idea it was so late: the evening had certainly seemed to me to be going on for an eternity, but I had lost all sense of actual time. And Kemp-Lore hadn't come back. His show had been

227

over for hours, and he hadn't come back. The bloody, murdering bastard, I thought.

I sat down on the floor of the box and leaned gingerly against the wall beside the telephone, with my head resting on the coin box. Exercise and the bitter wind outside, inactivity and shelter inside; one looked as cold a prospect as the other. But I was too tired to walk any more if I didn't have to, so the choice was easy.

I put my hands up to my face and one by one bit my fingers. They were icy cold and yellowish white, and none of them had any feeling. They would curl and uncurl, but slowly and weakly, and that was all. I got to work on them seriously then, rubbing them up and down against my legs, bumping them on my knees, forcing them open and shut, but it seemed to make little difference. I persevered from fear that they should get worse if I didn't, and paid for it in various creaks from my sore and sorely misused shoulders.

There was a good deal to think about to take my mind off my woes. That sticking-plaster for instance. Why had he used it? The strip over my mouth, I had assumed, had been to stop me shouting for help; but when I got it off at last and shouted, there was no one to hear. No one could have heard however loud I yelled, because the stable was so far from the lane.

The strip over my eyes should have been to prevent my seeing where I was going, but why did it matter if I saw an empty yard and a deserted tack-room? What would have happened differently, I wondered, if I had been able to see and talk.

To see ... I would have seen Kemp-Lore's expression while he went about putting me out of action. I would have seen Kemp-Lore ... that was it! It was himself he had not wanted me to see, not the place.

If that were so it was conceivable that he had prevented me from talking simply so that he should not be trapped into answering. He had spoken only once, and that in a low, unrecognizable tone. I became convinced that he had not wanted me to hear and recognize his voice.

In that case he must have believed I did not know who had abducted me, that I didn't know who he was. He must still believe it. Which meant that he thought James had knocked Turniptop's doped sugar out of his hand by accident, that he hadn't heard about Tick-Tock and me going round all the stables, and that he didn't know that I had been asking about the Jaguar. It gave me, I thought, a fractional advantage for the future. If he had left any tracks anywhere, he would not see any vital, immediate need to obliterate them. If he didn't know he was due for destruction himself, he would not be excessively on his guard.

Looking at my bloodless hands and knowing that on top of everything else I still had to face the pain of their return to life, I was aware that all the civilized brakes were off in my conscience. Helping to build up what he had broken was not enough. He himself had hammered into me the inner implacability I had lacked to avenge myself and all the others thoroughly, and to do it physically and finally and without compunction.

She came, in the end.

I heard a car draw up and a door slam, and her quick tread on the road. The door of the telephone box opened, letting in an icy blast, and there she was, dressed in trousers and woolly boots and a warm blue padded jacket, with the light falling on her dark hair and making hollows of her eyes.

I was infinitely glad to see her. I looked up at her and did my best at a big smile of welcome, but it didn't come off very well. I was shivering too much.

She knelt down and took a closer look at me. Her face went stiff with shock.

'Your hands,' she said.

'Yes. Did you bring the scissors?'

Without a word she opened her handbag, took out a sensible-sized pair, and cut me free. She did it gently. She took the harness hook from between my knees and laid it on the floor, and carefully peeled from my wrists the cut pieces of rope. They were all more brown than white, stained with blood, and where they had been there were big corrugated raw patches, dark and deep. She stared at them.

'More bits of rope down there,' I said, nodding towards my feet.

She cut the pieces round my ankles, and I saw her rubbing my trouser leg between her fingers. The air had been too cold to dry them and my body had not generated enough heat, so they were still very damp.

'Been swimming?' she said flippantly. Her voice cracked.

There was a step on the road outside and a man's shape loomed up behind Joanna.

'Are you all right, miss?' he said in a reliable sounding Cockney voice.

'Yes, thank you,' she said. 'Do you think you could help me get my cousin into the taxi?'

He stepped into the doorway and looked down at me, his eyes on my wrists and my hands.

'Christ,' he said.

'Very aptly put,' I said.

He looked at my face. He was a big sturdy man of about fifty, weather-beaten like a sailor, with eyes that looked as if they had seen everything and found most of it disappointing.

'You've been done proper, haven't you?' he said.

'Proper,' I agreed.

He smiled faintly. 'Come on then. No sense in hanging about here.'

I stood up clumsily and lurched against Joanna, and put my arms round her neck to save myself from falling; and as I was there it seemed a shame to miss the opportunity, so I kissed her. On the eyebrow, as it happened.

'Did you say "cousin"?' said the taxi driver.

'Cousin,' said Joanna firmly. Much too firmly.

The driver held the door open. 'We'd better take him to a doctor,' he said.

'No,' I said. 'No doctor.'

Joanna said, 'You need one.'

'No.'

'That's frostbite,' said the driver pointing to my hands.

'No,' I said. 'It isn't freezing. No ice on the puddles. Just cold. Not frostbite.' My teeth were chattering and I could only speak in short sentences.

'What happened to your back?' asked the driver, looking at the tattered bits of shirt sticking to me.

'I . . . fell over,' I said. 'On some gravel.'

He looked sceptical.

'It's a terrible mess, and there's a lot of dirt in it,' said Joanna, peering round me and sounding worried.

'You wash it,' I said. 'At home.'

'You need a doctor,' said the driver again.

I shook my head. 'I need Dettol, aspirins and sleep.'

'I hope you know what you're doing,' said Joanna. 'What else?'

'Sweater,' I said.

'It's in the taxi,' she said. 'And some other clothes. You can change as we go along. The sooner you get into a hot bath the better.'

'I'd be careful about that, miss,' said the driver. 'Don't go warming those hands up too fast or the fingers will drop off.' A comforting chap. Inaccurate too, I trusted. Joanna looked more worried than ever.

We walked from the telephone box to the taxi. It was an ordinary black London taxi. I wondered what charm Joanna had used to get it so far out into the country in the middle of the night; and also, more practically, whether the meter was still ticking away. It was.

'Get in, out of the wind,' she said, opening the taxi door.

I did as I was told. She had brought a suitcase, from which she now produced a thin, pale blue cardigan of her own, and a padded man-size olive-coloured anorak which zipped up the front. She looked at me judiciously, and out came the scissors. Some quick snips and the ruins of my shirt lay on the seat beside me. She cut two long strips of it and wound them carefully round my wrists. The taxi driver watched.

'This is a police job,' he suggested.

I shook my head. 'Private fight,' I said.

He held up the harness hook, which he had brought across from the telephone box.

'What sort of thing is this?' he asked.

'Throw it in the ditch,' I said, averting my eyes.

'You'll be needing it for the police,' he insisted.

'I told you,' I said wearily, 'no police.'

His disillusioned face showed that he knew all about

people who got themselves beaten up but wouldn't report it. He shrugged and went off into the darkness, and came back without the hook.

'It's in the ditch behind the telephone box, if you change your mind,' he said.

'Thanks,' I said.

Joanna finished the bandages and helped my arms into both the garments she had brought, and fastened the fronts. The next thing the suitcase produced was a pair of fur lined mittens which went on without too much trouble, and after that a thermos flask full of hot soup, and some cups.

I looked into Joanna's black eyes as she held the cup to my mouth. I loved her. Who wouldn't love a girl who thought of hot soup at a time like that?

The driver accepted some soup too, and stamped his feet on the ground and remarked that it was getting chilly. Joanna gave him a pained look, and I laughed.

He glanced at me appraisingly and said, 'Maybe you can do without a doctor, at that.' He thanked Joanna for the soup, gave her back the cup, settled himself in the driving seat and, switching off the light inside the taxi, started to drive us back to London.

'Who did it?' said Joanna.

'Tell you later.'

'All right.' She didn't press. She bent down to the case and brought out some fleecy slippers, thick socks and a pair of her own stretchy trews. 'Take your trousers off.'

I said ironically, 'I can't undo the zip.'

'I forgot . . .'

'Anyway,' I said, 'I'll settle for the socks; can't manage the trousers.' Even I could hear the exhaustion in my voice, and Joanna without arguing got down on her knees in the swaying cab and changed my wet socks and shoes for dry ones.

'Your feet are freezing,' she said.

'I can't feel them,' I said. The moon shone clearly through the window and I looked at the slippers. They were too large for me, much too large for Joanna.

'Have I stepped into Brian's shoes?' I asked.

After a pause she said neutrally, 'They are Brian's, yes.'

'And the jacket?'

'I bought it for him for Christmas.'

So that was that. It wasn't the best moment to find out.

'I didn't give it to him,' she said after a moment, as if she had made up her mind about something.

'Why not?'

'It didn't seem to suit a respectable life in the outer suburbs. I gave him a gold tie-pin instead.'

'Very suitable,' I said dryly.

'A farewell present,' she said quietly.

I said sincerely, 'I'm sorry.' I knew it hadn't been easy for her.

She drew in a breath sharply. 'Are you made of iron, Rob?'

'Iron filings,' I said.

The taxi sped on.

'We had a job finding you,' she said. 'I'm sorry we were so long. It was such a big area, you see.'

'You came, though.'

'Yes.'

I found sitting in the swaying taxi very uncomfortable. My arms and shoulders ached unceasingly and if I leaned back too heavily the raw bits didn't like it. After a while I gave it up, and finished the journey sitting on the floor with my head and my hands in Joanna's lap.

I was of course quite used to being knocked about. I followed, after all, an occupation in which physical damage was a fairly frequent though unimportant factor; and, especially during my first season, when I was a less efficient jockey and most of the horses I rode were the worst to be had, there was rarely a time when some area of my body was not black and blue. I had broken several of the smaller bones, been kicked in tender places, and dislocated one or two joints. On my general sense of well-being, and on my optimism that I wouldn't crash unmendably, none of these things had made the slightest dent. It seemed that in common with most other jockeys I had been born with the sort of resilient constitution which could take a bang and be ready for business, if not the following day, at least a good deal quicker than the medical profession considered normal.

Practice had given me a certain routine for dealing with discomfort, which was mainly to ignore it and concentrate on something else: but this system was not operating very well that evening. It didn't work, for instance, when I sat for a while in a light armchair in Joanna's warm room with my elbows on my knees, watching my fingers gradually change colour from yellowy white to smudgy charcoal, to patchy purple, and finally to red.

It began as a tingle, faint and welcome, soon after we had got back and Joanna had turned both her powerful heaters on. She had insisted at once on removing my clammy trousers and also my pants, and on my donning her black trews, which were warm but not long enough by several inches. It was odd, in a way, letting her undress me, which she did matter-of-factly and without remark; but in another way it seemed completely natural, a throwback to our childhood, when we had been bathed together on our visits to each other's houses.

She dug out some rather powdery-looking aspirins in a bottle. There were only three of them left, which I swallowed. Then she made some black coffee and held it for me to drink. It was stiff with brandy.

'Warming,' she said laconically. 'Anyway, you've stopped shivering at last.'

It was then that my fingers tingled and I told her.

'Will it be bad?' she said prosaically, putting down the empty coffee mug.

'Possibly.'

'You won't want me to sit and watch you then,' she said.

I shook my head. She took the empty mug into the kitchen and was several minutes coming back with a full one for herself.

The tingle increased first to a burning sensation and then to a feeling of being squeezed in a vice, tighter and tighter, getting more and more agonizing until it felt that at any minute my fingers would disintegrate under the pressure. But there they were, harmlessly hanging in the warm air, with nothing to show for it except that they were turning slowly puce.

Joanna came back from the kitchen and wiped the sweat off my forehead.

'Are you all right?' she asked.

'Yes,' I said.

She nodded, and gave me a faint edition of the intimate smile that had had my heart doing flip-flaps from boyhood, and drank her coffee.

When the pulse got going, it felt as though my hands had been taken out of the vice, laid on a bench, and were being rhythmically hammered. It was terrible. And it went on too long. My head drooped.

When I looked up she was standing in front of me, watching me with an expression which I couldn't read. There were tears in her eyes.

'Is it over?' she said, blinking to disguise them.

'More or less.'

We both looked at my hands, which were now a fierce red all over.

'And your feet?' she asked.

'They're fine,' I said. Their awakening had been nothing.

'I'd better wash those grazes on your back,' she said.

'No,' I said. 'In the morning.'

'There's a lot of dirt in them,' she protested.

'It's been there so long already that a few more hours won't hurt,' I said. 'I've had four anti-tetanus injections in the last two years, and there's always penicillin ... and I'm too tired.'

She didn't argue. She unzipped and helped me take off the anorak, and made me get into her bed, still incongruously dressed in her black trews and blue cardigan and looking like a second-rate ballet dancer with a hangover. The sheets were rumpled from her lying in them before I had woken her up, and there was still a dent in her pillow where her head had been. I put mine there too, with an odd feeling of delight. She saw me grin, and correctly read my mind.

'It's the first time you've got into my bed,' she said. 'And it'll be the last.'

'Have a heart, Joanna,' I said.

She perched herself on the edge of the mattress and looked down at me.

'It's no good for cousins,' she said.

'And if we weren't cousins?'

'I don't know . . .' she sighed. 'But we are.'

She bent down to kiss me good night on the forehead.

I couldn't help it; I put my arms up round her shoulders and pulled her down on to my chest and kissed her properly, mouth to mouth. It was the first time I had ever done it, and into it went all the pent-up and suppressed desire I had ever felt for her. It was too hungry, too passionate, much too desperate. I knew it, but I couldn't stop it. For a moment she seemed to relax and melt and kiss me back, but it was so brief and passing that I thought I had imagined it, and afterwards her body grew rigid.

I let her go. She stood up abruptly and stared at me, her face scrubbed of any emotion. No anger, no disgust; and no love. She turned away without speaking and went across the room to the sofa, where she twisted a blanket around herself and lay down. She stretched out her hand to the table light and switched it off.

Her voice reached me across the dark room, calm, self-controlled. 'Good night, Rob.'

'Good night, Joanna,' I said politely.

There was dead silence.

I rolled over on to my stomach and put my face in her pillow.

CHAPTER THIRTEEN

I don't know whether she slept or not during the next four hours. The room was quiet. The time passed slowly.

The pulse in my hands went on throbbing violently for a while, but who cared? It was comforting, even if it hurt. I thought about all the fat red corpuscles forcing their way through the shrunken capillaries like water gushing along dry irrigation ditches after a drought. Very nice. Very life-giving. By tomorrow afternoon, I thought – correction, this afternoon – they might be fit for work. They'd got to be, that was all there was about it.

Some time after it was light I heard Joanna go into her narrow bathroom-kitchen where she brushed her teeth and made some fresh coffee. The warm roasted smell floated across to me. Saturday morning, I thought. Midwinter Cup day. I didn't leap out of bed eagerly to greet it; I turned over slowly from my stomach on to one side, shutting my eyes against the stiffness which afflicted every muscle from neck to waist, and the sharp soreness of my back and wrists. I really didn't feel very well.

She came across the room with a mug of steaming coffee and put it on the bedside table. Her face was pale and expressionless.

'Coffee,' she said unnecessarily.

'Thank you.'

'How do you feel?' she asked, a little too clinically.

'Alive,' I said.

There was a pause.

'Oh, go on,' I said. 'Either slosh me one or smile . . . one or the other. But don't stand there looking tragic, as if the Albert Hall had burned down on the first night of the Proms.'

'Damn it, Rob,' she said, her face crinkling into a laugh.

'Truce?' I asked.

'Truce,' she agreed, still smiling. She even sat down again on the edge of the bed. I shoved myself up into a sitting position, wincing somewhat from various aches, and brought a hand out from under the bedclothes to reach for the coffee.

As a hand it closely resembled a bunch of beef sausages. I produced the other one. It also was swollen. The skin on both felt very tender, and they were still unnaturally red.

'Blast,' I said. 'What's the time?'

'About eight o'clock,' she said. 'Why?'

Eight o'clock. The race was at two-thirty. I began

counting backwards. I would have to be at Ascot by at the latest one-thirty, preferably earlier, and the journey down, going by taxi, would take about fifty minutes. Allow an hour for hold-ups. That left me precisely four and a half hours in which to get fit enough to ride, and the way I felt, it was a tall order.

I began to consider ways and means. There were the Turkish baths, with heat and massage; but I had lost too much skin for that to be an attractive idea. There was a work-out in a gym; a possibility, but rough. There was a canter in the park – a good solution on any day except Saturday, when the Row would be packed with little girls on leading-reins – or better still a gallop on a racehorse at Epsom, but there was neither time to arrange it nor a good excuse to be found for needing it.

'What's the matter?' asked Joanna.

I told her.

'You don't mean it?' she said. 'You aren't seriously thinking of racing today?'

'I seriously am.'

'You're not fit to,' she said.

'That's the point. That's what we are discussing, how best to get fit,' I said.

'That isn't what I mean,' she protested. 'You look ill. You need a long, quiet day in bed.'

'I'll have it tomorrow,' I said, 'today I am riding Template in the Midwinter Cup.' She began more forcibly to try to dissuade me, so I told her why I was going to ride. I told her everything, all about Kemp-Lore's anti-jockey obsession and all that had happened on the previous evening before she found me in the telephone box. It took quite a time. I didn't look at her while I told her about the tack-room episode, because for some reason it embarrassed me to describe it, even to her, and I knew then quite certainly that I was not going to repeat it to anyone else.

When I had finished she looked at me without speaking for half a minute – thirty solid seconds – and then she cleared her throat and said, 'Yes, I see. We'd better get you fit, then.'

I smiled at her.

'What first?' she said.

'Hot bath and breakfast,' I said. 'And can we have the weather forecast on?' I listened to it every morning, as a matter of routine.

She switched on the radio, which was busy with some sickening matinée music, and started tidying up the room, folding the blanket she had slept in and shaking the sofa cushions. Before she had finished the music stopped, and we heard the eight-thirty news headlines, followed by the forecast.

'There was a slight frost in many parts of the country last night,' said the announcer smoothly, 'and more is expected tonight, especially in exposed areas. Temperatures today will reach five degrees centigrade, forty-one Fahrenheit, in most places, and the north-easterly wind will moderate slightly. It will be bright and sunny in the south. Further outlook: colder weather is expected in the next few days. And here is an announcement. The stewards at Ascot inspected the course at eight o'clock this morning and have issued the following statement. "Two or three degrees of frost were recorded on the racecourse last night, but the ground on both sides of the fences was protected by straw, and unless there is a sudden severe frost during the morning, racing is certain.'

Joanna switched off. She said, 'Are you absolutely determined to go?'

'Absolutely,' I said.

'Well... I'd better tell you... I watched that programme last night on television. *Turf Talk*.'

'Did you now!' I said, surprised.

'I sometimes do, since you were on it. If I'm in. Anyway I watched last night.'

'And?' I prompted.

'He,' she said, neither of us needing help to know who she meant, 'he talked about the Midwinter Cup nearly all the time; potted biographies of the horses and trainers, and so on. I was waiting to hear him mention you, but he didn't. He just went on and on about how superb Template is; not a word about you. But what I thought you'd like to know is that he said that as it was such an important race he personally would be commentating the finish today, and that he personally would also interview the winning jockey afterwards. If only you can win, he'll have to describe you doing it, which would be a bitter enough pill, and then congratulate you publicly in full view of several million people.'

I gazed at her, awestruck.

'That's a great thought,' I said.

'Like he interviewed you after that race on Boxing Day,' she added.

'That was the race that sealed my fate with him, I imagine,' I said. 'And you seem to have done some fairly extensive viewing, if I may say so.'

She looked taken aback. 'Well ... didn't I see you sitting unobtrusively at the back of a concert I gave in Birmingham one night last summer?'

'I thought those lights were supposed to dazzle you,' I said.

'You'd be surprised,' she said.

I pushed back the bedclothes. The black trews looked even more incongruous in the daylight.

'I'd better get going,' I said. 'What do you have in the way of disinfectant and bandages, and a razor?'

'Only a few minute bits of Elastoplast,' she said apologetically, 'and the razor I de-fuzz my legs with. There's a chemist two roads away though, who will be open by now. I'll make a list.' She wrote it on an old envelope.

'And A.P.C. tablets,' I said. 'They are better than just aspirins.'

'Right,' she said. 'I won't be long.'

When she had gone I got out of bed and went into

the bathroom. It's easy enough to say, but it wasn't all that easy to do, since I felt as if some over-zealous laundress had fed me several times through a mangle. It was exasperating, I thought bitterly, how much havoc Kemp-Lore had worked on my body by such simple means. I turned on the taps, took off the trews and socks, and stepped into the bath. The blue cardigan had stuck to my back and the shirt bandages to my wrists, so I lay down in the hot water without tugging at them and waited for them to soak off.

Gradually the heat did its customary work of unlocking the worst of the cramps, until I could rotate my shoulders and turn my head from side to side without feeling that I was tearing something adrift. Every few minutes I added more hot water, so that by the time Joanna came back I was up to my throat in it and steaming nicely, warm to the backbone and beyond.

She had dried my trousers and pants overnight, and she pressed them for me while I eased myself out of the blue cardigan and reluctantly got out of the bath. I put on the trousers and watched her setting out her purchases on the kitchen table, a dark lock of hair falling forward into her eyes and a look of concentration firming her mouth. Quite a girl.

I sat down at the table and she bathed the grazes with disinfectant, dried them, and covered them with large pieces of lint spread with zinc-and-castor-oil ointment which she stuck on with adhesive tape. She was neat and quick, and her touch was light.

'Most of the dirt came out in the bath luckily,' she observed, busy with the scissors. 'You've got quite an impressive set of muscles, haven't you? You must be strong ... I didn't realize.'

'At the moment I've got an impressive set of jellies,' I sighed. 'Very wobbly, very weak.' And aching steadily, though there wasn't any point in saying so.

She went into the other room, rummaged in a drawer, and came back with another cardigan. Pale green, this time; the colour suited my state of health rather well, I thought.

'I'll buy you some new ones,' I said, stretching it across my chest to do up the fancy buttons.

'Don't bother,' she said, 'I loathe both of them.'

'Thanks,' I said, and she laughed.

I put the anorak on again on top of the jersey and pushed the knitted cuffs up my forearms. Joanna slowly unwound the blood-stained bandages on my wrists. They still stuck a bit in spite of the soaking, and what lay underneath was a pretty disturbing sight, even to me, now that we could see it in daylight.

'I can't deal with this,' she said positively. 'You must go to a doctor.'

'This evening,' I said. 'Put some more bandages on, for now.'

'It's too deep,' she said. 'It's too easy to get it infected. You can't ride like this, Rob, really you can't.'

'I can,' I said. 'I'll dunk them in a bowl of Dettol for a while, and then you wrap them up again. Nice and flat, so they won't show.'

'Don't they hurt?' she said.

I didn't answer.

'Yes,' she said. 'Silly question.' She sighed, and fetched a bowl full of warm water, pouring in Dettol so that it turned a milky white, and I soaked my wrists in it for ten minutes.

'That's fixed the infection,' I said. 'Now . . . nice and flat.'

She did as I asked, fastening the ends of the bandages down with little gold safety pins. When she had finished the white cuffs looked tidy and narrow, and I knew they would be unnoticeable under racing colours.

'Perfect,' I said appreciatively, pulling down the anorak sleeves to cover them. 'Thank you, Florence.'

'And Nightingale to you, too,' she said, making a face at me. 'When are you going to the police?'

'I'm not. I told you,' I said. 'I'm not going at all. I meant what I said last night.'

'But why not; why not?' She didn't understand. 'You could get him prosecuted for assault or for causing grievous bodily harm, or whatever the technical term is.'

I said, 'I'd rather fight my own battles . . . and anyway, I can't face the thought of telling the police what happened last night, or being examined by their doctors, and photographed; or standing up in court, if it came to that, and answering questions about it in public, and having the whole rotten lot printed in gory detail in the papers. I just can't face it, that's all.'

'Oh,' she said slowly. 'I suppose it would be a bit of an ordeal, if you look at it like that. Perhaps you feel humiliated . . . is that it?'

'You may be rather bruisingly right,' I admitted grudgingly, thinking about it. 'And I'll keep my humiliation to myself, if you don't mind.'

She laughed. 'You don't need to feel any,' she said. 'Men are funny creatures.'

The pity about hot baths is that although they loosen one up beautifully for the time being, the effect does not last; one has to consolidate the position by exercise. And exercise, my battered muscles protested, was just what they would least enjoy; all the same I did a few rather half-hearted bend-stretch arm movements while Joanna scrambled us some eggs, and after we had eaten and I had shaved I went back to it with more resolution, knowing that if I didn't get on to Template's back in a reasonably supple condition he had no chance of winning. It wouldn't help anyone if I fell off at the first fence.

After an hour's work, though I couldn't screw myself up to swinging my arms round in complete circles, I did get to the stage where I could lift them above shoulder height without wanting to cry out.

Joanna washed up and tidied the flat, and soon after

ten o'clock, while I was taking a breather, she said, 'Are you going on with this health and beauty kick until you leave for Ascot?'

'Yes.'

'Well,' she said, 'it's only a suggestion, but why don't we go skating instead?'

'All that ice,' I said, shuddering.

She smiled. 'I thought you had to remount at once, after a fall?'

I saw the point.

'Anyway,' she said, 'it's good, warming exercise, and far more interesting than what you've been doing.'

'You're a blooming genius, my darling Joanna,' I said fervently.

'Er . . . maybe,' she said. 'I still think you ought to be in bed.'

When she was ready we went along to my family's flat where I borrowed one of my father's shirts and a tie and also his skates, which represented his only interest outside music. Then we called at the bank, since the taxi ride the night before had taken nearly all Joanna's cash, and apart from needing money myself I wanted to repay her. Lastly, we stopped at a shop to buy me a pair of brown, silk-lined leather gloves, which I put on, and finally we reached the ice rink in Queensway where we had both been members from the days when we were taken there as toddlers on afternoons too rainy for playing in the Park.

We had not skated together since we were sixteen,

and it was fascinating to see how quickly we fell back into the same dancing techniques that we had practised as children.

She was right about the exercise. After an hour of it I had loosened up from head to foot, with hardly a muscle that wasn't moving reasonably freely. She herself, sliding over the ice beside me, had colour in her cheeks and a dazzling sparkle in her eyes. She looked young and vivid.

At twelve o'clock, Cinderella-like, we slid off the rink.

'All right?' she asked, smiling.

'Gorgeous,' I said, admiring the clear, intelligent face turned up to mine.

She didn't know whether I meant her or the skating, which was perhaps just as well.

'I mean . . . how are the aches and pains?'

'Gone,' I said.

'You're a liar,' she said, 'but at least you don't look as grey as you did.'

We went to change, which for me simply meant substituting my father's shirt and tie for the pale green cardigan, and putting back the anorak on top, and the gloves. Necessary, the gloves. Although my fingers were less swollen, less red, and no longer throbbed, the skin in places was beginning to split in short thread-thin cracks.

In the foyer Joanna put the cardigan and my father's skates into her bag and zipped it up, and we went out into the street. She had already told me that she would not come to Ascot with me, but would watch on television. 'And mind you win,' she said, 'after all this.'

'Can I come back to your place, afterwards?' I said.

'Why, yes . . . yes,' she said, as if surprised that I had asked.

'Fine,' I said. 'Well . . . good-bye.'

'Good luck, Rob,' she said seriously.

CHAPTER FOURTEEN

The third cruising taxi driver that I stopped just round the corner in Bayswater Road agreed to take me all the way to Ascot. During the journey, which was quick and skilfully driven, I kept the warmth and flexibility going in my arms by some minor exercises and imaginary piano playing; and if the driver saw me at it in his mirror he probably imagined I was suffering from a sad sort of St Vitus dance.

He announced, when I paid him at the gate, that he thought as it was his own cab that he might as well stay and have a flutter on the races himself, so I arranged for him to drive me back to London again at the end of the afternoon.

'Got any tips?' he said, counting my change.

'How about Template, in the big race?' I said.

'I dunno,' he pursed his lips. 'I dunno as I fancy that Finn. They say as he's all washed up.'

'Don't believe all you hear,' I said, smiling. 'See you later.'

'Right.'

I went through the gate and along to the weighing-room. The hands of the clock on the tower pointed to five-past one. Sid, James's head travelling lad, was standing outside the weighing-room door when I got there, and as soon as he saw me he came to meet me, and said, 'You're here then.'

'Yes,' I said. 'Why not?'

'The governor posted me here to wait for you. I had to go and tell him at once if you came. He's having lunch ... there's a rumour going round that you weren't going to turn up, see?' He bustled off.

I went through the weighing-room into the changing-room.

'Hello,' said my valet. 'I thought you'd cried off.'

'So you came after all,' said Peter Cloony.

Tick-Tock said, 'Where in hell have you been?'

'Why did everyone believe I wouldn't get here?' I asked.

'I don't know. Some rumour or other. Everyone's been saying you frightened yourself again on Thursday and you'd chucked up the idea of riding any more.'

'How very interesting,' I said, grimly.

'Never mind that now,' said Tick-Tock. 'You're here, and that's that. I rang your pad this morning, but your landlady said you hadn't been back all night. I wanted to see if it was O.K. for me to have the car after racing today and for you to get a lift back with Mr Axminster. I have met,' he finished gaily, 'a smashing girl. She's here at the races and she's coming out with me afterwards.'

'The car?' I said. 'Oh ... yes. Certainly. Meet me outside the weighing-room after the last, and I'll show you where it is.'

'Super,' he said. 'I say, are you all right?'

'Yes, of course.'

'You look a bit night-afterish, to my hawk eyes,' he said. 'Anyway the best of luck on Template, and all that rot.'

An official peered into the changing-room and called me out. James was waiting in the weighing-room outside.

'Where have you been?' he said.

'In London,' I said. 'What's this rumour about me not turning up?'

'God knows,' he shrugged. 'I was sure you wouldn't have stayed away without at least letting me know, but ...'

'No,' I said. 'Of course not.' Not unless, I thought, I had still been hanging in a deserted tack-room in the process of being crippled for life.

He dismissed the subject and began to talk about the race. 'There's a touch of frost in the ground still,' he said, 'but that's really to our advantage.' I told him I had walked round the course the day before, and knew which parts were best avoided.

'Good,' he said.

I could see that for once he was excited. There was

a sort of uncharacteristic shyness about his eyes, and
the lower teeth gleamed in an almost perpetual half
smile. Anticipation of victory, that's what it is, I
thought. And if I hadn't spent such a taxing night and
morning I would have been feeling the same. As it
was, I looked forward to the race without much joy,
knowing from past experience that riding with injuries
never made them better. Even so, I wouldn't have
given up my place on Template for anything I could
think of.

When I went back into the changing-room to put
on breeches and colours, the jockeys riding in the first
race had gone out, leaving a lot of space and quiet
behind them. I went along to my peg, where all my
kit was set out ready, and sat down for a while on the
bench. My conscience ought to have been troubling
me. James and Lord Tirrold had a right to expect
their jockey to be in tip-top physical condition for so
important a race, and, to put it mildly, he wasn't.
However, I reflected wryly, looking down at my gloved
hands, if we all owned up to every spot of damage,
we'd spend far too much time on the stands watching
others win on our mounts. It wasn't the first time I
had deceived an owner and trainer in this way and yet
won a race, and I fervently hoped it wouldn't be the
last.

I thought about the Midwinter. Much depended on
how it developed, but basically I intended to start
on the rails, sit tight in about fourth place all the way

round, and sprint the last three furlongs. There was a new Irish mare, Emerald, who had come over with a terrific reputation and might take a lot of beating, especially as her jockey was a wily character, very clever at riding near the front and slipping the field by a hard-to-peg-back ten lengths round the last bend. If Emerald led into the last bend, I decided, Template would have to be close to her by then, not still waiting in fourth place. Fast though he was, it would be senseless to leave him too much to do up the straight.

It is not customary for jockeys to stay in the changing-room while a race is on, and I saw the valets looking surprised that I had not gone out to watch it. I stood up, picked up the under-jersey and Lord Tirrold's colours and went to change into them in the washroom. Let the valets think what they like, I thought. I wanted to change out of sight, partly because I had to do it more slowly than usual but mostly so that they shouldn't see the bandages. I pulled down the sleeves of the finely-knitted green and black jersey until they hid those on my wrists.

The first race was over and the jockeys were beginning to stream into the changing-room when I went back to my peg. I finished changing into breeches, nylons and boots and took my saddle and weight cloth along to the trial scales for Mike to adjust the amount of lead needed to bring me to twelve stone.

'You've got gloves on,' he pointed out.

'Yes,' I said mildly, 'it's a cold day. I'd better have some silk ones for riding in, though.'

'O.K.' he said. He produced from a hamper a bundle of whitish gloves and pulled out a pair for me.

I went along to the main scales to weigh out, and gave my saddle to Sid, who was standing there waiting for it.

He said, 'The governor says I'm to saddle Template in the stable, and bring him straight down into the parade ring when it's time, and not go into the saddling boxes at all.'

'Good,' I said emphatically.

'We've had two private dicks and a bloody great dog patrolling the yard all night,' he went on. 'And another dick came with us in the horse-box, and he's sitting in Template's box at this very minute. You never saw such a circus.'

'How's the horse?' I asked, smiling. Evidently James was splendidly keeping his word that Template would not be doped.

'He'll eat 'em,' Sid said simply. 'The Irish won't know what hit them. All the lads have got their wages on him. Yeah, I know they've been a bit fed up that you were going to ride him, but I saw you turn that Turniptop inside out on Thursday and I told 'em they've nothing to worry about.'

'Thanks,' I said, sincerely enough; but it was just one more ounce on a load of responsibility.

The time dragged. My shoulders ached. To take my

mind off that I spent some time imagining the expression on Kemp-Lore's face when he saw my name up in the number frame. He would think at first it was a mistake. He would wait for it to be changed. And at any moment now, I thought maliciously, he will begin to realize that I am indeed here.

The second race was run with me still sitting in the changing-room, the object of now frankly curious looks from the valets. I took the brown gloves off and put on the greyish white ones. They had originally been really white, but nothing could entirely wash out a season's accumulated stains of mud and leather. I flexed my fingers. Most of the swelling had gone, and they seemed to be getting fairly strong again in spite of the cracked and tender skin.

Back came the other jockeys again, talking, laughing, swearing, dealing out friendly and not so friendly abuse, yelling to the valets, dumping down their kit – the ordinary, comradely, noisy changing-room mixture – and I felt apart from it, as if I were living in a different dimension. Another slow quarter of an hour crawled by. Then an official put his head in and shouted, 'Jockeys out, hurry up there, please.'

I stood up, put on the anorak, fastened my helmet, picked up my whip, and followed the general drift to the door. The feeling of unreality persisted.

Down in the paddock where in June the chiffons and ribbons fluttered in the heat stood cold little bunches of owners and trainers, most of them muffled to the eyes against the wind. It seared through the bare branches of the trees beside the parade ring, leaving a uniformity of pinched faces among the people lining the rails. The bright winter sunshine gave an illusion of warmth which blue noses and runny eyes belied. But the anorak, as I had been pleased to discover, was windproof.

Lord Tirrold wore on his fine-boned face the same look of excited anticipation that I could still see on James's. They are both so sure, I thought uneasily, that Template will win. Their very confidence weakened mine.

'Well, Rob,' said Lord Tirrold, shaking me too firmly by the hand, 'this is it.'

'Yes, sir,' I agreed, 'this is it.'

'What do you think of Emerald?' he asked.

We watched her shamble round the parade ring with the sloppy walk and the low-carried head that so often denotes a champion.

'They say she's another Kerstin,' said James, referring to the best steeplechasing mare of the century.

'It's too soon to say that,' said Lord Tirrold: and I wondered if the same thought sprang into his mind as into mine, that after the Midwinter, it might not be too soon, after all. But he added as if to bury the possibility, 'Template will beat her.'

'I think so,' James agreed.

I swallowed. They were too sure. If he won, they

would expect it. If he lost, they would blame me; and probably with good cause.

Template himself stalked round the parade ring in his navy-blue rug, playing up each time as he came face on to the wind, trying to turn round so that it blew on his quarters, with his lad hanging on to his leading-rein like a small child on a large kite.

A bell rang, indicating it was time for the jockeys to mount. James beckoned to the boy, who brought Template across to us and took off his rug.

'Everything all right?' James asked.

'Yes, sir.'

Template's eyes were liquid clear, his ears were pricked, his muscles quivering to be off: the picture of a taut, tuned racing-machine eager to get on with the job he was born for. He was not a kind horse: there was no sweetness in his make-up and he inspired admiration rather than affection: but I liked him for his fire and his aggressiveness and his unswerving will to win.

'You've admired him long enough, Rob,' said James teasingly. 'Get up on him.'

I took off the anorak and dropped it on the rug. James gave me a leg up into the saddle and I gathered the reins and put my feet into the irons.

What he read in my face I don't know, but he said suddenly, anxiously, 'Is anything wrong?'

'No,' I said. 'Everything's fine.' I smiled down at him, reassuring myself as much as him.

Lord Tirrold said, 'Good luck,' as if he didn't think I needed it, and I touched my cap to him and turned Template away to take his place in the parade down the course.

There was a television camera on a tower not far down the course from the starting gate, and I found the thought of Kemp-Lore raging at the sight of me on his monitor set a most effective antidote to the freezing wind. We circled round for five minutes, eleven of us, while the assistant starter tightened girths and complained that anyone would think we were in perishing Siberia.

I remembered that Tick-Tock, the last time we had ridden together on the course on a cold day, had murmured 'Ascot's blasted Heath. Where are the witches?' And I thought of him now, putting a brave face on his inactivity on the stands. I thought briefly of Grant, probably hating my guts while he watched the race on television, and of Peter Cloony's wife, with no set to watch on at all, and of the jockeys who had given up and gone into factories, and of Art, under the sod.

'Line up,' called the starter, and we straightened into a ragged row across the course, with Template firmly on the inside, hugging the rails.

I thought of myself, driven to distraction by having it drummed into me that I had lost my nerve, and I thought of myself dragged over flinty ground and tied to a piece of galvanized chain; and I didn't need any more good reasons for having to win the Midwinter Cup.

I watched the starter's hand. He had a habit of stretching his fingers just before he pulled the lever to let the tapes up, and I had no intention of letting anyone get away before me and cut me out of the position I had acquired on the rails.

The starter stretched his fingers. I kicked Template's flanks. He was moving quite fast when we went under the rising tapes, with me lying flat along his withers to avoid being swept off, like other riders who had jumped the start too effectively in the past. The tapes whistled over my head and we were away, securely on the rails and on the inside curve for at least the next two miles.

The first three fences were the worst, as far as my comfort was concerned. By the time we had jumped the fourth – the water – I had felt the thinly healed crusts on my back tear open, had thought my arms and shoulder would split apart with the strain of controlling Template's eagerness, had found just how much my wrists and hands had to stand from the tug of the reins.

My chief feeling, as we landed over the water, was one of relief. It was all bearable; I could contain it and ignore it, and get on with the job.

The pattern of the race was simple from my point of view, because from start to finish I saw only three other horses, Emerald and the two lightly-weighted animals whom I had allowed to go on and set the pace. The jockeys of this pair, racing ahead of me nose for nose, consistently left a two-foot gap between themselves and the rails, and I reckoned that if they were still there by the time we reached the second last fence in the straight, they would veer very slightly towards the stands, as horses usually do at Ascot, and widen the gap enough for me to get through.

My main task until then was keeping Emerald from cutting across to the rails in front of me and being able to take the opening instead of Template. I left just too little room between me and the front pair for Emerald to get in, forcing the mare to race all the way on my outside. It didn't matter that she was two or three feet in front: I could see her better there, and Template was too clever a jumper to be brought down by the half-length trick – riding into a fence half a length in front of an opponent, causing him to take off at the same moment as oneself and land on top of the fence instead of safely on the ground the other side.

With the order unchanged we completed the whole of the first circuit and swept out to the country again. Template jumped the four fences down to Swinley Bottom so brilliantly that I kept finding myself crowding the tails of the pacemakers as we landed, and had to ease him back on the flat each time to avoid taking the lead too soon, and yet not ease him so much that Emerald could squeeze into the space between us.

From time to time I caught a glimpse of the grimness on Emerald's jockey's face. He knew perfectly well what I was doing to him, and if I hadn't beaten him to the rails and made a flying start, he would have done the same to me. Perhaps I had Kemp-Lore to thank that he hadn't even tried, I thought fleetingly; if the bonfire Kemp-Lore had made of my reputation had led the Irishman to misjudge what I would do, so much the better.

For another half-mile the two horses in front kept going splendidly, but one of the jockeys picked up his whip at the third last fence, and the other was already busy with his hands. They were dead ducks, and because of that they swung a little wide going round the last bend into the straight. The Irishman must have had his usual bend tactics too fixed in his mind, for he chose that exact moment to go to the front. It was not a good occasion for that manoeuvre. I saw him spurt forward from beside me and accelerate, but he had to go round on the outside of the two front horses who were themselves swinging wide, and he was wasting lengths in the process. The mare carried seven pounds less weight than Template, and on that bend she lost the advantage they should have given her.

After the bend, tackling the straight for the last time, with the second last fence just ahead, Emerald was in the lead on the outside, then the two tiring horses, then me.

There was a three foot gap then between the innermost pacemaker and the rails. I squeezed Template. He pricked his ears and bunched his colossal muscles and thrust himself forward into the narrow opening. He took off at the second last fence half a length behind and landed a length in front of the tiring horse, jumping so close to him on one side and to the wings on the other that I heard the other jockey cry out in surprise as I passed.

One of Template's great advantages was his speed away from a fence. With no check in his stride he sped smoothly on, still hugging the rails, with Emerald only a length in front on our left. I urged him a fraction forward to prevent the mare from swinging over to the rails and blocking me at the last fence. She needed two lengths' lead to do it safely, and I had no intention of letting her have it.

The utter joy of riding Template lay in the feeling of immense power which he generated. There was no need to make the best of things, on his back; to fiddle and scramble, and hope for others to blunder, and find nothing to spare for a finish. He had enough reserve strength for his jockey to be able to carve up the race as he wished, and there was nothing in racing, I thought, more ecstatic than that.

I knew, as we galloped towards the last fence, that Template would beat Emerald if he jumped it in anything like his usual style. She was a length ahead and showing no sign of flagging, but I was still holding Template on a tight rein. Ten yards from the fence, I let him go. I kicked his flanks and squeezed with the calves of my legs and he went over the birch like an angel, smooth, surging, the nearest to flying one can get.

He gained nearly half a length on the mare, but she didn't give up easily. I sat down and rode Template for my life, and he stretched himself into his flat-looking stride. He came level with Emerald half-way along the run in. She hung on grimly for a short distance, but Template would have none of it. He floated past her with an incredible increase of speed, and he won, in the end, by two clear lengths.

There are times beyond words, and that was one of them. I patted Template's sweating neck over and over. I could have kissed him. I would have given him anything. How does one thank a horse? How could one ever repay him, in terms he would understand, for giving one such a victory?

The two tall men were pleased all right. They stood side by side, waiting for us in the unsaddling enclosure, the same elated expression on both their faces. I smiled at them, and shook my feet out of the irons and slid off on to the ground. On to the ground: down to earth. The end of an unforgettable experience.

'Rob,' said James, shaking his big head. 'Rob.' He slapped Template's steaming shoulder and watched me struggle to undo the girth buckles with fingers shaking from both weakness and excitement.

'I knew he'd do it,' Lord Tirrold said. 'What a horse! What a race!'

I had got the buckles undone at last and had pulled the saddle off over my arm when an official came over and asked Lord Tirrold not to go away, as the Cup was to be presented to him in a few minutes. To me, he said, 'Will you come straight out again after you have weighed in? There's a trophy for the winning jockey as well.'

I nodded, and went in to sit on the scales. Now that the concentration of the race was over, I began to be aware of the extra damage it had done. Across the back of my shoulders and down my arms to the fingertips every muscle felt like lead, draggingly heavy, shot with stabbing and burning sensations. I was appallingly weak and tired, and the pain in my wrists had increased to the point where I was finding it very difficult to keep it all out of my face. A quick look revealed that the bandages were red again, and so were the cuffs of the silk gloves and parts of the fawn under-jersey. But if the blood had soaked through the black jersey as well, at least it didn't show.

With a broad smile Mike took my saddle from me in the changing-room and unbuckled my helmet and pulled it off my head.

'They are wanting you outside, did you know?' he said.

I nodded. He held out a comb. 'Better smarten your hair a bit. You can't let the side down.'

I obediently took the comb and tidied my hair, and went back outside.

The horses had been led away and in their place stood a table bearing the Midwinter Cup and other trophies, with a bunch of racecourse directors and stewards beside it.

And Maurice Kemp-Lore as well.

It was lucky I saw him before he saw me. I felt my scalp contract at the sight of him and an unexpectedly strong shock of revulsion ran right down my body. He couldn't have failed to understand it, if he had seen it.

I found James at my elbow. He followed my gaze.

'Why are you looking so grim?' he said. 'He didn't even try to dope Template.'

'No,' I agreed. 'I expect he was too tied up with his television work to be sure of having time to do it.'

'He has given up the whole idea,' said James confidently. 'He must have seen there was no chance any more of persuading anyone you had lost your nerve. Not after the way you rode on Thursday.'

It was the reckless way I had ridden on Thursday that had infuriated Kemp-Lore into delivering the packet I had taken on Friday. I understood that very well.

'Have you told anyone about the sugar?' I asked James.

'No, since you asked me not to. But I think

something must be done. Slander or no slander, evidence or not . . .'

'Will you wait,' I asked, 'until next Saturday? A week today? Then you can tell whoever you like.'

'Very well,' he said slowly. 'But I still think . . .'

He was interrupted by the arrival at the trophy table of the day's V.I.P., a pretty Duchess, who with a few well-chosen words and a genuinely friendly smile presented the Midwinter Cup to Lord Tirrold, a silver tray to James, and a cigarette box to me. An enterprising press photographer let off a flash bulb as the three of us stood together admiring our prizes, and after that we gave them back again to the clerk of the course, for him to have them engraved with Template's name and our own.

I heard Kemp-Lore's voice behind me as I handed over the cigarette box, and it gave me time to arrange my face into a mildly smiling blankness before turning round. Even so, I was afraid that I wouldn't be able to look at him without showing my feelings.

I pivoted slowly on my heels and met his eyes. They were piercingly blue and very cold, and they didn't blink or alter in any way as I looked back at them. I relaxed a little, inwardly, thankful that the first difficult hurdle was crossed. He had searched, but had not read in my face that I knew it was he who had abducted me the evening before.

'Rob Finn,' he said in his charming television voice, 'is the jockey you just watched being carried to victory

271

by this wonder horse, Template.' He was speaking into a hand microphone from which trailed yards of black flex, and looking alternately at me and at a camera on a scaffolding tower near by. The camera's red eye glowed. I mentally girded up my loins and prepared to forestall every disparaging opinion he might utter.

He said, 'I expect you enjoyed being his passenger?'

'It was marvellous,' I said emphatically, smiling a smile to outdazzle his. 'It is a great thrill for any jockey to ride a horse as superb as Template. Of course,' I went on amiably, before he had time to speak, 'I am lucky to have had the opportunity. As you know, I have been taking Pip Pankhurst's place all these months, while his leg has been mending, and today's win should have been his. He is much better now, I'm glad to say, and we are all delighted that it won't be long before he is riding again.' I spoke truthfully: whatever it meant to me in fewer rides, it would benefit the sport as a whole to have its champion back in action.

A slight chill crept into the corner of Kemp-Lore's mouth.

'You haven't been doing as well, lately . . .' he began.

'No,' I interrupted warmly. 'Aren't they extraordinary, those runs of atrocious luck in racing? Did you know that Doug Smith once rode ninety-nine losers in succession? How terrible he must have felt. It makes my twenty or so seem quite paltry.'

272

'You weren't worried, then, by ... er ... by such a bad patch as you've been going through?' His smile was slipping.

'Worried?' I repeated lightheartedly. 'Well, naturally I wasn't exactly delighted, but these runs of bad luck happen to everyone in racing, once in a while, and one just has to live through them until another winner comes along. Like today's,' I finished with a grin at the camera.

'Most people understood it was more than bad luck,' he said sharply. There was a definite crack in his jolly-chums manner, and for an instant I saw in his eyes a flash of the fury he was controlling. It gave me great satisfaction, and because of it I smiled at him more vividly.

I said, 'People will believe anything when their pockets are touched. I'm afraid a lot of people lost their money backing my mounts ... it's only natural to blame the jockey ... nearly everyone does, when they lose.'

He listened to me mending the holes he had torn in my life and he couldn't stop me without giving an impression of being a bad sport; and nothing kills the popularity of a television commentator quicker than obvious bad-sportsmanship.

He had been standing at right-angles to me with his profile to the camera, but now he took a step towards me and turned so that he stood beside me on my left side. As he moved there was a fleeting set to his mouth

273

that looked like cruelty to me, and it prepared me in some measure for what he did next.

With a large gesture which must have appeared as genuine friendship on the television screen, he dropped his right arm heavily across my shoulders, with his right thumb lying forward on my collar bone and his fingers spread out on my back.

I stood still, and turned my head slowly towards him, and smiled sweetly. Few things have ever cost me more effort.

'Tell us a bit about the race, then, Rob,' he said, advancing the microphone in his left hand. 'When did you begin to think you might win?'

His arm felt like a ton weight, an almost unsupportable burden on my aching muscles. I gathered my straying wits.

'Oh . . . I thought, coming into the last fence,' I said, 'that Template might have the speed to beat Emerald on the flat. He can produce such a sprint at the end, you know.'

'Yes, of course.' He pressed his fingers more firmly into the back of my shoulder and gave me what passed for a friendly shake. My head began to spin. Everything on the edge of my vision became blurred. I went on smiling, concentrating desperately on the fair, good-looking face so close to mine, and was rewarded by the expression of puzzlement and disappointment in his eyes. He knew that under his fingers, beneath two thin jerseys, were patches which

must be sore if touched, but he didn't know how much
or how little trouble I had had in freeing myself in the
tack-room. I wanted him to believe it had been none
at all, that the ropes had slipped undone or the hook
fallen easily out of the ceiling. I wanted to deny him
even the consolation of knowing how nearly he had
succeeded in preventing me from riding Template.

'And what are Template's plans for the future?'
He strove to be conversational, normal. The television
interview was progressing along well-trodden ways.

'There's the Gold Cup at Cheltenham,' I said. I was
past telling whether I sounded equally unruffled, but
there was still no leap of triumph in his face, so I went
on, 'I expect he will run there, in three weeks' time.
All being well, of course.'

'And do you hope to ride him again in that?' he
asked. There was an edge to his voice which just
stopped short of offensiveness. He was finding it as
nearly impossible to put on an appearance of affection
for me as I for him.

'It depends,' I said, 'on whether or not Pip is fit in
time ... and on whether Lord Tirrold and Mr
Axminster want me to, if he isn't. But of course I'd
like to, if I get the chance.'

'You've never yet managed to ride in the Gold Cup,
I believe?' He made it sound as if I had been trying
unsuccessfully for years to beg a mount.

'No,' I agreed. 'But it has only been run twice since

I came into racing, so if I get a ride in it so soon in my career I'll count myself very lucky.'

His nostrils flared and I thought in satisfaction, 'That got you squarely in the guts, my friend. You'd forgotten how short a time I've been a jockey.'

He turned his head away from me towards the camera and I saw the rigidity in his neck and jaw and the pulse which beat visibly in his temple. I imagined he would willingly have seen me dead: yet he was enough in command of himself to realize that if he pressed my shoulder any harder I would be likely to guess it was not accidental.

Perhaps if he had been less controlled at that moment I would have been more merciful to him later. If his professionally pleasant expression had exploded into the rage he was feeling, or if he had openly dug his nails with ungovernable vindictiveness into my back, I could perhaps have believed him more mad than wicked, after all. But he knew too well where to stop; and since I could not equate madness with such self-discipline, by my standards he was sane; sane and controlled, and therefore unlikely to destroy himself from within. I threw Claudius Mellit's plea for kid gloves finally overboard.

Kemp-Lore was speaking calmly towards the camera, finishing off his broadcast. He gave me a last, natural-looking little squeezing shake, and let his arm drop away from my shoulders. Slowly and methodically I silently repeated to myself the ten most obscene words I knew, and after that Ascot racecourse stopped attempting to whirl round and settled down again into brick and mortar and grass and people, all sharp and perpendicular.

The man behind the camera on the tower held up his thumb and the red eye blinked out.

Kemp-Lore turned directly to me again and said, 'Well, that's it. We're off the air now.'

'Thank you, Maurice,' I said, carefully constructing one last warm smile. 'That was just what I needed to set me back on top of the world. A big race win and a television interview with you to clinch it. Thank you very much.' I could rub my fingers in his wounds, too.

He gave me a look in which the cultivated habit of charm struggled for supremacy over spite, and still won. Then he turned on his heel and walked away, pulling his black microphone lead along the ground after him.

It is impossible to say which of us loathed the other more.

CHAPTER FIFTEEN

I spent most of the next day in Joanna's bed. Alone, unfortunately.

She gave me a cup of coffee for breakfast, a cosy grin, and instructions to sleep. So I lazily went on snoozing in the pyjamas she had bought me, dreaming about her on her own pillow, doing nothing more energetic than occasionally raise my blood pressure by thinking about Kemp-Lore.

I had arrived in a shaky condition on her doorstep the evening before, having first taken Tick-Tock and his space-age girlfriend by taxi to the boring White Bear at Uxbridge where, as I had imagined, the Mini-Cooper stood abandoned in the car park. It had seemed to me certain that Kemp-Lore had driven to the White Bear in his own car, had used the Mini-Cooper for his excursion to the abandoned stables, and had changed back again to his own car on the return journey. His route, checked on the map, was simple: direct almost. All the same I was relieved to find the little Mini safe and sound.

Tick-Tock's remarks about my carelessness with communal property trickled to a stop when he found my wrist-watch and wallet and the other things out of my pockets on the glove shelf, and my jacket and overcoat and a length of white nylon rope on the back seat.

'Why the blazes,' he said slowly, 'did you leave your watch and your money and your coats here? It's a wonder they weren't pinched. And the car.'

'It's the north-east wind,' I said solemnly. 'Like the moon, you know. I always do mad things when there's a north-east wind.'

'North-east my aunt fanny.' He grinned, picked up the coats, and transferred them to the waiting taxi. Then he surprisingly shovelled all my small belongings back into my trousers pockets, and put my watch into my gloved hand.

'You may have fooled everyone else, mate,' he said lightly, 'but to me you have looked like death inefficiently warmed up all day, and it's something to do with your maulers ... the gloves are new ... you don't usually wear any. What happened?'

'You work on it,' I said amiably, getting back into the taxi. 'If you haven't anything better to do.' I glanced across at his little hep-cat, and he laughed and flipped his hand, and went to help her into the Mini-Cooper.

The taxi-driver, in a good mood because he had backed three winners, drove me back to Joanna's mews without a single complaint about the roundabout journey. When I paid him and added a fat tip on top he said, 'Were you on a winner, too, then?'

'Yes,' I said. 'Template.'

'Funny thing that,' he said. 'I backed him myself, after what you said about not believing all you hear. You were quite right, weren't you? That fellow Finn's not washed up at all, not by a long chalk. He rode a hell of a race. I reckon he can carry my money again, any day.' He shifted his gears gently, and drove off.

Watching his tail-light bump away down the cobbled mews, I felt ridiculously happy and very much at peace. Winning the race had already been infinitely worth the cost, and the taxi-driver, not knowing who he was speaking to, had presented me with the bonus of learning that as far as the British racing public was concerned, I was back in business.

Dead beat but contented, I leaned against Joanna's door-post and rang her bell.

That wasn't quite the end of the most exhausting twenty-four hours of my life, however. My thoughtful cousin, anticipating correctly that I would refuse to turn out again to see a doctor, had imported one of her own. He was waiting there when I arrived, a blunt no-bedside manner Scot with bushy eyebrows and three warts on his chin.

To my urgent protests that I was in no state to withstand his ministrations, both he and Joanna turned deaf ears. They sat me in a chair, and off came my clothes again, the leather gloves and the silk racing ones I had not removed after riding, then the anorak, my father's shirt and the racing under-jersey, also not returned to Mike, then the bits of lint Joanna had stuck on in the morning, and finally the blood-soaked bandages round my wrists. Towards the end of all this rather ruthless undressing, the room began spinning as Ascot had done, and I regrettably rolled off the chair on to the floor, closer to fainting than I had been the whole time.

The Scotsman picked me up and put me back in the chair and told me to pull myself together and be a man.

'You've only lost a wee bit of skin,' he said sternly.

I began to laugh weakly, which didn't go down well, either. He was a joyless fellow. He compressed his mouth until the warts quivered when I shook my head to his enquiries and would not tell him what had happened to me. But he bound me up again comfortably enough and gave me some pain-killing pills which turned out to be very effective; and when he had gone I got into Joanna's bed and sank thankfully into oblivion.

Joanna worked at her painting most of the next day and when I surfaced finally at about four o'clock in the afternoon, she was singing quietly at her easel. Not the angular, spiky songs she specialized in, but a Gaelic ballad in a minor key, soft and sad. I lay and listened with my eyes shut because I knew she would stop if she found me awake. Her voice was true, even at a level not much above a whisper, the result of well-exercised vocal cords and terrific breath control. A proper Finn, she is, I thought wryly. Nothing done by halves.

She came to the end of the ballad, and afterwards began another. 'I know where I'm going, and I know who's going with me. I know who I love, but the dear knows who I'll marry. Some say he's black, but I say he's bonny . . .' She stopped abruptly and said quietly but forcefully, 'Damn, damn and blast.' I heard her throw down her palette and brushes and go into the kitchen.

After a minute I sat up in bed and called to her, 'Joanna.'

'Yes?' she shouted, without reappearing.

'I'm starving,' I said.

'Oh.' She gave a laugh which ended in a choke, and called, 'All right. I'll cook.'

And cook she did; fried chicken with sweet corn and pineapple and bacon. While the preliminary smells wafted tantalizingly out of the kitchen I got up and put my clothes on, and stripped her bed. There were clean sheets in the drawer beneath, and I made it up again fresh and neat for her to get into.

She carried a tray of plates and cutlery in from the kitchen and saw the bundle of dirty sheets and the smooth bed.

'What are you doing?'

'The sofa isn't good for you,' I said. 'You obviously haven't slept well . . . and your eyes are red.'

'That isn't . . .' she began, and thought better of it.

'It isn't lack of sleep?' I finished.

She shook her head. 'Let's eat.'

'Then what's the matter?' I said.

'Nothing. Nothing. Shut up and eat.'

I did as I was told. I was hungry.

She watched me finish every morsel. 'You're feeling better,' she stated.

'Oh, yes. Much. Thanks to you.'

'And you are not sleeping here tonight?'

'No.'

'You can try the sofa,' she said mildly. 'You might as well find out what I have endured for your sake.' I didn't answer at once, and she added compulsively, 'I'd like you to stay, Rob. Stay.'

I looked at her carefully. Was there the slightest chance, I wondered, that her gentle songs and her tears in the kitchen and now her reluctance to have me leave meant that she was at last finding the fact of our cousinship more troublesome than she was prepared for? I had always known that if she ever did come to love me as I wanted and also was not able to abandon her rigid prejudice against our blood relationship, it would very likely break her up. If that was what was happening to her, it was definitely not the time to walk out.

'All right,' I said smiling. 'Thank you. I'll stay. On the sofa.'

She became suddenly animated and talkative, and told me in great detail how the race and the interview afterwards had appeared on television. Her voice was quick and light. 'At the beginning of the programme he said he thought your name was a mistake on the number boards, because he had heard you weren't there, and I began to worry that you had broken down on the way and hadn't got there after all. But of course you had . . . and afterwards you looked like life-long buddies standing there with his arm round your shoulders and you smiling at him as if the sun shone out of his eyes. How did you manage it? But he was trying to needle you, wasn't he? It seemed like it to me, but then that was perhaps because I knew . . .' She stopped in mid-flow, and in an entirely different, sober tone of voice she said, 'What are you going to do about him?'

I told her. It took some time.

She was shaken. 'You can't,' she said.

I smiled at her, but didn't answer.

She shivered. 'He didn't know what he was up against, when he picked on you.'

'Will you help?' I asked. Her help was essential.

'Won't you change your mind and go to the police?' she said seriously.

'No.'

'But what you are planning . . . it's cruel.'

'Yes,' I agreed.

'And complicated, and a lot of work, and expensive.'

'Yes. Will you make that one telephone call for me?'

She sighed and said, 'You don't think you'll relent, once everything has stopped hurting?'

'I'm quite certain,' I said.

'I'll think about it,' she said, standing up and collecting the dirty dishes. She wouldn't let me help her wash up, so I went over to the easel to see what she had been working at all day: and I was vaguely disturbed to find it was a portrait of my mother sitting at her piano.

I was still looking at the picture when she came back.

'It's not very good, I'm afraid,' she said, standing beside me. 'Something seems to have gone wrong with the perspective.'

'Does Mother know you're doing it?' I asked.

'Oh no,' she said.

'When did you start it?'

'Yesterday afternoon,' she said.

There was a pause. Then I said, 'It won't do you any good to try to convince yourself your feelings for me are maternal.'

She jerked in surprise.

'I don't want mothering,' I said. 'I want a wife.'

'I can't . . .' she said, with a tight throat.

I turned away from the picture, feeling that I had

pressed her too far, too soon. Joanna abruptly picked up a turpentine-soaked rag and scrubbed at the still wet oils, wiping out all her work.

'You see too much,' she said. 'More than I understood myself.'

I grinned at her and after a moment, with an effort, she smiled back. She wiped her fingers on the rag, and hung it on the easel.

'I'll make that telephone call,' she said. 'You can go ahead with . . . with what you plan to do.'

On the following morning, Monday, I hired a drive-yourself car and went to see Grant Oldfield.

The hard overnight frost, which had caused the day's racing to be cancelled, had covered the hedges and trees with sparkling rime, and I enjoyed the journey even though I expected a reception at the end of it as cold as the day.

I stopped outside the gate, walked up the short path through the desolate garden, and rang the bell.

It had only just struck me that the brass bell push was brightly polished when the door opened and a neat dark-haired young woman in a green wool dress looked at me enquiringly.

'I came . . .' I said. 'I wanted to see . . . er . . . I wonder if you could tell me where I can find Grant Oldfield?'

'Indoors,' she said. 'He lives here; I'm his wife. Just a minute, and I'll get him. What name shall I say?'

'Rob Finn,' I said.

'Oh,' she said in surprise; and she smiled warmly. 'Do come in. Grant will be so pleased to see you.'

I doubted it, but I stepped into the narrow hall and she shut the door behind me. Everything was spotless and shining; it looked a different house from the one I remembered. She led the way to the kitchen and opened the door on to another area of dazzling cleanliness.

Grant was sitting at a table, reading a newspaper. He glanced up as his wife went in, and when he saw me his face too creased into a smile of surprised welcome. He stood up. He was much thinner and older-looking, and shrunken in some indefinable inner way; but he was, or he was going to be soon, a whole man again.

'How are you, Grant?' I said inadequately, not understanding their friendliness.

'I'm much better, thanks,' he said. 'I've been home a fortnight now.'

'He was in hospital,' his wife explained. 'They took him there the day after you brought him home. Dr Parnell wrote to me and told me Grant was ill and couldn't help being how he was. So I came back.' She smiled at Grant. 'And everything's going to be all right now. Grant's got a job lined up too. He starts in two weeks, selling toys.'

'Toys?' I exclaimed. Of all incongruous things, I thought.

'Yes,' she said, 'they thought it would be better for him to do something which had nothing to do with horses, so that he wouldn't start brooding again.'

'We've a lot to thank you for, Rob,' Grant said.

'Dr Parnell told me,' his wife said, seeing my surprise, 'that you would have been well within your rights if you'd handed him over to the police instead of bringing him here.'

'I tried to kill you,' Grant said in a wondering voice, as if he could no longer understand how he had felt. 'I really tried to kill you, you know.'

'Dr Parnell said if you'd been a different sort of person Grant could have ended up in a criminal lunatic asylum.'

I said uncomfortably, 'Dr Parnell appears to have been doing too much talking altogether.'

'He wanted me to understand,' she said, smiling, 'that you had given Grant another chance, so I ought to give him another chance too.'

'Would it bother you,' I said to Grant, 'if I asked you a question about how you lost your job with Axminster?'

Mrs Oldfield moved protectively to his side. 'Don't bring it all back,' she said anxiously, 'all the resentment.'

'It's all right, love,' Grant said, putting his arm around her waist. 'Go ahead.'

'I believe you were telling the truth when you told Axminster you had not sold information to that professional punter, Lubbock,' I said. 'But Lubbock did get information, and did pay for it. The question is, who was he actually handing over the money to, if he thought he was paying it to you?'

'You've got it wrong, Rob,' Grant said. 'I went over and over it at the time, and I went to see Lubbock and got pretty angry with him...' He smiled ruefully, 'and Lubbock said that until James Axminster tackled him about it he hadn't known for sure who he was buying information from. He had guessed it was me, he said. But he said I had given him the information over the telephone, and he had sent the payments to me in the name of Robinson, care of a Post Office in London. He didn't believe I knew nothing about it, of course. He just thought I hadn't covered myself well enough and was trying to wriggle out of trouble.' There was a remarkable lack of bitterness in his voice; his spell in a mental hospital, or his illness itself, seemed to have changed his personality to the roots.

'Can you give me Lubbock's address?' I asked.

'He lives in Solihull,' he said slowly. 'I might know the house again, but I can't remember the name of it, or the road.'

'I'll find it,' I said.

'Why do you want to?' he asked.

'Would it mean anything to you, if I happened to prove that you were telling the truth all along?'

His face came suddenly alive from within. 'I'll say it would,' he said. 'You can't imagine what it was like, losing that job for something I didn't do, and having no one believe in me any more.'

I didn't tell him that I knew exactly what it was like, only too well. I said, 'I'll do my best, then.'

'But you won't go back to racing?' his wife said to him anxiously. 'You won't start all over again?'

'No love. Don't worry,' he said calmly. 'I'm going to enjoy selling toys. You never know, we might start a toy shop of our own, next year, when I've learned the business.'

I drove the thirty miles to Solihull, looked up Lubbock in the telephone directory, and rang his number. A woman answered. She told me that he was not in, but if I wanted him urgently I would probably get hold of him at the Queen's Hotel in Birmingham, as he was lunching there.

Having lost my way twice in the one-way streets, I miraculously found a place to park outside the Queen's, and went in. I wrote a note on the hotel writing-paper, asking Mr Lubbock, whom I did not know even by sight, if he would be so very kind as to give me a few minutes of his time. Sealing the note in an envelope, I asked the head porter if he would have one of the page-boys find Mr Lubbock and give it to him.

'He went into the dining-room with another gentleman a few minutes ago,' he said. 'Here, Dickie, take this note in to Mr Lubbock.'

Dickie returned with an answer on the back of the note: Mr Lubbock would meet me in the lounge at two-fifteen.

Mr Lubbock proved to be a plumpish, middle-aged man with a gingery moustache and a thin section of lank hair brushed across a balding skull. He accepted from me a large brandy and a fat cigar with such an air of surprised irony that I was in no doubt that he was used to buying these things for jockeys, and not the other way about.

'I want to know about Grant Oldfield,' I said, coming straight to the point.

'Oldfield?' he murmured, sucking flame down the cigar. 'Oh yes, I remember, Oldfield.' He gave me a sharp upward glance. 'You ... er ... you still work for the same firm, don't you? Do you want a deal, is that it? Well, I don't see why not. I'll give you the odds to a pony for every winner you put me on to. No one could say fairer than that.'

'Is that what you paid Oldfield?' I said.

'Yes,' he said.

'Did you give it to him personally?' I asked.

'No,' he said. 'But then he didn't ask me personally. He fixed it up on the telephone. He was very secretive: he said his name was Robinson, and asked me to pay him in uncrossed money orders, and to send them to a Post Office for him to collect.'

'Which one?' I asked.

He took a swig at the brandy and gave me an assessing look. 'Why do you want to know?'

'It sounds a good idea,' I said casually.

He shrugged. 'I can't remember,' he said. 'Surely it's unimportant which Post Office it was? Somewhere in a London suburb, I know, but I can't remember where after all this time. NE7? N12? Something like that.'

'You wouldn't have a record of it?'

'No,' he said decisively. 'Why don't you ask Oldfield himself, if you need to know?'

I sighed. 'How many times did he give you information?' I asked.

'He told me the names of about five horses altogether, I should think. Three of them won, and I sent him the money on those occasions.'

'You didn't know it was Oldfield selling you tips, did you?' I asked.

'It depends what you mean by "know",' he said. 'I had a pretty good idea. Who else could it have been? But I suppose I didn't actually "know" until Axminster said "I hear you've been buying information from my jockey," and I agreed that I had.'

'So you wouldn't have told anyone before that that it was Oldfield who was selling you tips?'

'Of course not.'

'No one at all?' I pressed.

'No, certainly not.' He gave me a hard stare. 'You don't broadcast things like that, not in my business, and especially if you aren't dead sure of your facts. Just what is all this about?'

'Well . . .' I said. 'I'm very sorry to have misled you, Mr Lubbock, but I am not really in the market for information. I'm just trying to unstick a bit of the mud that was thrown at Grant Oldfield.'

To my surprise he gave a fat chuckle and knocked half an inch of ash off the cigar.

'Do you know,' he said, 'if you'd agreed to tip me off I'd have been looking for the catch? There's some jockeys you can square, and some you can't, and in my line you get an instinct for which are which. Now you . . .' he jabbed the cigar in my direction . . . 'you aren't the type.'

'Thanks,' I murmured.

'And more fool you,' he said nodding. 'It's not illegal.'

I grinned.

'Mr Lubbock,' I said, 'Oldfield was not Robinson, but his career and his health were broken up because you and Mr Axminster were led to believe that he was.'

He stroked his moustache with his thumb and forefinger of his left hand, wondering.

I went on, 'Oldfield has now given up all thought

293

of riding again, but it would still mean a great deal to him to have his name cleared. Will you help to do it?'

'How?' he said.

'Wouldn't you just write a statement to the effect that you saw no evidence at any time to support your guess that in paying Robinson, you were really paying Oldfield, and that at no time before James Axminster approached you did you speak of your suspicions as to Robinson's identity.'

'Is that all?' he said.

'Yes.'

'All right,' he said. 'It can't do any harm. But I think you're barking up the wrong tree. No one but a jockey would go to all that trouble to hide his identity. No one would bother, if his job didn't depend on not being found out. Still, I'll write what you ask.'

He unscrewed a pen, took a sheet of hotel writing-paper and in a decisive hand wrote the statement I had suggested. He signed it, and added the date and read it through.

'There you are,' he said. 'Though I can't see what good it will do.'

I read what he had written and folded the paper, and put it in my wallet.

'Someone told Mr Axminster that Oldfield was selling you information,' I said. 'If you hadn't told anyone at all – who knew?'

'Oh.' His eyes opened. 'I see, yes, I see. Robinson

294

knew. But Oldfield would never have let on ... so Oldfield was not Robinson.'

'That's about it,' I agreed, standing up. 'Thank you very much, Mr Lubbock, for your help.'

'Any time.' He waved the diminishing cigar, smiling broadly. 'See you at the races.'

CHAPTER SIXTEEN

On Tuesday morning I bought a copy of the *Horse and Hound* and spent a good while telephoning to a few of the people who had advertised their hunters for sale. With three of them I made appointments to view the animal in question in two days' time.

Next I rang up one of the farmers I rode for and persuaded him to lend me his Land-Rover and trailer on Thursday afternoon.

Then, having borrowed a tape measure out of Joanna's work-box – she was out at a rehearsal – I drove the hired car down to James's stables. I found him sitting in his office dealing with his paper work. The fire, newly lit in the grate, was making little headway against the raw chill in the air, and outside in the yard the lads looked frozen as they scurried about doing up their horses after the second morning exercise.

'No racing again today,' James remarked. 'Still, we've been extraordinarily lucky this winter up to now.'

He stood up and rubbed his hands, and held them out to the inadequate fire. 'Some of the owners have telephoned,' he said. 'They're willing to have you back. I told them...' and his lower teeth gleamed as he looked at me from under his eyebrows, '... that I was satisfied with your riding, and that you would be on Template in the Gold Cup.'

'What!' I exclaimed. 'Do you mean it?'

'Yes.' The glimmer deepened in his eyes.

'But... Pip...' I said.

'I've explained to Pip,' he said, 'that I can't take you off the horse when you've won both the King 'Chase and the Midwinter on him. And Pip agrees. I have arranged with him that he starts again the week after Cheltenham, which will give him time to get a few races in before the Grand National. He'll be riding my runner in that – the horse he rode last year.'

'It finished sixth,' I said, remembering.

'Yes, that's right. Now, I've enough horses to keep both Pip and you fairly busy, and no doubt you'll get outside rides as well. It should work out all right for both of you.'

'I don't know how to thank you,' I said.

'Thank yourself,' he said sardonically. 'You earned it.' He bent down and put another lump of coal on the fire.

'James,' I said, 'will you write something down for me?'

'Write? Oh, you'll get a contract for next season, the same as Pip.'

'I didn't mean that,' I said awkwardly. 'It's quite different ... would you just write down that it was Maurice Kemp-Lore who told you that Oldfield was selling information about your horses, and that he said he had learned it from Lubbock?'

'Write it down?'

'Yes. Please,' I said.

'I don't see ...' He gave me an intent look and shrugged. 'Oh, very well then.' He sat down at his desk, took a sheet of paper headed with his name and address, and wrote what I had asked.

'Signature and date?' he said.

'Yes, please.'

He blotted the page. 'What good will that do?' he said, handing it to me.

I took Mr Lubbock's paper out of my wallet and showed it to him. He read it through three times.

'My God,' he said. 'It's incredible. Suppose I had checked carefully with Lubbock? What a risk Maurice took.'

'It wasn't so big a risk,' I said. 'You wouldn't have thought of questioning what he put forward as a friendly warning. Anyway, it worked. Grant got the sack.'

'I'm sorry for that,' James said slowly. 'I wish there was something I could do about it.'

'Write to Grant and explain,' I suggested. 'He would appreciate it more than anything in the world.'

'I'll do that,' he agreed, making a note.

'On Saturday morning,' I said, taking back Lubbock's statement and putting it with his in my wallet, 'these little documents will arrive with a plop on the Senior Steward's doormat. Of course they aren't conclusive enough to base any legal proceedings on, but they should be enough to kick friend Kemp-Lore off his pedestal.'

'I should say you were right.' He looked at me gravely, and then said, 'Why wait until Saturday?'

'I ... er ... I won't be ready until then,' I said evasively.

He didn't pursue it. We walked out into the yard together and looked in on some of the horses, James giving instructions, criticism and praise – in that order – to the hurrying lads. I realized how used I had grown to the efficiency and prosperity of his organization, and how much it meant to me to be a part of it.

We walked slowly along one row of boxes, and James went into the tack-room at the end to talk to Sid about the cancellation of the following day's racing. Unexpectedly I stopped dead on the threshold. I didn't want to go in. I knew it was stupid, but it made no difference. Parts of me were still too sore.

The harness hook hung quietly from the centre of the ceiling, with a couple of dirty bridles swinging harmlessly on two of its curving arms. I turned my back on it and looked out across the tidy yard, and wondered if I would ever again see one without remembering.

Up in the rolling, grassy hills a mile or so away from his stable, James owned an old deserted keeper's cottage. In the past it had been the home allotted to the man who looked after the gallops, James had told me once on a journey to the races, but as it had no electricity, no piped water and no sanitation, the new groundsman preferred, not unnaturally, to live in comfort in the village below and go up the hill to work on a motor-bike.

The old cottage lay down an overgrown lane leading off a public but little used secondary road which led nowhere except up and along the side of the hill and down again to join the main road four miles further on. It served only two farms and one private house, and because of its quietness it was a regular route for the Axminster horses on roadwork days.

After leaving James I drove up to the cottage. I had not seen it at close quarters before, only a glimpse of its blank end wall from the end of the lane as I rode by. I now found it was a four-roomed bungalow, set in a small fenced garden with a narrow path leading from the gate to the front door. The neglected grass had been cropped short by sheep. There was one window to each room, two facing the front and two the back.

Getting in without a key presented no difficulty as most of the glass in the windows was broken; and opening one, I climbed in. The whole place smelt of fungus and rot, though faintly, as if the decay were only warming up for future onslaught. The walls and floorboards were still in good condition, and only one of the rooms was damp. I found that all four rooms opened on to a small central hall inside the front entrance; and as I made my tour I reflected that it could not have been more convenient if I had designed it myself.

I let myself out of the front door, and walking round to the back I took out Joanna's inch tape and measured the window frame; three feet high, four feet wide. Then I returned to the front, counted the number of broken panes of glass, and measured one of them. That done, I returned to James and asked him to lend me the cottage for a few days to store some things in for which there was no room at my digs.

'As long as you like,' he agreed absently, busy with paper work.

'May I mend some of the windows, and put on a new lock, to make it more secure?' I asked.

'Help yourself,' he said. 'Do what you like.'

I thanked him, and drove into Newbury, and at a builder's merchants waited while they made me up an order of ten panes of glass, enough putty to put them in with, several pieces of water pipe cut to a specified length, a bucket, some screws, a stout padlock, a bag of cement, a pot of green paint, a putty knife, a screwdriver, a cement trowel and a paint brush. Loaded to the axles with that lot I returned to the cottage.

I painted the weather-beaten front door and left it open to dry, reflecting that no one could blame a keeper, or his wife for that matter, for not wanting to live in that lonely, inconvenient cul-de-sac.

I went into one of the back rooms and knocked out all the panes of glass which still remained in their little oblong frames. Then, outside in the garden, I mixed a good quantity of cement, using water from the rain butt, and fixed six three-foot lengths of water pipe upright in a row across the window. That done, I went round into the hall, and on the doorpost and door of the same room screwed firmly home the fittings for the padlock. On the inside of the door I unscrewed the handle and removed it.

The final job was replacing the glass in the front windows, and it took me longest to do, chipping out all the old putty and squeezing on the new; but at last it was done, and with its whole windows and fresh green door the cottage already looked more cheerful and welcoming.

I smiled to myself. I retrieved the car from where I had parked it inconspicuously behind some bushes, and drove back to London.

The Scots doctor was drinking gin with Joanna when I let myself in.

'Oh no,' I said unceremoniously.

'Oh yes, laddie,' he said. 'You were supposed to come and see me yesterday, remember.'

'I was busy,' I said.

'I'll just take a look at those wrists, if you don't mind,' he said, putting down the gin and standing up purposefully.

I sighed and sat down at the table, and he unwrapped the bandages. There was blood on them again.

'I thought I told you to take it easy,' he said sternly. 'How do you expect them to heal? What have you been doing?'

I could have said 'Screwing in screws, chipping out putty and mixing cement,' but instead I rather unco-operatively muttered, 'Nothing.'

Irritated, he slapped a new dressing on with unnecessary force and I winced. He snorted, but he was gentler with the second one.

'All right,' he said, finishing them off. 'Now, rest them a bit this time. And come and see me on Friday.'

'Saturday,' I said. 'I won't be in London on Friday.'

'Saturday morning then. And mind you come.' He picked up his glass, tossed off the gin, and said a friendly good night exclusively to Joanna.

She came back laughing from seeing him out. 'He isn't usually so unsympathetic,' she said. 'But I think he suspects you were engaged in some sort of sadistic,

disgusting orgy last week, as you wouldn't tell him
how you got like that.'

'And he's dead right,' I said morosely. He had
stirred up my wrists properly, and they hadn't been
too good to start with, after my labours at the cottage.

For the third night I went to bed on the sofa and
lay awake in the darkness, listening to Joanna's soft
sleeping breath. Every day she hesitantly asked me if
I would like to stay another night in her flat, and as I
had no intention of leaving while there was any chance
of thawing her resistance, I accepted promptly each
time, even though I was progressively finding that no
bread would have been more restful. Half a loaf, in
the shape of Joanna padding familiarly in and out
of the bathroom in a pretty dressing-gown and going
to bed five yards away, was decidedly unsatisfying.
But I could easily have escaped and gone to a non-
tantalizing sleep in my own bed in my family's flat half
a mile away; if I didn't, it was my own fault, and
I pointed this out to her when every morning she
remorsefully apologized for being unfair.

On Wednesday morning I went to a large photographic
agency and asked to see a picture of Maurice Kemp-
Lore's sister Alice. I was given a bundle of
photographs to choose from, varying from Alice front-
view in spotted organza at a Hunt Ball to Alice
back-view winning over the last fence in a point to

point. Alice was a striking girl, with dark hair, high cheek-bones, small fierce eyes, and a tight aggressive mouth. A girl to avoid, as far as I was concerned. I bought a copy of a waist-length photograph which showed her watching some hunter trials, dressed in a hacking jacket and headscarf.

Leaving the agency, I went to the city offices of my parents' accountants, and talked 'our Mr Stuart' in the records department into letting me use first a typewriter and then his photo-copying machine.

On plain typing paper I wrote a bald account of Kemp-Lore's actions against Grant Oldfield, remarking that as a result of Axminster's relying on the apparent disinterestedness of Kemp-Lore's accusation, Oldfield had lost his job, had subsequently suffered great distress of mind, and had undergone three months' treatment in a mental hospital.

I made ten copies of this statement and then on the photo-copier printed ten copies each of the statements from Lubbock and James. I thanked 'our Mr Stuart' profusely and returned to Joanna's mews.

When I got back I showed her the photograph of Alice Kemp-Lore, and explained who she was.

'But,' said Joanna, 'she isn't a bit like her brother. It can't have been her that the ticket-collector saw at Cheltenham.'

'No,' I said. 'It was Kemp-Lore himself. Could you draw me a picture of him wearing a head-scarf?'

She found a piece of cartridge paper and with

concentration made a recognizable likeness in charcoal of the face I now unwillingly saw in dreams.

'I've only seen him on television,' she said. 'It isn't very good.' She began to sketch in a head-scarf, adding with a few strokes an impression of a curl of hair over the forehead. Then, putting her head on one side and considering her work, she emphasized the lips so that they looked dark and full.

'Lipstick,' she murmured, explaining. 'How about clothes?' Her charcoal hovered over the neck.

'Jodhpurs and hacking jacket,' I said. 'The only clothes which look equally right on men and women.'

'Crumbs,' she said, staring at me. 'It was easy, wasn't it? On with head-scarf and lipstick, and exit the immediately recognizable Kemp-Lore.'

I nodded. 'Except that he still reminded people of himself.'

She drew a collar and tie and the shoulders of a jacket with revers. The portrait grew into a likeness of a pretty girl dressed for riding. It made my skin crawl.

I found Joanna's eyes regarding me sympathetically.

'You can hardly bear to look at him, can you?' she said. 'And you talk in your sleep.'

I rolled up the picture, bounced it on the top of her head, and said lightly, 'Then I'll buy you some ear plugs.'

'He was taking a big risk, all the same, pretending to be a girl,' she said, smiling.

'I don't suppose he did it a minute longer than he

had to,' I agreed. 'Just long enough to get from Timberley to Cheltenham without being recognized.'

I filled ten long envelopes with the various statements, and stuck them down. I addressed one to the Senior Steward and four others to influential people on the National Hunt Committee. One to the Chairman of Universal Telecast, one to John Ballerton, and one to Corin Kellar, to show them their idol's clay feet. One to James. And one to Maurice Kemp-Lore.

'Can't he get you for libel?' asked Joanna looking over my shoulder.

'Not a chance,' I said. 'There's a defence in libel actions called justification, which roughly means that if a man has done something dishonest you are justified in disclosing it. You have to prove it is true, that's all.'

'I hope you are right,' she said dubiously, sticking on some stamps.

'Don't worry. He won't sue me,' I said positively.

I stacked nine of the envelopes into a neat pile on the bookshelf and propped the tenth, the unstamped one for Kemp-Lore, up on end behind them.

'We'll post that lot on Friday,' I said. 'And I'll deliver the other one myself.'

At eight-thirty on Thursday morning Joanna made the telephone call upon which so much depended.

I dialled the number of Kemp-Lore's London flat.

307

There was a click as soon as the bell started ringing, and an automatic answering device invited us to leave a recorded message. Joanna raised her eyebrows; I shook my head, and she put down the receiver without saying anything.

'Out,' I said unnecessarily. 'Damn.'

I gave her the number of Kemp-Lore's father's house in Essex and she was soon connected and talking to someone there. She nodded to me and put her hand over the mouthpiece, and said, 'He's there. They've gone to fetch him. I ... I hope I don't mess it up.'

I shook my head encouragingly. We had rehearsed pretty thoroughly what she was going to say. She licked her lips, and looked at me with anxious eyes.

'Oh? Mr Kemp-Lore?' She could do a beautiful cockney-suburban accent, not exaggerated and very convincing. 'You don't know me, but I wondered if I could tell you something that you could use on your programme in the newsy bits at the end? I do admire your programme, I do really. It's ever so good, I always think ...'

His voice clacked, interrupting the flow.

'What information?' repeated Joanna. 'Oh, well, you know all the talk there's been about athletes using them pep pills and injections and things, well I wondered if you wanted to know about jockeys doing it too ... one jockey, actually that I know of, but I expect they all do it if the truth were known ... Which jockey? Oh ... er ... Robbie Finn, you know, the one you talked to on the telly on Saturday after he won that race. Pepped to the eyebrows as usual he was, didn't you guess? You was that close to him I thought you must have ... How do I know? Well I do know ... you want to know how I know ... well ... it's a bit dodgy, like, but it was me got some stuff for him once. I work in a doctor's surgery ... cleaning you see ... and he told me what to take and I got it for him. But now look here, I don't want to get into no trouble, I didn't mean to let on about that ... I think I'd better ring off ... Don't ring off? You won't say nothing about it then, you know, me pinching the stuff?

'Why am I telling you? ... Well, he don't come to see me no more, that's why.' Her voice was superbly loaded with jealous spite. 'After all I've done for him ... I did think of telling one of the newspapers, but I thought I'd see if you were interested first. I can tell them if you'd rather ... Check, what do you mean check? ... You can't take my word for it on the telephone? Well, yes, you can come and see me if you want to ... no, not today, I'm at work all day ... yes, all right, tomorrow morning then.

'How do you get there? ... Well, you go to Newbury and then out towards Hungerford ...' She went on with the directions slowly while he wrote them down. 'And it's the only cottage along there, you can't miss it. Yes, I'll wait in for you, about eleven o'clock, all right then. What's my name? ... Doris Jones. Yes, that's right. Mrs Doris Jones ... Well ta-ta then.' The telephone clicked and buzzed as he disconnected.

She put the receiver down slowly, looking at me with a serious face.

'Hook, line and sinker,' she said.

When the banks opened I went along and drew out one hundred and fifty pounds. As Joanna had said, what I was doing was complicated and expensive; but complication and expense had achieved top-grade results for Kemp-Lore, and at least I was paying him the compliment of copying his methods. I grudged the money not at all: what is money for, it not to get what you want? What I wanted, admirable or not, was to pay him in his own coin.

I drove off to the Bedfordshire farmer who promised to lend me his Land-Rover and trailer. It was standing ready in the yard when I arrived at noon, and before I left I bought from the farmer two bales of straw and one of hay, which we stowed in the back of the Land-Rover. Then, promising to return that evening, I started away to the first of my appointments with the *Horse and Hound* advertisers.

The first hunter, an old grey gelding in Northamptonshire, was so lame that he could hardly walk out of his box and he was no bargain even at the sixty pounds they were asking for him. I shook my head, and pressed on into Leicestershire.

The second appointment proved to be with a brown mare, sound in limb but noisy in wind, as I discovered when I cantered her across a field. She was big, about twelve years old and gawky, but quiet to handle and not too bad to look at, and she was for sale only because she could not go as fast as her ambitious owner liked. I haggled, bringing him from the hundred he had advertised her for down to eighty-five pounds, and clinched the deal. Then I loaded the mare, whose name, her ex-owner said, was Buttonhook, into the trailer and turned my face south again to Berkshire.

Three hours later, at half-past five in the afternoon, I turned the Land-Rover into the lane at the cottage, and bumped Buttonhook to a standstill on the rough ground behind the bushes beyond the building. She had to wait in the trailer while I got the straw and spread it thickly over the floorboards in the room with the water pipes cemented over the window, and again while I filled her a bucket of water out of the rain butt and carried an armful of hay into the room and put it in the corner behind the door.

She was an affectionate old thing, I found. She came docilely out of the trailer and made no fuss when I led her up the little garden path and in through the front door of the cottage and across the little hall into the room prepared for her. I gave her some sugar and rubbed her ears, and she butted her head playfully against my chest. After a while, as she seemed quite content in her unusual and not very spacious loose box, I went out into the hall, shut the door, and padlocked her in. Then I walked round the outside of the cottage and shook the water-pipe bars to see if they were secure, as the frosty air might have prevented the cement from setting properly. But they were all immovably fixed.

The mare came to the window and tried to poke her muzzle through the glassless squares of the window frame and through the bars outside them, but the maze defeated her. I put my hand through and fondled her muzzle, and she blew contentedly down her nostrils. Then she turned and went over to the corner where her hay was, and quietly and trustfully put her head down to eat.

I dumped the rest of the hay and straw in one of the front rooms of the cottage, shut the front door, manoeuvred the trailer round with some difficulty into the lane again, and set off back to Bedfordshire. In due course I delivered the Land-Rover and trailer to their owner, thanked him, and drove the hired car back to Joanna's mews.

When I went in, she kissed me. She sprang up from the sofa where she had been sitting reading, and kissed me lightly on the mouth. It was utterly spontaneous; without thought: and it was a great surprise to both of us. I put my hands on her arms and smiled incredulously down into her black eyes, and watched the surprise there turn to confusion and the confusion to panic. I took my hands away and turned my back on her to give her time, taking off the anorak and saying casually over my shoulder, 'The lodger is installed in the cottage. A big brown mare with a nice nature.'

I hung up the anorak in the cupboard.

'I was just ... glad to see you back,' she said in a high voice.

'That's fine,' I said lightly. 'Can I rustle up an egg, do you think?'

'There are some mushrooms for an omelette,' she said, more normally.

'Terrific,' I said, going into the kitchen. 'Not peeled, by any chance?'

'Damn it, no,' she said, following me and beginning to smile. She made the omelette for me and I told her about Buttonhook, and the difficult moment passed.

Later on she announced that she was coming down to the cottage with me when I went in the morning.

'No,' I said.

'Yes,' she nodded. 'He is expecting Mrs Doris Jones to open the door to him. It will be much better if she does.'

I couldn't budge her.

'And,' she said, 'I don't suppose you've thought of putting curtains in the windows? If you want him to walk into your parlour, you'll have to make it look normal. He probably has a keen nose for smelling

313

rats.' She fished some printed cotton material out of the drawer and held it up. 'I've never used this . . . we can pin it up to look like curtains.' She busily collected some drawing pins and scissors, and then rolled up the big rag rug which the easel stood on and took a flower picture off the wall.

'What are those for?' I said.

'To furnish the hall, of course. It's got to look right.'

'Okay, genius,' I said, giving in. 'You can come.'

We put all the things she had gathered into a tidy pile by the door, and I added two boxes of cubed sugar from her store cupboard, the big electric torch she kept in case of power cuts, and a broom.

After that springing kiss, the sofa was more of a wasteland than ever.

CHAPTER SEVENTEEN

We set off early and got down to the cottage before nine, because there was a good deal to be done before Kemp-Lore arrived.

I hid the car behind the bushes again, and we carried the rug and the other things indoors. Buttonhook was safe and sound in her room, and was delighted to see us, neighing purringly in her throat when we opened her door. While I tossed her straw and fetched her some more hay and water, Joanna said she would clean the windows at the front of the cottage, and presently I heard her humming softly as she wiped away the grime of years.

The putty round the new panes had hardened well, and after I had finished Buttonhook, and Joanna was stepping back admiring the sparkle of the glass, I fetched the paint and began the tedious job of covering the patchwork of old decayed black paint and pale new putty with a bright green skin. Joanna watched me for a while and then went indoors. She put down the rug in the little hall, and I heard her banging a

nail into the wall to hang up the picture just inside
the front door where no visitor could fail to see it.
After that she worked on the inside of the windows
while I painted their outsides. She cut the flowery
material into lengths and pinned it so that it hung like
curtains.

When we had both finished we stood at the gate in
front of the cottage admiring our handiwork. With its
fresh paint, pretty curtains, and the rug and picture
showing through the half-open door, it looked well
cared for and homely.

'Has it got a name?' Joanna asked.

'I don't think so. It's always called "The Keeper's
Cottage," as far as I know,' I said.

'We should name it Sundew,' she said.

'After the Grand National winner?' I said, puzzled.

'No,' she said soberly, 'the carnivorous plant.'

I put my arm round her waist. She didn't stir.

'You will be careful, won't you?' she said.

'Yes, I will,' I assured her. I looked at my watch. It
was twenty minutes to eleven. 'We'd better go indoors
in case he comes early.'

We went in and shut the front door and sat on the
remains of the hay bale in the front room, giving
ourselves a clear view of the front gate.

A minute or two ticked by in silence. Joanna
shivered.

'Are you too cold?' I said with concern. There had
been another frost during the night and there was, of

course, no heating in the cottage. 'We should have brought a stove.'

'It's nerves as much as cold,' she said, shivering again.

I put my arm round her shoulders. She leaned comfortably against me, and I kissed her cheek. Her black eyes looked gravely, warily into mine.

'It isn't incest,' I said.

Her eyelids flickered in shock, but she didn't move.

'Our fathers may be brothers,' I said, 'but our mothers are not related to them or to each other.'

She said nothing. I had a sudden feeling that if I lost this time I had lost for ever, and a leaden chill of despair settled in my stomach.

'No one forbids marriage between cousins,' I said slowly. 'The Law allows it and the Church allows it, and you can be sure they wouldn't if there were anything immoral in it. And in a case like ours, the medical profession raises no objection either. If there were a good genetic reason why we shouldn't marry, it would be different. But you know there isn't.' I paused, but she still looked at me gravely and said nothing. Without much hope I said, 'I don't really understand why you feel the way you do.'

'It's instinct,' she said. 'I don't understand it myself. It's just that I've always thought of it as wrong . . . and impossible.'

There was a little silence.

I said, 'I think I'll sleep in my digs down here in

the village tonight, and ride out at exercise with the horses tomorrow morning. I've been neglecting my job this week . . .'

She sat up straight, pulling free of my arm.

'No,' she said abruptly. 'Come back to the flat.'

'I can't. I can't any more,' I said.

She stood up and went over to the window and looked out. Minutes passed. Then she turned round and perched on the window-sill with her back to the light, and I couldn't see her expression.

'It's an ultimatum, isn't it?' she said shakily. 'Either I marry you or you clear out altogether? No more having it both ways like you've given me this past week . . .'

'It isn't a deliberate ultimatum,' I protested. 'But we can't go on like this for ever. At least, I can't. Not if you know beyond any doubt that you'll never change your mind.'

'Before last week-end there wasn't any problem as far as I was concerned,' she said. 'You were just something I couldn't have . . . like oysters, which give me indigestion . . . something nice, but out of bounds. And now'—she tried to laugh—'now it's as if I've developed a craving for oysters. And I'm in a thorough muddle.'

'Come here,' I said persuasively. She walked across and sat down again beside me on the hay bale. I took her hand.

318

'If we weren't cousins, would you marry me?' I held my breath.

'Yes,' she said simply. No reservations, no hesitation any more.

I turned towards her and put my hands on the sides of her head and tilted her face up. There wasn't any panic this time. I kissed her; gently, and with love.

Her lips trembled, but there was no rigidity in her body, no blind instinctive retreat as there had been a week ago. I thought, if seven days can work such a change, what could happen in seven weeks?

I hadn't lost after all. The chill in my stomach melted away. I sat back on the hay bale, holding Joanna's hand again and smiling at her.

'It will be all right,' I said. 'Our being cousins won't worry you in a little while.'

She looked at me wonderingly for a moment and then unexpectedly her lips twitched at the corners. 'I believe you,' she said, 'because I've never known anyone more determined in all my life. You've always been like it. You don't care what trouble you put yourself to to get what you want ... like riding in the race last Saturday, and fixing up this fly-trap of a cottage, and living with me how you have this week ... so my instinct against blood relatives marrying, wherever it is seated, will have to start getting used to the idea that it is wrong, I suppose, otherwise I'll find myself being dragged by you along to Claudius Mellit to be psychoanalysed or brain-washed, or something.

I will try,' she finished more seriously, 'not to keep you waiting very long.'

'In that case,' I said, matching her lightheartedness, 'I'll go on sleeping on your sofa as often as possible, so as to be handy when the breakthrough occurs.'

She laughed without strain. 'Starting tonight?' she asked.

'I guess so,' I said smiling. 'I never did like my digs much.'

'Ouch,' she said.

'But I'll have to come back here on Sunday evening in any case. As James has given me my job back, the least I can do is show some interest in his horses.'

We went on sitting on the hay bale, talking calmly as if nothing had happened; and nothing had, I thought, except a miracle that one could reliably build a future on, the miracle that Joanna's hand now lay intimately curled in mine without her wanting to remove it.

The minutes ticked away towards eleven o'clock.

'Suppose he doesn't come?' she said.

'He will.'

'I almost hope he doesn't,' she said. 'Those letters would be enough by themselves.'

'You won't forget to post them when you get back, will you?' I said.

'Of course not,' she said, 'but I wish you'd let me stay.'

I shook my head. We sat on, watching the gate. The

minute hand crept round to twelve on my watch, and passed it.

'He's late,' she said.

Five past eleven. Ten past eleven.

'He isn't coming,' Joanna murmured.

'He'll come,' I said.

'Perhaps he got suspicious and checked up and found there wasn't any Mrs Doris Jones living in the Keeper's Cottage,' she said.

'There shouldn't be any reason for him to be suspicious,' I pointed out. 'He clearly didn't know at the end of that television interview with me last Saturday that I was on to him, and nothing I've done since should have got back to him, and James and Tick-Tock promised to say nothing to anyone about the doped sugar. As far as Kemp-Lore should know, he is unsuspected and undiscovered. If he feels as secure as I am sure he does, he'll never pass up an opportunity to learn about something as damaging as pep pills . . . so he'll come.'

A quarter past eleven.

He had to come. I found that all my muscles were tense, as if I were listening for him with my whole body, not only my ears. I flexed my toes inside my shoes and tried to relax. There were traffic jams, breakdowns, detours, any number of things to delay him. It was a long way, and he could easily have misjudged the time it would take.

Twenty past eleven.

Joanna sighed and stirred. Neither of us spoke for ten minutes. At eleven-thirty, she said again, 'He isn't coming.'

I didn't answer.

At eleven-thirty-three, the sleek cream nose of an Aston Martin slid to a stop at the gate and Maurice Kemp-Lore stepped out. He stretched himself, stiff from driving, and glanced over the front of the cottage. He wore a beautifully cut hacking jacket and cavalry twill trousers, and there was poise and grace in his every movement.

'Glory, he's handsome,' breathed Joanna in my ear. 'What features! What colouring! Television doesn't do him justice. It's difficult to think of anyone who looks so young and noble doing any harm.'

'He's thirty-three,' I said, 'and Nero died at twenty-nine.'

'You know the oddest things,' she murmured.

Kemp-Lore unlatched the garden gate, walked up the short path and banged the knocker on the front door.

We stood up. Joanna picked a piece of hay off her skirt, swallowed, gave me a half-smile, and walked unhurriedly into the hall. I followed her and stood against the wall where I would be hidden when the front door opened.

Joanna licked her lips.

'Go on,' I whispered.

322

She put her hand on the latch, and opened the door.

'Mrs Jones?' the honey voice said. 'I'm so sorry I'm a little late.'

'Won't you come in, Mr Kemp-Lore?' said Joanna in her cockney-suburban accent. 'It's ever so nice to see you.'

'Thank you,' he said stepping over the threshold. Joanna took two paces backwards and Kemp-Lore followed her into the hall.

Slamming the front door with my foot, I seized Kemp-Lore from behind by both elbows, pulling them backwards and forcing him forwards at the same time. Joanna opened the door of Buttonhook's room and I brought my foot up into the small of Kemp-Lore's back and gave him an almighty push. He staggered forwards through the door and I had a glimpse of him sprawling face downwards in the straw before I had the door shut again and the padlock firmly clicking into place.

'That was easy enough,' I said with satisfaction. 'Thanks to your help.'

Kemp-Lore began kicking the door.

'Let me out,' he shouted. 'What do you think you're doing?'

'He didn't see you,' said Joanna softly.

'No,' I agreed, 'I think we'll leave him in ignorance while I take you into Newbury to catch the train.'

'Is it safe?' she said, looking worried.

'I won't be away long,' I promised. 'Come on.'

Before driving her down to Newbury I moved Kemp-Lore's car along and off the lane until it was hidden in the bushes. The last thing I wanted was some stray inquisitive local inhabitant going along to the cottage to investigate. Then I took Joanna to the station and drove straight back again, a matter of twenty minutes each way, and parked in the bushes as usual.

Walking quietly I went along the side of the cottage and round to the back.

Kemp-Lore's hands stuck out through the glassless window frames, gripping the water pipe bars and shaking them vigorously. They had not budged in their cement.

He stopped abruptly when he saw me and I watched the anger in his face change to blank surprise.

'Who did you expect?' I said.

'I don't know what's going on,' he said. 'Some damn fool of a woman locked me in here nearly an hour ago and went away and left me. You can let me out. Quickly.' His breath wheezed sharply in his throat. 'There's a horse in here,' he said looking over his shoulder, 'and they give me asthma.'

'Yes,' I said steadily, without moving. 'Yes. I know.'

It hit him then. His eyes widened.

'It was you . . . who pushed me . . .'

'Yes,' I said.

He stood staring at me through the criss-cross of window frame and bars.

'You did it on purpose? You put me in here with a horse on purpose?' His voice rose.

'Yes,' I agreed.

'Why?' he cried. He must have known the answer already, but when I didn't reply he said again, almost in a whisper, 'Why?'

'I'll give you half an hour to think about it,' I said, turning to walk away.

'No,' he exclaimed. 'My asthma's bad. Let me out at once.' I turned back and stood close to the window. His breath whistled fiercely, but he had not even loosened his collar and tie. He was in no danger.

'Don't you have some pills?' I said.

'Of course. I've taken them. But they won't work with a horse so close. Let me out.'

'Stand by the window,' I said, 'and breathe the fresh air.'

'It's cold,' he objected. 'This place is like an ice house.'

I smiled. 'Maybe it is,' I said. 'But then you are fortunate . . . you can move about to keep warm, and you have your jacket on . . . and I have not poured three bucketfuls of cold water over your head.'

He gasped sharply, and it was then, I think, that he began to realize that he was not going to escape lightly or easily from his prison.

Certainly, when I returned to him after sitting on

the hay bale for half an hour listening to him alternately kicking the door and yelling for help out of the window, he was no longer assuming that I had lured him all the way from London and gone to the trouble of converting a cottage room into a loose box merely to set him free again at his first squawk.

When I walked round to the window I found him fending off Buttonhook, who was putting her muzzle affectionately over his shoulder. I laughed callously, and he nearly choked with rage.

'Get her away from me,' he screamed. 'She won't leave me alone. I can't breathe.'

He clung on to a bar with one hand, and chopped at Buttonhook with the other.

'If you don't make so much noise she'll go back to her hay.'

He glared at me through the bars, his face distorted with rage and hate and fright. His asthma was much worse. He had unbuttoned the neck of his shirt and pulled down his tie and I could see his throat heaving.

I put the box of sugar cubes I was carrying on the inner window-sill, withdrawing my hand quickly as he made a grab at it.

'Put some sugar on her hay,' I said. 'Go on,' I added, as he hesitated. 'This lot isn't doped.'

His head jerked up. I looked bitterly into his staring eyes.

'Twenty-eight horses,' I said, 'starting with

Shantytown. Twenty-eight sleepy horses who all ate some sugar from your hand before they raced.'

Savagely he picked up the box of sugar, tore it open, and sprinkled the cubes on the pile of hay at the other end of the room. Buttonhook, following him, put her head down and began to crunch. He came back to the window, wheezing laboriously.

'You won't get away with this,' he said. 'You'll go to jail for this. I'll see you're pilloried for this.'

'Save your breath,' I said brusquely. 'I've a good deal to say to you. After that, if you want to complain to the police about the way I've treated you, you're welcome.'

'You'll be in jail so quick you won't know what hit you,' he said, the breath hissing through his teeth. 'Now, hurry up and say whatever it is you want to say.'

'Hurry?' I said slowly. 'Well now, it's going to take some time.'

'You'll have to let me out by two-thirty at the latest,' he said unguardedly. 'I've got rehearsals today at five.'

I smiled at him. I could feel it wasn't a pleasant smile.

I said, 'It isn't an accident that you are here on Friday.'

His jaw literally dropped. 'The programme . . .' he said.

'Will have to go on without you,' I agreed.

'But you can't,' he shouted, gasping for enough breath, 'you can't do that.'

'Why not?' I said mildly.

'It's ... it's television,' he shouted, as if I didn't know. 'Millions of people are expecting to see the programme.'

'Then millions of people are going to be disappointed,' I said.

He stopped shouting and took three gulping, wheezing breaths.

'I know,' he said, with a visible effort at moderation and at getting back to normal, 'that you don't really mean to keep me here so long that I can't get to the studio in time for the programme. All right then,' he paused for a couple of wheezes, 'if you let me go in good time for the rehearsals, I won't report you to the police as I threatened. I'll overlook all this.'

'I think you had better keep quiet and listen,' I said. 'I suppose you find it hard to realize that I don't give a damn for your influence or the pinnacle the British public have seen fit to put you on, or your dazzling, synthetic personality. They are a fraud. Underneath there is only a sick mess of envy and frustration and spite. But I wouldn't have found you out if you hadn't doped twenty-eight horses I rode and told everyone I had lost my nerve. And you can spend this afternoon reflecting that you wouldn't be missing your programme tonight if you hadn't tried to stop me riding Template.'

He stood stock still, his face pallid and suddenly sweating.

'You mean it,' he whispered.

'Indeed I do,' I said.

'No,' he said. A muscle in his cheek started twitching. 'No. You can't. You did ride Template... you must let me do the programme.'

'You won't be doing any more programmes,' I said. 'Not tonight or any night. I didn't bring you here just for a personal revenge, though I don't deny I felt like killing you last Friday night. I brought you here on behalf of Art Mathews and Peter Cloony and Grant Oldfield. I brought you because of Danny Higgs, and Ingersoll, and every other jockey you have hit where it hurts. In various ways you saw to it that they lost their jobs; so now you are going to lose yours.'

For the first time, he was speechless. His lips moved but no sound came out except the high, asthmatic whine of his breathing. His eyes seemed to fall back in their sockets and his lower jaw hung slack, making hollows of his cheeks. He looked like a death's-head caricature of the handsome charmer he had been.

I took the long envelope addressed to him out of my pocket and held it to him through the bars. He took it mechanically, with black fingers.

'Open it,' I said.

He pulled out the sheets of paper and read them. He read them through twice, though his face showed from the first that he understood the extent of the disaster. The haggard hollows deepened.

'As you will see,' I said, 'those are photostat copies. More like them are in the post to the Senior Steward and to your boss at Universal Telecast, and to several other people as well. They will get them tomorrow morning. And they will no longer wonder why you failed to turn up for your programme tonight.'

He still seemed unable to speak, and his hands shook convulsively. I passed to him through the bars the rolled up portrait Joanna had drawn of him. He opened it, and it was clearly another blow.

'I brought it to show you,' I said, 'so that you would realize beyond any doubt that I know exactly what you have been doing. All along you have found that having an instantly recognizable face was a big handicap when it came to doing things you couldn't explain away, like ramming an old Jaguar across Peter Cloony's lane.'

His head jerked back, as if it still surprised him that I knew so much.

I said calmly, 'A ticket collector at Cheltenham said you were pretty.'

I smiled faintly. He looked very far from pretty at that moment.

'As for that Jaguar,' I said, 'I haven't had time yet to find out where it came from, but it can be done. It's only a question of asking. Advertising its number in the trade papers . . . tracing its former owner . . . that sort of thing. Tedious, I dare say, but definitely possible, and if necessary I will do it. No one would forget having you for a customer.

'You must have bought it in the week after the tank

carrier blocked Cloony's lane, because that is what gave you the idea. Do you think you can explain away the time sequence of acquiring the Jaguar and abandoning it exactly where and when and how you did? And disappearing from the scene immediately afterwards?'

His mouth hung open and the muscle twitched in his cheek.

'Most of your vicious rumours,' I said, changing tack, 'were spread for you by Corin Kellar and John Ballerton, who you found would foolishly repeat every thought that you put into their heads. I hope you know Corin well enough to realize that he never stands by his friends. When the contents of the letter he will receive in the morning sink into that rat-brain of his, and he finds that other people have had letters like it, there won't be anyone spewing out more damaging truth about you than him. He will start telling everyone, for instance, that it was you who set him at loggerheads with Art Mathews. There won't be any stopping him.

'You see,' I finished after a pause, 'I think it is only justice that as far as possible you should suffer exactly what you inflicted on other people.'

He spoke at last. The words came out in a wheezing croak, and he was past caring what admissions he made. 'How did you find it out?' he said disbelievingly. 'You didn't know last Friday, you couldn't see . . .'

'I did know last Friday,' I said, 'I knew just how far you had gone to smash Peter Cloony, and I knew you hated me enough to give yourself asthma doping my mounts. I knew the dope business had gone sour on you when it came to Turniptop at Stratford. And you may care to learn that it was no accident that James Axminster jogged your arm and stepped on the sugar lumps; I asked him to, and told him what you were doing. I knew all about your curdled, obsessive jealousy of jockeys. I didn't need to see you last Friday to know you ... there wasn't anyone else with any reason to want me out of action.'

'You can't have known all that,' he said obstinately, clinging to it as if it mattered. 'You didn't know the next day when I interviewed you after the race ...' His voice tailed off in a wheeze and he stared at me hopelessly through the bars.

'You aren't the only one who can smile and hate at the same time,' I said neutrally. 'I learned it from you.'

He made a sound like a high-pitched moan, and turned his back towards me with his arms bent upwards and folded over his head in an attitude of the utmost misery and despair. It may be regrettable, but I felt no pity for him at all.

I walked away from his window, round the cottage and in at the front door, and sat down again on the hay in the front room. I looked at my watch. It was a quarter to two. The afternoon stretched lengthily ahead.

Kemp-Lore had another spell of screaming for help through the window, but no one came; then he tried the door again, but there was no handle on his side of it for him to pull, and it was too solidly constructed for him to kick his way through. Buttonhook grew restive again from the noise and started pawing the ground, and Kemp-Lore shouted to me furiously to let him out, let him out, let him out.

Joanna's great fear had been that his asthma would make him seriously ill, and she had repeatedly warned me to be careful; but I judged that while he had enough breath for so much yelling he was in no real danger, and I sat and listened to him without relenting. The slow hours passed, punctuated only by the bursts of fury from the back room, while I stretched myself comfortably across the hay and day-dreamed about marriage to my cousin.

At about five o'clock he was quiet for a long time. I got up and walked round the outside of the cottage and looked in through the window. He was lying face down in the straw near the door, not moving at all.

I watched him for a few minutes and called his name, but as he still did not stir I began to be alarmed, and decided I would have to make sure he was all right. I returned to the hall, and having shut the front door firmly behind me, I unlocked the padlock on the back room. The door swung inwards, and Buttonhook, lifting her head, greeted me with a soft whinny.

Kemp-Lore was alive, that at least was plain. The sound of his high, squeezed breath rose unmistakably from his still form. I bent down beside him to see into just how bad a spasm he had been driven, but I never did get around to turning him over or feeling his pulse. As soon as I was down on one knee beside him he heaved himself up and into me, knocking me sprawling off balance, and sprang like lightning for the door.

I caught his shoe as it zipped across three inches from my face and yanked him back. He fell heavily on top of me and we rolled towards Buttonhook, with me trying to pin him down on the floor and he fighting like a tiger to get free. The mare was frightened. She cowered back against the wall to get out of our way, but it was a small room and our struggles took us among Buttonhook's feet and under her belly. She stepped gingerly over us and made cautiously for the open door.

Kemp-Lore's left hand was clamped round my right wrist, a circumstance which hindered me considerably. If he'd been clairvoyant he couldn't have struck on anything better calculated to cause me inconvenience. I hit him in the face and neck with my left hand, but I was too close to get any weight behind it and was also fairly occupied dodging the blows he aimed at me in return.

After he had lost the advantage of surprise, he seemed to decide he could only get free of me by lacing his fingers in my hair and banging my head against the wall, for this he tried repeatedly to do. He was staggeringly strong, more than I would have believed possible in view of his asthma, and the fury and desperation which fired him blazed in his blue eyes like a furnace.

If my hair hadn't been so short he would probably have succeeded in knocking me out, but his fingers kept slipping when I twisted my head violently in his grasp, and the third time my ear grazed the plaster I managed at last to wrench my right hand free as well.

After that, hauling off a fraction, I landed a socking right jab in his short ribs, and the air whistled out of his lungs screeching like an express train. He went a sick grey-green colour and fell slackly off me, gasping and retching and clawing his throat for air.

I got to my feet and hauled him up, and staggered with him over to the window, holding him where the fresh cold air blew into his face. After three or four minutes his colour improved and the terrifying heaving lessened, and some strength flowed back into his sagging legs.

I clamped his fingers round the window frames and let go of him. He swayed a bit, but his hands held, and after a moment I walked dizzily out of the room and padlocked the door shut behind me.

Buttonhook had found her way into the front room and was placidly eating the hay. I leaned weakly against the wall and watched her for a while, cursing myself for the foolish way I had nearly got myself locked into my own prison. I was badly shaken, not only by the fight itself but by the strength with which Kemp-Lore had fought and by the shocking effect my last blow had had on him. I ought to have had more sense, I knew, than to hit an asthmatic with that particular punch.

There was no sound from the back room. I straightened up and walked round to the window. He was standing there, holding on to the frames where I had put him, and there were tears running down his cheeks.

He was breathing safely enough, the asthma reduced to a more manageable wheeze, and I imagined it would not get any worse from then on, as Buttonhook was no longer in the room with him.

'Damn you,' he said. Another tear spilt over. 'Damn you. Damn you.'

There wasn't anything to say.

I went back to Buttonhook, and put on her halter. I had meant to deal with her later, after I had let Kemp-Lore go, but in the changed circumstances I decided to do it straight away, while it was still light. Leading her out of the front door and through the gate, I jumped on to her back and rode her away up past the two cars hidden in the bushes and along the ridge of the hill.

A mile further on I struck the lane which led up to the Downs, and turning down that came soon to a gate into a field owned by a farmer I had often ridden for. Slipping off Buttonhook I opened the gate, led her through and turned her loose.

She was so amiable that I was sorry to part with

her, but I couldn't keep her in the cottage, I couldn't stable an elderly hunter in James's yard and expect his lads to look after her, I couldn't find a snap buyer for her at six o'clock in the evening; and I frankly didn't know what else to do with her. I fondled her muzzle and patted her neck and fed her a handful of sugar. Then I slapped her on the rump and watched my eighty-five quid kick up her heels and canter down the field like a two-year-old. The farmer would no doubt be surprised to find an unclaimed brown mare on his land, but it would not be the first time a horse had been abandoned in that way, and I hadn't any doubt that he would give her a good home.

I turned away and walked back along the hill to the cottage. It was beginning to get dark, and the little building lay like a shadow in the hollow as I went down to it through the trees and bushes. All was very quiet, and I walked softly through the garden to the back window.

He was still standing there. When he saw me he said quite quietly 'Let me out.'

I shook my head.

'Well at least go and telephone the company, and tell them I'm ill. You can't let them all wait and wait for me to come, right up to the last minute.'

I didn't answer.

'Go and telephone,' he said again.

I shook my head.

He seemed to crumple inside. He stretched his

hands through the bars and rested his head against the window frames.

'Let me out.'

I said nothing.

'For pity's sake,' he said, 'let me out.'

For pity's sake.

I said, 'How long did you intend to leave me in that tack-room?'

His head snapped up as if I'd hit him. He drew his hands back and gripped the bars.

'I went back to untie you,' he said, speaking quickly, wanting to convince me. 'I went back straight after the programme was over, but you'd gone. Someone found you and set you free pretty soon, I suppose, since you were able to ride the next day.'

'And you went back to find the tack-room empty?' I said. 'So you knew I had come to no harm?'

'Yes,' he said eagerly. 'Yes, that's what happened. I wouldn't have left you there very long, because of the rope stopping your circulation.'

'You did think there was some danger of that, then?' I said innocently.

'Yes, of course there was, and that's why I wouldn't have left you there too long. If someone hadn't freed you first, I'd have let you go in good time. I only wanted to hurt you enough to stop you riding.' His voice was disgustingly persuasive, as if what he was saying were not abnormal.

'You're a liar,' I said calmly. 'You didn't go back to

untie me after your show. You would have found me
still there if you had. In fact it took me until midnight
to get free, because no one came. Then I found a
telephone and rang up for a car to fetch me, but by
the time it reached me, which was roughly two o'clock,
you had still not returned. When I got to Ascot the
following day, everyone was surprised to see me. There
was a rumour, they said, that I wouldn't turn up. You
even mentioned on television that my name in the
number frames was a mistake. Well . . . no one but you
had any reason to believe that I wouldn't arrive at the
races: so when I heard that rumour I knew that you
had not gone back to untie me, even in the morning.
You thought I was still swinging from that hook, in
God knows what state . . . and as I understand it, you
intended to leave me there indefinitely, until someone
found me by accident . . . or until I was dead.'

'No,' he said faintly.

I looked at him without speaking for a moment,
and then turned to walk away.

'All right,' he screamed suddenly, banging on the
bars with his fists. 'All right. I didn't care whether you
lived or died. Do you like that? Is that what you want
to hear? I didn't care if you died. I thought of you
hanging there with your arms swelling and going
black . . . with the agony going on and on . . . and I
didn't care. I didn't care enough to stay awake. I went
to bed. I went to sleep. I didn't care. I didn't care . . .
and I hope you like it.'

His voice cracked, and he sank down inside the room so that all I could see in the gathering dusk was the top of his fair head and the hands gripping the bars with the knuckles showing white through the skin.

'I hope you like it,' he said brokenly.

I didn't like it. Not one little bit. It made me feel distinctly sick.

I went slowly round into the front room and sat down again on the hay. I looked at my watch. It was a quarter-past six. Still three hours to wait: three hours in which the awful truth would slowly dawn on Kemp-Lore's colleagues in the television studio, three hours of anxious speculation and stop-gap planning, culminating in the digging out of a bit of old film to fill in the empty fifteen minutes and the smooth announcement, 'We regret that owing to the – er – illness of Maurice Kemp-Lore there will be no *Turf Talk* tonight.'

Or ever again, mates, I thought, if you did but know it.

As it grew dark the air got colder. It had been frosty all day, but with the disappearance of the sun the evening developed a sub-zero bite, and the walls of the unlived-in cottage seemed to soak it up. Kemp-Lore began kicking the door again.

'I'm cold,' he shouted. 'It's too cold.'

'Too bad,' I said, under my breath.

'Let me out,' he yelled.

I sat on the hay without moving. The wrist which

he had latched on to while we fought was uncomfortably sore, and blood had seeped through the bandage again. What the Scots doctor would have to say when he saw it I hated to think. The three warts would no doubt quiver with disapproval. I smiled at the picture.

Kemp-Lore kicked the door for a long time, trying to break through it, but he didn't succeed. At the same time he wasted a good deal of breath yelling that he was cold and hungry and that I was to let him out. I made no reply to him at all, and after about an hour of it the kicking and shouting stopped, and I heard him slither down the door as if exhausted and begin sobbing with frustration.

I stayed where I was and listened while he went on and on moaning and weeping in desolation. I listened to him without emotion; for I had cried too, in the tack-room.

The hands crawled round the face of my watch.

At a quarter to nine, when nothing could any longer save his programme, and even a message explaining his absence could scarcely be telephoned through in time, Kemp-Lore's decreasing sobs faded away altogether, and the cottage was quiet.

I got stiffly to my feet and went out into the front garden, breathing deeply in the clear air, with an easing sense of release. The difficult day was over, and the stars were bright in the frosty sky. It was a lovely night.

I walked along to the bushes and started Kemp-Lore's car, turning it and driving it back to the gate. Then for the last time I walked round the cottage to talk to him through the window, and he was standing there already, his face a pale blue behind the window frames.

'My car,' he said hysterically. 'I heard the engine. You're going to drive away in my car and leave me.'

I laughed. 'No. You are going to drive it away yourself. As fast and as far as you like. If I were you, I'd drive to the nearest airport and fly off. No one is going to like you very much when they've read those letters in the morning, and it will be only a day or two before the newspapers get on to it. As far as racing goes, you will certainly be warned off. Your face is too well-known in Britain for you to hide or change your name or get another job. And as you've got all night and probably most of tomorrow before the storm breaks and people start eyeing you with sneers and contempt, you can pack up and skip the country quite easily, without any fuss.'

'You mean ... I can go? Just go?' He sounded astounded.

'Just go,' I said, nodding. 'If you go quickly enough, you'll avoid the enquiry the stewards are bound to hold, and you'll avoid any charge they might think of slapping on you. You can get away to some helpful distant country where they don't know you, and you can start again from scratch.'

'I suppose I haven't much choice,' he murmured. His asthma was almost unnoticeable.

'And find a country where they don't have steeplechasing,' I finished.

He moaned sharply, and crashed his fists down on the window frame.

I went round into the cottage and in the light of Joanna's big torch unlocked the padlock and pushed open the door. He turned from the window and walked unsteadily towards me across the straw, shielding his ravaged face from the light. He went through the door, passed me without a glance, and stumbled down the path to his car; and I walked down the path behind him, shining the torch ahead. I propped the torch on top of the gate-post so as to leave my hands free in case I needed to use them, but there didn't seem to be much fight left in him.

He paused when he was sitting in his car, and with the door still wide open looked out at me.

'You don't understand,' he said, his voice shaking. 'When I was a boy I wanted to be a jockey. I wanted to ride in the Grand National, like my father. And then there was this thing about falling off... I'd see the ground rushing past under my horse and there would be this terrible sort of pain in my guts, and I sweated until I could pull up and get off. And then I'd be sick.'

He made a moaning noise and clutched his stomach at the memory. His face twisted. Then he said suddenly, fiercely, 'It made me feel good to see jockeys looking worried. I broke them up all right. It made me feel warm inside. Big.'

He looked up at me with renewed rage, and his voice thickened venomously.

'I hated you more than all the others. You rode too well for a new jockey and you were getting on too quickly. Everyone was saying "Give Finn the bad horses to ride, he doesn't know what fear is". It made me furious when I heard that. So I had you on my programme, remember? I meant to make you look a fool. It worked with Mathews, why not with you? But Axminster took you up and then Pankhurst broke his leg . . . I wanted to smash you so much that it gave me headaches. You walked about with that easy confidence of yours, as if you took your strength for granted, and too many people were getting to say you'd be champion one day . . .

'I waited for you to have a fall that looked fairly bad, and then I used the sugar. It worked. You know it worked. I felt ten feet tall, looking at your white face and listening to everyone sniggering about you. I watched you find out how it felt. I wanted to see you writhe when everyone you cared for said . . . like my father said to all his friends . . . that it was a pity about you . . . a pity you were a snivelling little coward, a pity you had no nerve . . . no nerve . . .'

His voice died away, and his hollowed eyes were

wide, unfocused, as if he were staring back into an unbearable past.

I stood looking down at the wreck of what could have been a great man. All that vitality, I thought; all that splendid talent wasted for the sake of hurting people who had not hurt him.

Such individuals could be understood, Claudius Mellit had said. Understood, and treated, and forgiven.

I could understand him in a way, I supposed, because I was myself the changeling in a family. But my father had rejected me kindly, and I felt no need to watch musicians suffer.

Treated . . . The treatment I had given him that day might not have cured the patient, but he would no longer spread his disease, and that was all I cared about.

Without another word I shut the car door on him and gestured to him to drive away. He gave me one more incredulous glance as if he still found it impossible that I should let him go, and began to fumble with the light switches, the ignition, and the gears.

I hoped he was going to drive carefully. I wanted him to live. I wanted him to live for years, thinking about what he had thrown away. Anything else would be too easy, I thought.

The car began to roll, and I caught a last glimpse of the famous profile, the eclipsed, exiled profile, as he slid away into the dark. The brake lights flashed red as he paused at the end of the lane, then he turned out into the road, and was gone. The sound of his engine died away.

I took the torch from the gate-post and walked up the path to the quiet cottage, to sweep it clean.

Forgiveness, I thought. That was something else again.

It would take a long time to forgive.

SMOKESCREEN

With thanks to Jane and Christopher Coldrey

INTRODUCTION

In 1971 I was asked to go to South Africa to take part in the Johannesburg International Horse Show, a two-week-long entertainment similar to the Olympia and Wembley indoor horse shows in London and Canada's Royal Winter Fair in Toronto. The invited party of about twenty international horse people included Olympic show-jumpers Piero d'Inzeo and Anneli Drummond Hay, who jumped local borrowed horses to dazzling effect. I went in the capacity of judge of varying classes of riding horses, a task which meant setting the horses in order according to their looks, and then riding them to see if they moved with presence, appointing winners overall.

My wife Mary and I stayed with the Show Director Christopher Coldrey on his farm out in the country, and in between performances he introduced us to South African private life. We spent a free weekend of three scorching days in the Kruger Park Game Reserve, eyeball to eyeball with lion, elephant, impala and giraffe, and were shown the back roads and hidden places by one of the senior game wardens. Naturally (for me) we went also to race meetings, and there met a man who invited us down his gold mine, offering a private conducted tour and invaluable knowledge.

Smokescreen, written after our return to England, unsurprisingly unfolds against a background of South African racing, a gold mine and blazing heat in the Kruger Park Game Reserve; and to this day, if I glance into the book, the beauty and the powerful sweet scent of the South African countryside fill my memory.

Edward Lincoln, the chief character, is an English film star, and for the authentic background of his job my wife and I went to the British film studios at Pinewood, where we were comprehensively shown how movies are made. We already counted many actors among our friends, as Mary had earlier worked behind the scenes in the theatre, so usefully I knew how good actors behave and think.

As a mix of all these experiences, together with humour and, of course, make believe, *Smokescreen* evolved.

This is not a political book, just a matter of fun and suspense.

CHAPTER ONE

Sweating, thirsty, hot, uncomfortable, and tired to the point of explosion.

Cynically, I counted my woes.

Considerable, they were. Considerable, one way and another.

I sat in the driving seat of a custom-built aerodynamic sports car, the cast-off toy of an oil sheik's son. I had been sitting there for the best part of three days. Ahead, the sun-dried plain spread gently away at some distant brown and purple hills, and hour by hour their hunched shapes remained exactly where they were on the horizon, because the 150 mph Special was not moving.

Nor was I. I looked morosely at the solid untarnishable handcuffs locked round my wrists. One of my arms led through the steering wheel, and the other was outside it, so that in total effect I was locked on to the wheel, and in consequence firmly attached to the car.

There was also the small matter of seat belts. The Special would not start until the safety harness was fastened. Despite the fact that the key was missing from

1

the ignition, the harness was securely fastened: one strap over my stomach, one diagonally across my chest.

I could not bring my legs up from their stretched-forward sports car position in order to break the steering wheel with my feet. I had tried it. I was too tall, and couldn't bend my knees far enough. And apart from that, the steering wheel was not of possibly breakable plastic. People who built spectacularly expensive cars like the Special didn't mess around with plastic wheels. This was one of the small-diameter leather-covered metal type, as durable as the Mont Blanc.

I was thoroughly fed up with sitting in the car. Every muscle in my legs, up my spine and down my arms protested energetically against the constraint. A hard band of heaviness behind my eyes was tightening into a perceptible ache.

It was time to make another determined effort to get free, though I knew from countless similar attempts that it couldn't be done.

I tugged, strained, used all my strength against the straps and the handcuffs: struggled until fresh sweat rolled down my face; and couldn't, as before, progress even a millimetre towards freedom.

I put my head back against the padded headrest, and rolled my face around towards the open window beside me, on my right.

I shut my eyes. I could feel the slash of sunlight cut across my cheek and neck and shoulder with all the vigour of 15.00 hours in July at 37° North. I could feel the heat on my left eyelid. I let lines of frustration and pain develop across my forehead, put a certain grimness into my mouth, twitched a muscle along my jaw, and swallowed with an abandonment of hope.

After that I sat still, and waited.

The desert plain was very quiet.

I waited.

Then Evan Pentelow shouted 'Cut' with detectable reluctance, and the cameramen removed their eyes from the view-finders. No whisper of wind fluttered the large bright-coloured umbrellas which shielded them and their apparatus. Evan fanned himself vigorously with his shooting schedule, creating the breeze that nature had neglected, and others in the small group in the shade of portable green polystyrene sun-shelters came languidly to life, the relentless heat having hours ago drained their energy. The sound mixer took off his ear-phones, hung them over the back of his chair, and fiddled slowly with the knobs on his Nagra recorder, and the electricians kindly switched off the clutch of minibrute lamps which had been ruthlessly reinforcing the sun.

I looked into the lens of the Arriflex which had been recording every sweating pore at a distance of six feet from my right shoulder. Terry, behind his camera, mopped his neck with a dusty handkerchief, and Simon added to his Picture Negative Report for the processing laboratory.

Further back, from a different angle, the Mitchell, with its thousand-feet magazine, had shot the same scene. Lucky, who operated it, was busily not meeting my eye, as he had been since breakfast. He believed I was angry with him, because, although he swore it was not his fault, the last lot of film he had shot the day before had turned out to be fogged. I had asked him quite mildly in the circumstances just to be sure that today there should be no more mishaps, as I reckoned I couldn't stand many more retakes of Scene 623.

Since then, we had retaken it six times. With, I grant you, a short break for lunch.

Evan Pentelow had apologized to everyone, loudly and often, that we would just have to go on and on shooting the scene until I got it right. He changed his mind about how it should go after every second take, and although I followed a good many of his minutely detailed directions, he had not yet once pronounced himself satisfied.

Every single member of the team who had come to southern Spain to complete the location shots was aware of the animosity behind the tight-reined politeness with which he spoke to me, and behind that with which I answered him. The unit, I had heard, had opened a book on how long I would hang on to my temper.

The girl who carried the precious key to the handcuffs walked slowly over from the furthest green shelter, where the continuity, make-up, and wardrobe girls sat exhaustedly on spread-out towels. Tendrils of damp hair clung to the girl's neck as she opened the door of the car and fitted the key into the hole. They were regulation

British police handcuffs, fastening with a stiffish screw instead of a ratchet, and she always had some difficulty in pushing the key round its last few all-important turns.

She looked at me apprehensively, knowing that I couldn't be far from erupting. I achieved at least the muscle movements of a smile, and relief at not being bawled at gave her impetus to finish taking off the handcuffs smoothly and quickly.

I unfastened the seat harness and stood up stiffly outside in the sun. It was a good ten degrees cooler than inside the Special.

'Get back in,' Evan said. 'We'll have to take it again.'

I inhaled a lungful straight from the Sahara, and counted five in my mind. Then I said, 'I'm going over to the caravan for a beer and a pee, and we'll shoot it again when I come back.'

They wouldn't pay out the pool on that, I thought in amusement. That might be a crack in the volcano, but it wasn't Krakatoa. I wondered if they would let me take a bet on the flashpoint myself.

No one had bothered to put the canvas over the Mini-moke, to shield it from the sun. I climbed into the little buggy where it was parked behind the largest shelter, and swore as the seat leather scorched through my thin cotton trousers. The steering wheel was hot enough to fry eggs.

The legs of my trousers were rolled up to the knee, and on my feet were flip-flops. They contrasted oddly with the formal white shirt and dark tie which I wore above, but then the Arriflex angle cut me off at the knee, and the Mitchell higher still, above the waist.

I drove the Moke without haste to where the semi-circle of caravans was parked, two hundred yards away in a hollow. An apology for a tree cast a patch of thinnish shade that was better than nothing for the Moke, so I stopped it there and walked over to the caravan assigned to me as a dressing-room.

The air-conditioning inside hit like a cold shower, and felt marvellous. I loosened my tie, undid the top button of my shirt, fetched a can of beer from the refrigerator, and sat down wearily on the divan to drink it.

Evan Pentelow was busy paying off an old resent-ment, and unfortunately there was no way I could stop him. I had worked with him only once before, on his first major film and my seventh, and by the end of it we had detested each other. Nothing had improved by my subsequently refusing to sign for films if he were to direct, a circumstance which had cut him off from at least two smash hits he might otherwise have collared.

Evan was the darling of those critics who believed that actors couldn't act unless the director told them inch by inch what to do. Evan never gave directions by halves: he liked to see his films called 'Evan Pentelow's latest', and he achieved that by making the gullible believe that step by tiny step the whole thing stemmed from his talent, and his alone. Never mind how old a hand an actor was, Evan remorselessly taught him his business. Evan never *discussed* how a scene should be played, how a word should be inflected. He dictated.

He had cut some great names down to size, down to notices like 'Pentelow has drawn a sympathic performance from Miss Five-Star Blank ...' He resented everyone, like me, who wouldn't give him the chance.

There was no doubt that he was an outstanding director in that he had a visual imagination of a very high quality. Most actors positively liked to work with him, as their salaries were generous and his films never went unsung. Only uncompromising bloody asses like myself believed that at least nine-tenths of a performance should be the actor's own work.

I sighed, finished the beer, visited the loo, and went out to the Moke. Apollo still raged away in the brazen sky, as one might say if one had a taste for that sort of thing.

The original director of the glossy action thriller on which we were engaged had been a quiet-spoken sophisticate who usually lifted the first elbow before breakfast and had died on his feet at 10 AM, from a surfeit of Scotch. It happened during a free weekend which I had spent alone in Yorkshire walking on the hills, and I had returned to the set on Tuesday to find Evan already ensconced and making his stranglehold felt.

There was about an eighth of the film still to do. The sly smile that he had put on when he saw me arrive had been pure clotted malice.

Protestations to the management had brought sooth-ing noises but no joy.

'No one else of that calibre was free ... can't take risks with the backers' money, can we, not as things are these days ... got to look at it realistically ... Sure, Link, I know you won't work with him ordinarily, but this is a *crisis*, dammit ... it isn't actually in your contract in black and white this time, you know, because I checked ... well, actually, we were relying on your good nature, I suppose ...'

I interrupted dryly, 'And on the fact that I'll be collect-ing four per cent of the gross?'

The management cleared its throat. 'Er, we wouldn't ourselves have made the mistake of reminding you ... but since you mention it ... yes.'

Amused, I had finally given in, but with foreboding, as the location scenes of the car all lay ahead. I had known Evan would be difficult: hadn't reckoned, though, that he would be the next best thing to sadistic.

I stopped the Moke with a jerk behind the shelter and pulled the canvas cover over it to stop it sizzling. I had been away exactly twelve minutes, but when I walked round into the shelter Evan was apologizing to the camera crews for my keeping them hanging around in this heat. Terry made a disclaiming gesture, as I could see perfectly well that he had barely finished loading the Arriflex with a fresh magazine out of the ice box. No one bothered to argue. At a hundred degrees in the shade, no one but Evan had any energy.

'Right,' he said briskly. 'Get into the car, Link. Scene 623, Take 10. And let's for hell's sake get this one right.'

I said nothing. Of the nine previous takes, three had been fogged: that left today's six; and I knew, as everyone else knew, that Evan could have used any one of them.

I got into the car. We retook the scene twice more.

Evan managed to shake his head dubiously even after that, but the head cameraman told him the light was getting too yellow, and even if they took any more it would be no good, as they wouldn't be able to match it to the scene which went before. Evan gave in only because he could come up with no possible reason for going on, for which Apollo had my thanks.

The unit packed up. The girl came limply across and undid the handcuffs. Two general duty men began to wrap up the Special in dust-sheets and pegged-down tarpaulins, and Terry and Lucky began to dismantle their cameras and pack them in cases, to take them away for the night.

In twos and threes everyone straggled across to the caravans, with me driving Evan in the Moke and saying not a word to him on the way. The coach had arrived from the small nearby town of Madroledo, bringing the two night-watchmen. Coach was a flattering word for it: an old airport runabout bus with a lot of room for equipment and minimum comfort for passengers. The company said they had stipulated a luxury touring coach with air-conditioning, but the bone-shaker was what had actually turned up.

The hotel in Madroledo where the whole unit was staying was in much the same category. The small inland town, far from the tourist beat, offered amenities that package holiday operators would have blanched at; but the management had had to install us there, they said, because the best hotels on the coast at Almeria were booked solid by hundreds of Americans engaged on making an epic western in the next bit of desert to ours.

In fact I much preferred even the rough bits of this film to the last little caper I had been engaged on, a misty rock-climbing affair in which I had spent days and days clinging to the ledges while the effects men showered buckets of artificial rainstorm over my head. It was never much good my complaining about the occasional wringers I got put through: I'd started out as a sort of stunt man, they said, so what was a little cold, a little heat? Get out there on the ledges, they said. Get out there in the car. And just concentrate on how much lolly you're stacking away to comfort you later through arthritis. Never fear, they said, we won't let you come to any real harm, not so long as the insurance premiums are so high, and not so long as almost every film you make covers its production costs in the first month of showing. Such charming people, those managements, with dollar signs for eyes, cash registers for hearts.

Cooler and cleaner, the entire unit met for before-dinner drinks in Madroledo's idea of an American Bar.

Away out on the plain in the warm night the Special sat under its guarding floodlights, a shrouded hump, done with the day. By tomorrow night, I thought, or at least the day after, we would have completed all the scenes which needed me stuck in the driving seat. Provided Evan could think of no reason for reshooting Scene 623 yet again, we only had 624 and 625 to do, the cavalry-to-the-rescue bits. We had done Scenes 622 and 621, which showed the man waking from a drugged sleep and assessing his predicament, and the helicopter shots were also in the can; the wide-circling and then narrowing aerial views which established the Special in its bare lonely terrain, and gave glimpses of the man slumped inside. Those were to be the opening shots of the film and the background to the credits, the bulk to the story being told afterwards in one long flashback to explain why the car and the man were where they were.

In the bar Terry and the Director of Photography were holding a desultory discussion about focal lengths, punctuating every wise thought with draughts of sangria. The Director, otherwise known professionally as the lighting cameraman, and personally as Conrad, patted me gently on the shoulder and pressed an almost cold glass into my hand. We had all grown to like this indigenous thirst quencher, a rough red local wine diluted by ice and a touch of the fruit salads.

'There you are, dear boy, it does wonders for the dehydration,' he said, and then in the same breath finished his broken-off sentence to Terry. 'So he used

11

an eighteen-millimetre wide-angle and of course every scrap of tension evaporated from the scene.'

Conrad spoke from the strength of an Oscar on the sideboard, and called everyone 'dear boy', from chairmen downwards. Aided by a naturally resonant bass voice and a droopy cultivated moustache, he had achieved the notable status of 'a character' in a business which specialized in them, but behind the flamboyance there was a sharp technician's mind which saw life analytically at twenty-four frames per second and thought in Eastman-colour.

Terry said, 'Beale Films won't use him now because of the time he shot two thousand feet one day at Ascot without an 85 filter, and there wasn't another race meeting due there until a month after they ran into compensation time . . .'

Terry was fat, bald, forty, and had given up earlier aspirations to climb to Director of Photography with his name writ large in credits. He had settled instead for being a steady, reliable, experienced, and continually in-work craftsman, and Conrad always liked to have him on his team.

Simon joined us and Conrad gave him, too, a glass of sangria. Simon, the clapper/loader of Terry's crew, had less assurance than he ought to have had at twenty-three, and was sometimes naïve to the point where one speculated about arrested development. His job entailed operating the clapper board before every shot, keeping careful records of the type and footage of film used, and loading the raw film into the magazines which were used in the cameras.

Terry himself had taught him how to load the magazines, a job which meant winding unexposed film on to reels, in total darkness and by feel only. Everyone, to begin with, learned how to do it with unwanted exposed film in a well-lit room, and practised it over and over until they could do it with their eyes shut. When Simon could do this faultlessly, Terry sent him to load some magazines in earnest, and it was not until after a long day's shooting that the laboratory discovered all the film to be completely black.

Simon, it appeared, had done exactly what he had been taught: gone into the loading room and threaded the film on to the magazine with his eyes shut. And left the electric light on while he did it.

He took a sip of his pink restorer, looked at the others in bewilderment, and said, 'Evan told me to write "print" against every one of those shots we took today.' He searched their faces for astonishment and found none. 'But, I say,' he protested, 'if all the first takes were good enough to print, why on earth did he go on doing so many?'

No one answered except Conrad, who looked at him with pity and said, 'Work it out, dear boy. Work it out.' But Simon hadn't the equipment.

The bar room was large and cool, with thick white-painted walls and a brown tiled floor: pleasant in the daytime, when we were seldom there, but too stark at night because of the glaring striplighting some insensitive soul had installed on the ceiling. The four girls, sitting languidly round a table with half-empty glasses of lime juice and Bacardi and soda, took on a greenish tinge as the sunlight faded outside, and aged ten years. The pouches beneath Conrad's eyes developed shadows, and Simon's chin receded too far for flattery.

Another long evening stretched ahead, exactly like the nine that had gone before: several hours of shop and gossip punctuated by occasional brandies, cigars and a Spanish-type dinner. I hadn't even any lines to learn for the next day, as my entire vocal contribution to Scenes 624 and 625 was to be a variety of grunts and mumbles. I would be glad, I thought, by God I would be glad, to get back home.

We went in to eat in a private dining-room as uninviting as the bar. I found myself between Simon and the handcuffs girl, two-thirds of the way along one side of the long table at which we all sat together haphazardly. About twenty-five of us, there were: all technicians of some sort except me and the actor due to amble to the rescue as a Mexican peasant. The group had been cut to a minimum, and our stay scheduled for as short a time as possible: the management had wanted even the desert scenes shot at Pinewood like the rest of the film, or at least on some dried-up bit of England, but the original director had stuck out for the authentic shimmer of real heat, damn and bless his departed spirit.

There was an empty space around the far side of the table.

No Evan.

'He's telephoning,' the handcuffs girl said. 'I think he's been telephoning ever since we came back.'

I nodded. Evan telephoned the management most evenings, though not normally at great length. He was probably having difficulty getting through.

'I'll be glad to go home,' the girl said, sighing. Her first location job, which she had looked forward to, was proving disappointing; boring, too hot and no fun. Jill – her real name was Jill, though Evan had started calling her Handcuffs, and most of the unit had copied him – slid a speculative look sideways at my face, and added, 'Won't you?'

'Yes,' I said neutrally.

Conrad, sitting opposite, snorted loudly. 'Handcuffs, dear girl, that's cheating. Anyone who prods him has her bet cancelled.'

'It wasn't a prod,' she said defensively.

'Next best thing.'

'Just how many of you are in this pool?' I asked sarcastically.

'Everyone except Evan,' Conrad admitted cheerfully. 'Quite a healthy little jackpot it is.'

'And has anyone lost their money yet?'

Conrad chuckled. 'Most of them, dear boy. This afternoon.'

'And you,' I said, 'have you?'

He narrowed his eyes at me and put his head on one side. 'You've a temper that blows the roof off, but usually on behalf of someone else.'

'He can't answer your question, you see,' Jill explained to me. 'That's against the rules too.'

But I had worked with Conrad on three previous films, and he had indeed told me where he had placed his bet.

Evan came back from telephoning, walked purposefully to his empty chair, and splashed busily into his turtle soup. Intent, concentrated, he stared at the table and either didn't hear, or didn't wish to hear, Terry's tentative generalities.

I looked at Evan thoughtfully. At forty he was wiry, of medium height and packed with aggressive energy. He had undisciplined black curling hair, a face in which even the bones looked determined, and fierce hot brown eyes. That evening the eyes were looking inwards, seeing visions in his head; and the tumultuous activity going on in there showed unmistakably in the tension in his muscles. His spoon was held in rigid fingers, and his neck and back were as stiff as stakes.

I didn't like his intensity, not at any time or in any circumstances. It always set up in me the unreasonable reaction of wanting to avoid doing what he was pressing for, even when his ideas made good sense. That evening he was building up a good head of steam, and my own antipathy rose to match.

He shovelled his way briskly through the anglicized

paella which followed, and pushed his empty plate away decisively.

'Now . . .' he said: and everybody listened. His voice sounded loud and high, strung up with his inner urgency. It would have been impossible to sit in that room and ignore him.

'As you know, this film we are making is called *Man in a Car.*'

We knew.

'And as you know, the car has figured in at least half the scenes that have been shot.'

We knew that too, better than he did, as we had been with it all through.

'Well . . .' he paused, looking round the table, collecting eyes. 'I have been talking to the producer, and he agrees . . . I want to change the emphasis . . . change the whole shape of the film. There are going to be a number of flashbacks now, and not just one. The story will jump back every time from the desert scene and each desert shot will give an impression of the days passing, and show the man growing weaker. There is to be no rescue, as such. This means, I'm afraid, Stephen . . .' He looked directly at the other actor, '. . . that your part is out entirely, but you will of course be paid what was agreed.' He turned back to the unit in general. 'We are going to scrap those cool witty scenes of reunion with the girl that you did at Pinewood. Instead, we will end the film with the reverse of the opening. That is to say, a helicopter shot that starts with the car in close-up and gradually

17

recedes from it until it is merely a dot on the plain. The view will widen just at the end to indicate a peasant walking along a ridge of hill, leading a donkey, and everyone who sees the film can decide for himself whether the peasant rescues the man, or passes by without seeing him.'

He cleared his throat into a wholly attentive silence. 'This of course means that we shall have to do much more work here on location. I estimate that we will be here for at least another two weeks, as there will have to be many more scenes of Link in the car.'

Someone groaned. Evan looked fiercely in the direction of the protest, and silenced it effectively. Only Conrad made any actual comment.

'I'm glad I'm behind the camera, and not in front of it,' he said slowly. 'Link's showing wear and tear already.'

I pushed the last two bits of chicken around with my fork, not really seeing my plate. Conrad was staring across at me: I could feel his eyes. And all the others', too. It was the actor in me, I knew, which kept them waiting while I ate a mouthful, drank some wine, and finally looked up again at Evan.

'All right,' I said.

A sort of quiver ran through the unit, and I realized they had all been holding their breath for the explosion of the century. But setting my own feelings aside, I had to admit that what Evan had suggested made excellent film sense, and I trusted to that instinct, if not to his humanity. There was a lot I would do, to make a good film.

He was surprised at my unconditional agreement, but also excited by it. Visions poured out of him, faster than his tongue.

'There will be tears . . . and skin cracks, and sun blisters . . . and terrible thirst . . . and muscles and tendons quivering with strain like violin strings, and hands curled with cramp . . . and agony and frightful despair . . . and the scorching, inexorable, thunderous silence . . . and towards the end, the gradual disintegration of a human soul . . . so that even if he is rescued he will be different . . . and there won't be a single person who sees the film who doesn't leave exhausted and wrung out and filled with pictures he'll never forget.'

The camera crews listened with an air of we've-seen-all-this-before and the make-up girl began looking particularly thoughtful. It was only I who seemed to see it from the inside looking out, and I felt a shudder go through my gut as if it had been a real dying I was to do, and not pretence. It was foolish. I shook myself; shook off the illusion of personal involvement. To be any good, acting had to be deliberate, not emotional.

He paused in his harangue, waiting with fixed gaze for me to answer him, and I reckoned that if I were not to let him stampede all over me it was time to contribute something myself.

'Noise,' I said calmly.

'What . . .?'

19

'Noise,' I repeated. 'He would make a noise, too, at first. Shouting for help. Shouting from fury, and hunger, and terror. Shouting his bloody head off.'

Evan's eyes widened and embraced the truth of it.

'Yes,' he said. He took a deep ecstatic breath at the thought of his idea taking actual shape. '. . . Yes.'

Some of the inner furnace died down to a saner, more calculating heat.

'Will you do it?' he said.

I knew he meant not Would I just get through the scenes somehow, but Would I put into them the best I could. And he might well ask, after his behaviour to me that day. I would, I thought; I would make it bloody marvellous; but I answered him flippantly.

'There won't be a dry eye in the house.'

He looked irritated and disappointed, which would do no harm. The others relaxed and began talking, but some undercurrent of excitement had awoken, and it was the best evening we had had since we arrived.

So we went back to the desert plain for another two weeks, and it was lousy, but the glossy little adventure turned into an eventual box-office blockbuster which even the critics seemed to like.

I got through the whole fortnight with my temper intact; and in consequence Conrad, who had guessed right, won his bet and scooped the pool.

CHAPTER TWO

England in August seemed green and cool in comparison when I got back. At Heathrow I collected my car, a production line BMW, darkish blue, ordinarily jumbled registration number, nothing Special about it, and drove westwards into Berkshire with a feeling of ease.

Four o'clock in the afternoon.

Going home.

I found myself grinning at nothing in particular. Like a kid out of school, I thought. Going home to a summer evening.

The house was middle-sized, part old, part new, built on a gentle slope outside a village far up the Thames. There was a view down over the river, and lots of evening sun, and an unsignposted lane to approach by, that most people missed.

There was a boy's bicycle lying half on the grass, half on the drive, and some gardening tools near a half-weeded flowerbed. I stopped the car outside the garage, looked at the shut front door, and walked round the house to the back.

I saw all four of them before they saw me; like looking in through a window. Two small boys splashing in the pool with a black and white beach ball. A slightly faded sun umbrella nearby, with a little girl lying on an air bed in its shade. A young woman with short chestnut hair, sitting on a rug in the sun, hugging her knees.

One of the boys looked up and saw me standing watching them from across the lawn.

'Hey,' he shouted. 'Dad's home,' and ducked his brother.

I walked towards them, smiling. Charlie unstuck herself from the rug and came unhurriedly to meet me.

'Hi,' she said. 'I'm covered in oil.' She put her mouth forward for a kiss and held my face between the insides of her wrists.

'What on earth have you been doing with yourself?' she asked. 'You look terribly thin.'

'It was hot in Spain,' I said. I walked back to the pool beside her, stripping off my loosened tie, and then my shirt.

'You didn't get very sunburned.'

'No . . . Sat in the car most of the time . . .'

'Did it go all right?'

I made a face. 'Time will tell . . . How are the kids?'

'Fine.'

I had been away a month. It might have been a day. Any father coming home to his family after a day's work.

Peter levered himself out of the pool via his stomach and splashed across the grass.

22

'What did you bring us?' he demanded.

'Pete, I've *told* you . . .' Charlie said, exasperated. 'If you ask, you won't *get*.'

'You won't get much this time anyway,' I told him. 'We were miles from any decent shops. And go and pick your bike up off the drive.'

'Oh, honestly,' he said. 'The minute you're home, we've done something wrong.' He retreated round the house, his backview stiff with protest.

Charlie laughed. 'I'm glad you're back . . .'

'Me too.'

'Dad, look at me. Look at me do this, Dad.'

I obediently watched while Chris turned some complicated sort of somersault over the beach ball and came up with a triumphant smile, shaking water out of his eyes and waiting for praise.

'Jolly good,' I said.

'Watch me again, Dad . . .'

'In a minute.'

Charlie and I walked over to the umbrella, and looked down at our daughter. She was five years old, brown-haired, and pretty. I sat down beside the air bed and tickled her tummy. She chuckled, and smiled at me deliciously.

'How's she been?'

'Same as usual.'

'Shall I take her in the pool?'

'She came in with me this morning . . . but she loves it. It wouldn't do her any harm to go again.'

Charlie squatted down beside her. 'Daddy's home, little one,' she said. But to Libby, our little one, the words themselves meant almost nothing. Her mental development had slowed to a snail's pace after the age of ten months, when her skull had been fractured. Peter, who had been five then, had lifted her out of her pram, wanting to be helpful and bring her indoors for lunch. But Charlie, going out to fetch her, had seen him trip and fall and it had been Libby's head which struck the stone step on the terrace of the flat we then occupied in London. The baby had been stunned, but after an hour or two the doctors could find nothing wrong with her.

It was only two or three weeks later that she felt sick, and later still, when she was surviving a desperate illness, that the hospital doctors told us she had had a hair-line fracture at the base of the brain, which had become infected and given her meningitis. We were so relieved that she was alive that we scarcely took notice of the cautiously phrased warnings . . . 'We must not be surprised if she were a little late in developing . . .' Of course she would be a little late after being so ill. But she would soon catch up, wouldn't she? And we dismissed the dubious expression, and that unfamiliar word 'retarded'.

During the next year we learned what it meant, and in facing such a mammoth disaster had also discovered much about ourselves. Before the accident, our marriage had been shaking towards disintegration under the onslaughts of prosperity and success: after it, we had gradually cemented ourselves together again, with a much clearer view of what was really important, and what was not.

We had left the bright lights, the adulation, and the whoopee, and gone to live in the country, where anyway both of us had our original roots. Better for the kids, we said; and knew it was better for us, too.

Libby's state no longer caused us any acute grief. It was just part of life, accepted and accustomed. She was treated with good humour by the boys, with love by Charlie, and with gentleness by me; and as she was seldom ill and seemed to be happy enough, it could have been a lot worse.

It had proved harder in the end to grow skins against the reactions of strangers, but after all these years neither Charlie nor I gave a damn what anyone said. So maybe Libby couldn't talk yet, couldn't walk steadily, fed herself messily, and was not reliably continent: but she was our daughter, and that was that.

I went into the house, changed into swimming trunks, and took her with me into the pool. She was slowly learning to swim, and had no fear of the water. She splashed around happily in my grasp, patted my face with wet palms and called me 'Dada', and wound her arms around my neck and clung to me like a little limpet.

After a bit I handed her over to Charlie to dry, and played water polo (of sorts) with Peter and Chris, and after twenty minutes of that decided that even Evan Pentelow was a lesser task master.

25

'More, Dad,' they said, and 'I *say*, Dad, you aren't getting out already, are you?'

'Yes,' I said firmly, and dried myself sitting beside Charlie on the rug.

She put the kids to bed while I unpacked, and I read them stories while she cooked, and we spent the evening by ourselves, eating chicken and watching an old movie (from before my days) on television. After that we stacked the dishes in the washer and went to bed.

We had no one else living in the house with us. On four mornings a week a woman walked up from the village to help with the chores, and there was also a retired nurse there who would always come to look after Libby and the boys if we wanted to go out. These arrangements were Charlie's own choice: I had married a quiet, intelligent girl who had grown into a practical, down-to-earth, and, to her own surprise, domesticated woman. Since we had left London she had developed an added strength which one could only call serenity, and although she could on occasion lose her temper as furiously as I could, her foundations were now built on rock.

A lot of people in the film world, I knew, thought my wife unexciting and my home life a drag, and expected me to break out in blondes and red-heads, like a rash. But I had very little in common with the sort of larger-than-life action man I played in film after film. They were my work, and I worked hard at them, but I didn't take them home.

Charlie snuggled beside me under the duvet and put

26

her head on my chest. I smoothed my hands over her bare skin, feeling the ripple deep in her abdomen and the faint tremble in her legs.

'OK?' I asked, kissing her hair.

'Very . . .'

We made love in the simple, ordinary way, as we always did; but because I had been away a month it was one of the best times, one of the breathtaking, fundamental, indescribable times which became a base to live from. Certainty begins here, I thought. With this, what else did one need?

'Fantastic,' Charlie sighed. 'That was *fantastic*.'

'Remind us to do it less often.'

She laughed. 'It does improve with keeping . . .'

'Mm.' I yawned.

'I say,' she said, 'I was reading a magazine in the dentist's waiting-room this morning while Chris was having his teeth done, and there was a letter in it on the sob-stuff page, from a woman who had a bald fat middle-aged husband she didn't fancy, and she was asking for advice on her sex life. And do you know what advice they gave her?' There was a smile in her voice. 'It was, "Imagine you are sleeping with Edward Lincoln".'

'That's silly.' I yawned again.

'Yeah . . . Actually, I thought of writing in and asking what advice they would give *me*.'

'Probably tell you to imagine you're sleeping with some fat bald middle-aged man you don't fancy.'

She chuckled. 'Maybe I will be, in twenty years' time.'

'You are so kind.'

'Think nothing of it.'

We drifted contentedly to sleep.

I had a racehorse, a steeplechaser, in training with a thriving stable about five miles away, and I used to go over when I was not working and ride out with the string at morning exercise. Bill Tracker, the energetic trainer, did not in general like to have owners who wanted to ride their horses, but he put up with my intermittent presence on the same two counts as his stable lads did, namely that my father had once been a head lad along in Lambourn, and that I had also at one time earned my living by riding, even if not in races.

There wasn't much doing in August, but I went over, a couple of days after my return, and rode out on the Downs. The new jumping season had barely begun, and most of the horses, including my own, were still plodding round the roads to strengthen their legs. Bill generously let me take out one of the more forward hurdlers which was due to have its first run in two weeks or so, and as usual I much appreciated the chance he gave me to ride to some useful purpose, and to shake the dust off the one skill I had been born with.

I had learned to ride before I could walk, and had grown up intending to be a jockey. But the fates weren't kind: I was six feet tall when I was seventeen, and whatever special something it took to be a racer, I hadn't got.

The realization had been painful. The switch to jigging along in films, a wretched second best.

Ironic, to remember that.

The Downs were wide and windy and covered in breathable air: nice and primaeval still, except for the power station on the horizon and the distant slash of the motorway. We walked and trotted up to the gallops, cantered, galloped where and when bidden, and walked down again, cooling the horses off; and it was absolutely great.

I stayed to breakfast with the Trackers and rode my own horse afterwards with the second lot round the roads, cursing like the rest of the lads at the cars which didn't slow down to pass. I relaxed easily in the saddle and smiled as I remembered how my father had yelled himself hoarse at me – 'Sit *up*, you bloody boy. And keep your elbows *in*.'

Evan Pentelow and Madroledo were in another world.

When I got back the boys were squabbling noisily over whose turn it was with the unbroken roller skates, and Charlie was making a cake.

'Hi,' she said. 'Did you have a good ride?'

'Great.'

'Fine . . . Well there weren't any calls, except Nerissa rang . . . Will you two be *quiet*, we can't hear ourselves think . . .'

29

'It's *my* turn,' Peter yelled.

'If you two don't both shut up I'll twist your ears,' I said.

They shut up. I'd never carried out the often repeated threat, but they didn't like the idea of it. Chris immediately pinched the disputed skates and disappeared out of the kitchen, and Peter gave chase with muted yells.

'Kids!' Charlie said disgustedly.

I scooped out a fingerful of raw cake mixture and got my wrist slapped.

'What did Nerissa want?'

'She wants us to go to lunch.' Charlie paused, with the wooden spoon dropping gouts of chocolate goo into the bowl. 'She was a bit . . . well . . . odd, in a way. Not her usual brisk self. Anyway, she wanted us to go today . . .'

'Today!' I said, looking at the clock.

'Oh, I told her we couldn't, that you wouldn't be back until twelve. So she asked if we could make it tomorrow.'

'Why the rush?'

'Well, I don't know, darling. She just said, could we come as soon as poss. Before you got tied up in another film, she said.'

'I don't start the next one until November.'

'Yes, I told her that. Still, she was pretty insistent. So I said we'd love to go tomorrow unless you couldn't, in which case I'd ring back this lunch time.'

'I wonder what she wants,' I said. 'We haven't seen her for ages. We'd better go, don't you think?'

'Oh yes, of course.'

So we went.

It is just as well one can never foresee the future.

Nerissa was a sort of cross between an aunt, a god-mother, and a guardian, none of which I had ever actually had. I had had a stepmother who loved her two precious children exclusively, and a busy father nagged by her to distraction. Nerissa, who had owned three horses in the yard where my father reigned, had given me first sweets, then pound notes, then encouragement, and then, as the years passed, friendship. It had never been a close relationship, but always a warmth in the background.

She was waiting for us, primed with crystal glasses and a decanter of dry sherry on a silver tray, in the summer sitting-room of her Cotswold house, and she rose to meet us when she heard her manservant bringing us through the hall.

'Come on, my dears, come in,' she said. 'How lovely to see you. Charlotte, I love you in yellow . . . and Edward, how very thin you are . . .'

She had her back to the sunlight which poured in through the window framing the best view in Gloucestershire, and it was only when we each in turn kissed her offered cheek that we could see the pitiful change in her.

The last time I had seen her she had been an attract-ive woman of fifty plus, with young blue eyes and an apparently indestructible vitality. Her walk seemed to be on the edge of dancing, and her voice held a wise sense of humour. She came from the blue-blooded end of the Stud Book and had what my father had succinctly described as 'class'.

But now, within three months, her strength had vanished and her eyes were dull. The gloss on her hair, the spring in her step, the laugh in her voice: all were gone. She looked nearer seventy than fifty, and her hands trembled.

'Nerissa,' Charlie exclaimed in a sort of anguish, for she, like me, held her in much more than affection.

'Yes, dear. Yes,' Nerissa said comfortingly. 'Now sit down, dear, and Edward shall pour you some sherry.'

I poured all three of us some of the fine pale liquid, but Nerissa hardly sipped hers at all. She sat in a gold brocade chair in a long-sleeved blue linen dress, with her back to the sun and her face in shadow.

'How are those two little monkeys?' she asked. 'And how is dear little Libby? And Edward, my dear, being so thin doesn't suit you . . .' She talked on, making practised conversation and looking interested in our answers, and gave us no opening to ask what was the matter with her.

When she went into the dining-room it was with the help of a walking stick and my arm, and the feather-light lunch which had been geared to her needs did nothing to restore my lost pounds. Afterwards, we went slowly back to the summer-room for coffee.

'Do smoke, Edward dear . . . There are some cigars in

the cupboard. You know how I love the smell . . . and so few people smoke here, nowadays.'

I imagined they didn't because of her condition, but if she wanted it, I would, even though I rarely did, and only in the evening. They were Coronas, but a little dry from old age. I lit one, and she inhaled the smoke deeply, and smiled with real pleasure.

'That's so good,' she said.

Charlie poured the coffee but again Nerissa hardly drank. She settled back gently into the same chair as before, and crossed her elegant ankles.

'Now, my dears,' she said calmly, 'I shall be dead by Christmas.'

We didn't even make any contradictory noises. It was all too easy to believe.

She smiled at us. 'So sensible, you two are. No silly swooning, or making a fuss.' She paused. 'It appears I have some stupid ailment, and they tell me there isn't much to be done. As a matter of fact, it's what they *do* do which is making me feel so ill. Before, it wasn't so bad . . . but I have had to have X-rays so often . . . and now all these horrid cytotoxic drugs, and really, they make me most unwell.' She managed another smile. 'I've asked them to stop, but you know what it's like . . . if they can, they say they must. Quite an unreasonable view to take, don't you think? Anyway, my dears, that need not trouble you . . .'

'But you would like us to do something for you?' Charlie suggested.

Nerissa looked surprised. 'How did you know I had anything like that in mind?'

'Oh . . . Because you wanted us in a hurry . . . and you must have known for weeks how ill you were.'

'Edward, how clever your Charlotte is,' she said. 'Yes, I do want something . . . want Edward to do something for me, if he will.'

'Of course,' I said.

A dry amusement crept back into her voice. 'Wait until you hear what it is, before you promise so glibly.'

'OK.'

'It is to do with my horses.' She paused to consider, her head inclined to one side. 'They are running so badly.'

'But,' I said, in bewilderment, 'they haven't been out yet, this season.'

She still had two steeplechasers trained in the yard where I had grown up, and although since my father's death I had no direct contact with them, I knew they had won a couple of races each the season before.

She shook her head. 'Not the jumpers, Edward. My other horses. Five colts and six fillies, running on the flat.'

'On the flat? I'm sorry . . . I didn't realize you had any.'

'In South Africa.'

'Oh.' I looked at her a bit blankly. 'I don't know anything about South African racing. I'm awfully sorry. I'd love to be of use to you . . . but I don't know enough to begin to suggest why your horses there are running badly.'

'It's nice of you, Edward dear, to look disappointed. But you really can help me, you know. If you will.'

'Just tell him how,' Charlie said, 'and he'll do it. He'll do anything for you, Nerissa.'

At that time, and in those circumstances, she was right. The finality of Nerissa's condition made me sharply aware of how much I had always owed her: not in concrete terms as much as in the feeling that she was *there*, interested and caring about what I did. In my motherless teens, that had meant a lot.

She sighed. 'I've been writing to my trainer out there about it, and he seems very puzzled. He doesn't know why my horses are running badly, because all the others he trains are doing all right. But it takes so long for letters to pass . . . the postal services at both ends seem to be so erratic these days. And I wondered, Edward, my dear, if you could possibly . . . I mean, I know it's a good deal to ask . . . but could you possibly give me a week of your time, and go out there and find out what's happening?'

There was a small silence. Even Charlie did not rush to say that of course I would go, although it was clear already that it would have to be a matter of how, not of whether.

Nerissa went on persuasively, 'You see, Edward, you do know about racing. You know what goes on in a stable, and things like that. You could see, couldn't you, if there is something wrong with their training? And then of course you are so good at investigating things . . .'

'I'm what?' I asked. 'I've never investigated anything in my life.'

She fluttered a hand. 'You know how to find things out, and nothing ever deflects you.'

'Nerissa,' I said suspiciously, 'you've been seeing my films.'

'Well, of course. I've seen nearly all of them.'

'Yes, but that's not me. Those investigating supermen, they're just acting.'

'Don't be silly, Edward dear. You couldn't do all the things you do in films without being brave and determined and very clever at finding things out.'

I looked at her in a mixture of affection and exasperation. So many people mistook the image for the man, but that she should . . .

'You've known me since I was eight,' I protested. 'You know I'm not brave or particularly determined. I'm ordinary. I'm me. I'm the boy you gave sweets to, when I was crying because I'd fallen off a pony, and said "never mind" to, when I didn't have the nerve to be a jockey.'

She smiled indulgently. 'But since then you've learned to fight. And look at that last picture, when you were clinging to a ledge by one hand with a thousand foot drop just below you . . .'

'Nerissa, dear Nerissa,' I interrupted her. 'I'll go to South Africa for you. I really will. But those fights in films . . . most of the time that isn't me, it's someone my size and shape who really does know judo. I don't. I can't fight at all. It's just my face in close-ups. And those ledges I was clinging to . . . certainly they were on a real rock face, but I was in no danger. I wouldn't have fallen a thousand feet, but only about ten, into one of those nets they use under trapeze acts in circuses. I did fall, two or three times. And there wasn't really a thousand feet below me; not sheer anyway. We filmed it in the Valley of Rocks in North Devon, where there are a lot of little plateaux among the rock faces, to stand the cameras on.'

She listened with an air of being completely unconvinced. I reckoned it was useless to go on: to tell her that I was not a crack shot, couldn't fly an aeroplane or beat Olympic skiers downhill, couldn't speak Russian or build a radio transmitter or dismantle bombs, and would tell all at the first threat of torture. She knew different, she'd seen it with her own eyes. Her expression told me so.

'Well, all right,' I said, capitulating. 'I do know what should and should not go on in a racing stable. In England, anyway.'

'And,' she said complacently, 'you can't say it wasn't you who did all that trick riding when you first went into films.'

I couldn't. It was. But it had been nothing unique.

'I'll go and look at your horses, and see what your trainer says,' I said; and thought that if had no reasons to offer, I would be most unlikely to find any.

'Dear Edward, so kind . . .' She seemed suddenly weaker, as if the effort of persuading me had been too much. But when she saw the alarm on Charlie's face, and on mine, she raised a reassuring smile.

'Not yet, my dears. Another two months, perhaps . . . Two months at least, I think.'

Charlie shook her head in protest, but Nerissa patted her hand. 'It's all right, my dear. I've come to terms with it. But I want to arrange things . . . which is why I want Edward to see about the horses, and I really ought to explain . . .'

'Don't tire yourself,' I said.

'I'm not . . . tired,' she said, obviously untruthfully. 'And I want to tell you. The horses used to belong to my sister, Portia, who married and went to live in South Africa thirty years ago. After she was widowed she stayed there because all her friends were there, and I've been out to visit her several times over the years. I know I've told you about her.'

We nodded.

'She died last winter,' I said.

'Yes . . . a great sorrow.' Nerissa looked a good deal more upset about her sister's death than about her own. 'She had no close relatives except me, and she left me nearly everything she had inherited from her husband. And all her horses, too.' She paused, as much to gather her forces as her thoughts. 'They were yearlings. Expensive ones. And her trainer wrote to me to ask if I wanted to sell them, as of course owing to the African horsesick-

38

ness quarantine laws we cannot bring South African horses to England. But I thought it might be fun ... interesting ... to run them in South Africa, and then sell them for stud. But now ... well, now I won't be here when they are old enough for stud, and meanwhile their value has dropped disastrously.'

'Dearest Nerissa,' Charlie said. 'Does it matter?'

'Oh yes. Yes, my dear, it does,' she said positively. 'Because I'm leaving them to my nephew, Danilo, and I don't like the idea of leaving him something worthless.'

She looked from one of us to the other. 'I can't remember – have you ever met Danilo?'

Charlie said, 'No,' and I said, 'Once or twice, when he was a small boy. You used to bring him to the stables.'

'That's right, so I did. And then of course my brother-in-law divorced that frightful woman, Danilo's mother, and took him to live in California with him. Well ... Danilo has been back in England recently, and he has grown into such a nice young man. And isn't that lucky, my dears? Because, you see, I have so few relatives. In fact, really, Danilo is the only one, and even he is not a blood relative, his father being dear John's youngest brother, do you see?'

We saw. John Cavesey, dead sixteen years or more, had been a country gent with four hunters and a sense of humour. He had also had Nerissa, no children, one brother, one nephew, and five square miles of Merrie England.

After a pause Nerissa said, 'I'll cable to Mr Arknold

39

. . . that's my trainer . . . to tell him you're coming to look into things, and to book some rooms for you.'

'No, don't do that. He might resent your sending anyone, and I'd get no cooperation from him at all. I'll fix the rooms, and so on. And if you cable him, just say I might be calling in, out of interest, while I'm in South Africa on a short visit.'

She smiled slowly and sweetly, and said, 'You see, my dear, you do know how to investigate, after all.'

CHAPTER THREE

I flew to Johannesburg five days later, equipped with a lot of facts and no faith in my ability to disentangle them.

Charlie and I had driven home from Nerissa's in a double state of depression. Poor Nerissa, we said. And poor us, losing her.

'And you've only just come home,' Charlie added.

'Yes,' I sighed. 'Still . . . I couldn't have said no.'

'No.'

'Not that it'll do much good.'

'You never know, you might spot something.'

'Very doubtful.'

'But,' she said with a touch of anxiety, 'you will do your best?'

'Of course, love.'

She shook her head. 'You're cleverer than you think.'

'Yeah,' I said. 'Sure.'

She made a face, and we went some way in silence. Then she said, 'When you went out to look at those two young chasers in her paddock, Nerissa told me what is the matter with her.'

41

'Did she?'

Charlie nodded. 'Some ghastly thing called Hodgkin's disease, which makes her glands swell, or something, and turn cellular, whatever that really means. She didn't know very clearly herself, I don't think. Except that it is absolutely fatal.'

Poor Nerissa.

'She also told me,' Charlie went on, 'that she has left us a keepsake each in her will.'

'Has she really?' I turned my head to look at Charlie. 'How kind of her. Did she say what?'

'Keep your eyes on the road, for heaven's sake. No, she didn't say what. Just something to remember her by. She said she had quite enjoyed herself, drawing up her new will and giving people presents in it. Isn't she amazing?'

'She is.'

'She really meant it. And she is so pleased that her nephew has turned out well. I've never seen anyone like that before . . . dying, and quite calm about it . . . and even enjoying things, like making a will . . . and knowing . . . knowing . . .'

I glanced at her sideways. Tears on Charlie's cheeks. She seldom cried, and didn't like to be watched.

I kept my eyes on the road.

I telephoned my agent and stunned him.

'But,' he stuttered, 'you never go anywhere, you

always refuse . . . you thumped my table and shouted about it . . .'

'Quite,' I agreed. 'But now I want a good reason for going to South Africa, so are any of my films due to open there soon, or are they not?'

'Well . . .' he sounded thoroughly disorganized. 'Well, I'll have to look it up. And are you sure,' he added in disbelief, 'that if one of them is due to open, you really and truly want me to tell them you'll turn up in person?'

'That's what I said.'

'Yes. I just don't believe it.'

He rang back an hour later.

'There are two coming up. They are showing *One Way to Moscow* in Cape Town, starting Monday week. That's the first in a series of six revivals, so although *Moscow* itself is pretty old, you could turn up to give the whole lot a boost. Or there's the opening of *Rocks* in Johannesburg. But that's not until September 14th. Three weeks off. Is that soon enough?'

'Not really.' I pondered. 'It will have to be the Johannesburg one, though.'

'All right. I'll fix it. And . . . er . . . does the sudden change of heart extend to chat shows and newspaper interviews?'

'No, it does not.'

'I was afraid of that.'

*

I had taken home from Nerissa's house all her trainer's letters, all the South African Racing Calendars, newspaper cuttings and magazines she had been sent, and all the details of breeding and racing form of her eleven non-winning youngsters. A formidable bulk of paper, it had proved; and not miraculously easy to understand.

The picture which emerged, though, was enough to make anyone think, let alone the owner of the horses in question. Nine of the eleven had run nicely when they began their racing careers, and between December and May had clocked up a joint total of fourteen wins. Since the middle of May, none of them had finished nearer than fourth.

As far as I could judge from a limited squint at the leading-sires tables and the breeding notes section of the South African *Horse and Hound*, all of them were of impeccable pedigree, and certainly, from the amounts she had laid out, Nerissa's sister Portia had bought no bargains. None of them had so far won enough prize money to cover their purchase price, and with every resounding defeat their future stud value, too, slid a notch towards zero.

As a bequest, the South African horses were a lump of lead.

Charlie came with me to Heathrow to see me off, as I had been home only nine days, which hadn't been long enough for either of us. While we were waiting at the check-in counter half a dozen ladies asked for my autograph for their daughters – nephews – grandchildren –

and a few eyes swivelled our way; and presently a dark-uniformed airline official appeared at our side and offered a small private room for waiting in. They were pretty good about that sort of thing, as I came through the airport fairly often, and we accepted gratefully.

'It's like being married to two people,' Charlie sighed, sitting down. 'The public you, and the private you. Quite separate. Do you know, if I see one of the films, or even a clip of one on the box, I look at the pictures of you, and I think, I slept with that man last night. And it seems extraordinary, because that public you doesn't really belong to me at all, but to all the people who pay to see you. And then you come home again, and you're just you, my familiar husband, and the public you is some other fellow . . .'

I looked at her affectionately. 'The private me has forgotten to pay the telephone bill.'

'Well, damn it, I reminded you sixteen times . . .'

'Will you pay it, then?'

'Well, I suppose so. But the telephone bill is one of your jobs. Checking all those cables, and those phone calls to America – I don't know what they should be. We're probably being overcharged, if you don't check it.'

'Have to risk it.'

'Honestly!'

'It will be set off against tax, anyway.'

'I suppose so.'

I sat down beside her. The unpaid telephone bill was as good as anything else to talk about: we no longer

45

needed to say aloud what we were saying to each other underneath. In all our life together we had taken good-byes casually, and hellos, too. A lot of people mistook it for not caring. It was perhaps too much the opposite. We needed each other like bees and honey.

When I landed at Jan Smuts International Airport six-teen hours later, I was met by a nervous man with damp palms who introduced himself as the South African Dis-tribution Manager for Worldic Cinemas.

'Wenkins,' he said. 'Clifford Wenkins. So nice to see you.'

He had restless eyes and a clipped South African accent. About forty. Never going to be successful. Talk-ing a little too loudly, a little too familiarly, with the sort of uneasy bonhomie I found hardest to take.

As politely as possible I removed my sleeve from his grasp.

'Nice of you to come,' I said; and wished he hadn't.

'Couldn't let Edward Lincoln arrive without a recep-tion, you know.' He laughed loudly, out of nerves. I wondered idly why he should be so painfully self-conscious: as Distribution Manager he surely met film actors before breakfast every month of the year.

'Car over here.' He walked crabwise in front of me with his arms extended fore and aft, as if to push a path for me with the one and usher me along it with the other. There were not enough people around for it to be remotely necessary.

I followed him, carrying my suitcase and making an effort to suffer his attentions gladly.

'Not far,' he said anxiously, looking up placatingly at my face.

'Fine,' I said.

There was a group of about ten people just inside the main doors. I looked at them in disillusion: their clothes and the way they stood had 'media' stamped all over them, and it was without surprise that I saw the tape-recorders and cameras sprout all over as soon as we drew near.

'Mr Lincoln, what do you think of South Africa?'

'Hey, Link, how about a big smile . . .?'

'Is there any truth in the rumour . . .?'

'Our readers would like your views on . . .'

'Give us a smile . . .'

I tried not to stop walking, but they slowed us down to a crawl. I smiled at them collectively and said soothing things like 'I'm glad to be here. This is my first visit. I am looking forward to it very much,' and eventually we persevered into the open air.

Clifford Wenkins's dampness extended to his brow, though the sunshine at 6,000 feet above sea level was decidedly chilly.

'Sorry,' he said, 'but they would come.'

'Marvellous how they knew the right day and the

right time, when my flight was only booked yesterday morning.'

'Er . . . yes,' he agreed weakly.

'I expect they are often willing to arrange publicity for people, when you want them to.'

'Oh yes, indeed,' he agreed warmly.

I smiled at him. One could hardly blame him for using me as payment for past and future services, and I knew it was widely considered irrational that I preferred to avoid interviews. In many countries the media gave you a rough passage if you wouldn't let them milk you for copy, and the South Africans had been more civil than most.

Wenkins rubbed his beaded forehead with one of the damp palms, and said, 'Let me take your suitcase.'

I shook my head. 'It isn't heavy,' I said, and besides, I was a good deal bigger than he was.

We walked across the car park to his car, and I experienced for the first time the extraordinary smell of Africa. A blend of hot sweet odours with a kink of mustiness; a strong disturbing smell which stayed in my nostrils for three or four days, until my scenting nerves got used to it and disregarded it. But my first overriding impression of South Africa was the way it smelt.

Smiling too much, sweating too much, talking too much, Clifford Wenkins drove me down the road to Johannesburg. The airport lay east of the city, out on the bare expanses of the Transvaal, and we were a good half-hour reaching our destination.

'I hope everything will be all right for you,' Wenkins said. 'We don't often get . . . I mean, well . . .' He laughed jerkily. 'Your agent was telling me on the telephone not to arrange any receptions or parties or radio shows or anything . . . I mean, we usually put on that sort of show for visiting stars . . . that is, er, of course, if Worldic are handling their films . . . but, er, we haven't done anything like that for you, and it seems all wrong to me . . . but then, your agent insisted . . . and then, your room . . . not in the city, he said. Not in the city itself, and not in a private house, he said, so I hope you will like . . . I mean, we were shattered . . . er, that is, honoured . . . to hear you were coming . . .'

Mr Wenkins, I thought, you would get a lot further on in life if you didn't chatter so much. And aloud I said, 'I'm sure everything will be fine.'

'Yes, well . . . Er, if you don't want the usual round of things, though, what am I to arrange for you? I mean, there is a fortnight before the premiere of *Rocks*, don't you see? So what . . .?'

I didn't answer that one straight away. Instead I said, 'This premiere . . . How much of a thing are you making of it?'

'Oh.' He laughed again at nothing funny. 'Er, well, big, of course. Invitations. Tickets in aid of charity. All the glitter, old boy . . . er, I mean . . . sorry . . . er, well. Worldic said to push the boat right out, you see, once they'd got over the shock, that is.'

'I do see.' I sighed slightly. I had chosen to do the

damn thing, I thought. So I ought, in all fairness, to give them value for their trouble.

'Look,' I said, 'if you want to, and if you think anyone would want to come, go ahead and arrange some sort of drinks and canapés affair either before or after the showing of the film, and I'll go to that. And one morning soon, if you'd like to, you could ask all those good friends of yours at the airport, and any others in their trade that you want to include, to meet us somewhere for coffee or a drink or something. How would that do?'

For once he was dumb. I looked across at him. His mouth was opening and shutting like a fish.

I laughed in my throat. Nerissa had a lot to answer for.

'The rest of the time, don't worry about me. I'll amuse myself all right. For one thing, I'll go to the races.'

'Oh,' He finally overcame the jaw problem and got the two halves into proper working order. 'Er . . . I could get someone to take you there, if you like.'

'We'll see,' I said noncommittally.

The journey ended at the Iguana Rock, a very pleasant country hotel on the northern edge of the city. The management gave me a civil greeting and a luxurious room and indicated that a clap of the hands would bring anything from iced water to dancing girls, as required.

'I would like to hire a car,' I said, and Wenkins gushed forth to say it was all arranged, he had arranged it, a chauffeur-driven pumpkin would be constantly on call, courtesy of Worldic.

I shook my head. 'Courtesy of me,' I said. 'Didn't my agent tell you that I intended to pay all the expenses of my trip myself?'

'Well, he did, yes, but . . . Worldic say they'd like to pick up the tab . . .'

'No,' I said.

He laughed nervously. 'No . . . well, I see, er, I mean . . . yes.' He spluttered to a stop. The eyes darted around restlessly, the hands gestured vaguely, the meaningless smile twitched his mouth convulsively, and he couldn't stand still on his two feet. I didn't usually throw people into such a tizzy, and I wondered what on earth my agent could have said to him, to bring him to such a state.

He managed eventually to get himself out of the Iguana Rock and back to his car, and his departure was a great relief. Within an hour, however, he was on the telephone.

'Would tomorrow, er, morning . . . suit you for, er, I mean, the Press?'

'Yes,' I said.

'Then, er, would you ask your driver to take you to, er, Randfontein House, er . . . the Dettrick Room . . . that's a reception room, you see, which we hire for this, well, sort of thing.'

'What time?'

51

'Oh ... say eleven thirty. Could you ... er ... get there at about eleven thirty?'

'Yes,' I said briefly again, and after a few further squirms he said he would look forward ... er ... to seeing me then.

I put the receiver down, finished unpacking, drank some coffee, summoned up the pumpkin, and went briskly off to the races.

CHAPTER FOUR

Flat racing in South Africa took place on Wednesdays and Saturdays throughout the year, but only occasionally on other days. Accordingly, it had seemed good sense to arrive in Johannesburg on Wednesday morning and go to the only race-meeting in South Africa that day, at Newmarket.

I paid to go in and bought a race-card. One of Nerissa's constant failures, I saw, was due to have another go later in the afternoon.

Newmarket was Newmarket the world over. Stands, cards, horses, bookmakers; atmosphere of bustle and purpose; air of tradition and order. All were much the same. I wandered across to the parade ring, where the runners for the first race were already walking round. Same little clumps of owners and trainers standing in hopeful conversations in the middle. Same earnest race-goers leaning on the rails and studying the wares.

Differences were small. The horses, to English eyes, looked slightly smaller-framed and had very upright fetlocks, and they were led round, not by white stable lads in their own darkish clothes, but by black stable-boys in long white coats.

On the principle of only backing horses I knew something about, I kept my hands in my pockets. The jockeys in their bright silks came out and mounted, the runners went away down the track and scurried back, hooves rattling on the bone-dry ground, and I strolled down from the stands to search for and identify Nerissa's trainer, Greville Arknold. He had a runner in the following race, and somewhere he would be found, saddling it up.

In the event, I hardly had to look. On my way to the saddling boxes, a young man touched me on the arm.

'I say,' he said, 'Aren't you Edward Lincoln?'

I nodded and half smiled, and kept on walking.

'Guess I'd better introduce myself. Danilo Cavesey. I believe you know my aunt.'

That stopped me, all right. I put out my hand, and he shook it warmly.

'I heard you were coming, of course. Aunt Nerissa cabled Greville you were on your way out here for some film premiere, and would he look out for you at the races. So I was kind of expecting you, you see.'

His accent was a slow Californian drawl full of lazy warmth. It was instantly clear why Nerissa had liked him: his sun-tanned, good-looking face, his open, pleasant expression, his clean, casual, blond-brown hair, all were in the best tradition of American youth.

'She didn't say you were in South Africa,' I commented, surprised.

'Well, no.' He wrinkled his nose disarmingly. 'I don't believe she knows. I only flew out here a few days ago, on a vacation. Say, how is the old girl? She wasn't all that sprightly when I last visited with her.'

He was smiling happily. He didn't know.

I said, 'She's pretty ill, I'm afraid.'

'Is that so? I'm sure sorry to hear that. I must write her, tell her I'm out here, tell her I'm taking a look-see into the state of the horses.'

'The state of the horses?' I echoed.

'Oh sure. Aunt Nerissa's horses out here are not running good. Stinking bad, to be accurate.' He grinned cheerfully. 'I shouldn't bet on number eight in the fourth race, if you want to die rich.'

'Thanks,' I said. 'She did mention to me that they were not doing so well just now.'

'I'll bet she did. They wouldn't win if you gave them ten minutes start and nobbled the others.'

'Is there any reason for it, do you know?'

'Search me,' he shrugged. 'Greville's real chewed up about it. Says he hasn't had anything like this happen before.'

'Not a virus?' I suggested.

'Can't be. Otherwise all the others would get it too, not just Aunt Nerissa's. We've been talking it over, you see. Greville just hasn't an idea.'

'I'd like to meet him,' I said casually.

'Oh sure. Yes, indeed. But say, why don't we get out of this wind and have ourselves a beer or something?

Greville has this starter now, but he'll be happy to see us later on.'

'All right,' I agreed, and we went and had ourselves the beer. Danilo was right: the south wind was cold and spring was still a hint and a memory.

Danilo, I judged, was about twenty years old. He had bright blue eyes and blond-brown eyelashes, and his teeth were California-straight. He had the untouched air of one to whom the rigours of life had not yet happened; a boy not necessarily spoilt, but to whom much had been given.

He was at Berkeley University studying Political Science, he said, with one more year to do. 'This time next summer I'll be all through with college . . .'

'What do you plan to do after that?' I asked, making conversation.

There was a flash of amusement in the blue eyes. 'Oh, I guess I'll have to think of something, but I've nothing lined up right now.'

The future could take care of itself, I thought, and reflected that for golden boys like Danilo it usually did.

We watched the next race together. Greville's starter finished third, close up.

'Too bad,' Danilo sighed. 'I just had it on the nose, not across the boards.'

'Did you lose much?' I asked sympathetically.

'I guess not. Just a few rand.'

Rands came just under two to the pound sterling, or

a little over one to the dollar. He couldn't have done himself much harm.

We walked down from the stands and over towards the unsaddling enclosures. 'Do you know something?' he said. 'You're not a bit what I expected.'

'In what way?' I asked, smiling.

'Oh, I guess . . . For a big movie star, I expected some sort of, well, *presence*. You know?'

'Off the screen, movie actors are as dim as anyone else.'

He glanced at me suspiciously, but I wasn't laughing at him. I meant it. He had a much more naturally luminous personality than I had. I might have been an inch or two taller, an inch or two broader across the shoulders, but the plus factor had nothing to do with size.

The man stalking round the horse which had finished third, peering judiciously at its legs and running a probing hand along its loins, was a burly thickset man with an air of dissatisfaction.

'That's Greville,' Danilo nodded, following my gaze.

The trainer spoke briefly to a woman Danilo identified to me as the horse's owner. His manner, from twenty feet away, looked brusque and far from conciliatory. I knew trainers had to grow hard skins if they were to stay sane: one could not for ever be apologizing to owners if their horses got beaten, one had to make them realize that regardless of the oats and exercise crammed into them, maybe other people's horses could actually run faster: but Greville Arknold appeared plainly disagreeable.

After a while the horses were led away and the crowd thinned out. Arknold listened, with a pinched mouth and a stubborn backward tilt of the head, to what looked almost like apologies from the woman owner. She came to a stop, got no melting response from him, shrugged, turned slowly, and walked away.

Arknold's gaze rose from down his nose and fastened on Danilo. He stared for a moment, then raised his eyebrows questioningly. Danilo very slightly jerked his head in my direction, and Arknold transferred his attention to me.

Again the slow appraisal. Then he came across.

Danilo introduced us with an air of what fun it was for us to know each other. A mutual privilege.

Great.

I didn't take to Greville Arknold, neither then nor ever after. Yet he was pleasant enough to me: smiled, shook hands, said he was glad to meet me, said that Mrs Cavesey had cabled to say I might be coming to the races, and to look after me if I did.

He had a flat-sounding Afrikaaner accent, and like many South Africans he was, I discovered later, trilingual in English, Afrikaans and Zulu. He had a face formed of thick slabs of flesh, lips so thin that they hardly existed, the scars of old acne over his chin and down his neck, and a bristly ginger moustache one inch by two below his nose. And for all the smiling and the welcoming chat, he had cold eyes.

'Your horse ran well just then,' I suggested conversationally.

The recent anger reappeared at once in his manner. 'That stupid woman insisted that her horse ran today when I wanted to run it Saturday instead. He had a hard race at Turffontein last Saturday. He needed another three days' rest.'

'She looked as if she were apologizing,' I said.

'*Ja*. She was. Too late, of course. She should have had more sense. Decent colt, that. Would have won on Saturday. No sense. Owners always ought to do what a trainer says. They pay for expert knowledge, don't they? So they always ought to do what the experts say.'

I smiled vaguely, noncommittally. As an owner myself, even of only one moderate steeplechasing gelding, I disagreed with him about always. Sometimes, even usually, yes. But always, no. I knew of at least one Grand National winner which would never have gone to the start if the owner had paid attention to the trainer's advice.

'I see Mrs Cavesey has a runner in the fourth,' I said.

The dogmatic look faded to be replaced by a slight frown.

'*Ja*,' Arnold said. 'I expect she may have mentioned to you that her horses are not doing well.'

'She told me you had no idea why,' I nodded.

He shook his head. 'I cannot understand it. They get

the same treatment as all the others. Same food, same exercise, everything. They are not ill. I have had a veterinarian examine them, several times. It is worrying. Very.'

'It must be,' I agreed sympathetically.

'And dope tests!' he said. 'We must have had a hundred dope tests. All negative, the whole lot.'

'Do they look fit?' I asked. 'I mean, would you expect them to do better, from the way they look?'

'See for yourself.' He shrugged. 'That is . . . I don't know how much of a judge of a horse you are . . .'

'Bound to be a pretty good one, I'd say,' said Danilo positively. 'After all, it's no secret his old man was a stable hand.'

'Is that so?' he said. 'Then perhaps you would like to see round the stables? Maybe you could even come up with some suggestion about Mrs Cavesey's string, you never know.'

The irony in his voice made it clear that he thought that impossible. Which meant that either he really did not know what was the matter with the horses, or he did know, but was absolutely certain that I would not find out.

'I'd like to see the stables very much,' I said.

'Good. Then you shall. How about tomorrow evening? Walk round with me, at evening stables. Four-thirty?'

I nodded.

'That's fixed then. And you, Danilo. Do you want to come as well?'

'That would be just fine, Greville. I sure would like that.'

So it was settled; and Danilo said he would come and pick me up at the Iguana Rock himself.

Chink, Nerissa's runner in the fourth race, looked good enough in the parade ring, with a healthy bloom on his coat and muscles looking strong and free and loose. There wasn't a great deal of substance about him, but he had an intelligent head and strong, well-placed shoulders. Nerissa's sister Portia had given twenty-five thousand rand for him as a yearling on the strength of his breeding, and he had won only one race, his first, way back in April.

'What do you think of him, Link?' Danilo asked, leaning his hip against the parade ring rail.

'He looks fit enough,' I said.

'Yeah. They all do, Greville says.'

Chink was being led around by two stable lads, one each side. Nothing wrong with Arknold's security arrangements.

Because of the upright fetlocks I found it hard to judge the degree of spring in Chink's stride. All the horses looked to me as if they were standing on their toes, a condition I imagined was caused by living from birth on hard dry ground. Certainly he went down to the post moving no more scratchily than the others, and he lined up in the stalls and bounded out of them with no trouble. I watched every step of his journey through my Zeiss eight by fifties.

He took the first half mile without apparent effort, lying about sixth, nice and handy, just behind the leading bunch. When they turned into the straight for home, the leaders quickened, but Chink didn't. I saw the head of the jockey bob and the rest of his body become energetically busy trying to keep the horse going: but when a jockey has to work like that on a horse a long way out, he might as well not bother. Chink had run out of steam, and the best rider in the world could have done nothing about that.

I put down my race glasses. The winner fought a ding-dong, the crowd roared, and Chink returned unsung, unbacked, unwatched, and a good thirty lengths later.

With Danilo I went down to where he was being unsaddled, and joined Greville Arknold in his aura of perplexed gloom.

'There you are,' he said. 'You saw for yourself.'

'I did,' I agreed.

Chink was sweating and looked tired. He stood still, with drooping head, as if he felt the disgrace.

'What do you think?' Arknold asked.

I silently shook my head. He had in fact looked plainly like a slow horse, yet on his breeding, and the fast time of the race he had won, he should not be.

He and the other ten could not all have bad hearts, or bad teeth, or blood disorders, all undetected. Not after those thorough veterinary investigations. And not *all* of them. It was impossible.

They had not all been ridden every time by the same jockey. There were, I had discovered from Nerissa's racing papers, very few jockeys in South Africa compared with England: only thirteen jockeys and twenty-two apprentices riding on the Natal tracks near Durban, the supposed centre of the sport.

There were four main racing areas: the Johannesburg tracks in the Transvaal, the Pietermaritzburg-Durban tracks in Natal, the Port Elizabeth tracks in the Eastern Cape, and the Cape Town tracks in Cape Province. Various ones of Nerissa's horses had been to all four areas, had been ridden by the local bunch of jockeys, and had turned in the same results.

Fast until May, dead slow from June onwards.

The fact that they moved around meant that it probably could not be attributed to something in their base quarters.

No illness. No dope. No fixed address. No common jockey.

All of which pointed to one solution. One source of disaster.

The trainer himself.

It was easy enough for a trainer to make sure a horse of his didn't win, if he had a mind to. He merely had to give it too severe an exercise gallop too soon before a race. Enough races had in sober fact been lost that way by accident for it to be impossible to prove that anyone had done it on purpose.

Trainers seldom nobbled their own horses because they had demonstrably more to gain if they won. But it looked to me as if it had to be Arknold who was responsible, even if the method he was using turned out to be the simplest in the world.

I thought the solution to Nerissa's problem lay in transferring her string to a different trainer.

I thought I might just as well go straight home and tell her so.

Two nasty snags.

I was committed to a premiere two weeks off.

And I might guess who and how, about the horses.

But I had no idea *why*.

CHAPTER FIVE

The ladies and gentlemen of the Press (or in the other words a partially shaven, polo-neck-sweatered, elaborately casual and uniformed mob) yawned to their feet when I reached the Dettrick Room in Randfontein House within ticking distance of half past eleven.

Clifford Wenkins had met me in the hall, twittering as before, and with wetter than ever palms. We rode up in the lift together, with him explaining to me exactly whom he had asked, and who had come. Interviewers from two radio programmes. He hoped I wouldn't mind? They would be happy just to tape my answers to their questions. Just into a microphone. If I didn't mind? And then there were the dailies, the weeklies, the ladies' magazines, and one or two people who had flown up especially from Cape Town and Durban.

I wished I hadn't suggested it. Too late to run away.

The only thing to do, I thought, as the lift hissed to a halt and the doors slid open, was to put on a sort of performance. To act.

'Wait a minute,' I said to Wenkins.

He stopped with me outside the lift as the doors shut again behind us.

'What is it?' he asked anxiously.

'Nothing. I just need a few seconds, before we go in.'

He didn't understand, though what I was doing was not a process by any means confined to professional actors. Girding up the loins, the Bible called it. Getting the adrenalin on the move. Making the heart beat faster. Shifting the mental gears into top. Politicians could do it in three seconds flat.

'OK,' I said.

He sighed with relief, walked across the hallway, and opened a heavy polished door opposite.

We went in.

They unfolded themselves from sofas and carpet, pushed themselves tiredly off the walls, stubbed out one or two cigarettes and went on puffing at others.

'Hi,' said one of the men: and the others, like a sort of jungle pack, watched and waited. He was one of those who had been at the airport. He had no reason, as none of them had, to believe I would now be any different.

'Hullo,' I said.

Well, I could always do it, if I really wanted to. Almost every well-trained actor can.

I watched them loosen, saw the tiredness go out of their manner and the smile creep into their eyes. They wouldn't now chew me to bits in their columns, even if they still came across with those carefully sharpened questions they all had ready in their notebooks.

The man who had said hi, their apparently natural leader, put out his hand to be shaken, and said, 'I'm Roderick Hodge of the *Rand Daily Star*. Features Editor.'

Late thirties, but trying to ignore the passage of time: young hair-cut, young clothes, young affectation of speech. A certain *panache* about him, but also some of the ruthless cynicism of experienced journalists.

I shook his hand and smiled at him as a friend. I needed him to be one.

'Look,' I said. 'Unless you are all in a hurry, why don't we sit down again, and then you can all ask whatever you like, perhaps in groups, maybe I can move around a bit, and then everyone might have more time for things than if I just sort of stand here in front of you.'

They thought that was all right. No one was in much of a hurry, they said. Roderick said dryly that no one would go before the booze started flowing, and the atmosphere started mellowing nicely into an all-pals-together trade meeting.

They mostly asked the personal questions first.

According to their calculations, I was thirty-three. Was that right?

It was.

And married? Yes. Happily? Yes. My first or second marriage? First. And her first? Yes.

They wanted to know how many children I had, with their names and ages. They asked how many rooms my house had, and what it had cost. How many cars, dogs, horses, yachts I had. How much I earned in a year, how much I had been paid for *Rocks*.

How much did I give my wife to buy clothes with? Did I think a woman's place was in the home?

'In the heart,' I said flippantly, which pleased the women's mag girl who had asked, but was slightly sick-making to all the others.

Why didn't I go to live in a tax haven? I liked England. An expensive luxury? Very. And was I a millionaire? Perhaps some days, on paper, when share prices went up. If I was as rich as that, why did I work? To pay taxes, I said.

Clifford Wenkins had summoned up some caterers who brought coffee and cheese biscuits and bottles of Scotch. The Press poured the whisky into the coffee and sighed contentedly. I kept mine separate, but had great difficulty in explaining to the waiter that I did not like any liquor diluted in nine times as much water. In South Africa, I had already discovered, they tended to fill up the tumblers; and I supposed it made sense as a long drink in a hot climate, but while it was so cold it merely ruined good Scotch.

Clifford Wenkins eyed my small drink in its large glass.

'Let me get you some water.'

'I've got some. I prefer it like this . . .'

'Oh . . . really?'

He scuttled busily away and came back with an earnestly bearded man trailing a hand microphone and a long lead. There was no sense of humour behind the beard, which made, I thought, for a fairly stodgy interview, but he assured me that what I had said was just right, just perfect for a five minute slot in his Saturday evening show. He took back the microphone which I had been holding, shook me earnestly by the hand, and disappeared into a large array of recording equipment in one corner.

After that I was supposed to do a second interview, this time for a woman's programme, but some technical hitches had developed in the gear.

I moved, in time, right round the room, sitting on the floor, on the arms of chairs, leaning on the window-sills, or just plain standing.

Loosened by the Scotch, they asked the other questions.

What did I think of South Africa? I liked it.

What were my opinions of their political scene? I hadn't any, I said. I had been in their country only one day. One couldn't form opinions in that time.

Most people arrived with them already formed, they observed. I said I didn't think that was sensible.

Well, what were my views on racial discrimination? I said without heat that I thought any form of discrimination was bound to give rise to some injustice. I said I thought it a pity that various people found it necessary to discriminate against women, Jews, Aborigines, American Indians and a friend of mine in Nairobi who couldn't get promotion in a job he excelled at because he was white.

I also said I couldn't answer any more of that sort of question, and could we please get off politics and civil rights unless they would like me to explain the differences between the economic theories of the Tory and Labour parties.

They laughed. No, they said. They wouldn't.

They reverted to films and asked questions I felt better able to answer.

Was it true I had started as a stunt man? Sort of, I said. I rode horses across everything from Robin Hood via Bosworth Field to the Charge of the Light Brigade. Until one day when I was doing a bit of solo stuff a director called me over, gave me some words to say, and told me I was in. Good clean romantic stuff, for which I apologized. It did happen sometimes like that though.

And then? Oh, then I got given a better part in his next film. And how old was I at the time? Twenty-two, just married, living on baked beans in a basement flat in Hammersmith, and still attending part-time speech and drama classes, as I had for three years.

I was standing more or less in the centre of the room when the door opened behind me. Clifford Wenkins turned his head to see who it was, frowned with puzzlement and went busily across to deal with the situation.

'I'm afraid you can't come in here,' he was saying bossily. 'This is a private room. Private reception. I'm sorry, but would you mind . . . I say, you can't . . . this is a private room . . . I say . . .'

I gathered Wenkins was losing. Not surprising, really.

Then I felt the clump on the shoulder and heard the familiar fruity voice.

'Link, dear boy. Do tell this . . . er . . . person, that we are old buddy buddies. He doesn't seem to want me to come in. Now, I ask you . . .'

I turned round. Stared in surprise. Said to Wenkins, 'Perhaps you would let him stay. I do know him. He's a cameraman.'

Conrad raised his eyebrows sharply. 'Director of Photography, dear boy. A cameraman indeed!'

'Sorry,' I said ironically. 'Have a Scotch?'

'Now that, dear boy, is more like it.'

Wenkins gave up the struggle and went off to get Conrad a drink. Conrad surveyed the relaxed atmosphere, the hovering smoke, the empty cups and half-empty glasses, and the gentle communicators chatting in seated groups.

'My God,' he said. 'My great God. I don't believe it. I didn't, in fact, believe it when they told me Edward Lincoln was giving a Press conference right here in Johannesburg at this very moment. I bet on it not being true. So they told me where. In that ritzy room at the top of the Randfontein, they said. Go and see for yourself. So I did.'

A laugh began rumbling somewhere down in his belly and erupted in a coughing guffaw.

71

'Shut up,' I said.

He spread his arms wide, embracing the room. 'They don't know, they just don't know what they're seeing, do they? They've just no idea.'

'Be quiet, Conrad, damn it,' I said.

He went on wheezing away in uncontainable chuckles. 'My dear boy. I didn't know you could do it. Off the set, that is. Talk about a lot of tame tigers eating out of your hand . . . Just wait until Evans hears.'

'He isn't likely to,' I said comfortably. 'Not from five thousand or so miles away.'

He shook with amusement. 'Oh no, dear boy. He's right here in Johannesburg. Practically in the next street.'

'He can't be!'

'We've been here since Sunday.' He choked off the last of his laughter and wiped his eyes with his thumb. 'Come and have some lunch, dear boy, and I'll tell you all about it.'

I looked at my watch. Twelve-thirty.

'In a while, then. I've still got one more bit of taping to do, when they get hold of a spare microphone.'

Roderick Hodge detached himself from a group by one of the windows and brought a decorative female over with him, and Clifford Wenkins dead-heated with Conrad's drink.

The girl, the would-be interviewer from the woman's radio programme, had the sort of face that would have been plain on a different personality: but she also had a bushy mop of curly brown hair, enormous yellow-rimmed sunglasses, and a stick-like figure clad in an orange and tan checked trouser suit. The spontaneous friendliness in her manner saved her from any impression of caricature. Conrad took in her colour temperature with an appreciative eye, while explaining he had been engaged on four films with me in the recent past.

Roderick's attention sharpened like an adjusted focus.

'What is he like to work with?' he demanded.

'That's not fair,' I said.

Neither Roderick nor Conrad paid any attention. Conrad looked at me judiciously, pursed his lips, lifted up a hand, and bent the fingers over one by one as he rolled his tongue lovingly around the words.

'Patient, powerful, punctual, professional, and puritanical.' And aside to me he stage-whispered, 'How's that?'

'Ham,' I said.

Roderick predictably pounced on the last one. 'Puritanical. How do you mean?'

Conrad was enjoying himself. 'All his leading ladies complain that he kisses them with art, not heart.'

I could see the headlines writing themselves in Roderick's head. His eye was bright.

'My sons don't like it,' I said.

'What?'

'When the elder one saw me in a film kissing someone

73

who wasn't his mother, he wouldn't speak to me for a week.'

They laughed.

But at the time it had been far from funny. Peter had also started wetting his bed again at five years old and had cried a lot, and a child psychiatrist had told us it was because he felt insecure: he felt his foundations were slipping away, because Daddy kissed other ladies, and quarrelled with Mummy at home. It had happened so soon after Libby's accident that we wondered whether he was also worrying about that: but we had never told him Libby had been ill because he had dropped her, and never intended to. One couldn't burden a child with that sort of knowledge, because a pointless, unnecessary feeling of guilt could have distorted the whole of his development.

'What did you do about that?' the girl asked sympathetically.

'Took him to some good clean horror films instead.'

'Oh, yeah,' Conrad said.

Clifford Wenkins came twittering back from another of his darting foraging expeditions. Sweat still lay in pearl-sized beads in the furrows of his forehead. How did he cope, I vaguely wondered, when summer came.

He thrust a stick microphone triumphantly into my hands. Its lead ran back to the corner where the radio apparatus stood. 'There we are ... er ... all fixed, I mean.' He looked in unnecessary confusion from me to the girl. 'There we are, Katya dear. Er . . . all ready, I think.'

I looked at Conrad. I said, 'I learned just one word of Afrikaans at the races yesterday, and you can do it while I tape this interview.'

Conrad said suspiciously, 'What word?'

'*Voetsek*,' I said conversationally.

They all split themselves politely. *Voetsek* meant bugger off.

Conrad's chuckles broke out again like a recurring infection, when they explained.

'If only Evan could see this . . .' he wheezed.

'Let's forget Evan,' I suggested.

Conrad put his hand on Roderick's arm and took him away, each of them enjoying a separate joke.

Katya's smallish eyes were laughing behind the enormous yellow specs. 'And to think they said that at the airport you were the chilliest of cold fish . . .'

I gave her a sideways smile. 'Maybe I was tired . . .' I eyed the notebook she clutched in one hand. 'What sort of things are you going to ask?'

'Oh, only the same as the others, I should think.' But there was a mischievous glint of teeth that boded no good.

'All set, Katya,' a man called from the row of electronic boxes and dials. 'Any time you say.'

'Right.' She looked down at the notebook and then up at me. I was about three feet away from her, holding my glass in one hand and the microphone in the other.

She considered this with her curly head on one side, then took a large step closer. Almost touching.

'That's better, I think. There will be too much background noise if either of us is too far from that microphone. It's an old one, by the looks of it. Oh, and maybe I'd better hold it. You look a bit awkward . . .' She took the microphone and called across the room. 'OK, Joe, switch on.'

Joe switched on.

Katya jerked appallingly from head to foot, arched backwards through the air and fell to the floor.

The murmuring peaceful faces turned, gasped, cried out, screwed themselves up in horror.

'Switch off,' I shouted urgently. 'Switch everything off. At once.'

Roderick took two strides and bent over Katya with outstretched hands to help her, and I pulled him back.

'Get Joe to switch that bloody microphone off first, or you will take the shock as well.'

The Joe in question ran over, looking ill.

'I have,' he said. 'It's off now.'

I thought that all, that any of them would know what to do, and do it. But they all just stood and knelt around looking at me, as if it were up to me to know, to do, to be the resourceful man in all those films who always took the lead, always . . .

Oh God, I thought.

Just look at them, I thought. And there was no time to waste. No time at all. She was no longer breathing.

I knelt down beside her and took her glasses off. Pulled open the neck of her shirt. Stretched her head back. Put my mouth on hers, and blew my breath into her lungs.

'Get a doctor,' Roderick. 'And an ambulance . . . Oh Christ . . . Hurry. Hurry . . .'

I breathed into her. Not too hard. Just with the force of breath. But over and over, heaving her chest up and down.

A lethal electric voltage stops the heart.

I tried to feel a pulse beating in her neck, but couldn't find one. Roderick interpreted my fingers and picked up her wrist, but it was no good there, either. His face was agonized. Katya was a great deal more, it seemed, than just a colleague.

Two thousand years passed like two more minutes. Roderick put his ear down on Katya's left breast. I went on breathing air into her, feeling as the seconds passed that it was no good, that she was dead. Her flesh was the colour of death, and very cold.

He heard the first thud before I felt it. I saw it in his face. Then there were two separate jolts in the blood vessel I had my fingers on under her jaw, and then some uneven, jerky little bumps, and then at last, unbelievably, slow, rhythmic, and strengthening, the life-giving ba-boom ba-boom ba-boom of a heart back in business.

Roderick's mouth tightened and twisted as he raised his head, and the cords in his neck stood out with the effort he was putting into not weeping. But the tears of relief ran for all that down his cheeks, and he tried to get rid of them with his fingers.

I pretended not to see, if that was what he wanted. But I knew, heaven forgive me, that one day I would put that face, that reaction, into a film. Whatever one learned, whatever one saw, and however private it was, in the end, if one were an actor, one used it.

She breathed in, convulsively, on her own, while I was still breathing in myself, through my nose. It felt extraordinary, as if she were sucking the air out of me.

I took my mouth away from hers, and stopped holding her jaws open with my hands. She went on breathing: a bit sketchily at first, but then quite regularly, in shallow bodyshaking, audible gasps.

'She ought to be warmer,' I said to Roderick. 'She needs blankets.'

He looked at me dazedly. 'Yes. Blankets.'

'I'll get some,' someone said, and the breath-held quietness in the room erupted with sudden bustle. Frozen shock turned to worried shock, and that to relieved shock, and from that to revival via the whisky bottle.

I saw Clifford Wenkins looking down at Katya's still unconscious form. His face was grey and looked like putty oozing, as the sweat had not had time to dry. For once, however, he had been reduced to speechlessness.

Conrad, too, seemed temporarily to have run out of 'dear boys'. But I guessed sharply that the blankness in his face as he watched the proceedings was not the result of shock. He was at his business, as I had been at mine, seeing an electrocution in terms of camera angles, atmospheric shadows, impact-making colours. And at what point, I wondered, did making use of other people's agonies become a spiritual sin.

Someone reappeared with some blankets, and with shaking hands Roderick wrapped Katya up in them, and put a cushion under her head.

I said to him, 'Don't expect too much when she wakes up. She'll be confused, I think.'

He nodded. Colour was coming back to her cheeks. She seemed securely alive. The time of fiercest anxiety was over.

He looked suddenly up at me, then down at her, then up at me again. The first thought that was not raw emotion was taking root.

As if it were a sudden discovery, he slowly said, 'You're Edward Lincoln.'

For him too the dilemma of conscience arose: whether or not to make professional copy out of the near-death of his girlfriend.

I looked round the room, and so did he. There had been a noticeable thinning of the ranks. I met Roderick's eyes and knew what he was thinking: the Press had made for the telephones, and he was the only one there from the *Rand Daily Star*.

He looked down again at the girl. 'She'll be all right, now, won't she?' he said.

I made an inconclusive gesture with my hands and

didn't directly answer. I didn't know whether or not she would be all right. I thought her heart had probably not been stopped for much over three minutes, so with a bit of luck her brain would not be irreparably damaged. But my knowledge was only the sketchy remains of a long-past first-aid course.

The journalist in Roderick won the day. He stood up abruptly and said, 'Do me a favour . . .? Don't let them take her to hospital or anywhere before I get back.'

'I'll do my best,' I said; and he made a highly rapid exit.

Joe, the radio equipment man, was coiling up the lead of the faulty microphone, having disconnected it gingerly from its power socket. He looked at it dubiously and said, 'It's such an old one I didn't know we had it. It was just there, in the box . . . I wish to God I hadn't decided to use it. It just seemed quicker than waiting any longer for the replacement from the studio. I'll make sure it'll do no more damage, anyway. I'll dismantle it and throw it away.'

Conrad returned to my side and stood looking down at Katya, who began showing signs of returning consciousness. Her eyelids fluttered. She moved under the blankets.

Conrad said, 'You do realize, dear boy, that until very shortly before the accident you were holding that microphone yourself.'

'Yes,' I said neutrally. 'I do.'

'And,' said Conrad, 'just how many people in this

room showed the slightest sign of knowing that the only hope for the electrocuted is artificial respiration, instantly applied?'

I looked at him straightly.

'Did you know?'

He sighed. 'You are so cynical, dear boy. But no, I didn't.'

CHAPTER SIX

Danilo arrived at the Iguana Rock at four o'clock with a hired Triumph, a scarlet open-necked shirt and a suntanned grin.

I had been back there less than an hour myself, Conrad and I having dawdled over a beer and sandwich lunch in an unobtrusive bar. Katya had gone to hospital, with Roderick in frantic tow, and the other journalists were currently stubbing their fingernails on their typewriters. Clifford Wenkins had twittered off at some unmarked point in the proceedings, and when Conrad and I left we saw him, too, engaged in earnest conversation on the telephone. Reporting to Worldic, no doubt. I stifled a despairing sigh. Not a butterfly's chance in a blizzard that anyone would ignore the whole thing as uninteresting.

Danilo chatted in his carefree way, navigating us round the elevated Sir de Villiers Graaf ring road, that God's gift to the city's inhabitants which took the through traffic out of their way, over their heads.

'I can't imagine what Johannesburg was like before

they built this highway,' Danilo commented. 'They still have a big traffic problem downtown, and as for parking ... there's more cars parked along the streets down there than one-armed bandits in Nevada ...'

'You've been here quite a time, then?'

'Hell, no,' he grinned. 'Only a few days. But I've been here before, once, and anyway it sure only takes twenty minutes of searching around to teach you that all the car parks are permanently full and that you can never park within a quarter-mile of where you want to be.'

He drove expertly and coolly on what was to him the wrong side of the road.

'Greville lives down near Turffontein,' he said. 'We drop down off this elevated part soon now ... did that sign say Eloff Street Extension?'

'It did,' I confirmed.

'Great.' He took the turn and we left the South African M1 and presently passed some football fields and a skating rink.

'They call this "Wembley",' Danilo said. 'And over there is a lake called Wemmer Pan for boating. And say, they have a water organ there which shoots coloured fountains up into the air in time to the music.'

'Have you been there?'

'No ... Greville told me, I guess. He also says it's a great place for fishing out rotting corpses and headless torsos.'

'Nice,' I said.

He grinned.

83

Before we reached Turffontein he turned off down a side road which presently became hard impacted earth covered with a layer of dust.

'They've had no rain here for four–five months,' Danilo said. 'Everything's sure looking dry.'

The grass was certainly brownish, but that was what I expected. I was surprised to learn from Danilo that in a month's time, when the rain came and the days were warmer, the whole area would be lush, colourful, and green.

'It's sure sad you won't be here to see the jacarandas,' Danilo said. 'They'll flower all over, after you've gone.'

'You've seen them before?'

He hesitated. 'Well no, not exactly. Last time I was here, they weren't flowering. It's just that Greville says.'

'I see,' I said.

'Here it is. This is Greville's place, right in here.' He pointed, then turned in between some severe-looking brick pillars and drove up a gravel drive into a stable which looked at if it had been transplanted straight from England.

Arknold himself was already out in the yard talking to a black African whom he introduced as his head boy, Barty. Arknold's head lad looked as tough as himself: a solid strong-looking man of about thirty, with a short thick neck and unsmiling cold eyes. He was the first black African I had seen, I thought in mild surprise, whose natural expression had not been good-natured.

There was nothing in his manner, however, but

civility, and he nodded to Danilo's greeting with the ordinary acknowledgement of people who meet each other fairly often.

Arknold said that everything was ready, and we started looking round the boxes without more ado. The horses were all like those I had seen on the track; up on their toes, with slightly less bone all round than those at home.

There was nothing at all to distinguish Nerissa's horses from their stable-mates. They looked as well, had legs as firm, eyes as bright; and they were not all stabled in one block, but were scattered among the rest. Colts in one quadrangle, fillies in another. Everything as it should be, as it normally would be in England.

The lads – the boys – were all young and all black. Like lads the world over they were possessively proud of the horses they cared for, though alongside this pride there emerged a second, quite definite, pattern of behaviour.

They responded to me with smiles, to Arknold with respect, and to Barty with unmistakable fear.

I had no knowledge of what sort of tribal hold he had over them, and I never did find out, but in their wary eyes and their shrinking away at his approach, one could see he held them in a bondage far severer than any British head lad could have imposed.

I thought back to the iron hand my father had once wielded. The lads had jumped to what he said, the apprentices had scurried, and indeed I had wasted no time, but I could not remember that anyone had held him in actual physical fear.

I looked at Barty and faintly shivered. I wouldn't have liked to work under him, any more than Arknold's lads did.

'This is Tables Turned,' Arknold was saying, approaching the box door of a dark chestnut colt. 'One of Mrs Cavesey's. Running at Germiston on Saturday.'

'I thought I might go to Germiston,' I said.

'Great,' Danilo said with enthusiasm.

Arknold nodded more moderately, and said he would arrange for me to pick up free entrance tickets at the gate.

We went into the box and stood in the usual sort of appreciative pause, looking Tables Turned over from head to foot while Arknold noted how he was looking compared with the day before and I thought of something not too uncomplimentary to say about him.

'Good neck,' I said. 'Good strong shoulders.' And a bit rat-like about the head, I thought to myself.

Arknold shrugged heavily. 'I took him down to Natal for the winter season, along with all the others. Had nearly the whole string down there for getting on for three months, like we do every year. We keep them at Summerveld, do you see?'

'Where is Summerveld?' I asked.

'More like what is Summerveld,' he said. 'It's a large area with stabling for about eight hundred horses, at Shongweni, near Durban. We book a block of stables there for the season. They have everything in the area one could need – practice track, restaurants, hostels for the boys, everything. And the school for jockeys and apprentices is there, as well.'

'But you didn't do much good, this year?' I said sympathetically.

'We won a few races with the others, but Mrs Cavesey's string . . . Well, to be frank, there are so many of hers that I can't afford to have them all go wrong. Does my reputation no good, do you see?'

I did see. I also thought he spoke with less passion than he might have done.

'This Tables Turned,' he said, slapping the horse's rump, 'on his breeding and his early form he looked a pretty good prospect for the Hollis Memorial Plate in June . . . that's one of the top two-year-old races . . . and he ran just like you saw Chink do at Newmarket. Blew up five hundred metres from home and finished exhausted, though I'd have sworn he was as fit as any of them.'

He nodded to the boy holding the horse's head, turned on his heel, and strode out of the box. Further down the line we reached another of Nerissa's, who evoked an even deeper display of disgust.

'Now this colt, Medic, he should have been a proper world-beater. I thought once that he'd win the Natal Free Handicap in July, but in the end I never sent him to Clairwood at all. His four races before that were too shameful.'

I had a strong feeling that his anger was half genuine. It puzzled me. He certainly did seem to care that the horses had all failed, yet I was still sure that he not only knew why they had but had engineered it himself.

With Barty in attendance, pointing out omissions with a stabbing black forefinger to every intimidated stable boy, we finished inspecting every one of the string, and afterwards went across to the house for a drink.

'All of Mrs Cavesey's lot are now counted as three-year-olds, of course,' Arknold said. 'The date for the age-change out here is August 1st, not January 1st as with you.'

'Yes,' I said.

'There isn't much good racing here on Rand tracks during August. Nothing much to interest you, I dare say.'

'I find it all extremely interesting,' I said truthfully. 'Will you go on running Mrs Cavesey's string as three-year-olds?'

'As long as she cares to go on paying their training fees,' he said gloomily.

'And if she decides to sell?'

'She'd get very little for them now.'

'If she sold them, would you buy any of them?' I asked.

He didn't answer immediately as he was showing us the way into his office, a square room full of papers, form books, filing cabinets and hard upright chairs. Arknold's guests were not, it seemed, to be made so comfortable that they outstayed their limited welcome.

I repeated my question unwisely, and received the full glare of the Arknold displeasure.

'Look, Mister,' he said fiercely. 'I don't like what you're suggesting. You are saying that maybe I lose races so I can buy the horses cheap, then win races when I have them myself, and then sell them well for stud. That's what you're saying, Mister.'

'I didn't say anything of the sort,' I protested mildly.

'It's what you were thinking.'

'Well,' I agreed. 'It was a possibility. Looking at it from outside, objectively, wouldn't that have occurred to you, too?'

He still glowered, but the antagonism slowly subsided. I wished I could decide whether he had been angry because I had insulted him, or because I had come too near the truth.

Danilo, who had been tagging along all the way making sunny comments to no one in particular, tried to smooth his ruffled friend.

'Aw, c'mon Greville, he meant no harm.'

Arknold gave me a sour look.

'Hey, c'mon. Aunt Nerissa probably told him to poke around for reasons, if he got the chance. You can't blame her, when she's pouring all that money into bad horses, now can you, Greville?'

Arknold made a fair pretence at being pacified and offered us a drink. Danilo smiled hugely in relief and said it wouldn't do, it wouldn't do at all, for us to quarrel.

I sipped my drink and looked at the two of them.

Glossy young golden boy. Square surly middle-aged man. They both drank, and watched me over the rims of the glasses.

I couldn't see an inch into either of their souls.

Back at the Iguana Rock there was a hand-delivered letter waiting for me. I read it upstairs in my room, standing by the window which looked out over the gardens, the tennis courts, and the great African outdoors. The light had begun fading and would soon go quickly, but the positive handwriting was still easy to see.

Dear Mr Lincoln,

I have received a cable from Nerissa Cavesey asking me to invite you to dinner. My wife and I would be pleased to entertain you during your visit, if you would care to accept.

Nerissa is the sister of my late brother's wife, Portia, and has become close to us through her visits to our country. I explain this, as Mr Clifford Wenkins of Worldic Cinemas, who very reluctantly informed me of your whereabouts, was most insistent that you would not welcome any private invitations.

Yours sincerely,

Quentin van Huren.

Behind the stiffly polite sentences, one could feel the irritation with which he had written that note. It was not only I, it seemed, who would do things slightly against their will, for Nerissa's sake: and Clifford Wenkins, with his fussing misjudgement of his responsibilities, had clearly not improved the situation.

I went over to the telephone beside the bed and put a call through to the number printed alongside the address on the writing-paper.

The call was answered by a black voice who said she would see if Mr van Huren was home.

Mr van Huren decided he was.

'I called to thank you for your letter,' I said. 'And to say that I would very much like to accept your invitation to dine with you, during my stay.' Two, I reckoned, could be ultra polite.

His voice was as firm as his handwriting, and equally reserved.

'Good.' He didn't sound overjoyed, however. 'It is always a pleasure to please Nerissa.'

'Yes,' I said.

There was a pause. The conversation could hardly be said to be rocketing along at a scintillating rate.

I said helpfully, 'I shall be here until a week next Wednesday.'

'I see. Yes. However, I shall be away from home all next week, and we are already engaged this Saturday and Sunday . . .'

'Then please don't worry,' I said.

He cleared his throat. 'I suppose,' he suggested doubtfully, 'that you would not be free tomorrow? Or,

91

indeed, this evening? My house is not far from the Iguana Rock . . . but of course I expect you are fully engaged.'

Tomorrow morning, I thought, all the newspapers would be flourishing a paragraph or two about Roderick Hodge's girlfriend. By tomorrow night, Mrs van Huren, if she felt like it, could fill her house with the sort of party I didn't like to go to. And tomorrow night I had agreed to have dinner with Conrad, though I could change that if I had to.

I said, 'If it is not too short notice, tonight would be fine.'

'Very well, then. Shall we say eight o'clock? I'll send my car to fetch you.'

I put down the receiver half regretting that I had said I would go, as his pleasure in my acceptance was about as intense as a rice-pudding. However, the alternatives seemed to be the same as the night before: either dine in the Iguana Rock restaurant with the sideways glances reaching me from the other tables, or upstairs alone in my room, wishing I was home with Charlie.

The house to which the van Hurens' car took me was big, old, and spelled money from the marble doorstep onwards. The hall was large, with the ceiling soaring away into invisibility, and round all four sides there was a graceful colonnade of pillars and arches: it looked like a small, splendid Italian piazza, with a roof somewhere over the top.

In the hall, from a door under the colonnade on the far side, came a man and a woman.

'I am Quentin van Huren,' he said. 'And this is my wife Vivi.'

'How do you do?' I said politely, and shook their hands.

There was a small hiatus.

'Yes ... well,' he said, making a gesture which was very nearly a shrug. 'Come along in.'

I followed them into the room they had come from. In the clearer light there, Quentin van Huren was instantly identifiable as a serious man of substance, since about him clung that unmistakable aura of know-how, experience and ability that constitutes true authority. As solidity and professionalism were qualities I felt at home with, I was immediately prepared to like him more than it seemed probable he would like me.

His wife Vivi was not the same: elegant-looking, but not in the same league intellectually.

She said, 'Do sit down, Mr Lincoln. We are so pleased you could come. Nerissa is such a very dear friend ...'

She had cool eyes and a highly practised social manner. There was less warmth in her voice than in her words.

'Whisky?' van Huren asked, and I said 'Thank you,' and got the tumbler full of water with the tablespoon of Scotch.

'I'm afraid I haven't seen any of your films,' van

Huren said, without sounding in the least sorry about it, and his wife added, 'We seldom go to the cinema.'

'Very wise,' I said without inflection, and neither of them knew quite how to take it.

I found it easier on the whole to deal with people intent on taking me down a peg rather than with the sycophantically over-flattering. Towards the snubbers I felt no obligation.

I sat down on the gold-brocaded sofa which she had indicated, and sipped my enervated drink.

'Has Nerissa told you she is . . . ill?' I asked.

They both sat without haste. Van Huren shifted a small cushion out of his way, twisting in his armchair to see what he was doing, and answered over his shoulder.

'She wrote a little while ago. She said she had something wrong with her glands.'

'She's dying,' I said flatly, and got from them their first genuine response. They stopped thinking about me. Thought about Nerissa. About themselves. The shock and regret in their faces were real.

Van Huren still held the cushion in his hand.

'Are you sure?' he said.

I nodded. 'She told me herself. A month or two, she says, is all she has.'

'Oh no,' Vivi said, her grief showing through the social gloss like a thistle among orchids.

'I can't believe it,' van Huren exclaimed. 'She is always so full of life. So gay. So vital.'

I thought of Nerissa as I had left her: vitality gone and life itself draining away.

'She is worried about her racehorses,' I said. 'The ones Portia left her.'

Neither of them was ready to think about racehorses. Van Huren shook his head, finished putting the cushion comfortably in his chair, and stared into space. He was a well-built man, at a guess in his fifties, with hair going neatly grey in distinguished wings above his ears. Seen in profile his nose was strongly rounded outwards from the bridge, but stopped straight and short with no impression of a hook. He had a firm, full-lipped, well-defined mouth, hands with square well-manicured nails, and a dark grey suit over which someone had taken a lot of trouble.

The door from the hall opened suddenly and a boy and a girl, quite remarkably alike, came in. He, about twenty, had the slightly sullen air of one whose feelings of rebellion had not carried him as far as actually leaving his palatial home. She, about fifteen, had the uncomplicated directness of one to whom the idea of rebellion had not yet occurred.

'Oh sorry,' she said. 'Didn't know we had anyone for dinner.' She came across the room in her jeans and a pale yellow tee-shirt, with her brother behind her dressed very much the same.

Van Huren said, 'This is my son Jonathan, and my daughter Sally . . .'

I stood up to shake hands with the girl, which seemed to amuse her.

'I say,' she said. 'Did anyone ever tell you you look like Edward Lincoln?'

'Yes,' I said. 'I am.'

'You are what?'

'Edward Lincoln.'

'Oh yeah.' She took a closer look. 'Oh golly. Good heavens. So you are.' Then doubtfully, afraid I was making a fool of her. 'Are you really?'

Her father said, 'Mr Lincoln is a friend of Mrs Cavesey . . .'

'Aunt Nerissa! Oh yes. She told us once that she knew you well . . . She's such a darling, isn't she?'

'She is,' I agreed, sitting down again.

Jonathan looked at me steadily with a cold and unimpressed eye.

'I never go to see your sort of film,' he stated.

I smiled mildly and made no answer: it was typical of the putting-down brand of remark made to me with varying degrees of aggression almost every week of my life. Experience had long ago shown that the only unprovocative reply was silence.

'Well, I do,' Sally said. 'I've seen quite a few of them. Was it really you riding that horse in *Spy Across Country*, like the posters said?'

I nodded, 'Mm.'

She looked at me consideringly. 'Wouldn't you have found it easier in a hackamore?'

96

I laughed involuntarily. 'Well, no. I know the script said the horse had a very light mouth, but the one they actually gave me to ride had a hard one.'

'Sally is a great little horsewoman,' her mother said unnecessarily. 'She won the big pony class at the Rand Easter show.'

'On Rojedda Reef,' Sally added.

The name meant nothing to me. But the others clearly thought it would. They looked at me expectantly, and in the end it was Jonathan who said with superiority, 'It's the name of our gold mine.'

'Really? I didn't know you had a gold mine.' I half deliberately said it with the same inflection that father and son had said they didn't see my films, and Quentin van Huren heard it. He turned his head quite sharply towards me, and I could feel the internal smile coming out of my eyes.

'Yes,' he said thoughtfully, holding my gaze. 'I see.' His lips twitched. 'Would you care to go down one? To see what goes on?'

From the surprised expressions on the rest of his family, I gathered that what he had offered was more or less the equivalent of my suggesting a Press conference.

'I'd like it enormously,' I assured him. 'I really would.'

'I'm flying down to Welkom on Monday morning,' he said. 'That's the town where Rojedda is . . . I'll be there the whole week, but if you care to come down with me Monday, you can fly back again the same evening.'

I said that would be great.

By the end of dinner the van Huren–Lincoln *entente* had progressed to the point where three of the family decided to go to Germiston that Saturday to watch Nerissa's horses run. Jonathan said he had more important things to do.

'Like what?' Sally demanded.

Jonathan didn't really know.

CHAPTER SEVEN

Friday turned out to be a meagre day for world news, which left a lot too much space for the perils of Katya. Seldom had the Press been invited in advance to such a spectacle, and in most papers it seemed to have made the front page.

One of them first unkindly suggested that it had all been a publicity stunt which had gone wrong, and then denied it most unconvincingly in the following paragraph.

I wondered, reading it, how many people would believe just that. I wondered, remembering that mischievous smile, whether Katya could possibly even have set it up herself. She and Roderick, between them.

But she wouldn't have risked her life. Not unless she hadn't realized she was risking it.

I picked up the *Rand Daily Star*, to see what they had made of Roderick's information, and found that he had written the piece himself. 'By our own *Rand Daily Star* eye-witness, Roderick Hodge' it announced at the top. Considering his emotional involvement it was not too highly coloured, but it was he, more than any of the others, who stressed, as Conrad had done, that if Katya had not taken the microphone away from me, it would have been I who got the shock.

I wondered how much Roderick wished I had done. For one thing, it would have made a better story.

With a twisting smile I read on to the end. Katya, he reported finally, was being detained in hospital over-night, her condition described as 'comfortable'.

I shoved the papers aside, and while I showered and shaved came to two conclusions. One was that what I had done was not particularly remarkable and certainly not worth the coverage, and the other was that after this I was going to have even more trouble explaining to Nerissa why all I could bring her were guesses, not proof.

Down at the reception desk I asked if they could get me a packed lunch and hire me a horse for the day out in some decent riding country. Certainly, they said, and waved a few magic wands: by mid-morning I was twenty-five miles north of Johannesburg setting out along a dirt road in brilliant sunshine on a pensioned-off race-horse who had seen better days. I took a deep contented breath of the sweet smell of Africa and padded along with a great feeling of freedom. The people who owned the horse had gently insisted on sending their head boy along with me so that I shouldn't get lost, but as he spoke little English and I no Bantu, I found him a most peaceful companion. George was small, rode well, and had a great line in banana-shaped smiles.

We passed a cross-roads where there was a large stall, all by itself, loaded with bright orange fruit and festooned with pineapples, with one man beaming beside them.

'*Naartjies*,' George said, pointing.

I made signs that I didn't understand. One thing about being an actor, it occasionally came in useful.

'*Naartjies*,' George repeated, dismounting from his horse and leading it towards the stall. I grasped the fact that George wanted to buy, so I called to him and fished out a five-rand note. George smiled, negotiated rapidly, and returned with a huge string bag of *naartjies*, two ripe pineapples, and most of the money.

In easy undemanding companionship we rode further, dismounted in some shade, ate a pineapple each, and cold chicken from the Iguana Rock, and drank some refreshing unsweet apple juice from tins George had been given to bring along. The *naartjies* turned out to be like large lumpy tangerines with green patches on the skin: they also tasted like tangerine, but better.

George ate his lunch thirty feet away from me. I beckoned to him to come closer, but he wouldn't.

In the afternoon we trotted and cantered a long way over tough scrubby brown dried grass, and finally, walking to cool the horses, found ourselves approaching the home stables from the opposite direction to the way we set out.

They asked ten rand for the hire of the horse, though the day I had had was worth a thousand, and I gave

George five rand for himself, which his employers whispered was too much. George with a last dazzling smile handed me the bag of *naartjies* and they all gave me friendly waves when I left. If only life were all so natural, so undemanding, so unfettered.

Five miles down the road I reflected that if it were, I would be bored to death.

Conrad was before me at the Iguana.

He met me as I came into the hall and surveyed me from head to foot, dust, sweat, *naartjies* and all.

'What on earth have you been doing, dear boy?'

'Riding.'

'What a pity I haven't an Arriflex with me,' he exclaimed. 'What a shot . . . you standing there looking like a gypsy with your back to the light . . . and those oranges . . . have to work it into our next film together, can't waste a shot like that . . .'

'You're early,' I remarked.

'Might as well wait here as anywhere else.'

'Come upstairs, then, while I change.'

He came up to my room and with unfailing instinct chose the most comfortable chair.

'Have a *naartjie*,' I said.

'I'd rather have a Martini, dear boy.'

'Order one, then.'

He rang for his drink and it came while I was in the shower. I towelled dry and went back into the bed-

102

room in underpants to find him equipped also with a Churchill-sized cigar, wreathed in smoke and smelling of London clubs and plutocracy. He was looking through the pile of newspapers which still lay tidily on the table, but in the end left them undisturbed.

'I've seen all those,' he said. 'How do you like being a real hero, for a change?'

'Don't be nutty. What's so heroic about first aid?'

He grinned. Changed the subject.

'What in hell's name made you come out here for a premiere after all those years of refusing to show your face off the screen?'

'I came to see some horses,' I said, and explained about Nerissa.

'Oh, well, then, dear boy, that does make more sense, I agree. And have you found out what's wrong?'

I shrugged. 'Not really. Don't see how I can.' I fished out a clean shirt and buttoned it on. 'I'm going to Germiston races tomorrow, and I'll keep my eyes open again, but I doubt if anyone could ever prove anything against Greville Arknold.' I put on some socks and dark blue trousers, and some slip-on shoes. 'What are you and Evan doing here, anyway?'

'Film making. What else?'

'What film?'

'Some goddam awful story about elephants that Evan took it into his head to do. It was all set up before he got roped in to finish *Man in a Car*, and since he chose to ponce around in Spain for all that time, we were late getting out here. Should be down in the Kruger Game Park by now.'

I brushed my hair.

'Who's playing the lead?'

'Drix Goddart.'

I glanced at Conrad over my shoulder. He smiled sardonically.

'Wax in Evan's hands, dear boy. Laps up direction like a well patted puppy.'

'Nice for you all.'

'He's so neurotic that if someone doesn't tell him every five minutes that he's brilliant, he thinks everyone hates him.'

'Is he here with you?'

'No, thank God. He was supposed to be, but now he comes out with all the rest of the team after Evan and I have sorted out which locations we want to use.'

I put down the brushes and fastened my watch round my wrist. Keys, change, handkerchief into trouser pockets.

'Did you see the rushes of the desert scenes while you were in England?' Conrad asked.

'No,' I said. 'Evan didn't invite me.'

'Just like him.' He took a long swallow and rolled the Martini round his teeth. He squinted at the long ash on the end of his mini-torpedo. He said, 'They were good.'

'So they damn well ought to be. We did them enough times.'

He smiled without looking at me. 'You won't like the finished film.'

After a pause, as he didn't explain, I said, 'Why not?'

'There's something in it besides and beyond acting.' He paused again, considering his words. 'Even to a jaundiced eye like mine, dear boy, the quality of suffering is shattering.'

I didn't say anything. He swivelled his eyes in my direction.

'Usually you do not reveal much of yourself, do you? Well, this time, dear boy, this time . . .'

I compressed my lips. I knew what I'd done. I'd known while I did it. I had just hoped that no one would be perceptive enough to notice.

'Will the critics see what you saw?' I asked.

He smiled lop-sidedly. 'Bound to, aren't they? The best ones, anyway.'

I stared despondently at the carpet. The trouble with interpreting scenes too well, with taking an emotion and making the audience feel it sharply, was that it meant stripping oneself naked in public. Nothing as simple as naked skin, but letting the whole world peer into one's mind, one's beliefs, one's experience.

To be able to reproduce a feeling so that others could recognize it, and perhaps understand it for the first time, one had to have some idea of what it felt like in reality. To show that one knew meant revealing what one had felt. Revealing oneself too nakedly did not come easily to a private man, and if one did not reveal oneself, one never became a great actor.

I was not a great actor. I was competent and popular, but unless I whole-heartedly took the step into frightening personal exposure, I would never do anything great. There was always for me, in acting beyond a certain limit, an element of mental distress. But I had thought, when I risked doing it in the car, that my own self would be merged indiscernibly with the trials the fictional character was enduring.

I had done it because of Evan: to spite him, more than to please him. There was a point beyond which no director could claim credit for an actor's performance, and I had gone a long way beyond that point.

'What are you thinking?' Conrad demanded.

'I was deciding to stick exclusively in future to unreal entertaining escapades, as in the past.'

'You're a coward, dear boy.'

'Yes.'

He tapped the ash off his cigar.

'No one is going to be satisfied, if you do.'

'Of course they are.'

'Uhuh.' He shook his head. 'No one will settle for paste after they see they could have the real thing.'

'Stop drinking Martinis,' I said. 'They give you rotten ideas.'

I walked across the room, picked up my jacket, put it on, and stowed wallet and diary inside it.

'Let's go down to the bar,' I said.

He levered himself obediently out of the chair.

'You can't run away from yourself for ever, dear boy.'

'I'm not the man you think I am.'

'Oh yes,' Conrad said. 'Dear boy, you are.'

At Germiston races the next day I found waiting for me at the gate not only the free entrance tickets promised by Greville Arknold, but also a racecourse official with a duplicate set and instructions to take me up to lunch with the Chairman of the Race Club.

I meekly followed where he led, and was presently shown into a large dining-room where about a hundred people were already eating at long tables. The whole van Huren family, including a sulky Jonathan, occupied chairs near the end of the table closer to the door, and when he saw me come in, van Huren himself rose to his feet.

'Mr Klugvoigt, this is Edward Lincoln,' he said to the man sitting at the end of the table: and to me added, 'Mr Klugvoigt is the Chairman.'

Klugvoigt stood up, shook hands, indicated the empty chair on his left, and we all sat down.

Vivi van Huren in a sweeping green hat sat opposite me, on the Chairman's right, with her husband beside her. Sally van Huren was on my left, with her brother beyond. They all seemed to know Klugvoigt well, and as a personality he had much in common with van Huren:

107

same air of wealth and substance, same self-confidence, same bulk of body and acuity of mind.

Once past the preliminaries and the politeness (how did I like south Africa: nowhere so comfortable as the Iguana Rock: how long was I staying) the conversation veered naturally back to the chief matter in hand.

Horses.

The van Hurens owned a four-year-old which had finished third in the Dunlop Gold Cup a month earlier, but they were giving it a breather during these less important months. Klugvoigt owned two three-year-olds running that afternoon with nothing much expected.

I steered the conversation round to Nerissa's horses without much difficulty, and from there to Greville Arknold, asking, but not pointedly, how he was in general regarded, both as man and trainer.

Neither van Huren nor Klugvoigt were of the kind to come straight out with what they thought. It was Jonathan who leant forward and let out the jet of truth.

'He's a rude bloody bastard with hands as heavy as a gold brick.'

'I have to advise Nerissa, when I get home,' I commented.

'Aunt Portia always said he had a way with horses,' Sally objected, in defence.

'Yeah. Backwards,' said Jonathan.

Van Huren gave him a flickering glance in which humour was by no means lacking, but he changed the subject immediately with the expertise of one thoroughly awake to the risk of slander.

'Your Clifford Wenkins, Link, telephoned to me yesterday afternoon to offer us all some tickets to your premiere.' He looked amused. I gratefully accepted that he had loosened with me to the point of dropping the meticulous 'Mr' and thought that in an hour or two I might get around to Quentin.

'Apparently he had had second thoughts about his abruptness to me when I asked for your address.'

'Probably been doing some belated homework,' agreed Klugvoigt, who seemed to know all about it.

'It's only a . . . an adventure film,' I said. 'You might not enjoy it.'

He gave me a dry sardonic smile. 'You won't accuse me again of condemning what I haven't seen.'

I smiled back. I considerably liked Nerissa's sister's husband's brother.

We finished the excellent lunch and wandered out for the first race. Horses were already being mounted, and Vivi and Sally hurried off to upset the odds with a couple of rand.

'Your friend Wenkins said he would be here today,' van Huren remarked.

'Oh dear.'

He chuckled.

Arknold, in the parade ring, was throwing his magenta-shirted jockey up into the saddle.

'How heavy is a gold brick?' I asked.

Van Huren followed my gaze. 'Seventy-two pounds, usually. You can't lift them as easily, though, as seventy-two pounds of jockey.'

Danilo was standing by the rails, watching. He turned as the mounted horses walked away, caught sight of us, and came straight across.

'Hi, Link. I've been looking out for you. How's about a beer?'

I said, 'Quentin,' (not two hours: ten minutes) 'this is Danilo Cavesey, Nerissa's nephew. And Danilo, this is Quentin van Huren, whose sister-in-law, Portia van Huren, was Nerissa's sister.'

'Gee,' Danilo said. His eyes widened and stayed wide, without blinking. He was more than ordinarily surprised.

'Good heavens,' van Huren exclaimed. 'I didn't even know she had a nephew.'

'I kinda dropped out of her life when I was about six, I guess,' Danilo said. 'I only saw her again this summer, when I was over in England from the States.'

Van Huren said he had only twice met Nerissa's husband, and never his brother, Danilo's father. Danilo said he had never met Portia. The two of them sorted out the family ramifications to their own content and seemed to meet in understanding in a very short time.

'Well, what do you know?' Danilo said, evidently pleased to the roots. 'Say, isn't that just too much?'

When Vivi and Sally and Jonathan rejoined us after the race they chattered about it like birds, waving their arms about and lifting their voices in little whoops.

'He's a sort of cousin,' said Sally positively. 'Isn't it the greatest fun?'

Even Jonathan seemed to brighten up at the idea of receiving the sunshine kid into the family, and the two of them presently bore him away on their own. I saw him looking back over his shoulder with a glance for me that was a lot older than anything Jonathan or Sally could produce.

'What a nice boy,' Vivi said.

'Nerissa is very fond of him,' I agreed.

'We must ask him over, while he is here, don't you think, Quentin? Oh look, do you see who's down there . . . Janet Frankenloots . . . haven't seen her for ages. Oh, do excuse me, Link . . .' The great hat swooped off to meet the long-lost friend.

Van Huren was too depressingly right about Clifford Wenkins being at the races. To say that the Distribution Manager approached as directly as Danilo had done would be inaccurate: he made a crabwise deprecating semicircle, tripping over his feet, and ended damply by my side.

'Er . . . Link, good to see you . . . er, would you be Mr van Huren? Pleased . . . er . . . to meet you, sir.'

He shook hands with van Huren, who from long social practice managed not to wipe his palm on his trousers afterwards.

'Now. Er . . . Link. I've tried to reach you a couple of times, but you never seem, er . . . I mean . . . I haven't

called you when you are . . . er . . . in. So I thought . . .
well, I mean, er . . . I would be certain to see you here.'

I waited without much patience. He pulled a batch of
papers hastily out of an inside pocket.

'Now, we want . . . that is to say, Worldic have
arranged . . . er . . . since you did the press interviews, I
mean . . . they want you to go to . . . let's see . . . there's a
beauty competition to judge next Wednesday for Miss
Jo'burg . . . and er . . . guest of honour at the Ladies'
Kinema Luncheon Club on Thursday . . . and on Friday
a fund-raising charity reception given by . . . er . . . our
sponsors for the premiere . . . er, that is Bow-Miouw
Pet-food, of course . . . and er . . . well . . . Saturday's . . .
the official opening of er . . . the Modern Homes'
Exhibition . . . all good publicity . . . er . . .'

'No,' I said. And for hell's sake don't lose your temper
here, I told myself severely.

'Er,' Wenkins said, seeing no danger signals. 'We . . .
er . . . that is, Worldic, do think . . . I mean . . . that you
really ought to cooperate . . .'

'Oh they do.' I slowed my breathing deliberately.
'Why do you think I won't let Worldic pay my
expenses? Why do you think I pay for everything
myself?'

He was extremely unhappy. Worldic must have been
putting on the pressure from one side, and now I am
resisting him from the other. The beads sprang out on
his forehead.

'Yes, but . . .' He swallowed. 'Well . . . I expect . . . I

mean . . . the various organizations might be prepared to offer . . . er . . . I mean . . . well, *fees.*'

I counted five. Squeezed my eyes shut and open. Said, when I was sure it would come out moderately, 'Mr Wenkins, you can tell Worldic that I do not wish to accept any of those invitations. In fact, I will go only to the premiere itself and a simple reception before or after, as I said.'

'But . . . We have told everybody that you will.'

'You know that my agent particularly asked you, right at the beginning, not to fix anything at all.'

'Yes, but Worldic·say . . . I mean . . .'

Stuff Worldic, I thought violently. I said, 'I'm not going to those things.'

'But . . . you can't . . . I mean . . . *disappoint* them all . . . not now . . . they will not go to your films, if you don't turn up when . . . er . . . we've . . . er . . . well . . . promised you will.'

'You will have to tell them that you committed me without asking me first.'

'Worldic won't like it . . .'

'They won't like it because it will hurt their own takings, if it hurts anything at all. But it's their own fault. If they thought they could make me go to those functions by a species of blackmail, they were wrong.'

Clifford Wenkins was looking at me anxiously and van Huren with some curiosity, and I knew that despite my best intentions the anger was showing through.

I took pity on Clifford Wenkins and a grip on myself.

'Tell Worldic I will not be in Johannesburg at all next week. Tell them that if they had had the common sense to check with me first, I could have told them I am committed elsewhere, until the premiere.'

He swallowed again and looked even unhappier.

'They said I must persuade you . . .'

'I'm sorry.'

'They might even fire me . . .'

'Even for you, Mr Wenkins, I can't do it. I won't be here.'

He gave me a spanked-spaniel look which I didn't find endearing, and when I said no more he turned disgustedly away and walked off, stuffing the papers roughly into the side pocket of his jacket.

Van Huren turned his handsome head and gave me an assessing look.

'Why did you refuse him?' he asked. No blame in his voice; simply interest.

I took a deep breath: got the rueful smile out, and stifled the irritation which Clifford Wenkins had raised like an allergic rash.

'I never do those things . . . beauty contests and lunches and opening things.'

'Yes. But why not?'

'I haven't the stamina.'

'You're big enough,' he said.

I smiled and shook my head. It would have sounded pretentious to tell him that so-called 'personal appearances' left me feeling invaded, battered, and devoured, and that complimentary introductory speeches gave me nothing in return. The only compliment I truly appreciated was the money plonked down at the box-office.

'Where are you off to, next week, then?' he asked.

'Africa is huge,' I said, and he laughed.

We wandered back to look at the next batch of hopefuls in the parade ring, and identified number eight as Nerissa's filly, Lebona.

'She looks perfectly all right,' van Huren commented.

'She will start all right,' I agreed. 'And run well for three-quarters of the way. Then she'll tire suddenly within a few strides and drop right out, and when she comes back her sides will be heaving and she'll look exhausted.'

He was startled. 'You sound as if you know all about it.'

'Only guessing. I saw Chink run like that at Newmarket on Wednesday.'

'But you think they are all running to the same pattern?'

'The form book confirms it.'

'What will you tell Nerissa, then?'

I shrugged. 'I don't know . . . Probably to change her trainer.'

In due course we returned to the stands and watched Lebona run as expected. Van Huren seeming in no haste to jettison me for more stimulating company, and I well content to have him as a buffer state, the two of us, passing the cluster of tables and chairs under sun umbrellas, decided to sit down there and order refreshers.

For the first day since I had arrived, the sunshine had grown hot. No breeze stirred the fringes round the flowered umbrellas, and ladies in all directions were shedding their coats.

Van Huren, however, sighed when I commented on the good weather.

'I like winter best,' he said. 'When it's cold, dry, and sunny. The summers are wet, and far too hot, even up here on the highveld.'

'One thinks of South Africa as always being hot.'

'It is, of course. Once you get down near to sea level, it can be scorching even as early as this.'

The shadows of two men fell across the table, and we both looked up.

Two men I knew. Conrad: and Evan Pentelow.

I made introductions, and they pulled up chairs and joined us; Conrad his usual flamboyant self, scattering dear boys with abandon, and Evan, hair as unruly as ever, and eyes as hot.

Evan weighed straight in. 'You won't now refuse to turn up at the premiere of my *Man in a Car*, I hope.'

'You sound very proprietary,' I said mildly. 'It isn't altogether yours.'

'My name will come first in the credits,' he asserted aggressively.

'Before mine?'

Posters of Evan's films were apt to have Evan Pentelow in large letters at the top, followed by the name of the film, followed, in the last third of the space, by the actors' names all squashed closely together. Piracy, it was, or little short.

Evan glared, and I guessed he had checked my contract for the film, and found, as I had done, that in the matter of billing my agent had made no mistakes.

'Before the other director,' he said grudgingly.

I supposed that was fair. Although he had directed less than a quarter, the shape of the finished film would be his idea.

Van Huren followed the sparring with amusement and attention.

'So billing does matter as much as they say.'

'It depends,' I smiled, 'on who is sticking knives into whose back.'

Evan had no sense of humour and was not amused. He began instead to talk about the film he was going to make next.

'It's an allegory . . . every human scene is balanced by a similar one involving elephants. They were supposed to be the good guys of the action, originally, but I've been learning a thing or two about elephants. Did you know they are more dangerous to man than any other animal in Africa? Did you know that nothing preys on them except ivory hunters, and as ivory hunting is banned in the Kruger Park, the elephants are in the middle of a population explosion? They are increasing by a thousand a year, which means that in ten years there

117

will be no room for any other animals, and probably no trees in the park, as the elephants uproot them by the hundred.'

Evan, as usual on any subject which took his attention, was dogmatic and intense.

'And do you know,' he went on, 'that elephants don't like Volkswagens? Those small ones, I mean. Elephants seldom attack cars ordinarily, but they seem to make a bee-line for Volkswagens.'

Van Huren gave a disbelieving smile which naturally stirred Evan to further passion.

'It's true! I might even incorporate it in the film.'

'Should be interesting,' Conrad said with more than a touch of dryness. 'Leaving a car around as bait at least makes a change from goats and tigers.'

Evan glanced at him sharply, but nodded. 'We go down to the park on Wednesday.'

Van Huren turned to me with a look of regret.

'What a pity you can't go down there too, Link, next week. You want somewhere to go, and you'd have liked it there. The game reserves are about all that's left of the old natural Africa, and the Kruger is big and open and still pretty wild. But I know the accommodation there is always booked up months ahead.'

I didn't think Evan would have wanted me in the least, but to my surprise he slowly said, 'Well, as it happens, we made reservations for Drix Goddart to be down there with us, but now he's not coming for a week or two. We haven't cancelled . . . there will be an empty bed, if you want to come.'

I looked at Conrad in amazement but found no clue in his raised eyebrows and sardonic mouth.

If it hadn't been for Evan himself I would have leapt at it; but I supposed that even he was a great deal preferable to Clifford Wenkins's programme. And if I didn't go to the Kruger, which very much appealed to me, where else?

'I'd like to,' I said. 'And thanks.'

CHAPTER EIGHT

Danilo fetched up at the sun-shade flanked by his two van Huren satellites.

Sally waited for no introductions to Conrad and Evan. She looked to see that she was not actually interrupting anyone in mid-sentence, and then spoke directly to her father.

'We told Danilo you were taking Link down the gold mine on Monday, and he wants to know if he could go too.'

Danilo looked slightly embarrassed to have his request put so baldly, but after only a fraction's hesitation van Huren said, 'Why, of course, Danilo, if you would like to.'

'I sure would,' he said earnestly.

'Gold mine?' said Evan intently, pouncing on the words.

'The family business,' explained van Huren, and scattered introductions all round.

'There could be great background material . . . a gold mine . . . something I could use one day.' He looked expectantly at van Huren who was thus landed unfairly with the choice of being coerced or ungracious. He took it in his stride.

'By all means join us on Monday, if you would care to.'

Evan gave him no chance to retract and included Conrad in the deal.

When they and the three young ones had all gone off to place their bets, I apologized to van Huren that his generosity should have been stretched.

He shook his head. 'It will be all right. We seldom take large parties of visitors down the mine as it slows or stops production too much, but we can manage four of you without a break in work, if you are all sensible, as I am sure you will be.'

By the end of the afternoon the number had grown to five, as Roderick Hodge also turned up at Germiston, and having learned of the expedition begged van Huren privately to be allowed to tag along with a view to a feature article in the *Rand Daily Star*.

I would have thought that gold mines were a stale topic in Johannesburg, but Roderick had his way.

I found him unexpectedly at my elbow while I was watching Tables Turned amble round the parade ring looking the prize colt he was not. Danilo and all the van Hurens had gone to tea with the Chairman, a meal I preferred to do without, and Conrad and Evan were away in the distance being accosted by the ever perspiring Clifford.

Roderick touched me on the arm, and said tentatively, 'Link?'

I turned. His fortyish face had grown new lines in the last few days and looked much too old for the length of his trendy hair and the boyish cut of his clothes.

'How is Katya?' I asked.

'She's fine. Remarkable, really.'

I said I was glad, and then asked if he often went to the races.

'No ... actually I came to see you. I tried to get you at the Iguana Rock but they said you were at the races ...'

'Did they indeed,' I murmured.

'Er ...' he explained. 'I have what you might call a *source* there. Keeps me informed, you see.'

I saw. All over the world there was a grey little army which tipped off the Press and got tipped in return: hotel porters, railway porters, hospital porters, and anyone within earshot of VIP lounges at airports.

'I live this side of the city, so I thought I might just as well drift along.'

'A nice day,' I said.

He looked up at the sky as if it would have been all one to him if it had been snowing.

'I suppose so ... Look, I got a call this morning from Joe ... that's the chap who was setting up the radio equipment at Randfontein House.'

'I remember,' I said.

'He said he had taken that microphone to pieces, and

there was nothing wrong with it. The outer wire of the coaxial cable was of course connected to the metal casing, though . . .'

'Ah,' I interrupted. 'And what exactly is a coaxial cable?'

'Don't you know? It's an electric cable made of two wires, but one wire goes up the centre like a core, and the other wire is circular, outside it. Television aerial cables are coaxial . . . you can see that by the ends, where you plug them into the sets.'

'Oh yes,' I agreed. 'I see.'

'Joe says he found the earth wire and the live wire had been fastened to the wrong terminals in the power plug of the recorder he was using for Katya. He says people are warned over and over again about the dangers of doing that, but they still do it. The current would go straight through the mike's casing, and earth itself through whoever was holding it.'

I thought. 'Wouldn't the whole recorder had been live too?'

He blinked. 'Yes. Joe says that inside it must have been. But no one would have got a shock from it. The casing of the recorder was plastic, the knobs were plastic, and Joe himself was wearing rubber-soled shoes, which he says he always does anyway, as a precaution.'

'But he must have used that recorder before,' I protested.

'He says not. He says he plugged it in because it was just standing there when something went wrong with his own. He didn't know whose it was, and no one seems to have claimed it since.'

Arknold gave his jockey a leg up on to Tables Turned and the horses began to move out for the race.

I said, 'It was all very bad luck.'

'Joe thinks so,' he agreed. There was, however, a shade of doubt in his voice, and I looked at him enquiringly. 'Well . . . it's an appalling thing to say, but Joe wondered whether it could possibly have been a publicity stunt that went too far. He says that Clifford Wenkins was fussing round the electronic equipment after your first broadcast, and that you yourself set up the conference, and you did get the most fantastic Press coverage for saving Katya . . .'

'I agree it's an appalling thing to say,' I said cheerfully. 'Consider me appalled. Consider also that I have already wondered whether it was a publicity stunt set up by you and Katya . . . which went too far.'

He stared. Then relaxed. Then ruefully smiled.

'All right,' he said. 'Neither of us fixed it. How about our Clifford?'

'You know him better than I do,' I said. 'But although he seems to have sold his soul to Worldic Cinemas, he doesn't strike me as having the nerve or the ingenuity to fix it all up.'

'You fluster him,' Roderick observed. 'He isn't always as futile-seeming as he's been since you arrived.'

Further along the rails from us stood Danilo, watching Nerissa's colt with a smile on his frank and bonny face. I thought that if he had known he was so soon to inherit them, he would have been anxious instead.

Arknold joined him, and together they walked on to the stands to watch. Roderick and I tailed along after. We all watched Tables Turned set off at a great rate, run out of puff two furlongs from home, and finish a spent force.

Arknold, muttering under his breath and looking like thunder, bumped into me as he made his way down the stand steps to hold a post-mortem with the jockey.

He focused on me and said abruptly, 'It's too much, Mister. It's too much. That's a bloody good colt and he should have won by a mile in that company.' He shut his mouth like a trap, brushed past me, and thrust his way down through the crowd.

'Whatever's all that about?' Roderick asked casually; so casually that I remembered the *Rand Daily Star*, and didn't tell him.

'No idea,' I said, putting on a bit of puzzle: but Roderick's sceptical expression said that he similarly was remembering where I worked.

We walked down from the stands. I considered ways and means, and decided Klugvoigt was the best bet for what I wanted. So I drifted Roderick gently to where Conrad and Evan were discussing adjourning to the bar, inserted him into their notice, and left as he began telling Conrad the theories of Joe and the coaxial cable.

The Chairman was in his private box surrounded by

ladies in decorative hats. He saw me hovering alone, beckoned to me to come up the adjacent stairs, and when I reached his side, pressed into my hand some drowned whisky in a warmish glass.

'How are you doing?' he asked. 'Winning, I hope.'

'Not losing, anyway.' I smiled.

'What do you fancy in the next?'

'I'd have to see them in the parade ring first.'

'Wise fellow,' he agreed.

I admired the facilities. 'The stands look new,' I commented.

'Not long built,' he agreed. 'Very much needed, of course.'

'And the weighing room . . . from the outside it looks so comfortable.'

'Oh, it is, my dear chap.' A thought struck him. 'Would you care to see round inside it?'

'How very kind of you,' I said warmly and made ready-to-go-at-once movements so that he shouldn't forget. After a moment or two we parked our unfinished drinks and strolled easily across to the large square administrative block which housed the weighing and changing rooms on the ground floor and the racecourse offices upstairs.

The whole thing was modern and comfortable, a long way from all too many English equivalents. There was a large room furnished with easy-chairs where owners and trainers could sit in comfort to plan their coups and dissect their flops, but Klugvoigt whisked me past it into the inner recesses.

The jockeys themselves shared in the bonanza, being supplied with man-sized wire lockers for their clothes (instead of a peg), a sauna bath (as well as showers) and upholstered daybeds to rest on (instead of a hard narrow wooden bench).

The man I had hoped to see was lying on one of the black leather-covered beds supporting himself on one elbow. He was known to me via the number boards as K. L. Fahrden. He was Greville Arknold's jockey.

I told Klugvoigt I would be interested to speak to him, and he said sure, go ahead, he would wait for me in the reception room by the door, as there was someone there he too wanted to speak with.

Fahrden had the usual sharp fine bones with the usual lack of fatty tissue between them and the skin. His wary, narrow-eyed manner changed a shade for the better when Klugvoigt told him my name, but underwent a relapse when I said I was a friend of Mrs Cavesey.

'You can't blame me for her horses running so stinking,' he said defensively.

'I don't,' I said patiently. 'I only wanted to ask you how they felt to you personally, so that I could tell Mrs Cavesey what you said.'

'Oh. Oh, well, then.' He considered, and came across. 'They give you a good feel, see, at the start. Full of running, and revelling in it. Then you go pick 'em up, see, and there's bloody nothing there. Put on the pressure, see, and they blow up instant like.'

'You must have given them a lot of thought,' I said. 'What do you think is wrong with them?'

He gave me a sideways look. 'Search me,' he said.

'You must have a theory,' I urged.

'Only the same as anyone would,' he agreed reluctantly. 'And I'm not saying more than that.'

'Mm . . . Well, what do you think of Mr Arknold's head lad?'

'Barty? That great brute. Can't say as I've ever thought much about him. Wouldn't want to meet him alone on a dark night, if that's what you mean.'

It wasn't entirely what I meant, but I let it go. I asked him instead how he got on with Danilo.

'A real nice guy, that,' he said, with the first sign of friendliness. 'Always takes a great interest in Arknold's horses, of course, seeing as how so many of them are his aunt's.'

'Did you meet him when he was over here before?' I asked.

'Oh sure. He stayed in the hotel down in Summerveld, for a couple of weeks. A great guy. Always good for a laugh. He said he'd just been staying with his aunt, and she was a great girl. He was the only cheerful thing around, when the horses started running badly.'

'When was that?' I asked with sympathy in my voice.

'Oh, way back in June sometime. Since then there's

been every investigation you could think of, into why they flop. Dope tests, vets, the lot.'

'Is Arknold a good man to ride for?' I asked.

He closed up at once. 'More than my job's worth to say different.'

I fielded Klugvoigt from the reception room, thanked him, and walked back with him towards the parade ring. Someone button-holed him on the way, so I wandered by myself right across the course to the simple stand of plain wooden steps on the far side. From there one had a comprehensive view of the whole lay-out: the long sweep of stands, the small patch of sun umbrellas, the block of private boxes. Behind them all, the parade ring and the weighing room.

And round and about, mingling, chatting, exchanging information and sipping at cooling glasses, went Danilo and Arknold, Conrad and Evan, Roderick and Clifford Wenkins, and Quentin, Vivi, Jonathan and Sally van Huren.

I booked a telephone call to Charlie when I got back to the Iguana Rock that evening, and it came through punctually the next morning, Sunday, at ten o'clock.

We could hear each other as clearly as if we had been six miles apart instead of six thousand. She said she was glad I had called and glad that I wasn't electrocuted: yes, she said, it had been in all the papers at home yesterday, and one or two disgustedly hinted that it had all been a put-up job.

'It wasn't,' I said. 'I'll tell you all about it when I get home. How are the kids?'

'Oh, fine. Chris says he's going to be an astronaut, and Libby has managed to say "pool" when she wants to go in the water.'

'That's great,' I said, meaning Libby's advance, and Charlie said yes, it was great, it really was.

'I do miss you,' I said lightly, and she answered with equal lack of intensity, 'It seems a lot longer than four days since you went away.'

'I'll be back straight after the premiere,' I said. 'Before that I'm taking a look round a gold mine and then going to the Kruger National Park for a few days.'

'Lucky sod.'

'After the kids have gone back to school, we'll have a holiday somewhere, just by ourselves,' I said.

'I'll hold you to it.'

'You can choose, so start planning.'

'OK,' she said it casually, but sounded pleased.

'Look . . . I really rang about Nerissa's horses.'

'Have you found out what's wrong with them?'

'I don't know,' I said. 'But I have had a fairly cataclysmic idea. I can't be sure I'm right, though, until, or in fact unless, you can do something for me in England.'

'Shoot,' she said economically.

'I want you to take a look at Nerissa's will.'

'Wow.' She drew in a sharp breath. 'How on earth do I do that?'

'Ask her. I don't know how you'll manage it, but if she's had fun drawing it up, she might not mind talking about it.'

'Well . . . what exactly do you want me to look for if she lets me see it?'

'I want to know particularly if besides the horses she has left the residue of her estate to Danilo.'

'All right,' she said doubtfully. 'Is it very important?'

'Yes and no.' I half laughed. 'Young Danilo is out here in South Africa at this moment.'

'Is he?' she exclaimed. 'Nerissa didn't tell us that.'

'Nerissa doesn't know,' I said. I described the golden Danilo to her, and also Arknold, and explained how the horses all lost to the same pattern.

'Sounds like the trainer nobbling them,' she commented.

'Yes. I thought so too, at first. But now . . . well, I think it's the Californian kid, our Danilo.'

'But it can't be,' she objected. 'Whatever could he have to gain?'

'Death duties,' I said.

After a pause Charlie said doubtfully, 'You can't mean it.'

'I do mean it. It's a theory, anyway. But I can't begin to prove it.'

'I don't really see . . .'

'Imagine,' I said, 'that when Danilo went to see

Nerissa in the early summer, their first reunion after all those years, she told him she had Hodgkin's disease. He had only to look it up in a medical directory . . . he would find out it is always fatal.'

'Oh dear,' she sighed. 'Go on.'

'Nerissa liked him very much,' I said. 'Well . . . he's an attractive boy in many ways. Supposing that, after she'd decided to, she told Danilo she was leaving him her horses, and some money as well.'

'It's an awful lot of supposing.'

'Yes,' I agreed. 'Would you ask Nerissa? Ask her if she told Danilo what illness she had, and also if she told him what she was leaving him.'

'Darling, she'd be terribly distressed, at this stage, to find she was wrong about him.' Charlie herself sounded upset. 'She is so very pleased to have him to leave things to.'

'Just get her chatting on the subject, if you can, and ask her casually. I agree that it's important not to distress her. It might actually be better to let Danilo get away with it. In fact, I've been thinking about that for most of the night. He has been defrauding her of the prize money she might have won. How much would she mind?'

'She might even laugh. Like you did just now. She might even think it was a pretty bright idea.'

'Yes . . . Of course he has also been defrauding the South African betting public, but I suppose it's up to the racing authorities here to deal with it, if they catch him.'

'What makes you think it is Danilo?'

'It's so insubstantial,' I said with frustration. 'Mostly a matter of chance remarks and impressions, and terribly few facts. Well . . . for one thing, Danilo was around the horses when they started doing badly. Their jockey told me Danilo was in Africa then, in June, for a fortnight, which must have been just after he had stayed with Nerissa, because he talked about having seen her. After that he presumably went back to the States for a while, but the horses went on losing, so obviously he was not doing the actual stopping himself. It's difficult to see how he could ever have the opportunity of doing it himself, anyway, but he seems to have an understanding with Arknold's head lad: and I'll admit that all I have to go on *there*, is the way they look at each other. Danilo never guards his face, by the way. He guards his tongue, but not his face. So suppose it is Barty, the head boy, who is arranging the actual fixing, with suitable rewards from Danilo.'

'Well . . . if you are right . . . how?'

'There are only two completely undetectable ways which can go on safely for a long time . . . over-exercising, which loses the race on the gallops at home (though in that case it is always the trainer who's guilty, and people notice and talk) . . . and the way I think Barty must be using, the plain old simple bucket of water.'

Charlie said, 'Keep a horse thirsty, maybe even put lashings of salt in its feed, and then give it a bucket or two of water before the race?'

'Absolutely. The poor things can't last the distance with three of four gallons sloshing around in their stomachs. And as for Barty . . . even if he were not always around to supply the water at the right time, he has all the other lads intimidated to such an extent that they'd probably cut off their own ears if he told them to.'

'But,' she objected, 'if the head lad has been doing this for weeks and weeks surely the trainer would have cottoned on?'

'I think he has,' I agreed. 'I don't think he likes it, but he's letting it pass. He said it was "too much" when one of Nerissa's best colts got beaten out of sight yesterday in a poor class race. And then he himself gave me a version of what might be going on, and what may happen in the future. He accused me of implying that he was losing with the horses so that Nerissa would sell them: he would then buy them cheap, start winning, and sell them at a vast profit for stud. I had only vaguely been thinking along those lines, but he crystallized it as though the thought were by no means new to him. It was that, really, which set me wondering about Danilo. That, and the way he was smiling while he watched one of the horses go out to race. That smile was all wrong. Anyway . . . if he can reduce the value of the horses to nearly nil by Nerissa's death, there will be a great deal less duty to pay on them than if they were all winning. The difference would run into many thousands, considering there are eleven horses. That would be a profit well worth the outlay on a couple of trips to South Africa and payola for the head lad. I think they are going to change the system, but as the tax laws stand at present he would have to be in line for the residue of the estate, for there to be any point in his doing it.'

'Unscramble my brains,' Charlie said.

I laughed. 'Well. Estate duty will be paid on everything Nerissa owns. Then the separate bequests will be handed out. Then what is left will be the residue. Even though the horses are in South Africa, estate duty on them will be levied in England, because Nerissa lives there. So if the estate has to pay out all those thousands in death duties on the horses, there will be that many thousands less in the residue for Danilo to inherit.'

'Gotcha,' she said. 'And wow again.'

'Then, after they are safely his, he stops the watering lark, lets them win, sells them or puts them to stud, and collects some more lolly.'

'Oh, neat. Very neat.'

'Pretty simple, too.'

'I say,' she said. 'Isn't there anything we could try along the same lines? All that mountain of surtax we pay . . . and then when one of us dies we lose another terrific chunk of what we've paid tax on once already.'

I smiled. 'Can't think of anything which fluctuates in value so easily as a horse.'

'Let's buy some more, then.'

'And of course you have to know, pretty well to a month, exactly when you are going to die.'

'Oh damn it,' Charlie said laughing. 'Life is a lot of little green apples and pains in the neck.'

'I wonder if "a pain in the neck" originated from the axe.'

'The axeman cometh,' she said. 'Or for axe, read tax.'

'I'll bring you back a nugget or two from the gold mine,' I promised.

'Oh thanks.'

'And I'll telephone again on ... say ... Thursday evening. I'll be down in the Kruger Park by then. Would Thursday be OK for you?'

'Yes,' she said soberly, the fun vanishing like mist. 'I'll go over to Nerissa's before then, and see what I can find out.'

CHAPTER NINE

You can't keep a good Dakota down.

There were two of them waiting at the small Rand Airport near Germiston racecourse, sitting on their tail wheels and pointing their dolphin snouts hopefully to the sky.

We onloaded one of them at eight on Monday morning, along with several other passengers and a sizeable amount of freight. Day and time were unkind to Roderick, making it clearer than ever that letting go of a semblance of youth was long overdue. The mature man, I reflected, was in danger of wasting altogether the period when he could look most impressive: if Roderick were not careful he would slip straight from ageing youth to obvious old age, a mistake more often found in show business than journalism.

He was wearing a brown long-sleeved suede jacket with fringes hanging from every possible edge. Under that, an open-necked shirt in an orange-tan colour, trousers which were cut to prove masculinity, and the latest thing in desert boots.

Van Huren, at the other end of the scale in a dark city suit, arrived last, took control easily, and shunted us all aboard. The Dakota trip took an hour, and landed one hundred and sixty miles south, at an isolated mining town which had Welkom on the mat and on practically everything else.

The van Huren mine was on the far side from the airport, and a small bus had come to fetch us. The town was neat, modern, geometrical, with straight bright rows of little square houses and acres of glass-walled super-markets. A town of hygienic packaging, with its life blood deep underground.

Our destination looked at first sight to be a collection of huge whitish grey tips, one with its railway track climbing to the top. Closer acquaintance revealed the wheel-in-scaffolding at the top of the shaft, masses of administration buildings and miners' hostels, and dozens of decorative date palms. The short frondy trees, their sunlit leaf-branches chattering gently in the light breeze, did a fair job at beating the starkness, like gift-wrapping on a shovel.

Van Huren apologized with a smile for not being able to go down the mine with us himself: he had meetings all morning which could not be switched.

'But we'll meet for lunch,' he promised, 'and for that drink which you will all need!'

The guide someone a couple of rungs down the hier-archy had detailed to show us round was a grumpy young Afrikaaner who announced that he was Pieter

Losenwoldt and a mining engineer, and more or less explicitly added that his present task was a nuisance, an interruption of his work, and beneath his dignity.

He showed us into a changing room where we were to sink all differences in white overalls, heavy boots, and high-domed helmets.

'Don't take anything of your own down the mine except your underpants and a handkerchief,' he said dogmatically. 'No cameras.' He glowered at the equipment Conrad had lugged along. 'Camera flashes are not safe. And no matches. No lighters. When I say nothing, I mean nothing.'

'How about wallets?' Danilo demanded, antagonized and showing it.

Losenwoldt inspected him, saw a better looking, richer, more obviously likeable person than himself, and reacted with an even worse display of chips on shoulder.

'Leave everything,' he said impatiently. 'The room will be locked. Everything will be quite safe until you get back.'

He went away while we changed, and came back in similar togs.

'Ready? Right. Now, we are going 4,000 feet down. The lift descends at 2,800 feet a minute. It will be hot in places underground. Anyone who feels claustrophobic or ill in any way is to ask to return to the surface straight away. Understand?'

He got five nods and no affection.

He peered suddenly at me, speculating, then

dismissed the thought with pursed lips and a shake of the head. No one enlightened him.

'Your light packs are on the table. Please put them on.'

The light packs consisted of a flat power pack which one wore slung over the lumbar region, and a light which clipped on to the front of the helmet. A lead led from one to the other. The power packs fastened round one's waist with webbing, and were noticeably heavy.

Much like the seven dwarfs we tramped forth to the mine. The cage we went down in had half-sides only, so that the realities of rock burrowing hit at once. No comfort. A lot of noise. The nasty thought of all that space below one's booted feet.

It presumably took less than two minutes to complete the trip, but, as I was jammed tight between Evan, whose hot eyes looked for once apprehensive, and a six-foot-four twenty-stone miner who had joined with several cronies at the top, I couldn't exactly check it by stop-watch.

We landed with a clang at the bottom and disembarked. Another contingent were waiting to go up, and as soon as we were out, they loaded and operated the system of buzzers which got them clanking on their way.

'Get into the trucks,' said Losenwoldt bossily. 'They hold twelve people in each.'

Conrad surveyed the two trucks, which looked like wire cages on wheels with accommodation for one large dog if he curled himself up, and said sideways to me: 'Sardines have struck for less.'

I laughed. But the trucks did hold twelve; just. The last man in had to sit in the hole that did duty as doorway, and trust to what he could find to hang on to that he didn't fall out. Evan was last in. He hung on to Losenwoldt's overalls. Losenwoldt didn't like it.

Loaded to the gunnels, the trucks trundled off along the tunnel which stretched straight ahead for as far as one could see. The walls were painted white to about four feet: then there was a two-inch-deep bright red line, then above that the natural grey rock.

Conrad asked Losenwoldt why the red line was there: he had to shout to be heard, and he had to shout twice, as Losenwoldt was in no hurry to answer.

Finally he crossly shouted back. 'It is a guide to the tunnellers. When the tunnel is painted like this, they can see that they are making it straight and level. The red line is an eye-line.'

Conversation lapsed. The trucks covered about two miles at a fast trot and stopped abruptly at nowhere in particular. It was suddenly possible to hear oneself speak again, and Losenwoldt said, 'We get out here, and walk.'

Everyone unsqueezed themselves and climbed out. The miners strode purposefully away down the tunnel, but there was, it seemed, a set pattern for instructing visitors. Losenwoldt said ungraciously (but at least he said it), 'Along the roof of the tunnel you can see the cables from which we have the electric lights.' The lights were spaced overhead at regular intervals so that the whole tunnel was evenly lit. 'Beside it there is a live electric rail.' He pointed. 'That provides power for the trucks which take the rock along to the surface. The rock goes up in a faster lift, at more than 3,000 feet a minute. That big round pipe up there carries air. The mine is ventilated by blowing compressed air into it at many points.'

We all looked at him like kids round a teacher, but he had come to the end of that bit of official spiel, so he turned his back on us and trudged away down the tunnel.

We followed.

We met a large party of black Africans walking the other way. They were dressed as we were except that they were wearing sports jackets on top of their overalls.

Roderick asked, 'Why the jackets?'

Losenwoldt said, 'It is hot down here. The body gets accustomed. Without a jacket, it feels cold on reaching the surface. You can catch chills.'

Evan nodded wisely. We went on walking.

Eventually we came to a wider space where a second tunnel branched off to the right. Another party of Africans was collecting there, putting on jackets and being checked against a list.

'They have finished their shift,' Losenwoldt said, in his clipped way, hating us. 'They are being checked to make sure none of them is still underground when blasting takes place.'

142

'Blasting, dear boy?' said Conrad vaguely.

The expert eyed him with disfavour. 'The rock has to be blasted. One cannot remove it with pickaxes.'

'But I thought this was a gold mine, dear boy. Surely one does not need blasting to remove gold? Surely one digs out gravel and sifts the gold from it.'

Losenwoldt looked at him with near contempt. 'In California and Alaska, and in some other places, this may be so. In South Africa the gold is not visible. It is in minute particles in rock. One has to blast out the gold-bearing rock, take it to the surface, and put it through many processes, to remove the gold. In this mine, one has to take three tons of rock to the surface to obtain one ounce of pure gold.'

I think we were all struck dumb. Danilo's mouth actually dropped open.

'In some mines here in the Odendaalsrus gold field,' Losenwoldt went on, seeming not to notice the stunned reaction, 'it is necessary to remove only one and a half tons to get one ounce. These mines are of course the richest. Some need more than this one: three and a half or four tons.'

Roderick looked around him. 'And all the gold has been taken from here? And from where we came?'

His turn for the look of pity-contempt.

'This tunnel is not made through gold-bearing rock. This tunnel is just to enable us to get to the gold-bearing rock, which is in this part of the mine. It can only be reached at more than 4,000 feet underground.'

'Good God,' Conrad said, and spoke for us all.

Losenwoldt plodded grudgingly on with his lecture, but his audience were riveted.

'The reef . . . that is to say, the gold-bearing rock . . . is only a thin layer. It slopes underground from the north, being deepest beyond Welkom, further south. It extends for about eight miles from east to west, and about fourteen miles from north to south, but its limits are irregular. It is nowhere more than three feet in depth, and in this mine it is on average thirteen inches.'

He collected a lot of truly astonished glances, but only Danilo had a question.

'I suppose it must be worth it,' he said doubtfully. 'All this work and equipment, just to get so little gold.'

'It must be worth it or we would not be here,' said Losenwoldt squelchingly, which I at least interpreted as ignorance of the profit and loss figures of the business. But it must be worth it, I reflected, or van Huren would not live in a sub-palace.

No one else said anything. Seldom had cheerful casual conversation been more actively discouraged. Even Evan's natural inclination to put himself in charge of everything was being severely inhibited; and in fact, after looking apprehensive in the lift he now seemed the most oppressed of us all at the thought of millions of tons of rocks pressing down directly above our heads.

'Right,' said Losenwoldt with heavy satisfaction at having reduced the ranks to pulped silence. 'Now, switch on your helmet lights. There are no electric lights further along there.' He pointed up the branch tunnel. 'We will go to see the tunnelling in progress.'

He strode off without checking to see that we all followed, but we did, though Evan gave a backward glance in the direction of the shaft which would have warned a more careful guide not to take too much for granted.

The tunnel ran straight for a while and then curved to the right. As we approached the corner we could hear a constantly increasing roaring noise, and round on the new tack it increased noticeably.

'What's that noise?' Evan asked in a voice still the safe side of active anxiety.

Losenwoldt said over his shoulder, 'Partly the air-conditioning, partly the drilling,' and kept on going. The spaced electric light bulbs came to an end. The lights on our helmets picked the way.

Suddenly, far ahead, we could discern a separate glimmer of light beyond the beams we were ourselves throwing. Closer contact divided the glimmer into three individual helmet lights pointing in the same direction as ours: but these lit only solid rock. We were coming to the end of the tunnel.

The walls at this point were no longer painted a comforting white with a red line, but became the uniform dark grey of the basic rock, which somehow emphasized the fanaticism of burrowing so deep in the earth's undisturbed crust, in search of invisible yellow dust.

The air pipe stopped abruptly, the compressed air

roaring out from its open mouth. Beyond that the noise of the drilling took over, as aggressive to the eardrums as six fortissimo discotheques.

There were three miners standing on a wooden platform, drilling a hole into the rock up near the eight-foot-high roof. Our lights shone on the sweat on their dark skins and reflected on the vests and thin trousers they wore in place of everyone else's thick white overalls.

The racket came from a compressor standing on the ground, as much as from the drill itself. We watched for a while. Evan tried to ask something, but it would have taken a lip reader to get anywhere.

Finally Losenwoldt, with a tight mouth and tired eyelids, jerked his head for us to go back. We followed him, glad about the lessening load on our ears. Walking last, I turned round where the air pipe ended, switched off my helmet light for a moment, and looked back. Three men on their scaffolding, intent on their task, enveloped in noise, and lit only by the glow-worms on their heads. When I had turned and gone, they would be alone with the primaeval darkness closing in behind them. I was left with a fanciful impression of a busy team of devils moleing along towards Inferno.

Once back in the wider section Losenwoldt continued our instruction.

'They were drilling holes about six feet deep, with tungsten drills. That,' he pointed, 'is a pile of drills.'

We looked where he pointed. The horizontal stack of six-foot rods by the tunnel wall had looked more like a heap of unused piping before: but they were solid metal rods about two inches in diameter with a blade of tungsten shining at the end of each.

'The rods have to be taken to the surface every day, to be sharpened.'

We nodded like wise owls.

'Those three men have nearly finished drilling for today. They have drilled many holes in the face of the tunnel. Each hole will receive its charge of explosive, and after the blasting the broken rock will be removed. Then the drillers return and start the process again.'

'How much tunnel can you make in one day?' Roderick asked.

'Eight feet a shift.'

Evan leant against the rock wall and passed a hand over a forehead that Clifford Wenkins could not have bettered.

'Don't you ever use pit-props?' he said.

Losenwoldt answered the face of the question and didn't see the fear behind it.

'Of course not. We are tunnelling not through earth, but through bedrock. There is no danger of the tunnel collapsing inwards. Occasionally, loosened slabs of rock fall from the roof or the wall. This usually happens in areas recently blasted. Where we see such loosened rocks, we pull them down, if we can, so that there is no danger of them falling on anyone later.'

Evan failed to look comforted. He dug out his handkerchief and mopped up.

'What sort of explosive do you use,' Danilo asked, 'for blasting?'

Losenwoldt still didn't like him, and didn't answer. Roderick, who was also interested, repeated the same question.

Losenwoldt ostentatiously stifled a sigh and replied in more staccato sentences than ever.

'It is Dynagel. It is a black powder. It is kept in locked red boxes fastened to the tunnel wall.'

He pointed to one of them a little further on. I had walked past two or three of them, padlocks and all, without wondering what they were for.

Danilo, with sarcasm, said to Roderick, 'Ask him what happens when they blast,' and Roderick did.

Losenwoldt shrugged. 'What would you expect? But no one sees the blasting. Everyone is out of the mine before the charges are detonated. No one returns down the mine for four hours after blasting.'

'Why not, dear boy?' drawled Conrad.

'Dust,' Losenwoldt said succinctly.

'When do we get to see this gold rock . . . this reef?' asked Danilo.

'Now.' Losenwoldt pointed along the continuation of the main tunnel. 'Further down there it will be very hot. There is a stretch with no air conditioning. Beyond that there is air again. Leave your helmet lights on, you will need them. Take care where you walk. The floor of the tunnel is rough in places.'

He finished with a snap and as before set off with his back to us.

Again we followed.

I said to Evan, 'Are you OK?' which irritated him into straightening his spine and flashing the eyes and saying of course he damn well was, did I think he was a fool.

'No,' I said.

'Right then.' He strode purposefully past me to get nearer to the pearls spat from Losenwoldt's lips and I again brought up the rear.

The heat further on was intense but dry, so that although one felt it, it produced no feeling of sweat. The tunnel at this point grew rough, with uneven walls, no painted lines, no lights, and a broken-up floor: it also sloped gradually downhill. We trudged on, boots crunching on the gritty surface.

The further we went, the more activity we came across. Men in white overalls were everywhere, busy, carrying equipment, with their helmet lights shining on other people's concentrated faces. The peak of each helmet tended to throw a dark band of shadow across every man's eyes, and once or twice I had to touch Roderick, who was in front of me, so that he would turn and reassure me that I was still following the right man.

At the end of the hot stretch it felt like stepping straight into the Arctic. Losenwoldt stopped there and consulted briefly with two other young miners he found talking to each other.

'We will split up here,' he said finally. 'You two with

me.' He pointed to Roderick and Evan. 'You two with Mr Anders.' He assigned Conrad and Danilo to a larger version of himself. 'You,' he pointed at me, 'with Mr Yates.'

Yates, younger than the others, appeared unhelpfully subservient to them, and spoke with a slight speech impediment in the order of a cleft palate. He gave me a twitchy smile and said he hoped I wouldn't mind, he wasn't used to showing people round, it wasn't usually his job.

'It's kind of you to do so,' I said soothingly.

The others were moving off in their little groups and were soon lost in the general crowd of white overalls.

'Come along then.'

We continued down the tunnel. I asked my new guide what the gradient was.

'About one in twenty,' he said. But after that he lapsed into silence, and I reckoned if I wanted to know any more I would have to ask. Yates did not know the conducted tour script like Losenwoldt, who in retrospect did not seem too bad.

Holes appeared from time to time in the left-hand wall, with apparently a big emptiness behind them.

'I thought this tunnel was through solid rock,' I observed. 'So what are those holes?'

'Oh . . . we are now in the reef. The reef has been removed from much of that portion behind that wall. In a minute I'll be able to show you better.'

'Does the reef slope at one in twenty, then?' I asked.

He thought it a surprising question. 'Of course,' he said.

'That tunnel which is still being drilled, back there, where is that going?'

'To reach another area of reef.'

Yes. Silly question. The reef spread laterally for miles. Quite. Removing the reef must be rather like chipping a thin slice of ham out of a thick bread sandwich.

'What happens when all the reef is removed?' I asked. 'There must be enormous areas with nothing holding up the layers of rock above.'

He answered willingly enough. 'We do not remove all supports. For instance, the wall of the tunnel is thick, despite the holes, which are for blasting and ventilation purposes. It will hold the roof up in all this area. Eventually, of course, when this tunnel is worked out and disused, the layers will gradually close together. I believe that most of Johannesburg sank about three feet, as the layers below it closed together, after all the reef was out.'

'Not recently?' I said, surprised.

'Oh, no. Long ago. The Rand gold fields are shallower and mining began there first.'

People were carrying tungsten rods up the tunnel and others were passing us down it.

'We are getting ready to blast,' Yates said without being asked. 'All the drilling is finished and the engineers are setting the charges.'

'We haven't very long, then,' I said.

'Probably not.'

'I'd like to see how they actually work the reef.'

'Oh . . . yes. Just down here a bit further, then. I will take you to the nearest part. There are others further down.'

We came to a larger than usual hole in the wall. It stretched from the floor to about five feet up, but one could not walk straight through it, as it sloped sharply upwards inside.

He said, 'You will have to mind your head. It is very shallow in here.'

'OK,' I said.

He gestured to me to crawl in ahead of him, which I did. The space was about three feet high but extended out of sight in two directions. A good deal of ham had already gone from this part of the sandwich.

Instead of a firm rock floor, we were now scrambling over a bed of sharp-edged chips of rock, which rattled away as one tried to climb up over them. I went some way into the flat cavern and then waited for Yates. He was close behind, looking across to our right where several men lower down were working along a curving thirty-foot stretch of the far wall.

'They are making final checks on the explosive charges,' he said. 'Soon everyone will begin to leave.'

'This loose stuff we are lying on,' I said. 'Is this the reef?'

'Oh . . . no, not exactly. These are just chips of rock. See, the reef used to lie about midway up the stope.'

'What is the stope?'

'Sorry . . . the stope is what we are now in. The place we take the reef from.'

'Well . . . down there, in the part which is not blasted yet, how do you tell which is the reef?'

The whole thing looked the same to me. Dark grey from top to bottom. Dark grey uneven roof curving down in dark grey uneven walls, merging into dark grey shingle floor.

'I'll get you a piece,' he said obligingly, and crawled crabwise on his stomach over to where his colleagues were working. It was barely possible to sit up in the stope. Just about possible to rise to hands and knees, if one kept one's head down. I supported myself on one elbow and watched him borrow a small hand pick and lever a sliver of rock out of the far wall.

He scrambled back.

'There you are . . . This is a piece of reef.'

We focused both our lights on it. A two-inch-long grey sharp-edged lump with darker grey slightly light-reflecting spots and streaks on its surface.

'What are those dark spots?' I said.

'That's the ore,' he said. 'The paler part is just ordinary rock. The more of those dark bits there are in the reef, the better the yield of gold per ton of rock.'

'Then is this dark stuff . . . gold?' I asked dubiously.

'It has gold in it,' he nodded. 'Actually it is made up of four elements: gold, silver, uranium and chrome. When the reef is milled and treated, they are separated out. There is more gold than silver or uranium.'

'Can I keep this piece?' I asked.

'Certainly.' He cleared his throat. 'I am sorry, but they have a job for me to do down there. Could you possibly find your own way back up the tunnel? You cannot get lost.'

'That's all right,' I said. 'You go on, I don't want to interfere with your job.'

'Thank you,' he said, and scrambled away in haste to please the people who really mattered to him.

I stayed where I was, for a while, watching the engineers and peering into the interminable dug-out space uphill. The light of my helmet couldn't reach its limits: it stretched away into impenetrable blackness.

The workers below me were thinning out, returning to the tunnel to make their way back towards the shaft. I put the tiny piece of reef in my pocket, took a last look round, and began to inch my way back to the hole where I had come in. I turned round to go into the tunnel feet first, but as I started to shuffle backwards I heard someone begin to climb into the stope behind me, the light from his helmet flashing on my overalls. I stopped, to let him go by. He made a little forward progress and I glanced briefly over my shoulder to see who it was. I could see only the peak of his helmet, and shadow beneath.

Then my own helmet tipped off forward and a large chunk of old Africa clobbered me forcefully on the back of the head.

Stunned, it seemed to me that consciousness ebbed

away slowly: I fell dizzily down endless mine shafts with flashing dots before my eyes.

I had blacked out completely long before I had hit the bottom.

CHAPTER TEN

Blackness.

Nothing.

I opened my eyes. Couldn't see. Put my hand to my face to feel if my eyelids were open.

They were.

Thought was entirely disconnected. I didn't know where I was, or why I was there, or why I couldn't see. Time seemed suspended. I couldn't decide whether I was asleep or not, and for a while I couldn't remember my own name.

Drifted away again. Came back. Snapped suddenly into consciousness. Knew I was awake. Knew I was me.

Still couldn't see.

I moved; tried to sit up. Discovered I was lying on my side. When I moved, I heard the crunching noise and felt the sharp rock chips shifting against my pressure.

In the stope.

Cautiously I put up a hand. The rock ceiling was a couple of feet above my head.

No helmet on my head. A tender lump on the back of it and a thumping pain inside it.

Bloody hell, I thought. I must have bashed my head. I'm in the stope. I can't see because there isn't any light. Everyone has left the mine. And the blasting charges will go off at any minute.

For a paralysing age I couldn't think beyond the fact that I was going to be blown to bits before I had even finished realizing it. After that I thought it might have been better if I'd been blown to bits before I woke up. At least I wouldn't now be awake worrying. After that, and not before time, I began wondering what to do.

Light, first.

I felt around to my back, found the lead from the power pack and gently pulled it. The other end scraped towards me over the choppy shingle, but when I picked up the torch I knew I wasn't going to get any light. The glass and the bulb were both smashed.

The light unit had come off the bracket on the helmet. I felt around with an outstretched hand, but couldn't find the helmet.

Must get out, I thought urgently, and in the same split second wondered . . . which way was out.

I made myself stay still. The last thing I remembered was agreeing with Yates that I could find my own way back. I must have been stupid enough to try to raise my head too high. Must literally have hit the roof. I couldn't remember doing it. The only thing that seemed clear was that I had smashed my helmet light when I fell, and that no one had seen me lying there in the dark.

Bloody fool, I cursed myself. Clumsy bloody fool, getting into this mess.

Gingerly, with one arm outstretched, I shifted myself a foot forward. My fingers found nothing to touch except stone chips.

I had to know which way I was going. Otherwise, I thought, I may be crawling away from safety, not towards it. I had to find the hole in the tunnel.

I picked up a handful of the flinty pebbles and began throwing them methodically round in a circle, starting on my right. It was an erratic process, as some hit the roof and some the ground, but enough went far enough before they fell to assure me that there was a small space all around me in front.

I rolled over on to my back and the power pack dug into me. I unfastened the webbing and pulled it off. Then I threw another lot of stones in arc round my legs.

The wall of the tunnel was there. A lot of the stones hit it.

My heart by then was thudding so much it was deafening me. Shut up, shut up, I said to myself. Don't be so bloody scared, it isn't of any practical use.

I threw more stones, this time not to find the wall, but the hole in it. I found it almost at once. Threw more stones to make sure: but there it had to be, just to the left of where my feet were pointing, because all the stones that went over there were falling further away, and clattering after they landed. They weren't round enough to roll, but heavy enough to continue downhill when they fell. Downhill . . . on the steep little slope from the stope into the tunnel.

More stones. I moved my feet, then my whole body, until the hole was straight in front over my toes. Then on my elbows and my bottom, keeping my head well back, I shuffled forwards.

More stones. Hole still there.

More shuffling. Another check.

It couldn't have been more than ten feet. Felt like ten miles.

I tentatively swept my arms around in the air. Could feel the roof, nothing else.

Went forward another two or three feet. Felt around with my arms. Touched solid rock. Ahead, to the right.

Another foot forward. Felt my feet turn abruptly downwards, bending my knees. Put both my hands out sideways and forwards and felt rock on both sides. Half-way out of the hole . . . and gingerly, lying flat, I inched forward until my feet scrunched on the tunnel floor. Even then I bent my knees and continued slithering without raising my head, all too aware of the hard sharpness of the rock above the vulnerability of my unhelmeted skull.

I ended on my knees in the tunnel, gasping and feeling as frightened as ever.

Think.

The holes had been in the left-hand wall, as we came

down. Once in the tunnel, Yates had said, I couldn't get lost.

OK. Turn right. Straight forward. Dead simple.

I stood up carefully, and with the hole at my back, turned left. Put my hand on the rough rock wall. Took a step forward.

The scrunch of my boot on the rock floor made me realize for the first time how quiet it was. Before, I had had both the stones and my own heart to fill my ears. Now, there was nothing. The silence was as absolute as the darkness.

I didn't waste time brooding about it. Scrunched ahead as fast as I dared, step by careful step. No sound . . . that meant that the air-conditioning had been switched off . . . which hardly mattered, there was a mineful still to breathe . . . even if it was hot.

My hand lost the wall suddenly, and my heart set up a fresh chorus. Taking a grip on my breath I took a step backwards. Right hand back on wall. OK. Breathe out. Now, kneel down, grope along floor, keep in contact with wall on right . . . navigate past another of the holes which led through to the stope.

Holes which would let the blast out of the stope, when the charges exploded.

Blast travelled far when confined in a long narrow space. Blast was a killing force, as deadly as flying rocks.

Oh God, I thought. Oh hell's bloody bells. What did one think about if one were probably going to die at any minute?

I thought about getting as far back up the mine as quickly as I could. I thought about not losing contact with the right-hand wall when I passed the holes in it, because if I did I might turn round in the darkness and find the other wall instead, and go straight back towards the explosion. I didn't think about anything else at all. Not even about Charlie.

I went on. The air became hotter and hotter. The stretch that had been hot coming down was now an assault on the nerve endings.

Struggling on, I couldn't tell how fast I was going. Very slowly, I imagined. Like in a nightmare, trying to flee from a terror at one's heels, and not being able to run.

I got back in the end to the wider space, and the explosion still hadn't happened. Another explosion was due to take place down the branch tunnel also . . . but the bend in the tunnel should disperse some of the blast.

Beginning at last to let hope creep in, and keeping my hand on the right-hand wall literally for dear life, I trudged slowly on. Two miles to go, maybe, to the bottom of the shaft . . . but every step taking me nearer to safety.

Those lethal pockets of dynagel never did explode; or not while I was down the mine.

One minute I was taking another step into darkness. The next, I was blinded by light.

I shut my eyes, wincing against the brightness, and I

stopped walking and leaned against the wall instead. When I opened my eyes again, the electric lights were blazing in all their glory, and the tunnel looked as solid, safe, and reassuringly painted, as it had done on the way in.

Weakened by relief, I shifted off the wall and went on again, with knees that were suddenly trembling, and a head that was back to aching like a hang-over.

There was a background hum now again in the mine, and from far away up the tunnel a separate noise detached itself and grew louder: the rattle of the wire cage trucks making the outward journey. Eventually it stopped and then there was the sound of several boots, and then finally, round a shallow curve, came four men in white overalls.

Hurrying.

They spotted me, and began to run. Slowed and stopped just before they reached me, with relief that I was mobile showing on their faces. Losenwoldt was one of them: I didn't know the others.

'Mr Lincoln . . . are you all right?' one of them asked anxiously.

'Sure,' I said. It didn't sound right. I said it again. 'Sure.' Much better.

'How did you get left behind?' Losenwoldt said reprovingly, shifting all possible blame from himself. Not that I would have allotted him any: he was just forestalling it.

I said, 'I'm sorry to have been such a nuisance . . . I

think I must have hit my head and knocked myself out, but I can't actually remember how ...' I wrinkled my forehead. 'So damned stupid of me.'

One of them said, 'Where were you, exactly?'

'In the stope,' I said.

'Good grief ... You probably lifted your head too sharply ... or maybe a piece of rock fell from the roof and caught you.'

'Yes,' I said.

Another of them said, 'If you were unconscious in the stope, however did you get back here?'

I told them about the stones. They didn't say anything. Just looked at each other.

One of them walked round my back and after a moment said, 'There's some blood on your hair and down your neck, but it looks dry ... I don't think you're still bleeding.' He came round to my side. 'Do you feel all right to walk to the trucks? We brought a stretcher ... just in case.'

I smiled. 'Guess I can walk.'

We walked. I asked, 'How did you discover I was down here?'

One of them said ruefully, 'Our system of checking everyone is out of the mine before blasting is supposed to be infallible. And so it is, as far as the miners are concerned. But visitors ... you see, we don't often have small groups of unofficial visitors, like today. Mr van Huren seldom invites anyone, and no one else is allowed to. Nearly all the visitors we have here are official tourist groups, of about twenty people, and the mine more or less stops while we show them round, but we only do that every six weeks or so. We don't usually blast at all, on those days. Today, though, one of your party felt ill and went back before the others, and I think everyone took it for granted that you had gone with him. Tim Yates said when he last saw you, you were just about to return up the tunnel.'

'Yes . . .' I agreed. 'I remember that.'

'The other three visitors went up together, and the checkers accounted for every miner, so we assumed everyone was out, and were all set to detonate . . .'

A tall thin man took up the story. 'Then one of the men who counts the numbers going up and down in the lift said that one more had gone down than had come up. The shift checkers said it was impossible, each group had been checked out by name. The lift man said he was sure. Well . . . that only left the visitors. So we checked them. The three in the changing room said you hadn't changed yet, your clothes were still there, so you must be in the first-aid room with one called Conrad, who had not felt well.'

'Conrad,' I exclaimed. I had thought they meant Evan. 'What was wrong with him?'

'I think they said he had an attack of asthma. Anyway, we went and asked him, and he said you hadn't come up with him.'

'Oh,' I said blankly. Certainly, if I had been with him I

would have gone up, but I hadn't seen him at all after we had separated at the beginning of the reef.

We came to the trucks and climbed in. A lot of space with only five people instead of twelve.

'The one who was ill,' Losenwoldt stated virtuously, 'the stout one with the droopy moustache, he was not with me. If he had been, of course I would have escorted him back to the trucks, and of course I would have known you were not with him.'

'Of course,' I said dryly.

We clattered back along the tunnel to the bottom of the shaft, and from there, after the exchange of signal buzzes, rose in the cage through three-quarters of a mile of rock up to the sunlight. Its brilliance was momentarily painful, and it was also cold enough to start me shivering.

'Jacket,' exclaimed one of my escorts. 'We took down a blanket . . . should have put it round you.' He hurried off into a small building by the shaft and came back with a much used tweed sports coat, which he held for me to put on.

There was an anxious-looking reception committee hovering around: Evan, Roderick, Danilo, and van Huren himself.

'My dear fellow,' he said, peering at me as if to reassure himself that I was real. 'What can I say?'

'For heaven's sake,' I said, 'it was my own fault and I'm terribly sorry to have caused all this fuss . . .' Van Huren looked relieved and smiled, and so did Evan, Roderick and Danilo. I turned back to the three strangers who had come down for me: Losenwoldt had already gone. 'Thank you,' I said. 'Thank you very much.'

They all grinned. 'We want payment,' one said.

I must have looked bewildered. I was wondering what was right. How much.

'Your autograph,' one of them explained.

'Oh . . .' I laughed. 'OK.'

One of them produced a notebook, and I wrote a thank-you to each of them, on three separate pages. And cheap at the price, I thought.

The mine's doctor swabbed stone dust from the cut on my head, said it wasn't deep, nothing serious, didn't need stitching, didn't need a plaster, even, unless I wanted one . . .

'I don't,' I said.

'Good, good. Swallow these, then. In case you develop a headache.'

I swallowed obediently. Collected Conrad, now breathing normally again, from a rest room next door, and followed directions to the bar and dining-room for lunch. On the way, we swopped operations, so to speak. Neither of us felt much pleased with himself.

The five of us sat at a table with Quentin van Huren, plus two other senior executives whose names I never learned. My narrow escape was chewed over by everyone all over again, and I said with feeling to Roderick that I would be much obliged if he would keep my embarrassment out of his inky columns.

He grinned. 'Yeah . . . Much better copy if you'd been blown up. Not much news value in a checker doing his job properly.'

'Thank God for that,' I said.

Conrad looked at me sideways. 'There must be a jinx on you in South Africa, dear boy. That's the second time you've been close to extinction within a week.'

I shook my head. 'No jinx. Just the opposite. I've survived twice. Look at it that way.'

'Only seven lives left,' Conrad said.

The talk worked back to gold. I suspected that in Welkom it always did, like Newmarket and horses.

'Say, how do you get it out of the rock?' Danilo demanded. 'You can't even see it.'

Van Huren smiled indulgently. 'Danilo, it is simple. You crush the rock in mills until it is powdered. You add cyanide of potassium, which holds the gold particles in solution. You add zinc, to which the gold particles stick. You then wash out the acid. You then separate the zinc from the gold again, using aqua regia, and finally you retrieve the gold.'

'Oh, simple,' Conrad agreed. 'Dear boy.'

Van Huren warmed to him, and smiled with pleasure. 'That is not exactly all. One still has to refine the gold . . . to remove impurities by melting it to white heat in giant crucibles, and pouring it out into bricks. The residue flows away, and you are left with the pure gold.'

Danilo did a rapid calculation. 'You'll have gotten around three thousand five hundred tons of reef out of the mine, for one little old brick.'

'That's so,' agreed van Huren, smiling. 'Give or take a ton or two.'

'How much do you bring out in a week?' Danilo asked.

'Just over forty thousand metric tons.'

Danilo's eyes flickered as he did the mental arithmetic. 'That means . . . er . . . about eleven and a half gold bricks every week.'

'Do you want a job in the accounting department, Danilo?' asked van Huren, much amused.

But Danilo hadn't finished. 'Each brick weighs 71 lbs, right? So that makes . . . let's see . . . around 800 lbs of gold a week. Say, what's the price of gold per ounce? Gee, this is sure the right business to be in. What a gas!' He was deeply stimulated, as he had been by the whole trip, with a strong inner excitement shining out of his eyes. An attraction towards money-making, and the calculations needed to work out estate-duty dodging, seemed to me to be all of a piece.

Van Huren, still smiling, said, 'You're forgetting the wages, the maintenance, and the shareholders. There are only a few grains of dust left after they've all taken their cut.'

Danilo's curving mouth showed he didn't believe it.

Roderick shot an orange cuff out of the brown suede sleeve to reveal half a ton of tiger's eye doing duty as a cufflink.

'Don't you own the mine altogether, then, Quentin?' he asked.

The executive and van Huren himself both smiled indulgently at Roderick for his naïvety.

'No,' van Huren said. 'My family own the land and the mineral rights. Technically, I suppose, we do own the gold. But it takes an enormous amount of capital, many millions of rands, to sink a shaft and build all the surface plant needed. About twenty-five years ago my brother and I floated a company to raise capital to start drilling, so the company has hundreds of private shareholders.'

'That mine doesn't look twenty-five years old,' I objected amiably.

Van Huren shifted his smiling eyes in my direction and went on explaining.

'The part you saw this morning is the newest tunnel, and the deepest. There are other tunnels at higher levels . . . in past years we have taken out all the up-slope areas of the reef.'

'And there's still a lot left?'

Van Huren's smile had the ease of one who would never be short of a thousand. 'It will see Jonathan out,' he said.

Evan chose to find the mechanics and economics less interesting than the purpose, and waved his arms about as he pinned every gaze down in turn with the fierce eyes and declaimed with his usual intensity.

'What is gold for, though? This is what we should be asking. What everyone should be asking. What is the *point*? Everyone goes to so much trouble to get it, and pays so much for it, and it has no real *use*.'

'Gold-plated lunar bugs,' I murmured.

Evan glared at me. 'Everyone digs it out of the ground here and puts it back underground at Fort Knox, where it never sees daylight again ... Don't you see ... the whole thing is *artificial*? Why should the whole world's wealth be based on a yellow metal which has no *use*?'

'Good for filling teeth,' I said conversationally.

'And for pure radio contacts in transistor units,' Roderick added, joining the game.

Van Huren listened and watched as if he found the entertainment a nice change for a Monday. I stopped baiting Evan, though, because after seeing the mine I half held his views.

I travelled back to Johannesburg in the Dakota that evening sitting next to Roderick and feeling a trifle worn. A hot afternoon spent walking round the surface buildings of a mine, watching gold being poured from a crucible, seeing (and hearing) the ore being crushed, and visiting one of the miners' hostels, had done no good at all to a throbbing head. Half a dozen times I had almost dropped out, but, especially with Roderick's ready typewriter in the background, I hadn't wanted to make a fuss.

The visit to the hostel had been best: lunch was being cooked for the next surface shift off work, and we tasted it in the kitchen. Vast vats of thick broth with a splendid flavour, vegetables I couldn't identify and hadn't the energy to ask about, and thick wads of cream-coloured mealie bread, a sort of fatless version of pastry.

From there we went next door into the hostel's bar, where the first of the returning shift were settling down to the serious business of drinking what looked like half-gallon plastic tubs of milky cocoa.

'That's Bantu beer,' said our afternoon guide, who had proved as sweet as Losenwoldt was sour.

We drank some. It had a pleasant dry flavour but tasted nothing like beer.

'Is it alcoholic, dear boy?' Conrad asked.

The dear boy said it was, but weak. Considering that we saw one man dispatch his whole tubful in two great draughts, the weakness was just as well.

Our guide beckoned to one of the men sitting at a table with his colleagues, and he got to his feet and came over. He was tall and not young, and he had a wide white grin which I found infectious.

The guide said, 'This is Piano Nyembezi. He is the checker who insisted we had left someone down the mine.'

'Was it you?' I asked with interest.

'*Yebo*,' he said, which I later learned meant yes in

Zulu. ('No' turned out to consist of a click, a glottal stop, and an 'aa' sound. As far as a European was concerned, it was impossible to say no in a hurry.)

'Well, Piano,' I said. 'Thank you very much.' I put out my hand and he shook it, an event which drew large smiles from his friends, an indrawn breath from our guide, a shake of the head from Roderick and no reaction whatsoever from Evan, Conrad or Danilo.

There was a certain amount of scuffling in the background, and then one of the others brought forward a well-thumbed copy of a film magazine.

'It is Piano's paper,' the newcomer said, and thrust it into his hands. Nyembezi looked embarrassed, but showed me what it was. Full page, and as boring-looking as usual.

Wrinkling my nose I took the magazine from him and wrote across the bottom of my picture, 'I owe my life to Piano Nyembezi', and signed my name.

'He'll keep that for ever,' the guide said.

Until tomorrow, perhaps, I thought.

The Dakota droned on. The evening sun fell heavily across my eyelids as we banked round on to a new course, and I gingerly lifted my head off the seat-back to put it down the other way. The cut on my head, though not deep, was sore.

For some reason the small movement triggered off a

few sleepy nerve cells, and in a quiet fashion I remembered that there had been someone with me in the stope.

I remembered I had been turning round to leave feet first, and had stopped to let someone else in. I remembered that I hadn't seen his face: didn't know who he was.

If he had been there when I bashed my head, why on earth hadn't he helped me?

Such was my fuzzy state of mind that it took me a whole minute more to move on to the conclusion that he hadn't helped me because he'd applied the rock himself.

I opened my eyes with a jolt. Roderick's face was turned towards mine. I opened my mouth to tell him. Then I shut it again, firmly. I did not in the least want to tell the *Rand Daily Star*.

CHAPTER ELEVEN

I used a lot of the time I could more profitably have spent sleeping that night in coming to terms with the thought that someone might have tried to kill me.

Didn't know who. Couldn't guess why. And still was not certain whether my memory was complete: perhaps the other man in the stope had gone away again, and I had forgotten it.

Also, even if I had been 100 per cent certain, I didn't know what I should do about it.

Telephone van Huren? Start an investigation? But there had been so many people down the mine, all dressed alike, and half in darkness. Any investigation was going to produce more talk and doubt than results, and 'Lincoln complains of attempted murder' were gossip-column snippets I could do without.

Twice within a week, Conrad had said, 'Close to extinction.'

It didn't make sense. It was only in films that the chaps I played got threatened and attacked, and made miraculous escapes.

Yet if I did nothing about it, what then? If someone really had been trying to kill me, there was nothing to stop him trying again. How could I possibly protect myself every minute of every day . . . especially against unforeseen things like microphones and rocks in gold mines?

If . . . and I wasn't altogether convinced . . . two murder attempts had been made, they had both been arranged to look like accidents. So it was of little use taking future precautions against things like poison and bullets and knives-in-the-back down dark alleys. One would have to beware instead of cars with no brakes, deadly insects in one's shoes, and disintegrating balconies.

I shied away for a long time from thinking about *who*, for it had to be someone who had been down in the mine.

A miner who didn't like my films taking steps to avoid sitting through any others? He wouldn't have to kill me: could simply vote with his feet.

Someone smouldering from ungovernable professional jealousy? The only person I knew of who regularly swore undying hatred was Drix Goddart, but he was not yet in South Africa, let alone 4,000 feet under Welkom.

None of the people working the mine had known I was going to be there, and before the incident, none of them had used my name.

That left . . . Oh hell, I thought. Well . . . it left

175

Evan . . . and Conrad . . . and Danilo . . . and Roderick. And also van Huren, who owned a lot of souls and could have things done by proxy.

As for *why* . . . Evan's professional resentment was surely not obsessive enough, and Danilo didn't know my guess of what he was up to with the horses; and in any case, even if he did, he wouldn't try to cover up such a minor crime with murder. More likely to confess and laugh, I would have thought, and meet a warning-off with a what-the-hell shrug.

Motives for Conrad, Roderick and van Huren took even less cogitation. I couldn't rake up a decent one between them.

They had all (except Conrad who had been in the surgery) looked relieved when I stepped safely out of the mine . . . could they possibly have looked relieved just because I said I couldn't remember how I got knocked out?

It all seemed so improbable. I couldn't imagine any of them plotting away in murky labyrinths of villainy. It didn't make sense. I must, I concluded, be imagining things. I had been involved in too much fiction, and I had begun to project it on to reality.

I sighed. Realized that my head had stopped aching and that the unsettled feeling of concussion was subsiding, and presently, imperceptibly, went to sleep.

In the morning the night thoughts seemed even more preposterous. It was Conrad who had suggested a connection between the mike and the mine; and Conrad had got it wrong.

Roderick telephoned at breakfast time. Would I care to have dinner at his flat, with Katya, just the three of us and no fuss: and when I hesitated for a few seconds over replying, he added quickly that it would all be strictly off the record, anything I said would not be taken down and used against me.

'OK,' I agreed, with a smile in my voice and reservations in my mind. 'Where do I find you?'

He told me the address, and said, 'That chauffeur of yours will know where to find it.'

'Oh. Yes,' I agreed.

I put the receiver down slowly: but there was no reason why he shouldn't know about the hired car-and-driver, and there was of course his source at the Iguana. Roderick had all along known where I was going, what I was doing, and how often I brushed my teeth.

Almost before I had taken my hand off it, the telephone rang again.

Clifford Wenkins. Could he, er, that was to say, would it be convenient for him to come to the club that morning to discuss, er, details, for the, er, premiere?

Er yes, I said.

After that, Conrad rang. Was I going to travel down to the Kruger Park with him and Evan?

'How long are you staying there?' I asked.

'About ten days, I should think.'

'No, then. I'll have to come back by next Tuesday, at the latest. I'll drive down separately. It will be better anyway to have two cars, with you and Evan concentrating on locations.'

'Yeah,' he said, sounding relieved: hadn't wanted to spend a week at close quarters keeping Evan and me off each other's throats, I imagined.

They would come around for a drink before lunch, he said. Evan, it appeared, was bursting with inspirations for his new film. (When was he not?)

After that, Arknold.

'Look, Mister Lincoln. About Mrs Cavesey's horses . . . Look . . .' He petered heavily out.

After waiting in vain for him to start up again I said, 'I'll be here all morning, if you'd care to come over.'

Three heavy breaths. Then he said, 'Perhaps. Might be as well. Yes. All right. About eleven, then, after I've watched the horses work.'

'See you,' I said.

Hot sunshine, blue sky.

I went downstairs and drank my coffee out on the terrace, and read the newspaper. Close columns filled with local issues, all assuming a background of common knowledge which I didn't have. Reading them was like going into a film halfway through.

A man had been murdered in Johannesburg: found two days ago, with a wire twisted round his neck.

With a shiver I put down the paper. No one was trying to murder me. I had decided it was nonsense. Another man's death had no business to be raising hairs on my skin. The trouble was, no one had told my subconscious that we were all through with red alerts.

'Morning,' said a fresh young voice in my ear. 'What are you doing?'

'Watching the flowers grow.'

She sat down opposite me, grinning all over her fifteen-year-old face.

'I've come to play tennis.'

She wore a short white dress, white socks, white shoes, and carried two racquets in zipped waterproof covers. Her dark shoulder-length hair was held back by a green head-band, and the van Huren wealth spoke as eloquently as ever in her natural confidence and poise.

'Coffee?' I suggested.

'Rather have orange juice.'

I ordered it.

'Didn't you just love the gold mine?' she demanded.

'I just did,' I agreed, imitating Danilo's accent, as she had done his turn of phrase.

She wrinkled her nose, amused. 'You never miss a damn thing, do you? Dad says you have an intuitive mind, whatever the hell that is.'

'It means I jump to conclusions,' I said.

She shook her head dubiously. 'Uhuh. He seemed to think it was good.'

The orange juice came and she drank some, clinking the ice. She had long dark eyelashes and more cream than peaches. I stifled as always the inner lurch of regret that young girls like Sally gave me: my own daughter might grow up as pretty, but the zest and the flash would be missing.

She put down the glass and her eyes searched the hotel buildings behind me.

'Have you seen Danilo anywhere?' she said. 'The swine said he'd be here at ten, and it's a quarter after already.'

'He was busy doing sums all yesterday,' I said gravely. 'I expect they wore him out.'

'What sums?' she said suspiciously.

I told her.

She laughed. 'He can't help doing sums, then, I shouldn't think. All Saturday at the races, he was doing it. A living computer, I called him.' She took another orange sip. 'I say, did you know he's a terrific gambler? He had ten rand on one of those horses. *Ten rand!*'

I thought van Huren had made a sensible job of her, if a ten-rand bet still seemed excessive.

'Mind you,' she added, 'The horse won. I went with him to collect the winnings. Twenty-five rand, would you believe it? He says he often wins. He was all sort of gay and laughing about it.'

'Everyone loses in the end,' I said.

180

'Oh, don't be such a downpour,' she exploded. 'Just like Dad.'

Her eyes suddenly opened wider, and she transferred her attention to somewhere behind me.

Danilo joined us. White shorts, sturdy sunburned legs, light blue windcheater hanging open.

'Hi,' he said happily, including us both.

'Hi,' echoed Sally, looking smitten.

She left me and the half-finished orange juice without a backward glance, and went off with the bright boy as girls have been going off since Eve. But this girl's father had a gold mine; and Danilo had done his sums.

Arknold came, and the reception desk directed him to the garden. He shook hands, sat down, huffed and puffed, and agreed to a beer. Away in the distance Danilo and Sally belted the ball sporadically over the net and laughed a lot in between.

Arknold followed my gaze, recognized Danilo, and consolidated his indecision in a heavy frown.

'I didn't know Danilo would be here,' he said.

'He can't hear you.'

'No . . . but . . . Look, Mister . . . Do you mind if we go indoors?'

'If you like,' I agreed; so we transferred to the lounge, where he was again too apprehensive to come to the boil, and finally up to my room. One could still see the tennis courts; but the tennis courts couldn't see us.

He sat, like Conrad, in the larger of the two armchairs, seeing himself as a dominant character. The slab-like features made no provision for subtle nuances of feeling to show in changing muscle tensions round eyes, mouth or jaw line, so that I found it as nearly impossible as always to guess what he was thinking. The overall impression was of aggression and worry having a ding-dong: the result, apparent indecision about whether to attack or placate.

'Look,' he said in the end. 'What are you going to tell Mrs Cavesey when you get back to England?'

I considered. 'I haven't decided.'

He thrust his face forward like a bulldog. 'Don't you go telling her to change her trainer.'

'Why precisely not?'

'There's nothing wrong with the way I train them.'

'They look well,' I agreed. 'And they run stinking. Most owners would have sent them to someone else long ago.'

'It's not my fault they don't win,' he asserted heavily. 'You tell her that. That's what I came to say. You tell her it's not my fault.'

'You would lose their training fees, if they went,' I said. 'And you would lose face, perhaps. But you would gain freedom from the fear of being prosecuted for fraud.'

'See here, Mister,' he began angrily, but I interrupted him.

'Alternatively, you could sack your head boy, Barty.'

Whatever he had been going to say remained unsaid. His trap-like mouth dropped open.

'Should you decide to sack Barty,' I said conversationally, 'I could advise Mrs Cavesey to leave the horses where they are.'

He shut his mouth. There was a long pause while most of the aggression oozed away and a tired sort of defeatism took its place.

'I can't do that,' he said sullenly, not denying the need for it.

'Because of a threat that you will be warned off?' I suggested. 'Or because of the profit to come?'

'Look, Mister . . .'

'See that Barty leaves before I go home,' I said pleasantly.

He stood heavily up, and gave me a hard stare which got him nowhere very much. Breathing loudly through his nose, he was inarticulate; and I couldn't guess from his expression whether what hung fire on his tongue was a stream of invective, a defence in mitigation, or even a plea for help.

He checked through the window that his buddy Danilo was still on the courts, then turned away abruptly and departed from my room without another word: a man on a three-pronged toasting fork if ever I saw one.

*

I returned to the terrace: found Clifford Wenkins walking indecisively about peering at strangers behind their newspapers.

'Mr Wenkins,' I called.

He looked up, nodded nervously, and scuttled around tables and chairs to reach me.

'Good morning ... er ... Link,' he began and half-held out one hand, too far away for me to shake it. I sketched an equally noncommittal welcome. His best friend must have been telling him, I thought.

We sat at one of the small tables in the shade of a yellow and white sun awning, and he agreed that ... er ... yes ... a beer would be fine. He pulled another untidy wad of papers out of an inner pocket. Consulting them seemed to give him strength.

'Er ... Worldic have decided ... er ... they think it would be best, I mean, to hold the reception before ... er ... the film, you see.'

I saw. They were afraid I would vanish during the showing, if they arranged things the other way round.

'Here ... er ... is a list of people ... er ... invited by Worldic ... and here ... somewhere here ... ah, yes, here is the Press list and ... er ... a list of people who have bought tickets to the reception . . . We limited the ... er ... numbers, but we have ... er ... had ... I mean ... it may be ... perhaps ... just a bit of a *crush*, if you see what I mean.'

He sweated. Mopped up with a neatly folded white square. Waited, apparently, for me to burn. But what could I say? I'd arranged it myself; and I supposed I was grateful that people actually wanted to come.

'Er . . . if that's all right . . . I mean . . . well . . . there are still some tickets left . . . er . . . for the premiere itself, you see . . . er . . . some at twenty rand . . .'

'Twenty rand?' I said. 'Surely that's too much?'

'It's for charity,' he said quickly. 'Charity.'

'What charity?'

'Oh . . . er . . . let's see . . . I've got it here somewhere . . .' But he couldn't find it. 'Anyway . . . for charity . . . so Worldic want you to . . . I mean, because there are still some tickets, you see, to . . . er . . . well, some sort of publicity stunt . . .'

'No,' I said.

He looked unhappy. 'I told them . . . but they said . . . er . . . well . . .' He faded away like a pop song, and didn't say that Worldic's attitude to actors had made the KGB seem paternal.

'Where is the reception to be?' I asked.

'Oh . . . er . . . opposite the Wideworld Cinema, in the Klipspringer Heights Hotel. I . . . er . . . I think you will like it . . . I mean . . . it is one of the best . . . er . . . hotels in Johannesburg.'

'Fine,' I said. 'I'll be back here by, say, six o'clock next Tuesday evening. You could ring me here for final arrangements.'

'Oh yes . . . er,' he said, 'but . . . er . . . Worldic said they would like . . . er . . . to know where you are staying . . . er . . . in the Kruger Park.'

'I don't know,' I said.

'Well, er . . . could you find out?' He looked unhappy. 'Worldic said . . . er . . . on no account . . . should I not find out . . .'

'Oh. Very well,' I said. 'I'll let you know.'

'Thank you,' he gasped. 'Now . . . er . . . well . . . I mean . . . er . . .' He was working himself into a worse lather than ever over what he was trying to say next. My mind had framed one large *No* before the thought of Worldic on his tail had goaded him to get it out.

'We . . . well, that is to say . . . Worldic . . . have fixed a . . . er . . . photographic . . . session for you . . . I mean . . . well, this afternoon, in fact.'

'What photographic session?' I asked ominously.

He had another mop. 'Just . . . well . . . photographs.'

He had a terrible time explaining, and a worse time when I got it straight, that what Worldic wanted were some pictures of me reclining in bathing trunks under a sun umbrella beside a bosomy model in a bikini.

'You just run along and tell Worldic that their promotion ideas are fifty years out of date, if they think cheese-cake will sell twenty-rand seats.'

He sweated.

'And furthermore you can tell Worldic that one more damn fool suggestion and I'll never again turn up at anything they handle.'

'But . . .' he stuttered. 'You see . . . after those pics in

186

the newspapers . . . of you giving Katya the kiss of life . . . after that . . . see . . . we were flooded . . . simply flooded . . . with enquiries . . . and all the cheaper seats went in a flash . . . and the reception tickets, too . . . all went . . .'

'But that,' I said slowly and positively, 'was not a publicity stunt.'

'Oh no.' He gulped. 'Oh no. Of course not. Oh no. Oh no . . .' He rocked to his feet, knocking his chair over. The beads were running down his forehead and his eyes looked wild. He was on the point, the very point of panic flight, when Danilo and Sally came breezily back from the courts.

'Hullo, Mr Wenkins,' Sally said in her adolescent unperceptive way. 'I say, you look almost as hot and sweaty as we do.'

Wenkins gave her a glazed, mesmerized look and fumbled around with his handkerchief. Danilo looked at him piercingly and thoughtfully and made no remark at all.

'Well . . . I'll . . . er, tell them . . . but they won't . . . like it.'

'You tell them,' I agreed. 'No stunts.'

'No stunts,' he echoed weakly; but I doubted whether he would ever have the nerve to pass on the message.

Sally watched his backview weave unsteadily into the club, as she sprawled exhaustedly in her garden chair.

'I say, he does get himself into a fuss, don't you think? Were you bullying the poor lamb, Link?'

'He's a sheep, not a lamb.'

'A silly sheep,' Danilo said vaguely, as if his thoughts were somewhere else.

'Could I have some orange juice?' Sally said.

Evan and Conrad arrived before the waiter, and the drinks order expanded. Evan was at his most insistent, waving his arms about and laying down the law to Conrad in the usual dominating I-am-the-director-and-the-rest-of-you-are-scum manner. Conrad looked half patient, half irritated: lighting cameramen were out-ranked by directors, but they didn't have to like it.

'Symbolism,' Evan was saying fiercely. 'Symbolism is what the film is all about. And post office towers are the new phallic symbol of national strength. Every virile country has to have its revolving restaurant . . .'

'It might be just because every country has one, that the one in Johannesburg is not news,' Conrad murmured, in a tone a little too carefully unargumentative.

'The tower is *in*,' stated Evan with finality.

'Even if you can't find an elephant that shape,' I said, nodding.

Conrad choked and Evan glared.

Sally said, 'What is a phallic symbol?' And Danilo told her kindly to look it up in the dictionary.

I asked Evan where exactly we would be staying in the Kruger Park, so that I could be found if necessary.

'Don't expect me to help,' he said unhelpfully. 'The production department made the bookings months ago.

Several different camps, starting in the south and working north, I believe.'

Conrad added casually, 'We do have a list, back at the hotel . . . I could copy it out for you, dear boy.'

'It isn't important,' I said. 'It was only Worldic who wanted it.'

'Not important!' Evans exclaimed. 'If Worldic wants it, of course they must have it.' Evan had no reservations towards companies that might screen his masterpieces. 'Conrad can copy the list and send it to them direct.'

I looked at Conrad in amusement. 'To Clifford Wenkins, then,' I suggested. 'It was he who asked.'

Conrad nodded shortly. Copying the list from friendliness was one thing and on Evan's orders another: I knew exactly how he felt.

'I don't suppose you are intending to bring the chauffeur Worldic gave you,' Evan said bossily to me. 'There won't be any rooms for him.'

I shook my head. 'No,' I said mildly. 'I'm hiring a car to drive myself.'

'All right, then.'

Even on a fine Tuesday morning with a healthy gin half-drunk and no pressure on him at all, he still flourished the hot eyes like lances and curled his fingers so that the tendons showed tight. The unruly curly hair sprang out vigorously like Medusa's snakes, and the very air around him seemed to quiver from his energy output.

Sally thought him fascinating. 'You'll love it in the

game park,' she told him earnestly. 'The animals are so sweet.'

Evan only knew how to deal with girls that young if he could bully them in front of a camera: and the idea that animals could be sweet instead of symbolic seemed to nonplus him.

'Er . . .' he said uncertainly, and sounded exactly like Wenkins.

Conrad cheered up perceptibly: smoothed his moustache and looked on Sally benignly. She gave him an uncomplicated smile and turned to Danilo.

'You'd love it too,' she said. 'Next time you come to South Africa, we must take you down there.'

Danilo could scarcely wait. Conrad asked him how much longer he was staying this time, and Danilo said a week or so, he guessed, and Sally insisted anxiously that he was staying until after Link's premiere, surely he remembered he was going to the reception with the van Hurens. Danilo remembered: he sure was.

He grinned at her. She blossomed. I hoped that the sun kid dealt in compassion alongside the mathematics.

Evan and Conrad stayed for lunch, endlessly discussing the locations they had picked throughout the city. They were, it appeared, going to incorporate a lot of *cinéma vérité*, with Conrad humping around a hand-held Arriflex to film life as it was lived. By the end of the cheese, the whole film, symbolism, elephants, and all, seemed to me doomed to be a crashing bore.

Conrad's interest was principally technical. Mine was non-existent. Evan's, as usual, inexhaustible.

'So we'll take the Arriflex with us, of course,' he was telling Conrad. 'We may see unrepeatable shots ... it would be stupid not to be equipped.'

Conrad agreed. They also discussed sound-recording equipment and decided to take that too. The production department had fixed up for a park ranger to show them round in a Land Rover, so there would be room to use everything comfortably.

Anything which they could not cram into their hired station wagon for the journey down, they said, could go in my car, couldn't it? It could. I agreed to drive to their hotel first thing in the morning to embark the surplus.

When they had gone I paid off the car and chauffeur Worldic had arranged, and hired a modest self-drive saloon instead. A man from the hiring company brought it to the Iguana, showed me the gear system, said it was a new car only just run-in and that I should have no trouble with it, and departed with the chauffeur.

I went for a practice drive, got lost, bought a map, and found my way back. The car was short on power uphill, but very stable on corners; a car for Sunday afternoons, airing Grandma in a hat.

CHAPTER TWELVE

The map and the car took me to Roderick's flat just as it was getting dark.

I tested the brakes before I set off, the car having stood alone in the car park for hours. Nothing wrong with them, of course. I sneered inwardly at myself for being so silly.

Roderick's flat was on the sixth floor.

It had a balcony.

Roderick invited me out first thing to look at the view.

'It looks marvellous at this time of night,' he said, 'with the lights springing up in every direction. In the daytime there are too many factories and roads and mining tips, unless of course you find the sinews of trade stimulating . . . and soon it will be too dark to see the shape of things in the dusk . . .'

I hovered, despite myself, on the threshold.

'Come on,' he said. 'Are you afraid of heights?'

'No.'

I stepped out there, and the view lived up to his commercial. The balcony faced south, with the kite-shaped Southern Cross flying on its side in the sky straight ahead; and orange lights stretching like a chain away towards Durban down the motorway.

Roderick was not leaning on the pierced ironwork which edged the balcony. With part of my mind shivering and the rest telling me not to be such an ass, I kept my weight nearer the building than his: I felt guilty of mistrust and yet couldn't trust, and saw that suspicion was a wrecker.

We went in. Of course, we went in. Safely. I could feel muscles relax in my jaw and abdomen that I hadn't known were tense. Silly fool, I thought: and tried to shut out the fact that for both mike and mine, Roderick had been there.

His flat was small but predictably full of impact. A black sack chair flopped on a pale olive carpet: khaki-coloured walls sprouted huge brass lamp brackets between large canvases of ultra simple abstracts in brash challenging colours: a low glass-topped table stood before an imitation tiger-skin sofa of stark square construction; and an Andy Warholish imitation can of beer stood waist-high in one corner. Desperately trendy, the whole thing; giving like its incumbent, the impression that way out was where it was all at, man, and if you weren't out there as far as you could go you might as well be dead. It seemed a foregone conclusion that he smoked pot.

Naturally, he had expensive stereo. The music he chose was less underground than could be got in

London, but the mix of anarchy and self-pity came across strongly in the nasal voices. I wondered whether it was just part of the image, or whether he sincerely enjoyed it.

'Drink?' he offered, and I said Yes, please.

Campari and soda, bitter-sweet pink stuff. He took it for granted I would like it.

'Katya won't be long. She had some recording session or other.'

'Is she all right now?'

'Sure,' he said. 'A hundred per cent.' He underplayed the relief, but I remembered his tormented tears: real emotions still lived down there under the with-it front.

He was wearing another pair of pasted-on trousers, and a blue ruffled close-fitting shirt with lacing instead of buttons. As casual clothes, they were as deliberate as signposts: the rugged male in his sexual finery. I supposed my own clothes too made a statement, as indeed everyone's did, always.

Katya's statement was as clear as a trumpet, and said, 'look at me'.

She arrived like a gust of bright and breezy show-biz, wearing an eye-stunning yellow catsuit which flared widely from the knees in black-edged ruffles. She looked like a flamenco dancer split up the middle, and she topped up the impression with a high tortoise-shell mantilla comb pegged like a tiara into her mop of hair.

Stretching out her arms she advanced on me with life positively spurting from every pore, as if instead of harming her the input of electric current had doubled her vitality.

'Link, darling, how marvellous,' she said extravagantly. And she had brought someone with her.

The barriers in my mind rose immediately like a hedge and prickled away all evening. Roderick and Katya had planted a bombshell to lead me astray, and were betraying their intention through the heightened mischief in Katya's manner. I didn't like the game, but I was an old hand at it, and nowadays I never lost. I sighed regretfully for the quiet no-fuss dinner which Roderick had promised. Too much ever to hope for, I supposed.

The girl was ravishing, with cloudy dark hair and enormous slightly myopic-looking eyes. She wore a soft floaty garment, floor-length and green, which swirled and lay against her as she moved, outlining now a hip, now a breast, and all parts in quite clearly good shape.

Roderick was watching my reactions sideways, while pretending to pour out more Camparis.

'This is Melanie,' Katya said as if inventing Venus from the waves; and there was perhaps a touch of the Botticellis in the graceful neck.

Christened Mabel, no doubt, I said to myself uncharitably, and greeted her with a lukewarm smile and a conventional handshake. Melanie was not a girl to be put off by a cool reception. She gave me a gentle flutter of lengthy lashes, a sweet curve of soft pink lips, and a smouldering promise in the smoky eyes. I thought: She's done this sort of thing before, and she is as aware of her power as I am when I act.

Melanie just happened to sit beside me on the tiger-skin sofa, stretching out languorously so that the green material revealed the whole slender shape. Just happened to have no lighter of her own, so that I had to help her with Roderick's orange globe table model. Just happened to have to cup my hand in both of her own to guide the flame to the end of her cigarette. Just happened to steady herself with a hand on my arm as she leant forward to flick off ash.

Katya gaily sparkled and Roderick filled my glass with gin when he thought I wasn't looking, and I began to wonder where he had hidden the tape-recorder. If this little lot was to be off the record, I was the plumber's mate.

Dinner was laid with candles on a square black table in a mustard-painted dining alcove. The food was great and the talk provocative, but mostly the three of them tossed the ball among themselves while I replied when essential with murmurs and smiles, which couldn't be picked on as quotes.

Melanie's scent was as subtle as Joy, and Roderick had laced my wine with brandy. He watched and spoke and attended to me with friendly eyes, and waited for me to deliver myself up. Go stuff the *Rand Daily Star*, I thought: my friend Roderick is a bastard and my tongue is my own.

Something of my awareness must have shown in my

eyes, for a thoughtful look suddenly crossed his forehead and he changed his tack in two sentences from sexual innuendo to meaningful social comment.

He said, 'What do you think of apartheid, now that you've been here a week?'

'What do you?' I replied. 'Tell me about it. You three who live here . . . you tell *me*.'

Roderick shook his head and Katya said it was what visitors thought that mattered, and only Melanie, who was playing different rules, came across with the goods.

'Apartheid,' she said earnestly, 'is necessary.'

Roderick made a negative movement, and I asked, 'In what way?'

'It means living separately,' she said. 'It doesn't mean that one race is better than the other, just that they are different, and should remain so. All the world seems to think that white South Africans hate the blacks and try to repress them, but it is not true. We care for them . . . and the phrase, "black is beautiful" was thought up by white Africans to give black Africans a sense of being important as individuals.'

I was intensely surprised, but Roderick reluctantly nodded. 'That's true. The Black Power Movement have adopted it as their own, but they didn't invent it. You might say, I suppose, that the phrase has achieved everything it was intended to, and a bit more besides.'

'To read foreign papers,' said Melanie indignantly, warming to her subject, 'you would think the blacks are a lot of illiterate cheap labour. And it isn't true.

Schooling is compulsory for both races, and factories pay the rate for the job, regardless of skin colour. And that,' she added, 'was negotiated by the white trade unionists.'

I liked her a lot better since she'd forgotten the sexpot role. The dark eyes held fire as well as smoke, and it was a change to hear someone passionately defending her country.

'Tell me more,' I said flippantly.

'Oh . . .' She looked confused for a moment, then took a fresh hold on enthusiasm, like a horse getting its second wind. 'Black people have everything the same as white people. Everything that they want to have. Only a minority have big houses because the majority don't like them: they like to live out of doors, and only go into shelters to sleep. But they have cars and businesses and holidays and hospitals and hotels and cinemas . . . everything like that.'

The white people on the whole had more money, I thought; and undoubtedly more freedom of action. I opened my mouth to make some innocuous remark about the many entrance doors marked 'non-whites' and 'whites only', but Melanie jumped right in to forestall any adverse comment, which was not in the least what Roderick wanted. He frowned at her. She was too busy to notice.

'I know what you're going to say,' she said inaccurately. 'You're going to talk about injustice. Everyone from England always does. Well, certainly, of course, there are injustices. There are in every country in the world, including yours. Injustices make the headlines. Justice is not news. People come here purposely seeking for injustice, and of course they find it. But they never report on the good things, they just shut their eyes and pretend there aren't any.'

I looked at her thoughtfully. There was truth in what she said.

'Every time a country like England attacks our way of life,' she said, 'they do more harm than good. You can feel the people here close their ranks and harden their attitude. It is stupid. It slows down the progress our country is gradually making towards partnership between the races. The old rigid type of apartheid is dying out, you know . . . and in five or ten years' time it will only be the militants and extremists on both sides who take it seriously. They shout and thump, and the foreign press listens and pays attention, like they always do to crackpots, and they don't see, or at any rate they never mention, the slow quiet change for the better which is going on here.'

I wondered how she would feel about it if she were black: even if things were changing, there was still no overall equality of opportunity. Blacks could be teachers, doctors, lawyers, priests. They couldn't be jockeys. Unfair, unfair.

Roderick, waiting in vain for me to jump in with both feet, was driven again to a direct question.

'What are your views, Link?'

I smiled at him.

'I belong to a profession,' I said, 'which never discriminates against blacks or Jews or women or Catholics or Protestants or bug-eyed monsters, but only against non-members of Equity.'

Melanie looked blank about Equity but she had a word to say about Jews.

'Whatever white South Africans may be accused of,' she contended, 'we have never sent six million blacks to the gas chamber.'

Which was rather like saying, I thought frivolously, that one might have measles, but had never infected anyone with whooping cough.

Roderick gave up angling for a quotable political commitment and tried to bounce Melanie back into sultry seduction. Her own instincts were telling her she would get further with me if she laid off the sex, because the doubt showed clearly in her manner as she attempted to do as he wanted. But evidently it was important to them both that she should persevere, and she refused to be discouraged by my lack of answering spark. She smiled a meek feminine smile to deprecate every opinion she had uttered, and bashfully lowered the thick black lashes.

Katya and Roderick exchanged eye-signals as blinding as lighthouses on a dark night, and Katya said she was going to make coffee. Roderick said he would help: and why didn't Melanie and Link move over to the sofa, it was more comfortable than sitting round the table.

Melanie smiled shyly. I admired the achievement: she was as shy underneath as a sergeant-major. She draped herself beautifully over the sofa with the green material swirling closely across the perfect bosom which rose and fell gently with every breath. She noted the direction of my eyes and smiled with pussy-cat satisfaction.

Premature, dearest Melanie, premature, I thought.

Roderick carried in a tray of coffee cups and Katya went out on to the balcony. When she came in, she shook her head. Roderick poured out the coffee and Katya handed it round: the suppressed inner excitement, absent during dinner, was fizzing away again in the corners of her smile.

I looked at my watch. A quarter past ten.

I said, 'I must be going soon. Early start tomorrow morning, I'm afraid.'

Katya said quickly, 'Oh no, you can't go yet, Link,' and Roderick handed me a bulbous glass with enough brandy to sink a battleship. I took a sip but made it look like a swallow, and reflected that if I'd drunk everything he'd given me I would have been in no state to drive away.

Melanie kicked off her golden slippers and flexed her toes. On them she wore pearly pink nail varnish and nothing else: and with a quick flash of bare ankle and calf she managed to plant the idea in my mind that under the green shift there were no other clothes.

The coffee was as good as the dinner: Katya was more expert a cook than conspirator. Within twenty minutes she again strolled out on to the balcony, and this time, when she came back, the message as a nod.

I looked at all three of them, wondering. Roderick with his old-young face, Katya yellow-frilly and irresponsible, Melanie conscientiously weaving her web. They had laid some sort of trap. The only thing was . . . what?

Twenty to eleven. I finished my coffee, stood up, and said, 'I really must go now . . .'

This time there was no resistance. They all three uncurled themselves to their feet.

'Thank you,' I said, 'for a great evening.'

They smiled.

'Marvellous food,' I said to Katya.

She smiled.

'Splendid drinks,' I said to Roderick.

He smiled.

'Superb company,' I said to Melanie.

She smiled.

Not a really genuine smile among them. They had watchful, expectant eyes. My mouth, for all the available liquid, felt dry.

We moved towards the lobby, which was an extension of the sitting-room.

Melanie said, 'Time I was going too . . . Roderick, would you order me a taxi?'

'Sure, love,' he said easily, and then, as if the thought was just striking, 'but you go the same way as Link . . . I'm sure he would give you a lift.'

They all looked at me, smiling.

'Of course,' I said. What else. What else could I say?

The smiles went on and on.

Melanie scooped up a tiny wrap from beside the front door, and Roderick and Katya saw us down the hall and into the lift, and were still waving farewell as the doors closed between us. The lift sank. One of those automatic lifts which stopped at every floor one had pre-selected. I pressed G for ground, and at G for ground it stopped.

Politely I let Melanie out first. Then I said, 'I say . . . terribly sorry . . . I've left my signet ring on the wash basin in Roderick's bathroom. I'll just dash back for it. You wait there, I won't be a second.'

The doors were closing before she could demur. I pressed the buttons for floors 2 and 6. Got out at 2. Watched the pointer begin to slide towards Roderick's floor at 6, and skipped quickly through the doors of the service stairs at the back of the hall.

The unadorned concrete and ironwork steps wound down round a small steep well and let me out into an area full of stacked laundry baskets, central-heating boilers, and rows of garbage cans. Out in the narrow street behind the covered yard I turned left, skirted the whole of the next door block at a fast pace, and finally, more slowly, inconspicuously walked in the shadows back towards Roderick's.

I stopped in a doorway a hundred yards away, and watched.

There were four men in the street, waiting. Two

opposite the front entrance of Roderick's apartment block. Two others patiently standing near my hired car. All of them carried objects which gleamed in the street lamps, and whose shapes I knew all too well.

Melanie came out of the apartment block and hurried across the road to talk to two of the men. The green dress clung to her body and appeared diaphanous to the point of transparency in the quality of light in the street. She and the men conferred agitatedly, and there was a great deal of shaking of heads.

All three of them suddenly looked up, and I followed the direction of their gaze. Roderick and Katya were standing out on the balcony, calling down. I was too far away to hear the exact words, but the gist was entirely guessable. The quarry had got away, and none of them was pleased.

Melanie and the two men turned and walked in my direction, but only as far as the other two beside my car. They all five went into a huddle which could produce no happiness, and in the end Melanie walked back alone and disappeared into the flats.

I sighed wryly. Roderick was no murderer. He was a newspaperman. The four men had come armed with cameras. Not knives. Not guns.

Not my life they were after; just my picture.

Just my picture outside a block of flats at night alone with a beautiful girl in a totally revealing dress.

I looked thoughtfully at the four men beside my car,

decided the odds were against it, turned on my heel, and quietly walked away.

Back at the Iguana Rock (by taxi), I telephoned Roderick.

He sounded subdued.

I said, 'Damn your bloody eyes.'

'Yes.'

'Have you got this telephone bugged?'

A pause. Then on a sigh again he said, 'Yes.'

'Too late for honesty, my friend.'

'Link . . .'

'Forget it,' I said. 'Just tell me why.'

'My paper . . .'

'No,' I said. 'Newspapers don't get up to such tricks. That was a spot of private enterprise.'

A longer pause.

'I guess I owe it to you,' he said slowly. 'We did it for Clifford Wenkins. The little runt is scared silly by Worldic, and he begged us, in return for favours he has done us from time to time, to set you up for him. He said Worldic would sack him if he couldn't persuade you to do a girly session to sell their twenty-rand seats, and he had asked you, and you had absolutely refused. Melanie is our top model girl, and he got her to help in a good cause.'

'That Wenkins,' I said bitterly, 'would sell his soul for publicity stunts.'

205

'I'm sorry, Link . . .'

'Not as sorry as he will be,' I said ominously.

'I promised him I wouldn't tell you . . .'

'Stuff both of you,' I said violently, and rattled the receiver into its cradle.

CHAPTER THIRTEEN

The next morning, the Iguana management having kindly sent someone with the keys to fetch my hired car from outside Roderick's flat, I packed what little I would need for the Kruger Park, and chuntered round to Evan and Conrad's hotel.

The loading of their station wagon was in process of being directed by Evan as if it were the key scene in a prestige production, and performed by Conrad at his most eccentric. Boxes, bags, and black zipped equipment littered the ground for a radius of ten yards.

'Dear boy,' Conrad said as I approached, 'for God's sake get some ice.'

'Ice?' I echoed vaguely.

'Ice.' He pointed to a yellow plastic box about two feet by one. 'In there. For the film.'

'What about beer?'

He gave me a sorrowful, withering glance. 'Beer in the red one, dear boy.'

The red thermal box had had priority; had already been clipped tight shut and lifted on to the car. Smiling,

I went into the hotel on the errand and returned with a large plastic bagful. Conrad laid the ice-pack in the yellow box and carefully stacked his raw stock on top. The yellow box joined the red one and Evan said that at this rate we wouldn't reach the Kruger by nightfall.

At eleven the station wagon was full to the gunnels but the ground was still littered with that extraordinary collection of wires, boxes, tripods and clips which seemed to accompany cameramen everywhere.

Evan waved his arms as if by magic wand and the whole lot would leap into order. Conrad pulled his moustache dubiously. I opened the boot of my saloon, shovelled the whole lot in unceremoniously, and told him he could sort it all out when we arrived.

After that we adjourned for thirst quenchers, and finally got the wheels on the road at noon. We drove east by north for several hours and descended from the high Johannesburg plateau down to a few hundred feet above sea level. The air grew noticeably warmer on every long downhill stretch, which gave rise to three or four more stops for sustenance. Conrad's cubic capacity rivalled the Bantus'.

By five we arrived at the Numbi gate, the nearest way into the park. The Kruger itself stretched a further two hundred miles north and fifty east with nothing to keep the animals in except their own wish to stay. The Numbi gate consisted of a simple swinging barrier guarded by two khaki-uniformed black Africans and a small office. Evan produced passes for two cars and reservations for staying in the camps, and with grins and salutes the passes were stamped and the gates swung open.

Brilliant scarlet and magenta bougainvillaea just inside proved misleading: the park itself was tinder dry and thorny brown after months of sun and no rain. The narrow road stretched ahead into a baked wilderness where the only man-made thing in sight was the tarmac itself.

'Zebras,' shouted Evan, winding down his window and screaming out of it.

I followed his pointing finger, and saw the dusty herd of them standing patiently under bare-branched trees, slowly swinging their tails and merging uncannily into the striped shade.

Conrad had a map, which was just as well. We were headed for the nearest camp, Pretoriuskop, but roads wound and cross-crossed as we approached it, unmade-up dry earth roads leading off at tangents to vast areas inhabited believably by lion, rhinoceros, buffalo and crocodile.

And, of course, elephant.

The camp turned out to be an area of several dozen acres, enclosed by a stout wire fence, and containing nothing so camplike as tents. Rather like Butlins gone native, I thought: clusters of round, brick-walled, thatched-roofed cabins like pink-coloured drums with wide-brimmed hats on.

'*Rondavels,*' Evan said in his best dogmatic manner, waving a hand at them. He checked in at the big reception office and drove off to search for the huts with the right numbers. There were three of them: one each. Inside, two beds, a table, two chairs, fitted cupboard, shower room, and air-conditioning. Every mod con in the middle of the jungle.

Evan banged on my door and said come out, we were going for a drive. The camp locked its gates for the night at six thirty, he said, which gave us forty minutes to go and look at baboons.

'It will take too long to unpack the station wagon,' he said. 'So we will all go in your car.'

I drove and they gazed steadfastly out of the windows. There were some distant baboons scratching themselves in the evening sunlight on a rocky hill, and a herd of impala munching away at almost leafless bushes, but not an elephant in sight.

'We'd better go back before we get lost,' I said, but even then we only whizzed through the gates seconds before closing time.

'What happens if you're late?' I asked.

'You have to spend the night outside,' Evan said positively. 'Once the gate is closed, it's closed.'

Evan, as usual, seemed to be drawing information out of air, though he gave the game away later by producing an information booklet he had been given in reception. The booklet also said not to wind down windows and scream 'zebra' out of them, as the animals didn't like it. Wild animals, it appeared, thought cars were harmless

210

and left them alone, but were liable to bite any bits of humans sticking out.

Conrad had had to unpack the whole station wagon to unload the red beer box, which was likely to reverse his priorities. We sat round a table outside the huts, cooling our throats in the warm air and watching the dark creep closer between the *rondavels*. Even with Evan there it was peaceful enough to unjangle the screwiest nerves . . . and lull the wariest mind into a sense of security.

Thursday, the following day, we set off at daybreak and breakfasted at the next camp, Skukuza, where we were to stay that night.

Skukuza was larger and boasted executive-status *rondavels*, which Evan's production company had naturally latched on to. They had also engaged the full-time attendance of a park ranger for the day, which would have been splendid had he not been an Afrikaner with incomplete English. He was big, slow-moving, quiet and unemotional, the complete antithesis of Evan's fiery zeal for allegory.

Evan shot questions and had to wait through silences for his answers: no doubt Haagner was merely translating the one into Afrikaans in his head, formulating the other and translating that into English, but the delay irritated Evan from the start. Haagner treated Evan with detachment and refused to be hurried, which gave

211

Conrad the (decently concealed) satisfaction of an underdog seeing his master slip on a banana skin.

We set off in Haagner's Range Rover, accompanied by the Arriflex, a tape recorder, half a dozen smaller cameras, and the red thermal box loaded with a mixed cargo of film, beer, fruit, and sandwiches in plastic bags. Evan had brought sketch pads, maps and notebooks, and six times remarked that the company should have equipped him with a secretary. Conrad murmured that we should be glad that we weren't equipped with Drix Goddart, but from the sour look Evan slid me he didn't necessarily agree.

'*Olifant*,' Haagner said, pointing, having been three times told of the aim of the expedition.

He stopped the van. 'There, in the valley.'

We looked. A lot of trees, a patch of green, a winding river.

'There, man,' he said.

Eventually our untrained eyes saw them: three dark hunched shapes made small by distance, flapping a lazy ear behind a bush.

'Not near enough,' Evan said disgustedly. 'We must get nearer.'

'Not here,' said Haagner. 'They are across the river. The Sabie river. *Sabie* is Bantu word: it means Fear.'

I looked at him suspiciously but he was not provoking Evan in any way; simply imparting information. The slow peaceful-looking water wound through the valley and looked as unfearful as the Thames.

Evan had no eyes for the various antelope-like species Haagner pointed out, nor for the blue jays or turkey buzzards or vervet monkeys or wildebeest, and particularly not for the herds of gentle impala. Only the implicitly violent took his attention: the vulture, the hyena, the wart-hog, the possibility of lion and the scarcity of cheetah.

And, of course, *olifants*. Even adopted the Afrikaans word as his own and rolled it round his tongue as if he alone had invented it. *Olifant* droppings on the road (fresh, said Haagner) excited him almost to orgasm. He insisted on us stopping there and reversing for a better view, and on Conrad sticking the Arriflex lens out of the window and exposing about fifty feet of film from different angles and with several focal lengths.

Haagner, patiently positioning the van for every shot, watched these antics and clearly thought Evan unhinged, and I laughed internally until my throat ached. Had the obliging elephant returned Evan would no doubt have directed him to defecate again for Scene 1, Take 2. He would have seen nothing odd in it.

Evan left the heap reluctantly and was working out how to symbolize it in an utterly meaningful way. Conrad said he could do with a beer, but Haagner pointed ahead and said 'Onder-Sabie', which turned out to be another rest camp like the others.

'*Olifant* in Saliji river,' said Haagner coming back from a chat with some colleagues. 'If we go now, you see them perhaps.'

Evan swept us away from the shady table and our half-empty glasses and scurried forth again into the increasing noonday heat. All around us, more sensible mortals were fanning themselves and contemplating siesta, but *olifants*, with Evan, came before sense.

The Range Rover was as hot as an oven.

'It is hot, today,' Haagner said. 'Hotter tomorrow. Summer is coming. Soon we will have the rain, and all the park will be green.'

Evan, alarmed, said, 'No, no. The park must be burned up, just like this. Inhospitable land, bare, hungry, predatory, aggressive and cruel. Certainly not soft and lush.'

Haagner understood less than a tenth. After a long pause he merely repeated the bad news: 'In one month, after the rains start, the park will be all green. Then, much water. Now, not much. All small rivers are dry. We find *olifant* near bigger rivers. In Saliji.'

He drove several miles and stopped beside a large wooden sun shelter built high at the end of a valley. Below, the Saliji river stretched away straight ahead, and the *olifants* had done Evan proud. A large family of them were playing in the water, squirting each other through their trunks and taking care of their kids.

As it was an official picnic place especially built in an area of cleared ground, we were all allowed out of the car. I stretched myself thankfully and dug into the red box for a spot of irrigation. Conrad had a camera in one hand and a beer in the other, and Evan brandished his enthusiasm over us all like a whip.

Haagner and I sat in ninety degrees in the shade at one of the small scattered tables and ate some of the packed sandwiches. He had warned Evan not to go too far from the shelter while filming as it presented an open invitation to a hungry lion, but Evan naturally believed that he would not meet one: and he didn't. He took Conrad plus Arriflex fifty yards downhill into the bush for some closer shots, and Haagner called him urgently to come back, telling me his job would be lost if Evan were.

Conrad soon climbed up again, mopping drops from his brow which were not all heat, and reported that 'something' was grunting down there behind some rocks.

'There are twelve hundred lion in the park,' Haagner said. 'When hungry, they kill. Lions alone kill thirty thousand animals in the park every year.'

'God,' said Conrad, visibly losing interest in Evan's whole project.

Eventually Evan returned unscathed, but Haagner regarded him with disfavour.

'More *olifant* in the north,' he said. 'For *olifant*, you go north.' Out of his district, his tone said.

Evan nodded briskly and set his mind at rest.

'Tomorrow. We set off northwards tomorrow, and tomorrow night we stay in a camp called Satara.'

Reassured, Haagner drove us slowly back towards

Skukuza, conscientiously pointing out animals all the way.

'Could you cross the park on a horse?' I asked.

He shook his head decisively. 'Very dangerous. More dangerous than walking, and walking is not safe.' He looked directly at Evan. 'If your car break down, wait for next car, and ask people to tell rangers at the next camp. Do not leave your car. Do not walk in the park. Especially do not walk in the park at night. Stay in car all night.'

Evan listened to the lecture with every symptom of ignoring it. He pointed instead to one of the several unmetalled side roads we had passed with 'no entry' signs on them, and asked where they led.

'Some go to the many Bantu ranger stations,' said Haagner after the pause for translation. 'Some to water holes. Some are fire breaks. They are roads for rangers. Not roads for visitors. Do not go down those roads.' He looked at Evan, clearly seeing that Evan would not necessarily obey. 'It is not allowed.'

'Why not?'

'The park is 8,000 square miles . . . visitors can get lost.'

'We have a map,' Evan argued.

'The service roads,' Haagner said stolidly, 'are not on the maps.'

Evan ate a packet of sandwiches mutinously and rolled down the window to throw out the plastic bag.

'Do not do that,' Haagner said sharply enough to stop him.

'Why not?'

'The animals eat them, and choke. No litter must be thrown. It kills the animals.'

'Oh very well,' said Evan ungraciously, and handed me the screwed-up bag to return to the red box. The box was clipped shut and tidy, so I shoved it in my pocket. Evan polished off the job of being a nuisance by throwing out instead the half-eaten crust of his cheese-and-tomato.

'Do not feed the animals,' said Haagner automatically.

'Why not?' Evan, belligerent, putting on an RSPCA face.

'It is unwise to teach animals that cars contain food.'

That silenced him flat. Conrad twitched an eyebrow at me and I arranged my face into as near impassiveness as one can get while falling about inside.

Owing to an *olifant* waving its ears as us within cricket-ball distance we did not get back to Skukuza before the gates shut. Evan, oblivious to the fast-setting sun, saw allegories all over the place and had Conrad wasting film by the mile, taking shots through glass. He had wanted Conrad to set up a tripod in the road to get steadier than hand-held pictures, but even he was slightly damped by the frantic quality in Haagner's voice as he told him not to.

'*Olifant* is the most dangerous of all the animals,' he

217

said earnestly, and Conrad equally earnestly assured him that for nothing on earth would he, Conrad, leave the safety of the Range Rover. Haagner wouldn't even have the window open and wanted to drive away at once. It appeared that when *olifants* waved their ears like that they were expressing annoyance, and since they weighed seven tons and could charge at 25 m.p.h., it didn't do to hang about.

Evan didn't believe that any animal would have the gall to attack such important humans as E. Pentelow, director, and E. Lincoln, actor. He persuaded Conrad to get clicking, and Haagner sat there with the engine running and his foot on the clutch. When the elephant finally took one step in our direction we were off down the road with a jolt that threw Conrad, camera and all, to the floor.

I helped him up, while Evan complained about it to Haagner. The ranger, nearing the end of his patience, stopped the car with an equal jerk and hauled on the hand brake.

'Very well,' he said. 'We wait.'

The elephant came out on to the road, a hundred yards behind us. The big ears were flapping like flags.

Conrad looked back. 'Do drive on, dear boy,' he said with anxiety in his voice.

Haagner folded his lips. The elephant decided to follow us. He was also accelerating to a trot.

It took more seconds than I cared before Evans cracked. He was saying 'For God's sake, where is the

Arriflex?' to Conrad, when it seemed at last to dawn on him that there might be some real danger.

'Drive away,' he said to Haagner urgently. 'Can't you see that that animal is charging?'

And it had tusks, I observed.

Haagner too decided that enough was enough. He had the hand brake off and the gears in mesh in one slick movement, and the elephant got a trunkful of dust.

'What about the next car coming along?' I asked. 'They'll meet it head on.'

Haagner shook his head. 'No cars will come this way any more today. It is too late. They will all be near the camps now. And that *olifant*, he will go straight away into the bush. He will not stay on the road.'

Conrad looked at his watch. 'How long will it take us to get back to Skukuza?'

'With no more stops,' Haagner said with bite, 'about half an hour.'

'But it is six fifteen already!' Conrad said.

Haagner made a noncommittal movement of his head and didn't answer. Evan appeared subdued into silence and a look of peaceful satisfaction awoke on the Afrikaner's face. For the whole of the rest of the way it stayed there, first in the quick dust, then in the reflected glow of the headlights. Before we reached Skukuza he swung the Range Rover down one of the no entry side roads, a detour which brought us after a mile or two suddenly and unexpectedly into a village of modern bungalows with tiny little flower gardens and street lighting.

We stared in amazement. A suburb, no less, set down greenly in the brown dry veldt.

'This is the ranger village,' Haagner said. 'My house is over there, the third down that road. All the whites who work in the camp, and the white rangers, we live here. The Bantu rangers and workers also have villages in the park.'

'But the lions,' I said. 'Are the villages safe, isolated like this?'

He smiled. 'It is not isolated.' The Range Rover came to the end of the houses, crossed about fifty unlit yards of road and sped straight into the back regions of Skukuza camp. 'But also, no, it is not entirely safe. One must not walk far from the houses at night. Lions do not normally come near the gardens ... and we have fences round them ... but a young Bantu was taken by a lion one night on that short piece of road between our village and the camp. I knew him well. He had been told never to walk ... it was truly sad.'

'Are people often ... taken ... by lions?' I asked, as he pulled up by our *rondavels*, and we unloaded ourselves, the cameras, and the red box.

'No. Sometimes. Not often. People who work in the park; never visitors. It is safe in cars.' He gave Evan one last meaningful stare. 'Do not leave your car. To do so is not safe.'

*

Before dinner in the camp restaurant I put a call through to England. Two hours' delay, they said, but by nine o'clock I was talking to Charlie.

Everything was fine, she said, the children were little hooligans, and she had been to see Nerissa.

'I spent the whole day with her yesterday . . . Most of the time we just sat, because she felt awfully tired, but she didn't seem to want me to go. I asked her the things you wanted . . . not all at once, but spread over . . .'

'What did she say?'

'Well . . . You were right about some things. She did tell Danilo she had Hodgkin's disease. She said she didn't know herself that it was fatal when she told him, but she doesn't think he took much notice, because all he said was that he thought only young people got it.'

If he knew that, I thought, he knew a lot more.

'Apparently he stayed with her for about ten days, and they became firm friends. That was how she described it. So she told him, before he went back to America, that she would be leaving him the horses as a personal gift, and also, as he was all the family she had, all the rest of her money after other bequests had been met.'

'Lucky old Danilo.'

'Yes . . . Well, he came to see her again, a few weeks ago, late July or early August. While you were in Spain, anyway. She knew by then that she was dying, but she didn't mention it to Danilo. She did show him her will, though, as he seemed interested in it. She said he was so

221

sweet when he had read it, and hoped not to be inheriting for twenty years.'

'Little hypocrite.'

'I don't know,' said Charlie doubtfully, 'because although you were right about so much, there is a distinct fly in the wood pile.'

'What's that?'

'It can't be Danilo who is making the horses lose. It simply cannot.'

'It must be,' I said. 'And why not?'

'Because when Nerissa told him she was worried about the way they were running, and wished she could find out what was wrong, it was Danilo himself who came up with the idea of sending *you*.'

'It can't have been,' I exclaimed.

'It definitely was,' Charlie said. 'She was positive about it. It was Danilo's own suggestion.'

'Blast,' I said.

'He wouldn't have suggested she send someone to investigate, if he'd been nobbling them himself.'

'No . . . I suppose not.'

'You sound depressed,' she said.

'I haven't any other answers for Nerissa.'

'Don't worry. You weren't anyway going to tell her her nephew was up to no good.'

'That's true,' I agreed.

'And it wasn't difficult for Danilo to read her will. She leaves it lying around all the time on that marquetry table in the corner of the sitting-room. She showed it to me immediately, as soon as I mentioned it, because it interests her a lot. And I saw what keepsakes she is leaving us, if you're interested.'

'What are they?' I asked idly, thinking about Danilo.

'She's leaving you her holding in something called Rojedda, and she's leaving me a diamond pendant and some earrings. She showed them to me . . . they are absolutely beautiful and I told her they were far too much, but she made me try them on so she would see how I looked. She seemed to be so pleased . . . so happy . . . isn't she incredible? I can hardly bear . . . oh . . . oh dear . . .'

'Don't cry, darling,' I said.

There were some swallowing noises.

'I . . . can't . . . help it. She is already much worse than when we saw her before, and she's very uncomfortable. One of her swollen glands is pressing on things in her chest.'

'We'll go and see her as soon as I get back.'

'Yes.' She sniffed away the tears. 'God, I do miss you.'

'Me too,' I said. 'Only one more week. I'll be home a week today, and we'll take the kids down to Cornwall.'

After the call I went outside and walked slowly past our *rondavels* and out on to the rough grassy area beyond. The African night was very quiet. No roar of traffic from any distant city, just the faint steady hum of the generator supplying Skukuza with electricity, and the energetic music of cicadas.

Nerissa had given me my answers.

I saw what they meant, and I didn't want to believe it.

A gamble. No more, no less.

With my life as the stake.

I went back to the telephone and made one more call. Van Huren's manservant said he would see, and Quentin came on the line. I said I knew it was an odd thing to ask, and I would explain why when next I saw him, but could he possibly tell me what size Nerissa's holding in Rojedda was likely to be.

'The same as my own,' he said without hesitation. 'She has my brother's holding, passed to her by Portia.'

I thanked him numbly.

'See you at the premiere,' he said. 'We are looking forward to it very much.'

For hours, I couldn't go to sleep. Yet where could I be safer than inside a guarded camp, with Evan and Conrad snoring their heads off in the huts next door?

But when I woke up, I was no longer in bed.

I was in the car I had hired in Johannesburg.

The car was surrounded by early daylight in the Kruger National Park. Trees, scrub, and dry grass. Not a *rondavel* in sight.

Remnants of an ether smell blurred my senses, but one fact was sharp and self-evident.

One of my arms lay through the steering wheel, and my wrists were locked together in a pair of handcuffs.

CHAPTER FOURTEEN

This had to be some ghastly practical joke. Evan, being malicious.

This had to be Clifford Wenkins thinking up some frightful publicity stunt.

This had to be anything but real.

But I knew, deep down in some deathly cold core, that this time there was no girl called Jill coming to set me free.

This time the dying was there to be done. Staring me in the face. Straining already across my shoulders and down my arms.

Danilo was playing for his gold mine.

I felt sick and ill. Whatever anaesthetic had been used on me had been given crudely. Probably far too much for the purpose. Not that that was likely to worry anyone but me.

For an age I could think no further. The dizziness kept coming back in clammy pea-green waves. My physical wretchedness blocked any other thought; took up all my attention. Bouts of semi-consciousness brought me each time to a fresh awakening, to renewed awareness of my plight, to malaise and misery.

The first objective observation which pierced the fog was that I had gone to bed wearing shorts, and now had clothes on. The trousers I had worn the day before, and the shirt. Also, upon investigation, socks and slip-on shoes.

The next discovery, which had been knocking at the door of consciousness for some time but had been shut out as unwelcome, was that the car's seat belts were fastened. Across my chest and over my lap, just as in the Special.

They weren't tightly fastened, but I couldn't reach the clip.

I tried. The first of many tries at many things. The first of many frustrations.

I tried to slide my hands out of the handcuffs: but, as before, they were the regulation British police model, designed precisely not to let people slide their hands out. My bones, as before, were too big.

I tried with all my strength to break the steering wheel, but although this one looked flimsy compared with the one in the Special, I still couldn't do it.

I could move a shade more than in the film. The straps were not so tight and there was more room round my legs. Apart from that, there was little in it.

For the first of many times I wondered how long it would be before anyone set out to look for me.

Evan and Conrad, when they found me missing,

would surely start a search. Haagner, surely, would alert every ranger in the park. Someone would come along very soon. Of course they would. And set me free.

The day began to warm up, the sun in a cloudless sky shining brightly through the window on my right. The car was therefore facing north . . . and I groaned at the thought, because in the southern hemisphere the sun shone at midday from the north, and I should have its heat and light full in the face.

Perhaps someone would come before midday.

Perhaps.

The worst of the sickness passed in an hour or two, though the tides of unease ebbed and flowed for much longer. Gradually, however, I began to think again, and to lose the feeling that even if death were already perched on my elbow I was too bilious to care.

Clear thought number one was that Danilo had locked me in this car so that I should die and he would inherit Nerissa's half share in the van Huren gold mine.

Nerissa was leaving her Rojedda holding to me in her will, and Danilo, having read the will, knew.

Danilo was to inherit the residue. Should I die before Nerissa, the Rojedda bequest would be void, and the holding would become part of his residue. Should I live, he stood to lose not only a share of the mine, but hundreds of thousands of pounds besides.

As the law stood then, and would still stand when Nerissa died, estate duty on everything she possessed would be paid out of the residue. Danilo personally stood to lose every penny of the estate duty paid on the inheritance which Nerissa was leaving to me.

If only, I thought uselessly, she had told me what she was doing: I could have explained why she shouldn't. Perhaps she hadn't realized how immensely valuable the Rojedda holding was: she had only recently received it from her sister. Perhaps she hadn't understood how estate duty worked. Certainly, in view of the enjoyment she had found in her long-lost nephew, she had not intended me to prosper out of all proportion at Danilo's expense.

Any accountant would have told her, but wills were usually drawn up by solicitors, not accountants, and solicitors didn't give financial advice.

Danilo, with his mathematical mind, had read the will and seen the barbs in it, as I would have done. Danilo must have begun plotting my death from that very moment.

He had only had to tell me what she had written. But how could he know that? If he himself in reversed positions would have stuck two fingers up in my face, perhaps he thought that I, that anyone, would do that too.

Nerissa, I thought. Dear, dear Nerissa. Meaning good to everyone, and happily leaving them presents, and landing me in consequence in the most unholy bloody mess.

Danilo the gambler. Danilo the bright lad who knew that Hodgkin's disease was fatal. Danilo the little schemer who started by lowering the value of a string of racehorses to pay less estate duty on them, and who, when he found that the real stakes were much higher, had the nerve to move at once into the senior league.

I remembered his fascination down the mine, his questions about quantities at lunch, and his tennis game with Sally. He was after the whole works, not just half. Inherit one half and marry the other. No matter that she was only fifteen: in two more years it would be a highly suitable alliance.

Danilo . . .

I tugged uselessly, in sudden shaking fury, at the obstinate steering wheel. Such cruelty was impossible. How could he . . . how could anyone . . . lock a man in a car and leave him to die of heat and thirst and exhaustion? It only happened in films . . . in one film . . . in *Man in a Car*.

Don't get out of the car, Haagner had said. It is not safe to get out of the car. And a right bloody laugh that was. If I could get out of this car I would take my chance with the lions.

All that screaming and shouting I had done in the film. I remembered it coldly. The agony of spirit I had imagined and acted. The disintegration of a soul, a process I had dissected into a series of pictures to be presented one by one until the progression led inexorably to the empty shell of a man too far gone to recover his mind, even if his body were saved.

The man in the Special had been a fictional character. The man had been shown as reacting to every situation throughout the story with impulsive emotion, which was why his weeping fits *in extremis* had been valid. But I was not like the man: in many respects, diametrically opposite. I saw the present problem in mainly practical terms, and intended to go on doing so.

Someone, sometime, would find me. I would just have to try, in any way I could, to be alive – and sane – when they did so.

The sun rose high and the car grew hot; but this was only a secondary discomfort.

My bladder was full to bursting.

I could stretch my hands round the wheel to reach and undo the fly zip fastener, which I did. But I couldn't move far on the seat and even if I managed to open the door with my elbow, there would be no chance of clearing the car. Although there was no sense in it, I postponed the inevitable moment until continence was nearer a pain than a nuisance. But reluctance had its limits. When in the end I had to let go, a lot went as far as the floor, but a lot of it didn't, and I could feel the wetness soaking into my trousers from crutch to knee.

Sitting in a puddle made me extremely angry. Quite unreasonably, forcing me to mess myself seemed a more callous act than putting me in the car in the first place. In the film, we had glossed over this problem as being secondary to the mental state. We had been wrong. It was part of it.

The net result on me was to make me more resolved than ever not to be defeated. It made me mean and revengeful.

It made me hate Danilo.

The morning wore on. The heat became a trial and I got tired of sitting still. I had, however, I told myself, spent three weeks in Spain in precisely this position. There, in fact, it had been much hotter. I wilfully ignored the thought that in Spain we had knocked off for lunch.

Lunchtime was pretty near, by my watch. Well . . . maybe someone would come . . .

And how would they get there, I wondered. Ahead of me there was no road, just small trees, dry grass and scrubby undergrowth. To each side, just the same. But the car must have been driven there, not dropped by a passing eagle . . . Twisting my neck and consulting the reflection in the mirror, I saw that the road, such as it was, lay directly at my back. It was an earth road showing no sign of upkeep and all too many of desertion, and it petered out completely twenty yards or so from where I sat. My car had been driven straight off the end of it into the bush.

In less than a month it would rain: the trees and the grass would grow thick and green, and the road turn to mud. No one would find the car, if it were still there when the rains came.

If I . . . were still there when the rains came.

I shook myself. That way led straight towards the mental state of the man in the film, and of course I had decided to steer clear of it.

Of course.

Perhaps they would send a helicopter . . .

It was a grey car; nondescript. But surely any car would show up, from the air. There was a small aerodrome near Skukuza, I'd seen it marked on the map. Surely Evan would send a helicopter . . .

But where to? I was facing north, off the end of an abandoned track, I could be anywhere.

Maybe if I did after all make a noise, someone would hear . . . All those people driving along miles away in their safe little cars with the engines droning and the windows securely shut.

The car's horn . . . Useless. It was one of those cars which had to have the ignition on before the horn would sound.

In the ignition . . . no keys.

Lunchtime came and went. I could have done with a nice cold beer.

A heavy swishing in the bush behind me sent my head twisting hopefully in its direction. Someone had come . . . Well, hadn't I known they would?

No human voices, though, exclaimed over me, bringing freedom. My visitor, in fact, had no voice at all, as he was a giraffe.

The great fawn sky-scraper with paler patches rolled rhythmically past the car and began pulling at the sparse leaves scattering the top of the tree straight ahead. He was so close that his bulk shut out the sun, giving me a welcome oasis of shade. Huge and graceful, he stayed for a while, munching peacefully and pausing now and then to bend his great horned head towards the car, peering at it from eyes fringed by outrageously long lashes. The most seductive lady would be reduced to despair by a giraffe's eyelashes.

I found myself talking to him aloud. 'Just buzz off over to Skukuza, will you, and get our friend Haagner to come here in his Range Rover at the bloody double.'

The sound of my voice startled me, because in it I heard my own conviction. I might hope that Evan or Conrad or Haagner or the merest passing stranger would soon find me, but I didn't believe it. Unconsciously, because of the film, I was already geared to a long wait.

But what I did believe was that in the end someone would come. The peasant would ride by on his donkey, and see the car, and rescue the man. That was the only tolerable ending. The one I had to cling to, and work for.

For in the end, people would search.

If I didn't turn up at the premiere, there would be questions and checks, and finally a search.

The premiere was next Wednesday.

Today, I supposed, was Friday.

People could live only six or seven days without water.

I stared sombrely at the giraffe. He batted the fantastic eyelashes, shook his head gently as if in sorrow, and ambled elegantly away.

By Wednesday night I would have spent six whole days without water. No one would find me as soon as the Thursday.

Friday or Saturday, perhaps, if they were clever.

It couldn't be done.

It had to be.

When the giraffe took away with him his patch of shade I realized how fierce the sun had grown. If I did nothing about it, I thought, I would have me a nasty case of sunburn.

The parts of me most relentlessly in the sun were oddly enough my hands. As in most hot-country cars, the top third of the windscreen was tinted green against glare, and if I rolled my head back I could get my face out of the direct rays; but they fell unimpeded on to my lap. I solved the worst of that by unbuttoning my shirt cuffs and tucking my hands in the opposite sleeves, like a muff.

After that I debated the wisdom of taking my shoes and socks off, and of opening a window to let in some fresh and cooler air. I could get my feet, one at a time, up to my hands to get my socks off. I could also swivel enough in my seat to wind the left-hand window handle with my toes.

It wasn't the thought of invasion by animals that stopped me doing it at once, but the niggling subject of humidity.

The only water available to me for the whole of the time I sat there would be what was contained at that moment in my own body. With every movement and every breath I was depleting the stock, releasing water into the air about me in the form of invisible water vapour. If I kept the windows shut, the water vapour would mostly stay inside the car. If I opened them, it would instantly be lost.

The outside air, after all those rainless months, was as dry as Prohibition. It seemed to me that though I couldn't stop my body losing a lot of moisture, I could to some extent re-use it. It would take longer, in damper air, for my skin to crack in dehydration. Re-breathing water vapour would go some small way to postponing the time when the mucous linings of nose and throat would dry raw.

So what with one thing and another, I didn't open the window.

Like a man with an obsession I turned back again and again to the hope–despair see-saw of rescue, one minute convinced that Evan and Conrad would have sent out sorties the moment they found me gone, the next that they would simply have cursed my rudeness and set off by themselves towards the north, where Evan would become so engrossed with *olifant* that E. Lincoln would fade from his mind like yesterday's news.

No one else would miss me. Everyone back in Johannesburg – the van Hurens, Roderick, Clifford Wenkins – knew I had gone down to the game reserve for the rest of the week. None of them would expect to hear from me. None of them would expect me back before Tuesday.

The only hope I had lay in Evan and Conrad . . . and the peasant passing by with his donkey.

At some point during the long afternoon I thought of seeing if I still had in my trouser pockets the things I had had there the day before. I hadn't emptied the pockets when I undressed, I had just laid my clothes on the second bed.

Investigation showed that my wallet was still buttoned into my rear pocket, because I could feel its shape if I pushed back against the seat. But money, in these circumstances, was useless.

By twisting, lifting myself an inch off the seat, and tugging, I managed to get my right-hand pocket round to centre front, and, carefully exploring, brought forth a total prize of a packet of Iguana Rock book matches, with four matches left, a blue rubber band, and a three-inch stub of pencil with no point.

I put all these carefully back where they came from, and reversed the tugging until I could reach into the left-hand pocket.

Two things only in there. A handkerchief . . . and the forgotten screwed-up plastic bag from Evan's sandwiches.

'Don't throw plastic bags out of car windows,' Haagner had said. 'They can kill the animals.'

And save the lives of men.

Precious, precious plastic bag.

Never cross a desert without one.

I knew how to get half a cup of water every twenty-four hours from a sheet of plastic in a hot climate, but it couldn't be done by someone strapped into a sitting position inside a car. It needed a hole dug in the ground, a small weight, and something to catch the water in.

All the same, the principle was there, if I could make it work.

Condensation.

The hole in the ground method worked during the night. In the heat of the day one dug a hole, making it about eighteen inches deep, and in diameter slightly smaller than the available piece of plastic. One placed a cup in the hole, in the centre. One spread the sheet of plastic over the hole, and sealed it down round the edges with the dug-out earth or sand. And finally one placed a small stone or some coins on the centre of the plastic, weighing it down at a spot directly over the cup.

After that, one waited.

Cooled by the night, the water vapour in the hot air trapped in the hole condensed into visible water droplets, which formed on the cold unporous plastic, trickled downhill to the weighted point, and dripped from there into the cup.

A plastic bagful of hot air should produce a teaspoonful of water by dawn.

It wasn't much.

After a while I pulled one hand towards me as far as it would go, and leaned forward hard against the seat belt, and found I could reach far enough to blow into the bag if I held its gathered neck loosely with an O of forefinger and thumb.

For probably half an hour I breathed in through my nose, and out through my mouth, into the plastic bag. At the end of that time there were hundreds of small water droplets sticking to the inside of the bag . . . the water vapour out of my lungs, trapped there instead of escaping into the air.

I turned the bag inside out and licked it. It was wet. When I'd sucked off as much as I could, I laid the cool damp surface against my face, and perhaps because of the paltriness of what I had achieved, felt the first deep stab of desolation.

I fished out the blue rubber band again, and while the sunlit air was still hot, filled the bag with it, twisting the neck tight and fastening it with the band to one side of the steering wheel. It hung there like a fool's balloon, bobbing lightly away if I touched it.

I had been thirsty all day, but not unbearably.

After dark some hovering internal rumbles identified themselves as hunger. Again, not unbearably.

The bladder problem reappeared and was again a disaster. But time, I supposed, would lessen the difficulty: no input, less output.

Hope had to be filed under 'pending', after dark. Twelve hours to be lived before one could climb on to the will-they-won't-they treadmill again. I found them long, lonely, and dreadful.

The cramps which I had so imaginatively constructed for the film began to afflict my own body in earnest, once the heat of the day drained away and let my muscles grow stiff.

At first I warmed up by another dozen wrenching

attempts to break the steering wheel off the control column, the net result of which was considerable wear and tear on me, and none on the car. After that I tried to plan a sensible series of isometric exercises which would keep everything warm and working, but I only got about half of them done.

Against all the odds, I went to sleep.

The nightmare was still there when I woke up.

I was shivering with cold, creakingly stiff, and perceptibly hungrier.

I had nothing to eat but four matches, a handkerchief, and a blunt pencil.

After a small amount of thought I dug out the pencil, and chewed that. Not exactly for the food value, but to bare the lead. With that pencil, I decided, I could bring Danilo down.

Before dawn the realization crept slowly in that Danilo could not have abandoned me in the car without help. He would have needed someone to drive him away when he had finished locking me in. He wouldn't have walked through the game reserve, not only because of the danger from animals, but because a man on foot would have been as conspicuous as gallantry.

So someone had helped him.

Who?

241

Arknold . . .

He had shut his eyes to Danilo's fraud, when he had discovered it: had kept silent, because by not arranging better security he had put his licence at risk. But would he step down into murder to save himself a suspension?

No. He wouldn't.

Barty, for money?

I didn't know.

One . . . any . . . of the van Hurens, for any reason at all?

No.

Roderick, for news? Or Katya, or Melanie?

No.

Clifford Wenkins, for publicity?

If it was him, I was safe, because he wouldn't leave me there much longer. He wouldn't dare. Worldic, for a start, wouldn't want the merchandise turning up in a damaged state. I wished I believed it was Wenkins, but I didn't.

Evan? Conrad?

I couldn't face it.

They had both been there. On the spot. Sleeping next door. Handy for breaking in in the night and smothering me with ether.

One of them could have done it while the other slept. But which? And why?

If it were either Evan or Conrad I was going to die, because only they could save me.

The dawn came up on this bleakest of thoughts and showed me that my theories on water vapour were correct. I could see nothing of the Kruger National Park, because all the windows were fogged and beaded with condensation.

I could reach the glass beside me, and I licked it. It felt great. The dryness of my tongue and throat became instantly less aggravating, though I could still have done with a pint of draught.

I looked through the licked patch. Same old wilderness. Same old no one there.

My spoonful of water had formed all right inside the now cold plastic bag. Carefully I loosened its neck in the rubber band and squeezed the shrunken air out, to prevent it expanding again when the day grew hot, and reabsorbing the precious liquid. I wouldn't drink it until later, I decided. Until things got worse.

*

With all the precious humidity clinging to the inside of the windows, it was safe to embark on a change of air. I took off my sock and turned the handle with my toes, and opened the left-hand window a scant inch. Couldn't risk not being able to shut it again: but when the sun came up I got it shut without much trouble. When the growing heat cleared the windows by re-evaporating the water, at least I had such comfort as there was in knowing it was all still inside the car, doing its best.

The pencil I had chewed in the night (and stowed for safe storage under my watch strap) was showing signs of usefulness. One more session with the incisors, and it had enough bare lead at the tip to write with.

The only thing to write on that I had in my pockets was the inside of the book of matches, which was room enough for 'Danilo did it', but not for my whole purpose. There were maps and car documents, however, in the glove compartment in front of the passenger seat, and after a long struggle, tying my toes in knots and using up a great deal too much precious energy, I collected into my hands a large brown envelope, and a book of maps with nice blank end papers.

There was a lot to write.

CHAPTER FIFTEEN

Danilo had suggested to Nerissa that I go to South Africa because there, far from home, he could take or make any opportunity that offered to bring me to an accidental-looking death. He had lured me to the killing ground with a bait he knew I would take – a near-dying request from a woman I liked and was grateful to.

A death which was clearly a murder would have left him too dangerously exposed as a suspect. An obvious accident would be less suspiciously investigated . . . like a live microphone.

Danilo hadn't been there, in Randfontein House.

Roderick had been there, and Clifford Wenkins, and Conrad. And fifty others besides. If Danilo had provided the live mike, someone at the Press interview must have steered it into my hands. Luck alone had taken it out again.

Down the mine, at the suddenly opportune moment . . . bash.

Except for the steadfastness of a checker called Nyembezi, that attempt would have come off.

This wouldn't look like a natural accident, though. The handcuffs couldn't be called accidental.

Perhaps Danilo intended to come back, after I was dead, and take them away. Perhaps people would believe then that I had lost my way in the park and had died in the car rather than risk walking.

But the time span was tight. He couldn't wait a week to make sure I was dead before coming back, because by then everyone would be searching for me, and someone might have reached me before he did.

I sighed dispiritedly.

None of it made any sense.

The day proved an inferno compared with the one before. Much worse even than Spain. The scorching fury of the heat stunned me to the point where thought became impossible, and cramps wracked my shoulders, arms and stomach.

I tucked my hands into my sleeves and rolled my head back out of the direct rays and just sat there enduring it, because there was nothing else to do.

So much for my pathetic little attempts at water management. The brutal sun was shrivelling me minute by minute, and I knew that a week was wildly optimistic. In this heat, a day or two would be enough.

My throat burned with thirst and saliva was a thing of the past.

A gallon of water in the car's radiator . . . as out of reach as a mirage.

When I couldn't swallow without wincing or breathe without feeling the intaken air cut like a knife, I untied the plastic bag and poured the contents into my mouth. I made the divine H_2O last as long as possible; rolled it round my teeth and gums, and under my tongue. There was hardly enough left to swallow, and when it was gone I felt wretched. There was nothing, now, between me and nightfall.

I turned the bag inside out and sucked it, and held it against my mouth until the heat had dried it entirely, and then I filled it again with hot air, and with trembling fingers fumbled it back into the rubber band on the steering wheel.

I remembered that the boot of the car still held, as far as I knew, a lot of oddments of Conrad's equipment. Surely he would need it, would come looking for that, if not for me.

Evan, I thought, for God's sake come and find me.

But Evan had gone north in the park which stretched two hundred miles to the boundary on the great grey-green greasy Limpopo river. Evan was searching there for his Elephant's Child.

And I . . . I was sitting in a car, dying for a gold mine I didn't want.

*

Night came, and hunger.

People paid to be starved in health farms, and people went on hunger strikes to protest about this or that, so what was so special about hunger?'

Nothing. It was just a pain.

The night was cool, was blessed. In the morning, when I had licked as much of the window as I could reach, I went on with the writing. I wrote everything I could think of which would help an investigation into my death.

The heat started up before I had finished. I wrote 'give my love to Charlie', and signed my name, because I wasn't certain that by that evening I would be able to write any more. Then I slid the written papers under my left thigh so that they wouldn't slip out of reach on the floor, and tucked the little pencil under my watch strap, and collapsed the air out of the plastic bag to keep the next teaspoonful safe, and wondered how long, how long I would last.

By midday I didn't want to last.

I held out until then for my sip of water, but when it was gone I would have been happy to die. After the bag had dried against my face it took a very long time, and a great effort of will, for me to balloon it out and fix it again to the steering wheel. Tomorrow, I thought, the

thimbleful would form again, but I would be past
drinking it.

We had been wrong in the film, I thought. We had
focused on the mental state of the man too much, to the
neglect of the physical. We hadn't known about legs like
lead and ankles swollen to giant puffballs. I had long ago
shed my socks, and would have had as much chance of
forcing my shoes on again as of flying.

We hadn't known the abdomen would become agon-
izingly distended with gas or that the seat belts would
strain across it like hawsers. We hadn't guessed that the
eyes would feel like sand paper when the lachrymal
glands dried up. We had underestimated what dehydration did to the throat.

The overwhelming heat battered all emotions into
numbness. There was nothing anywhere but pain, and
no prospect that it would stop.

Except, of course, in death.

In the late afternoon an elephant came and uprooted
the tree the giraffe had browsed from.

That should be allegorical enough for Evan, I thought
confusedly. Elephants were the indestructible destroyers
of the wilderness.

But Evan was miles away.

249

Evan, I thought, Evan . . . Oh God, Evan . . . come . . . and find me.

The elephant ate a few succulent leaves off the tree and went away and left it with its roots in the air, dying for lack of water.

Before dark I did write a few more sentences. My hands trembled continually, and folded into tight cramps, and were in the end too weak to hold the pencil.

It fell down on the floor and rolled beneath my seat. I couldn't see it, or pick it up with my swollen toes.

Weeping would have been a waste of water.

Night came again and time began to blur.

I couldn't remember how long I had been there, or how long it was until Wednesday.

Wednesday was as far away as Charlie, and I wouldn't see either of them. I had a vision of the pool in the garden with the kids splashing in it, and it was the car that seemed unreal, not the pool.

Tremors shook my limbs for hours on end.

The night was cold. Muscles stiffened. Teeth chattered. Stomach shrieked to be fed.

In the morning, the condensation on the windows was so heavy that water trickled in rivulets down the glass. I could only, as ever, reach the small area near my head. I licked it weakly. It wasn't enough.

I hadn't the energy any more to open the window for a change of air: but cars were never entirely airtight, and it wouldn't be asphyxiation which saw me off.

The inevitable sun came back in an innocent rosy dawn, gentle prelude to the terrifying day ahead.

I no longer believed that anyone would come.

All that remained was to suffer into unconsciousness, because after that there would be peace. Even delirium would be a sort of peace, because the worst torment was to be aware, to understand. I would welcome a clouded mind, when it came. That, for me, would be the real death. The only one that mattered. I wouldn't know or care when my heart finally stopped.

Heat bullied into the car like a battering ram.

I burned.

I burned.

CHAPTER SIXTEEN

They did come.

When the sun was high, Evan and Conrad came in the station wagon. Evan stampeding about in a frenzy of energy, waving his arms about, with his hair sticking out crazily and his eyes too hot for comfort. Conrad, puffing slightly under the droopy moustache, mopping his forehead with a handkerchief.

They simply walked up to the car and opened the door. Then they stood still. And stared.

I thought they were unreal; the onset of delusion. I stared back, waiting for them to vanish.

Then Evan said, 'Where the hell have you been? We've been searching the whole bloody park for you since yesterday morning.'

I didn't answer him. I couldn't.

Conrad was saying, 'My God, my God, dear boy, my God . . .' as if the needle had stuck.

Evan went back to the station wagon, drove it across the grass, and parked it alongside the car I was in. Then he scrambled into the back and unclipped the red ice box.

'Will beer do?' he shouted. 'We didn't bring any water.'

Beer would do.

He poured it from a can into a plastic cup and held it to my mouth. It was cold; alive; incredible. I only drank half, because it hurt to swallow.

Conrad opened the left-hand door and sat on the seat beside me.

'We haven't a key for the handcuffs,' he said apologetically.

A laugh twitched somewhere inside me, the first for a long time.

'Phew,' Evan said, 'You do stink.'

They saw I couldn't talk. Evan poured more beer into the cup and held it for me, and Conrad got out of the car and rummaged about in the boot. He came back with four short lengths of strong wire and a roll of insulating tape, and with these he proceeded to set me free.

He stuck the four wires into the barrel of the handcuff lock, bound the protruding ends tightly together to give a handle for leverage, and began to turn. The makeshift key did a grand job. With a lot of swearing and a couple of fresh starts when the wires slipped out, Conrad got the ratchet on my right wrist opened.

And who cared about the other? It could wait.

They unclipped the seat belts and tried to help me out of the car, but I had been sitting in the same restricted position for over eighty hours, and like concrete my body seemed to have set in the mould.

Evan said doubtfully, 'I think one of us should go and find a doctor.'

I shook my head decidedly. There were things I wanted to tell them before the outside world broke in. I felt jerkily under my thigh for the papers I had written, and made writing motions with my hands. Conrad silently produced the gold ballpoint he always carried, and I shakily wrote on an unused corner of brown envelope, '*If you do not tell anyone you have found me, we can catch the man who put me here.*' And as an afterthought, I added, '*I want to do that.*'

They read the uneven words and stood wondering, almost literally scratching their heads.

I wrote a bit more. '*Please put something over the windscreen.*'

That at least made sense to them. Conrad draped the front of the car with a heavy groundsheet which effectively brought the temperature down by ten degrees.

Evan saw the plastic bag hanging from the steering wheel and pulled it off its rubber band.

'What the hell is this?' he said.

I pointed to the still undrunk mouthful of water lurking in one corner. Evan understood, and looked completely appalled.

He took the written pages out of my hand, and read them. I drank some more beer, holding the cup with trembly fingers but feeling life flowing back through all the dying channels with every difficult swallow.

He read right to the end and handed the pages to Conrad. He stared at me with stunned speechlessness. An unaccustomed state for Evan. After a long time he said slowly, 'Did you really think Conrad or I had helped to leave you here?'

I shook my head.

'And you can cross off poor old Clifford Wenkins, too, because he's dead. They fished him out of the Wemmer Pan on Saturday afternoon. He went boating, and drowned.'

The news took a while to percolate. I thought, no more stuttering, no more damp palms, no more nervous little man . . . poor little nervous man . . .

I lifted Conrad's golden pen, and Evan gave me one of his ubiquitous notebooks to write on.

'*I'd like to lie down. In the station wagon?*'

'Sure,' he said, seeming to be glad of an excuse for activity. 'We'll make you a bed.'

He hopped into the estate car again and hauled all their equipment to one side. In the cleared space he constructed a mattress from the back seats of both cars, and made a thick pillow out of coats and sweaters.

'The Ritz,' he said, 'is at your service.'

I tried a smile and caught sight of it in the driving mirror.

Ghastly. I had a four-day beard and sunken pinkish eyes and looked as grey and red as a sunburned ghost.

With more gentleness than I would have thought either of them had in their natures, they helped me out of the car and carried more than supported me over to the station wagon. Bent double, creaking in every muscle, and feeling that my lumbar vertebrae were breaking, I completed the journey, and once lying on the makeshift bed began the luxuriously painful process of straightening myself out. Evan took the groundsheet off my car and spread it over the roof of the station wagon, as much to shut out the heat as for shade.

I wrote again. '*Stay here, Evan*', because I thought they might start my car with a jump lead, and drive off for help. He looked doubtful, so I added with a fair amount of desperation, '*Please don't leave me.*'

'Christ,' he said, when he read that. 'Christ, mate, we won't leave you.' He was clearly emotionally upset, which surprised me. He didn't even like me, and in the Special had heaped on the discomfort without mercy.

I drank some more beer, mouthful by separate mouthful. My throat still beat a raging case of tonsillitis out of sight, but the lubrication was slowly taking effect. I could move my tongue better, and it was beginning to feel less like a swollen lump of liver.

Evan and Conrad sat in the front seats of the estate car and began discussing where to go. They had no accommodation reserved at Skukuza, which it appeared was still the nearest camp, and it was two hours' drive to the beds booked at Satara.

256

Satara and the beds won, which seemed good enough for me.

Evan said, 'We might as well get going, then. It's too bloody hot here. I've had enough of it. We'll find a patch of decent shade along the road, and stop for lunch. It's after two, already, and I'm hungry.'

That was a lot more like the Evan I knew and detested. With an inward smile, I had another go with the pen.

'*Remember how to get back here.*'

'Someone else can fetch the car,' said Evan impatiently. 'Later.'

I shook my head. '*We must come back.*'

'Why?'

'*To catch Danilo Cavesey.*'

They looked from the pad to my face. Then Evan merely said, 'How?'

I wrote down how. They read it. The air of excited intensity reawoke in Evan, and rapid professional calculations furrowed Conrad's forehead, for what I was asking them to do was much to their liking. Then a separate, secondary thought struck both of them, and they looked at me doubtfully.

'You can't mean it, dear boy,' Conrad said.

I nodded.

'What about the person who helped him?' Evan asked. 'What are you going to do about him?'

'*He's dead, now.*'

'Dead?' He looked incredulous. 'You don't mean . . . Clifford Wenkins?'

I nodded. I was tired. I wrote '*Tell you when I can talk.*'

They agreed to that. They shut the doors of my car, climbed into the front seats of the station wagon, turned it, and set off along the dirt road which had for so long for me been just a reflection in a three-by-six inch looking glass.

Conrad drove, and Evan made a map. They seemed to have found me by the merest chance, as I had been a mile up a side branch of an equally unkempt road leading to a now dry water hole. The water hole road joined into another, which led finally back to the roads used by visitors. Evan said he could find the way straight back to my car: it was easy. They had searched, he added, every side road they could find between Skukuza and Numbi, and that had been yesterday. Today, they had tried the dry sparse land to the south of the Sabie river, and they had found me on the fifth no-entry they had explored.

After five or six miles we came to a small group of trees throwing some dappled shade: Conrad at once pulled in and stopped the car, and Evan without more ado started burrowing into the red box. They had brought more sandwiches, more fruit, more beer.

I thought I would postpone sandwiches and fruit. Beer was doing wonders. I drank some more.

The other two munched away as if the whole picnic were routine. They opened the windows wide, reckoning that any sensible animal would be sleeping in this heat, not looking out for unwary humans.

No cars passed. Every sensible human, too, was busy at siesta in the air-conditioned camps. Evan, of course, was impervious to heat, and Conrad had to lump it.

I wrote again, '*What made you start looking for me?*'

Evan spoke round bits of ham sandwich. 'We kept wanting the things of Conrad's which were in your car. It became most annoying not to have them. So yesterday morning we telephoned the Iguana to tell you how selfish you had been to take them away with you.'

'They said you weren't there,' Conrad said. 'They said they understood you were going to the Kruger Park for several days.'

'We couldn't understand it,' Evan nodded. 'In view of your note.'

'What note?' I tried automatically to say the words, but my throat still wouldn't have it. I wrote them instead.

'The note you left,' Evan said impatiently. 'Saying you had gone back to Johannesburg.'

'*I left no note.*'

He stopped chewing and sat with his mouth full as if in suspended animation. Then he took up chewing again, and said, 'No. That's right. You couldn't have.'

'We thought you had, anyway,' Conrad said. 'It was just a piece of paper, written in capital letters, saying, "*Gone back to Johannesburg. Link.*" Bloody rude and ungrateful, dear boy, we thought of it. Packing all your gear and buzzing off at the crack of dawn without even bothering to say good-bye.'

'*Sorry.*'

Conrad laughed. 'After that we tried to reach Clifford Wenkins, because we thought he might know where you were, but all we got at his number was some hysterical woman saying he'd been drowned in the Wemmer Pan.'

'We tried one or two other people,' Evan went on. 'The van Hurens, and so on.'

'*Danilo?*' I wrote.

'No.' Evan shook his head. 'Didn't think of him. Wouldn't know where he's staying, for a start.' He ate a mouthful, reflecting. 'We thought it a bit unhelpful of you to go off without letting anyone know where you could be found, and then we thought perhaps you'd been damn bloody careless and got lost in the park, and never got back to Johannesburg at all. So after a bit of argy-bargy we persuaded the reception office at Satara to check what time you went out of the Numbi gate on Friday morning, and the gate keeper said that according to their records you hadn't gone out at all.'

'We telephoned Haagner, dear boy,' Conrad said, 'and explained the situation, but he didn't seem to be much worried. He said people often talked their way out of Numbi without papers, even though one was supposed to produce receipts to show one had paid for staying in camps. Mr Lincoln would only have to say, Haagner said, that Evan and Conrad were still in the park, and had paid for him. The Numbi men would check with Skukuza, and then let Mr Lincoln go. He also said you couldn't be lost in the park. You were too sensible, he said, and only fools got lost. People who drove miles down no-entry roads and then had their cars break down.'

And that, I presumed, was what they thought had happened. But I wouldn't grumble.

They opened cans of beer and gulped. I went on sipping.

'We had sure enough paid for you at Skukuza,' Evan said accusingly. 'Including the window you broke.'

I only had to pick up the pen.

'My God,' Evan said, before I got it to the paper. 'Danilo Cavesey broke the window . . . to get into your *rondavel*.'

I supposed so. He had got past the locked door without waking me.

'You're a fairly valuable property, dear boy,' Conrad said, finishing the saga. 'So we decided we ought perhaps to spend a day or so looking for you.'

'We saw a splendid herd of elephants yesterday afternoon,' said Evan, pointing out that the delay to their original plans had not been an entire waste. 'And we might see some more today,' he said.

They helped me into the *rondavel* in Satara and I asked them to turn the air-conditioning off, as to me the hut felt cold. If I got cold again I would get stiff again, which

261

would only add to my aches . . . I lay on one of the beds with three blankets over me and felt lousy.

Conrad fetched a glass of water and he and Evan stood around looking helpless.

Evan said, 'Let's take your stinking clothes off. You'd embarrass a pig, as you are.'

I shook my head.

'If we bring you some water, would you like to wash?'

No, again.

Evan wrinkled his nose. 'Well, you won't mind if neither of us sleeps in here with you?'

I shook my head. My smell was offensive to myself as well, now that I'd breathed so much clean fresh air.

Conrad went off to the camp shop to find something I could swallow and presently came back with a pint of milk and a tin of chicken soup. The only opener they had was the beer can opener, but they got the soup out into a jug in the end. There was nothing to heat the soup with, so they tipped in half the milk and stirred it around until it was runny. Then they poured out a glassful, and, grateful for their clumsy care, I drank it bit by bit.

'Now,' said Evan briskly, satisfied that they had done the best possible for me, 'let's get on with planning the trap.'

This time, when I tried, some semblance of speech came out.

'Danilo is staying at the Vaal Majestic,' I said.

'What did you say?' Evan demanded. 'Thank God you can talk again, but I couldn't understand a word of it.'

I wrote it down.

'Oh. Right.'

I said, 'Telephone in the morning, and tell him . . .' It was a croak, rough and cracked.

'Look,' Evan interrupted. 'We'll get along quicker if you write it.'

I nodded. Much easier on my throat, if he preferred it that way.

'*At breakfast time, tell Danilo you are trying to find out where I am, because I have Conrad's equipment in my car. Tell him I also have Conrad's gold pencil in my pocket, and he especially wants it back. Tell him I also have one of your notebooks, and you need your notes. Tell him you are worried because I had some theory that someone I knew had been trying to kill me.*'

Evan read, and looked dubious. 'Are you sure that will bring him?'

I wrote: '*Would you risk my being able to write down that theory, if you knew I had pencil and paper within reach?*'

He considered. He said, 'No. I wouldn't.'

'*I did do it.*'

'So you did.'

Conrad sat heavily down in the armchair, nodding.

'What next, dear boy?'

I wrote: *'This evening, telephone Quentin van Huren. Tell him where and in what state you found me. Say I wrote some notes. Read them to him. Tell him about the trap for Danilo. Ask him to tell the police. With his authority, he can arrange it properly.'*

'Sure. Sure.' Evan, with undaunted wiry energy, collected up my writings from the car and his notebook with all our plans, and strode off at once to the telephone in the main buildings.

Conrad stayed behind and lit a cigar, no doubt to fend off evil odours.

'It was Evan who insisted on looking for you, dear boy,' he said. 'Absolutely fanatical, he was. You know how he never lets up when he gets an idea. We went up every unlikely track . . . bloody silly, I thought . . . until we found you.'

'Who,' I said slowly, trying to speak clearly, 'told Danilo about the film . . . *Man in the Car?*'

He shrugged a little uncomfortably. 'Maybe I did. At Germiston. They were all asking about your latest work . . . the van Hurens, Clifford Wenkins, Danilo . . . everybody.'

It didn't matter. Wenkins could have got hold of the film's plot easily enough, through Worldic.

'Dear boy,' Conrad said thoughtfully. 'The make-up is all wrong in the film.' He puffed the cigar. 'Mind you,' he said, 'what you actually look like would be pretty poor box-office.'

'Thanks.'

He smiled. 'Have some more soup?'

Evan was gone a long time and came back looking earnest and intense.

'He wants me to ring back later. He was pretty incoherent when I'd finished.' Evan raised his eyebrows, surprised that anyone should need time to assimilate so many unwelcome facts. 'He said he would think over what ought to be done. And oh yes, he said to ask you why you now thought it was Clifford Wenkins who helped Danilo.'

I said, 'Clifford Wenkins would have helped . . .'

'Write it down,' said Evan impatiently. 'You sound like a crow with laryngitis.'

I wrote: '*Clifford Wenkins would do anything for publicity stunts. He would exchange recording gear and microphones, for instance. I do not believe he thought anyone would be killed, but if I got an electric shock at a Press conference, it would put my name and the purpose of my visit in the papers. I believe Danilo put it all into his head, and gave him the live equipment. Wenkins was terrified when Katya was so badly shocked and afterwards I saw him telephoning, looking very worried. I thought he was calling Worldic, but he might have been telling Danilo that the stunt had gone wrong.*'

'It went better, dear boy, from Worldic's point of view,' Conrad commented.

'*Worldic drove Clifford Wenkins unmercifully to arrange publicity stunts . . . so if Danilo suggested to him that they should kidnap me and lock me in a car, just like in my new film, he would have been foolish enough to agree.*

'*When I'd been in the car for three days, I did not think it could be Wenkins who'd been helping Danilo because I knew Wenkins would not leave me there very long. But once Wenkins was dead, no one but Danilo knew where I was. He had only to leave me there . . .*

'*After my body was discovered, people would work out that it had been a publicity stunt planned by Wenkins and myself, which went wrong because he drowned and could not set in motion the necessary search.*

'*I expect it was in Wenkins's car that he and Danilo drove into the park, so that the Numbi gate office would have it on record that he had been there.*'

Evan practically tore the notebook out of my hands, as he had been striding around with impatience while I wrote. He read to the end and handed the notebook to Conrad.

'Do you realize,' he demanded, 'that you are practically accusing Danilo of killing Clifford Wenkins, so that you shouldn't be found?'

I nodded.

'I think he did,' I croaked. 'For a gold mine.'

*

They left me with water and soup to hand and went off to dinner in the restaurant. When they came back, Evan had telephoned again to van Huren.

'He'd grasped everything a bit better,' Evan allowed condescendingly. 'I read him what you wrote about Wenkins, and he said he thought you could be right. He said he was upset about Danilo, because he had liked him, but he would do as you asked. He said that he himself would come down here . . . he's flying down to the Skukuza airstrip first thing in the morning. The police will be properly genned up. Conrad and I will meet them and van Huren at Skukuza, and go on from there, if it looks likely that Danilo has taken the bait.'

We were going to call Danilo in the morning. Even if he, too, flew down as fast as possible, everyone should be in position before he came.

The night was paradise compared with its predecessors, but still far short of heaven. In the morning I felt a good deal stronger; there were no more cramps and the fire in my throat would no longer frighten Celsius. I got myself to the bathroom looking as bent as old Adam the gardener, but I got there; and I ate the banana which Conrad brought me for breakfast.

Evan had gone to telephone Danilo, Conrad said, and Evan came later with a satisfied smile.

'He was there,' he said. 'And I'd say there was no doubt he swallowed it. He sounded pretty worried . . .

267

sharp voice, that sort of thing. He asked why I was so sure about the gold pencil. Can you believe it? I said Conrad had lent it to you Thursday evening and I'd seen you put it in your pocket. Then, Friday morning, you went off to Johannesburg without giving it back.'

CHAPTER SEVENTEEN

The hardest thing I ever did was to get back into that car.

We reached it at half past ten, and Evan and Conrad busily rigged up various bits and pieces, including a warning buzzer which would tell me when Danilo was approaching.

Half an hour later, when they had finished, the day was stoking up to another roaster. I drank the whole of the bottle of water we had brought from Satara and ate another banana.

Evan danced up and down. 'Come on. Come on. We haven't got all day. We've got to hurry to Skukuza to meet van Huren.'

I left the station wagon, hobbled across to the car, sat in the front seat, and fastened the seat belts.

The dying aches flared up at once.

Conrad approached with the handcuffs, and my throat closed. I couldn't look at him, couldn't look at Evan ... at anything. Couldn't do it ... all my nerves and muscles revolted.

Couldn't.

Conrad, watching me, said practically, 'You haven't got to, Link. It's your own idea, dear boy. He will come, whether you are here or not.'

'Don't try and dissuade him,' Evan said crossly. 'Not now we've gone to all this trouble. And as Link pointed out himself, if he isn't in the car when Danilo comes, nothing will be conclusive.'

Conrad still hesitated. My fault.

'Get on with it,' Evan said.

I put my arm through the steering wheel. It was trembling.

Conrad clicked the handcuffs shut first on one wrist and then the other, and I shuddered from head to foot.

'Dear boy . . .' Conrad said doubtfully.

'Come on,' Evan urged.

I didn't say anything. I thought that whatever I might start to say, it would come out as a screaming plea that they wouldn't leave me. Leave me, however, they must.

Evan shut the car door brusquely, and jerked his head for Conrad to follow him into the estate car. Conrad went with his head turned backwards, looking to see if I were calling him.

They climbed into the front seat, reversed, turned, drove away. The silence of the tinder-dry park settled around me.

I wished I had never suggested this plan. The car seemed hotter than ever, the heat more intolerable.

Within an hour, and in spite of the quantities of water I had drunk that morning, fierce thirst returned.

Cramps began again in my legs. My spine protested. My shoulders pulled with strain.

I cursed myself.

Supposing he took all day, I thought. Supposing he didn't fly down, but drove. Eight o'clock, when Evan telephoned him. At least five hours' drive to Numbi, another hour and a half to reach me . . . He might not come until three or four . . . which meant five hours in the car . . .

I tucked my hands into my shirt sleeves and rolled my head back out of the sun.

There was no water vapour, no plastic bag, to keep my mind occupied. The pencil-written sheets lay on my knees, with Conrad's gold pencil, companion to his pen, clipping them together. There was no leaping from hope to despair and back again, which was certainly a blessed relief, but unexpectedly left too much time free for pure feeling.

Every minute dragged.

The premiere, I thought, was due to be held the following night. I wondered who would be arranging everything, with poor Clifford Wenkins in his watery grave. I wondered if I would get to the Klipspringer Heights Hotel on time. In another twenty-four hours, shaved, bathed, rested, watered and fed, perhaps I might just make it. All those people paying twenty rand for a seat . . . unfair not to turn up, if I could . . .

Time crawled. I looked at my watch. It wasn't trying.

One o'clock came. One o'clock went.

Conrad had fixed a radio transmitter with a button for me to press if I simply could not stand any more. But if I pressed it, the whole of today's effort would be wasted. If I pressed it, the cohorts would rush to my rescue, but Danilo would see the activity, and would never come near.

I wished Conrad hadn't insisted on that button. Evan said it was necessary, so that he and van Huren and the police would know for certain that Danilo had come, if they should by some mischance miss him on the road.

One buzz was to mean that Danilo had come.

Two buzzes that he had left again.

A series of short buzzes would bring them instantly at any time to set me free.

I would wait another ten minutes before I gave up, I thought.

Then another ten.

Then another.

Ten minutes was always possible.

Conrad's warning buzzer sounded like a wasp in my ear and jerked me into action.

*

Danilo drove up beside me and stopped where the station wagon had been.

I pressed the buttons taped within reach on the steering column.

I put all the actor's art I had into looking not far from death: and didn't have to elaborate all that much on what I knew of the real thing. A couple of vultures had conveniently flapped and spiralled down, and now perched on a nearby tree like brooding anarchists awaiting the revolution. I eyed them sourly, but Danilo was reassured.

He opened the door and through slit eyes I saw him draw back when the unmitigated heat-stoked stench met his nostrils. It had been worth not washing, not changing my clothes. There was nothing about me to show I hadn't sat in that spot continuously since he had left me there, and a great deal to prove I had.

He looked at my lolling head, my flaccid hands, my bare swollen feet. He showed no remorse whatever. The sun blazed on the bright blond head, giving him a halo. The clean-featured all-American boy, as shiny, cold and ruthless as ice.

He bent down and practically snatched the papers off my lap. Unclipped the pencil and threw it on the back seat of the car. Read what I had written, right to the end.

'So you did guess . . . you did write . . .' he said. 'Clever Ed Lincoln, too clever by half. Too bad no one will ever read this . . .' He peered down into my half shut eyes to make sure I could hear him, could see him. Then

273

he took out a cigarette lighter, flicked the flint, and set the corners of the papers into the flame.

I shook feebly in my seat, in mute protest. It pleased him.

He smiled.

He turned the papers, burning them all up, and then ground the ashes into just more dust in the dusty grass.

'There,' he said cheerfully.

I made a small croak. He paid attention.

I said, 'Let . . . me . . . go.'

'Not a chance.' He put his hand in his pocket and brought out a bunch of keys. 'Keys to the car.' He held them up, jingling. 'Key to the handcuffs.' He waved it in front of my eyes.

'Please . . .' I said.

'You're worth too much to me dead, pal. Sorry and all that. But there it is.'

He put the keys in his pocket, shut the door on me, and without another glance, drove heartlessly away.

Poor Nerissa, I thought. I hoped she would die before she found out about Danilo; but life was not always kind.

In time, four cars rolled back into the reflection in the driving mirror, and stopped in a cluster round my car.

Evan and Conrad's estate wagon. A chauffeur-driven car with van Huren. Two police cars; the first containing, I later discovered, their photographer and their surgeon; the second, three senior police officers . . . and Danilo Cavesey.

They all stood up outside the cars; a meal and a half for any passing pride of lion. Wild animals, however, kept decently out of sight. Danilo outdid them all for savagery.

Conrad bustled over and pulled open the door.

'You all right, dear boy?' he said anxiously.

I nodded.

Danilo was saying loudly and virtuously, 'I told you, I'd just found him, and I was driving away to get help.'

'Oh yeah,' Conrad muttered, digging out his bits of wire.

'He has the key of the handcuffs in his pocket,' I said.

'You don't mean it, dear boy?' He saw I did mean it. He went over and told the police, and after a short scuffle they found the key. Also the car keys. And now, perhaps Mr Cavesey would explain why he was driving away, when he had in his pocket the means of freeing Mr Lincoln?

Mr Cavesey glowered and declined. He had been going for help, he said.

Evan, enjoying himself immensely, walked over to the tree the elephant had uprooted, and from its withering foliage disentangled the Arriflex on its tripod.

'Everything you did here, we filmed,' he told Danilo. 'Link had a cable to the car. He started the camera when you arrived.'

Conrad fished his best tape-recorder out from under the car and unhitched the sensitive microphone from just inside the door frame.

'Everything you said here,' he echoed, with equal satisfaction, 'we recorded. Link switched on the recorder, when you came.'

The police produced a pair of handcuffs of their own, and put them on Danilo, who had gone blue-white under the sun-tan.

Quentin van Huren walked over to the car and looked down at me. Conrad had forgotten the small detail of bringing back the key to free me. I still sat, locked and helpless, where I had begun.

'For God's sake . . .' van Huren looked appalled.

I smiled lop-sidedly and shook my head. 'For gold's sake,' I said.

His mouth moved, but no words came out.

Gold, greed and gilded boys . . . a thoroughly bad mixture.

Evan was strutting around looking important, intense, and satisfied, as if he had stage-managed and directed the entire performance. But he saw that I was still tethered, and for once some twitch of compassion reached him. He went to fetch the handcuff key and brought it over.

He stood beside van Huren for a second, staring down at me as if seeing something new. For the first time ever he smiled with a hint of friendship.

'Cut,' he said. 'No re-takes, today.'